WOL'
OF THE
IRISH SEA

WOLVES OF THE IRISH SEA

VOL. 2

WRATH OF KINGS

CONOR BRENNAN

This novel is a work of historical fiction.
Although most of the characters, places and incidents portrayed in it are factually correct,
much of the work is of the author's imagination.
The reference maps are based on the authors interpretation of the places at the time.

Published by Conor Brennan.

ISBN: 978-0-6454716-7-0

Editor: Robin Seavill

Cover design, illustration, maps and interior formatting:
Mark Thomas / Coverness.com

For Henry

IRELAND

VIKING ERA BRITAIN & IRELAND

BRITAIN

PROLOGUE

THE VISION OF RAGNALL
(910 AD)

Three of the most fearsome Viking leaders in the world knelt before the dais and Ragnall the King of the Ui Imair stood above them. Godfrith Ivarsson and Sihtric the Scourge of Ireland, his formidable twin brothers, stood by his side.

Olga the Valkyrie, Gragabai the Bastard, and Oitir Iarla the Black One had sailed to Lieurpul to swear their allegiance to the Ui Imair, each for different reasons. The fearsome Valkyrie had been driven from the river systems of Francia by the emergence of Rollo the Walker as the predominant Viking ruler on the River Seine. In an alliance with a Francish nobleman, the Walker had attacked the Valkyrie's longfort in the night and murdered many of her warriors including her two chief lieutenants, Henri the Cat and Ramshaw the Saxon. She barely survived the assault and had led her much diminished warband out to sea and away from the brutal Franco-Norse warlord. On learning of the fate of the Kings of Yorvik she had no option but to approach the strongest Viking power in the region for protection and opportunity; and that by default was Ragnall Ivarsson.

Gragabai was similarly constricted in his choices. He had fallen foul of his bloodthirsty half-brother Erik Bloodaxe and had fled the fjords of Norway before his brother's wrath. His father Harald Fairhair had not even tried to intercede on Gragabai's behalf, leaving his bastard son high and dry. As with the Valkyrie, he had no option but to bend the knee to the strongest Viking power he could find, away from his murderous brother's reach.

The most famous of the three supplicants before the lord of the Ui Imair was Oitir Iarla, the Black One. For a decade he had ravaged the Christian coastal kingdoms of Asturia and the Muslim caliphate of Al Andalus from his base in Brittany. Eventually his notoriety unified the Bretons, and his entire fleet was driven off. He spent the next couple of years launching attacks upon the lands around the mouth of the Severn River in Britain, but eventually, the Wessexian Fyrd was risen against him, and a portion of his host was destroyed. Just like the other two, he had been forced to limp north to Lieurpul to bend the knee to Ragnall for protection. Olga the Valkyrie, Gragabai the Bastard and Oitir the Black; three of the most powerful Viking war-leaders in northern Europe, with more than five hundred warriors each to command and dozens of ships, were all in Lieurpul to swear allegiance to the Ui Imair. All Ragnall Ivarsson could do was smile. *Odin is with me.*

The three of them swore an oath upon their arm rings that they would fight for the Ui Imair in exchange for a share of any spoils or tribute. Once the formalities were out of the way, Ragnall and his brothers ordered ale, wine and mead to the hall and the thousands of warriors present at Lieurpul raised their horns in salute at the incredible conjunction of Viking power that had just taken place. Many men in their cups whispered conspiratorially that the influence of the Gods was surely at hand, as how could so many legendary warlords and Viking warriors come together under the banner of the Ui Imair just as their power waxed. The battle of Odinsfield had been a disaster for sure, but the Ui Imair had quickly moved to fill the power vacuum and no Saxon opponent was currently capable of opposing them. Every single Viking warrior in Lieurpul that night sensed it; destiny was afoot and the veil between Midgard and Asgard had thinned. And no one sensed it more than the three surviving sons of Ivar Ivarsson.

Later that night at the back of the hall, the three mighty brothers sat hunched over a map of the Irish Sea with a cup of Francian wine each in hand. Ragnall the eldest spoke. "Brothers, we now command directly almost five thousand men and can exert influence upon twice that if it came to it. Now is the time to strike."

The two younger twin brothers exchanged a worried glance before Sihtric questioned him: "What do you intend, brother?"

Ragnall smiled before answering, "Firstly, we will go north into the Hebrides and Scottish Western Isles. Already their young warriors flock to our banners. They will not have the strength to withstand us and will have no choice but to bend the knee. We have Yorvik, we have Loidis, we have Cumbria and the west of Northumbria. We have more than a dozen longforts up and down the Irish Sea who pay us tribute. The leader of the Hebrides will have to see sense, bind himself to us and bolster our numbers."

Godfrith stared at Ragnall. "You mean to go further". It was a statement rather than a question, as the twins each knew the moods of their fearsome brother.

"You are of course right, Godfrith. For too long we have had to suffer humiliation and indignity from various warlords, kings and chieftains who would never have dreamed of defying our grandfather, the Boneless. It is our time now though. The Welsh will be the next to fall. These peasants are owed a great debt by our people, and we will repay it tenfold. And Sihtric, you have told me in detail how weak the kingdoms of Munster, Leinster and Osraige are in Ireland. They will fall to us as well. We will then bring the Isle of Mann back into the fold. Our distant cousins have paid us no tribute for years and I have never forgotten how they drove us off after the fall of Dublin. They sent us out to sea to die, brothers." Sihtric and Godfrith both nodded at this, their anger rising at Ragnall's words. "We had women, children, and elderly folk amongst us, starving to death upon the Irish Sea. Bairid mac Oitir and his sons will yield to us, or we will descend upon them and wipe them all out to a man." Ragnall's voice rose at his last declaration, and he slammed his fist onto the table where the map lay, to emphasise his point. His twin brothers nodded eagerly.

"We will then take back the city our ancestors founded. Our home, our birthright, is Dublin and the Ui Neill do not have the power to stop us. Flann Sinna is old, Sihtric, and I intend to honor my promise to you. I will not hit the lands under his control until he has died and one of his wretched sons has taken over. We hear that his lands are in turmoil and civil war rages in the entire northern half of Ireland. No one king will have the power to defeat us, and even Niall Glundub does not have the numbers or support to offer us battle if we strike quickly and decisively. We will come from the south and when the time is right, we will take Dublin by force."

Godfrith and Sihtric looked at each other excitedly at their brother's vision. It was outrageous, it was incredible, but it was doable and Ragnall emanated total belief.

"Once we have Dublin, we will subdue Wexford and Limerick. When we smash the remaining coastal Welsh kingdoms and the Ulaid, we will control the entire Irish Sea." Ragnall stood then, his voice rising in pitch and volume. "We will then come for the Scots and take our revenge upon Constantine for the death of our father and brothers. We will sack Mercia and burn that witch Aethelfled out of her hovel in Tamworth." Ragnall paused momentarily and closed his eyes. He bent over and leaned on the table with the map. Staring into his twin brothers' eyes, he drew his dagger and slammed it into the table. The twins looked down to see the blade quivering and instantly noticed where the blow had fallen. It was Tara, the capital of Ireland. Ragnall whispered then, "And when we have assembled our entire strength and destroyed our enemies, we will conquer the Ui Neill. The rest of Ireland will have a choice. Submit to the Ui Imair or burn".

PART 6

THE FUTILE WARS OF THE HIGH KING FLANN SINNA

DRAMATIS PERSONAE:

Aed Findliath (*Aid-fin-lee-at*) – Long-deceased King of the Cenel nEoghain and the Northern Ui Neill. Son of Niall Caille and father of Niall Glundub.

Aed mac Mael Padraig (*Aid-mac-male-paw-rig*) – Nobleman of the Ui Fhiachrach tribe of Connaught.

Aethelfled of Mercia (*A-thel-fled*) – Saxon Queen of Mercia and sister of the King of Wessex.

Aethelstan (*A-thel-stan*) – Young Saxon prince and Mercian commander.

Alphonso – The King of Asturia in Al Andalus.

Augaire mac Aililla (*Ag-wear-a-mac-al-lila*) – Ferocious young Irish warlord and bother in law to the Ui Imair princes.

Auisle Ragnarsson (*Ow-shla*) – Long-deceased former joint ruler of Dublin, son of Ragnar Lodbrok.

Bairid Oitirsson (*Bar-rid-oh-tier-son*) – Called Bairid mac Oitir by the Irish, distant kin to the Ui Imair as his grandfather Auisle was half-brother to Ivar the Boneless. Ruler of the powerful Kingdom of Mann in the Irish Sea.

Brunbolg Headtaker (*Brun-bulg-head-taker*) – Physically gigantic Viking warlord, subject to the influence of the Ui Imair.

Cairpre Cromm (*Car-pray-crom*) – Bishop Superior of Clonmacnoise

Caolan mac Murchu (*Kay-lawn-mac-mur-ku*) – South Bregan warrior and bodyguard of King Flann Sinna.

Cathal mac Conchobar (*Ca-hal-mac-con-co-bar*) – Over-king of all Connaught, subservient to the High King Flann Sinna of Meath.

Cearnachan mac Duiligen (*Kyer-na-cawn-mac-dil-i-gen*) – Renegade Argiallan chieftain.

Cearnachan mac Tighernain (*Kyer-na-cawn-mac-tier-nan*) – Brother of the King of Breffni.

Cerbaill mac Mael Ruanaid (*Ker-bal-mac-male-ruin-ad*) – Grandson of the High King Flann Sinna.

Charles the Simple – The King of West Francia, descendant of Charlemagne.

Charlemagne (*Sharl-a-main*) – Deceased leader of the Holy Roman Empire, which encompassed most of the land between the Danube and the Atlantic in Europe.

Conaing mac Niall (*Co-ning-mac-niall*) – Prince of the Cenel nEoghain, son of Niall Glundub.

Conchobar mac Flann (*Con-co-bar-mac-flann*) – Youngest son of the High King Flann Sinna.

Constantine mac Aed – Over-king of all Scotland.

Cormac mac Cuilennain (*Cor-mac-mac-cul-in-ann*) – Deceased King of the Eoghanachta tribes and over-king of Munster. Killed at the battle of Beallach Mughna.

Cuchulainn (*Coo-cull-en*) – Mythical Irish warrior, leader of the famous Red Branch Knights.

Cumuscach mac Mael Mocheirgi (*Cum-as-scok-mac-male-mo-hergi*) – Prince of the Leth Cathail tribe of the Ulaid.

Diarmuid – Young monk from Meath.

Domnall mac Aed (*Donal-mac-aid*) – Eldest son of Aed Findliath and Prince of the Cenel nEoghain, joint ruler with Niall Glundub of the Northern Ui Neill.

Donnchadh Donn mac Flann (*Dun-na-ka-dun-mac-flan-sinna*) – Powerful King of the Caille Follamain tribe in Meath, son of the High King Flann Sinna.

Edward the Elder – King of Wessex.

Eithigen mac Fingen (*Eth-I-gen-mac-fin-gen*) – High-ranking clergyman in Meath.

Erik Haraldsson – Also known as Erik Bloodaxe. Fearsome Viking marauder and raider, young son of the King of Norway.

Finn mac Cumhaill (*Finn-mac-cool*) – Mythical Irish hero and leader of the legendary Fianna.

Flann mac Tighernain (*Flan-mac-tier-nan*) – Opportunistic King of Breffni, sworn to the Northern Ui Neill.

Flann Sinna – High King of Ireland and over-king of Meath and the Southern Ui Neill.

Fogartach mac Tolarg (*Fo-gar-tach-mac-tol-arg*) – King of South Brega, under-king of the Southern Ui Neill.

Godfrith Ivarsson (*God-frith-ivarson*) – Twin brother of Sihtric, the youngest sons of the former King of Dublin, Ivar Ivarsson. Commander of the Ui Imair under his brother Ragnall.

Gorm – Ruler of the Norse-Gael town of Linn on the east coast of Ireland.

Gormlaith ingen Flann (*Gorm-la-ingen-flan*) – Princess of the Southern Ui Neill and wife of Niall Glundub.

Gragabai the Bastard (*Grag-a-by*) – Notorious Viking raider and alleged bastard son of Harald Fairhair.

Harald Fairhair – King of all Norway.

Heimdall – Major deity of the Scandinavian pantheon.

Henri the Cat – Lieutenant of the raider Olga the Valkyrie.

Iron Knee – Deceased savage Viking warlord, former ruler in Dublin, enemy of both the Kings of Meath and the Ui Imair.

Ivar the Boneless – Long-deceased former King of Dublin and a legendary son of Ragnar Lodbrok.

Louis the Child – Young King of East Francia.

Mael Ciaran mac Niall (*Male-kee-rawn*) – Prince of the Cenel nEoghain, son of Niall Glundub.

Mael Craobh (*Male-crave*) – King of Argialla and under-king of the Northern Ui Neill, son of the Black Fox.

Mael Mithig mac Flannacain – (*Male-mith-ig-mac-flan-na-cawn*) – Shrewd and charismatic King of North Brega, son-in-law to the High King Flann Sinna.

Mael Muire ingen Cinead (*Male-mwir-a-ingen-cin-aid*) – Princess of Scotland and Queen of Ireland, wife of Flann Sinna.

Mael Seachnaill mac Mael Ruanaid (*Male-shock-nail-mac-male-ruin-ad*) – Deceased High King of Ireland and the Southern Ui Neill and father of Flann Sinna.

Magnus Long-Tooth – Norse-Gael trader from the town of Linn.

Medb – Semi mythological Queen of Connaught, long dead.

Muirchertach mac Niall (*Mwir-her-tach-mac-niall*) – Formidable young son of Niall Glundub and Prince of the Northern Ui Neill and the Cenel nEoghain. His reputation as a warrior was such that the people of the north called him the "Hector" of Ireland.

Niall Caille (*Niall-kile-ya*) – Deceased King of the Northern Ui Neill and former High King of Ireland. Father of Aed Findliath.

Niall Glundub mac Aed Findliath – Newly returned Northern Ui Neill joint-king and powerful general.

Odin – Known as the Allfather, chief god of the Scandinavian pantheon.

Oengus mac Flann (*Ong-gus-mac-flann*) – Prince of the Southern Ui Neill, son of the High King and heir designate of all Ireland.

Oitir the Black (*Oh-tier*) – Brutal Viking warlord, operational all across Western Europe.

Owain ap Dyfnwal (*Oh-wain-ap-dyf-n-wal*) – King of Strathclyde, under-king of Constantine of Scotland.

Ragnall Ivarsson (*Rag-nal-ivarson*) – Leader of the Ui Imair.

Ragnar Lodbrok (*Ragnar-lod-brok*) – Long-deceased legendary Viking sea king and ravager, ancestor of multiple Viking warlords.

Ramshaw – Saxon Lieutenant of raider Olga the Valkyrie. Originally from Loidis, but banished to sell his sword on the Seine due to gambling debts.

Rollo the Walker – Notorious Viking warlord that plagued the Francian river systems.

Ruaidhri mac Murchu – (*Roo-ree-mac-murk-ku*) – South Bregan warrior, guardsman of the High King Flann Sinna.

Sihtric Ivarsson (*Si-tric-ivarson*) – Known as Sihtric the Scourge by the Irish. Warlord under the nominal command of his brother Ragnall.

Tadg mac Cathal (*Ty-g-mac-ca-hal*) – Prince of Connaught.

Thor – Major deity of the Scandinavian pantheon.

Thorsten the Cruel (*Thor-stin*) – Violent Viking warlord, active in the Irish Sea.

CHAPTER 1

THE BURNING OF THE UI FHIACHRACH (911 AD)

Flann Sinna's hand shook as he stared into the stone hearth in Tara's great hall. He neither recalled when the shakes had started nor even when he had taken his ease by the flames. A great wave of sadness washed over him; evidence was mounting that his body and mind were clearly diminishing, and the depreciation of great age ever gnawed at his vigor. His pride denied him the ability to request help from his servants, his wife, his sons and even his most trusted warriors, the outward showing of weakness being anathema to him. At night he occasionally found himself lost in his own halls and he would come to, under the stars outside in his night attire.

So far he had succeeded in assuaging any worries his immediate kin had harboured about his wellbeing but there was no doubt about it; he was in a downward spiral. Liver spots dotted his skin and although he could still ride a horse, his skill at arms had long departed. He insisted on campaigning himself though, every battle summer, as to show weakness to any of his rivals or peers would be catastrophic in his mind, in a perilous time. *I must will myself onward,* he thought.

The winter of 910 had been a rain-lashed brute of a season and the beginning of 911 had remained inclement, but the usual Christian Holy periods and the festivals and traditions of the old gods had been observed and finished on Tara. Although predictably nothing was received from the Northern Ui Neill and their client kingdoms, tribute had been made by most of his under-kings, from not just Connaught, Meath, Osraige and Leinster, but also Dublin and Munster. The defeat of Munster in 908 at the Battle of Beallach Mughna had devastated the numbers of fighting men that province could field, and the surviving kings and chieftains had shown wisdom enough to pay tribute to Tara.

Who else would protect them now against the ever-growing threat of the Northmen, apart from Flann? Munster was ripe for the sacking. Word had reached him in Tara of the great battle at Tettenhall between the Saxon King Edward the Elder in alliance with his sister Aethelfled, against the Norse and Danes of East Anglia, the five Boroughs and Yorvik. A Norse Gael trader by the name of Magnus Long-Tooth had brought word to Tara up the River Boyne, on his monthly trade route into the heart of Meath. When the trader had informed Flann of the escape of the Ui Imair who held the rearguard, he had tried to remain impassive and nonchalant, but the news of Sihtric the Scourge's survival when so many Vikings had been slain had made him exult inside. No matter what had occurred between them, he loved Sihtric and he was proud of the man he had become, Viking raider or no. The survival of his brothers Godfrith and Ragnall Ivarsson had given him less satisfaction: *those two could stand a bit of dying for the good of all Christian realms,* he mused to himself.

Ragnall was a fiend and a pirate and the threat he posed to peace and stability across both sides of the Irish sea was unparalleled. His legend grew month by month and Flann guessed that great lords from Rus to Byzantine, from Francia to Cordoba, trembled in their strongholds at his name. Powerful chieftains flocked to his banner from around the Viking world. Oitir the Black-Hearted and Gragabai the Bastard had sworn their warbands to Ragnall's cause. Sihtric also concerned Flann but in a different manner. Although he was sure that Sihtric's influence would at least temporarily keep the Ui Imair from raiding the lands of Meath, the young Ui Imair prince knew everything there was to know about the various Irish kingdoms, the way they fought, the key forts and the men who guarded them. This was all valuable information at Ragnall's disposal should he deign to use it. Sihtric had learned at Flann Sinna's side, absorbing the mechanics of rulership like a sponge. If ever Ragnall was to fall, Flann hoped it was Godfrith or one of the other barbarians such as Gragabai or Garangr who assumed leadership of the Ui Imair and not Sihtric, who was already a master tactician and a peerless warrior. The Ui Imair would have to be dealt with Flann knew, *but perhaps it may not have to be me who does it? Sihtric will steer them away from my lands, at least for now,* he hoped.

He was interrupted from his geopolitical ponderings by his chief bodyguard Caolan mac Murchu of South Brega. The robust soldier executed the old three-fingered salute of respect to the forehead before addressing Flann:

"My King, two men are here to consult with you. One of them is Tipraite son of Mael Finn, the Bishop Superior of Imlech Ibuir with news from abroad. The other is Prince Tadg mac Cathal of Connaught. The prince looks impatient for an audience but has insisted that the clergyman enter first."

Flann raised his eyebrows at that but decided against making a remark, *surely it was up to the High King as to whom would be allowed to petition him first within his own hall?* Flann nodded in agreement for expediency at his man. Caolan fetched the clergyman and brought him to a chair side by side with Flann's, by the fire. The Bishop of Imlech Ibuir was almost of an age with Flann and seemed every bit as decrepit and weather-beaten. He wore the simple robes of a monk with a stained travelling cloak draped across his shoulders. He had a large nose, veined through the consumption of mead like as not, and a large belly like a boulder. Flann indicated the clergyman should sit and called a servant to fetch them two cups of mead. Once the Bishop was settled Flann began:

"What can I do for you, Lord Bishop? I believe you have some news of import that you wish to tell me?"

A worried look creased the old bishop's visage, and he took a gulp of mead before answering.

"I have news from at home and abroad, my King. You may or may not be aware of some or all of it, but I felt it was imperative that I meet with you and inform you of what I know."

The Bishop shuffled nervously in his seat before speaking again.

"A member of my order has brought me news from Francia, Muslim Africa and Andalusia. I also have news from our brothers at the monastery near the Kingdom of Kerry, at the tip of Munster."

It was Flann's turn to shift uneasily in his chair.

"Say on, Lord Bishop, tell me of my own lands first."

The Bishop nodded ponderously and spoke. "There have been many Viking raids on the coastal villages across the Kingdom of Kerry. The chief villain appears to be a heathen barbarian known as Gragabai the Bastard. Many of the countryfolk have fled to our monastery for protection as the menfolk are much depleted from their wars with you, my King".

Flann was affronted by this accusation and interrupted the Bishop angrily.

"Those battles were justified as the Eoghanachta were raiding and killing my subjects. They reaped what they sowed. And as for Cormac mac Cuilennain declaring himself the Bishop of Cashel, that was a sham title, a clear attempt to curry favour with the clergy and the countryside, against my rightful rule as the chief King of the Ui Neill and the High King of this island."

Suitably chastened, the Bishop drank from his cup and spoke more carefully.

"Be that as it may, my King, the people are frightened and vulnerable, and the chieftains and Kings of Munster are no longer able to protect them. The Norse Gael Kingdom of Limerick is not being touched by these raids and some of the peasants feel that the Vikings are being harboured there in exchange for exclusion from the raids. If that fell kingdom should rise again to its prior strength, Flann of the Shannon, nobody upon the river from which you are named will be safe. Gragabai the Bastard needs to be put to the sword, my King, as if he feels that he has the run of the province, more terrible warlords will begin to appear, and Munster will drown in blood and slavery."

The King nodded in understanding, more to cozen the Bishop after lashing out at him moments before, than indicate surprise at new information. All this news, if not quite known to him, was going to happen at some point inevitably in his opinion.

"Lord Bishop, I will send envoys to the Kings of Munster and help in whatever way I can. If the Vikings land in force and make camp in a more permanent manner, I will summon my armies and march upon them, you can be sure of that."

The Lord Bishop seemed mollified by this and continued with the rest of his news.

"King Flann, as to the news from Francia."

Instantly Flann sat up straight. He prided himself on foreseeing what systematically would affect Ireland due to international events.

"There was a siege on the Francian city of Chartres. The forces of Charles the Simple were subdued by the pagan Rollo the Walker, a sacker of cities and a fiend amongst Christian women. An agreement has been reached between them. Rollo has been granted the lands around Rouen and made a count in perpetuity, in exchange for him and his commanders taking Christ as their Lord and swearing to obliterate any fleets of heathens who dare the river systems of northwest Francia. To all intents and purposes Rollo and his supporters are now landed nobility and will abandon the Viking way of life."

Flann did not need the Lord Bishop to elaborate further. If the rich plains of Francia were denied to parties of Vikings, where else would they go and who would they follow? Apart from King Harald Fairhair himself and his monstrous son the Bloodaxe, only Ragnall of the Ui Imair stood on par in terms of infamy.

"We have received news from Andalusia also. Asturias has had a civil war between their King Alphonso and his impatient sons, and his progeny have won. King Alphonso has been deposed."

The King grimaced at that. It did not take a subtle man to perceive the similarities of that kingdom with his own. He had been king for decades now and he had three surviving sons of his own with a partial claim to leadership. Flann boiled a little too, as he suspected that it was intended as a slight by the Lord Bishop who Flann recalled had kin amongst the Deise of Munster, a warlike tribe who had certainly suffered casualties at Beallach Mughna.

"What else, Lord Bishop?" he asked to move the conversation along and to deny the clergyman his small victory.

"The Fatamids of Egypt have attacked Sicily and have looked to take it from the Eastern Roman Empire, but they are simultaneously fighting a battle against recalcitrant Berber tribesmen in the Aifric, who chafe at their domination. As you know, my King, the Fatamids are Shi'ite and the Umayyads of Cordoba are followers of Sunni Islam. Soon there could be a war between them that could engulf the entire Mediterranean."

Flann had always kept an eye upon the goings-on of the southern Muslim kingdoms and those of the Aifric. For almost a century, Vikings had been slaving Irish people to these terrible kingdoms but when war engulfed them, demand tended to fall giving the Irish people a reprieve from their predations. This news was all to the good.

The Bishop continued, "The Eastern German kingdoms have come under the control of the Hungarian Magyars and their horse nomad allies. Louis the Child, the noble Christian child emperor, has been defeated at the Battle of Augsburg and his rule is at an end."

When the news petered out, Flann thanked the Bishop and called for his man Caolan to see to the Lord Bishop's needs and provide the clergyman's party with food and shelter and whatever they required for their journey back to the monastery at Imlech Ibuir. The Bishop made his abeyances to Flann and departed the room as quickly as he had come. In moments Caolan returned with the second petitioner, Prince Tadg of Connaught.

The prince did not deign to sit and when Flann looked up into his face, illuminated by the fire, the young man's countenance was set in a hard, sombre stare that could only mean war.

"High King Flann of the Shannon, my father has sent me to Tara to beg your intervention in the raids on his border. He does not have the men to patrol everywhere at once, nor the supplies to keep armed men ready at all times, as spring is just around the corner and the crops must be planted. He begs you to move west to help us, with as much strength as you can muster. Flann mac Tighearnan and his deviant brother Cernachan of Breffni are ravaging our northern borders. They are stealing our crops and livestock that we have stored away and our northern chieftains are hard pressed to feed their people. Already farmers are moving south seeking refuge in my father's lands and he has not the stores to feed them either. This is the work of Niall Glundub, my King. He sends his Breffni puppets, the two brothers and the other clans like the treacherous Ui Ruairc against us knowing that come battle season we will be much depleted from hardship. My father begs you now, to come to our aid despite it being early in the season. If you do not, when you call your banners to answer some threat, my father fears Connaught will not have the strength to assist you as we will have been undermined and perhaps conquered. Glundub may install one of our under-kings in our place and loyal to Aileach not Tara."

Flann absorbed all of what the young prince had said. He waved his hand at the prince indicating for the Connaught man to sit and reluctantly he did.

"Your father has been loyal to me throughout his life and I will never forget this. I agree this threat must be answered. For too long Glundub has sent his minions against you, looking to strengthen his allies and weaken mine. But first we must discover what the appropriate response must be, Prince Tadg. I also must face the realities of logistics as does your father. Even with the tribute I receive I can only house and feed a force of roughly five hundred men at any one time. It takes time to gather a force and take men from my chieftains and away from the land."

The Connaught prince interrupted, "Our need is great, King Flann, anything that you could provide would be appreciated. We only wish to defend our lands; we cannot oppose the armies of Breffni and the Northern Ui Neill further north."

Flann could only agree.

"I will send three hundred men west in two days, once provisions can be arrayed for them, and we will send the Breffni men fleeing from the lands of Connaught."

The Connaught prince sagged into his chair in relief.

"Who will lead your force, King Flann? The Scourge has abandoned you, we have heard, but the renown of a man such as Donnchadh Donn or Oengus at the head of this warband will put the Breffni men to flight."

The King shook his head. Unsteadily, hands and arms shaking, he rose from his seat. The Connaught man stood up from his chair also. Flann still topped six feet two and pleasingly exceeded the young man by several inches.

"No, Prince Tadg, it will be me who leads the force. I Flann of the Shannon will ride to the defence of my friends of Connaught and protect our people."

The early spring weather was cold and sharp, and frost lay on the ground in the mornings. At the break of each day Flann's joints ached as he rose from his tent and spasms of agony ripped through his back. His wife insisted that he bring two young lads with him to ensure the stress of the march did not overwhelm him. One of them was a grandson of his, Cerbaill, son of his murdered son Mael Ruanaid. The lad, although only ten, looked the spit of his deceased son and every time he saw the boy's face, despair and regret struck him. It was a recalcitrant tribe of Connaught who had trapped Mael Ruanaid and his retainers in a church on that desperate day and set fire to it. Flann shuddered involuntarily, the manner of his son's death was horrendous and yet here he was, more as like as not, coming to the aid of some of those who had committed that atrocity. But that was leadership he knew, the ability to compromise with your enemies and deprive your friends for the good of everybody, despite personal grievances.

His wife Mael Muire would take care of the day-to-day operations of Tara while he was away and in truth, she did that anyway while Flann was in residence. She presided over disputes, saw to the provisioning, and commanded the household. She oversaw the tithes and taxes and helped forge new laws for situations that arose. Age had come for her as rabidly as it did for Flann, but she still stood straight and tall, a woman of rare nobility. She had borne him his three youngest children, two daughters and his mighty son Conchobar mac Flann, the de facto ruler of Clan Colman. Conchobar was fiery and violent but ironclad in his honour, much like his half-brother, Niall Glundub. The Northern Ui Neill warlord himself, Niall Glundub mac Aed Findliath, gave Flann Sinna sleepless nights. Many times throughout every single day Flann found himself thinking about him, every thought bent to discovering his intentions, his will, and their entwined future. Despite being married to his mother and having a daughter married to the northern king, Flann could not seem to force Glundub to see sense.

The main bones of contention appeared to be Flann's refusal to resume the ancient tradition of alternating the High Kingship between the Northern and Southern Ui Neill, Flann's willingness to trade with elements of the Norse-Gaels and various Viking factions in the region, and his protection of Dublin, a city Niall insisted should be sacked and burned to the ground. Glundub was renowned as a Viking slayer beyond anything ever seen, a formidable fighter neark as notorious as Ivar the Boneless himself. In Flann's eyes though, it was this very uncompromising nature and happiness to resort to violence that made Niall Glundub unsuitable to be High King of the entire island. The Norse-Gael were here to stay and that was certain. In parts of the country, you would be hard-pressed to tell the Irish and the Scandinavians apart as they mingled intergenerationally. Glundub refused to accept this truth, his position was black and white whereas Flann knew that most of the situation was grey. Conchobar, Flann's son and Glundub's half-brother, echoed the same traits as Niall, which also made him unsuitable for rulership. He was a warmonger and unbendable. Hard policy decisions that compromised his personal honour were impossible for Conchobar. Of his surviving sons, only Oengus was sufficiently malleable to rule the land.

Flann had also been spending time with the young King of North Brega, who was married to his youngest daughter Maeve. His name was Mael Mithig mac Flannacain. With the murder of Mael Ruanaid, Flann had learned by the hardest of ways that you should not count your chickens until they hatch. Should Oengus fall before his time, Flann had privately decided that he would make Mael Mithig the heir designate before his other sons, Donnchadh Donn and Conchobar. He would not cede the throne to either of his other sons, nor would he allow Niall Glundub to force his return to the old ways, despite his fondness for his grandson, Glundub's heir and champion, Hector mac Niall. There was no denying it in Flann's mind, a resolution must be reached between the Northern Ui Neill and the Southern Ui Neill. Ragnall of the line of Ivar the

Boneless was coming and either the country would unite to oppose him, or it would fall to his will, bit by bit. And after the storm that was Ragnall of the Ui Imair passed, would Aethelfled of the Saxons or her brother look west? Who knew?

*

It had taken the party of warriors from Tara six days to reach the banks of the Shannon at the closest point to Rathcroghan the capital fort of Connaught, the seat of the Ui Briuin Sil Muiredaig. It took a further half a day to cross the river by barge as those warriors on horseback had to control their skittish mounts onto the barges without causing catastrophe. Prince Tadg of Connaught was there to meet Flann with an honour-guard and they then travelled together toward the house of King Cathal mac Conchobar. In a few hours, the party approached the great fort itself, visible across the plains and drumlins of Connaught. It was not so much a defensive fort as a populous town; the great seat of the warrior queen Medb, of the famous saga of the Tain Bo Cuailinge. Those who still worshipped the old gods or at least feared them, believed that Rathcroghan protected one of the entrances to the otherworld where the fairy folk and the Tuatha de Danann still held court. The otherworld was also the abode of the Morrigan, the great demoness who controlled and lorded over the dead. There were worrying signs apparent to Flann Sinna of the externalities of war all around, stark against the majesty of the capital of Connaught. Starving children shivered in the lee of the fort, huddled against their mothers' skirts. Gaunt-faced men and boys looked on hopefully at the warriors approaching, no doubt wishing that their lands and herds could be returned to them.

The King himself was waiting for the war party with his own retinue. Flann was pleased to see that Cathal had assembled a significant force to augment the elite of Tara. It also pleased Flann that the King did not bother with feasts and pageantry. They were here on serious business to secure the borders of Connaught, not to celebrate when Irish people were suffering. The men made camp for an hour, refuelling with food and fodder for the horses but by midday the swollen band of warriors was on the move once more. Flann and his bodyguard alongside the King and Prince of Connaught were on horseback in the vanguard. They travelled north and slightly east until the host of warriors re-joined the banks of the Shannon once more, as its course approached Lough Allen. They camped at dusk on the lake's shore, careful to set multiple sentries in case a force of Breffni men came upon them in the dark.

The night passed uneventfully, but bad dreams plagued Flann's sleep, visions of death and suffering. His body in the morning had finally begun to adjust once more to life in the saddle. The first few days upon leaving Tara with his retinue had crippled him physically but he refused to allow his retainers to see his weakness and infirmity. It was imperative that all saw him as the mighty Flann of the Shannon, the immortal and indomitable King who ruled with fairness but with an iron fist.

In the afternoon, the horror of the situation struck home. As the party turned around a forlorn hill, crowned with a copse of trees, a ferocious sight assailed them. A small fort stood burned and ruined with smoke still floating through the air. Flann and Prince Tadg issued commands for their men to deploy and surround the fort, looking for any assailants while simultaneously rounding up any survivors. King Cathal and Flann rode through the remnants of the gates alone to witness what had occurred first. Several huts and halls were burned to ash while others smouldered in the gloom. Smears of blood were splashed on the ground in random spots with great flocks of crows and other carrion birds circling overhead, wary of the two men. The centre square revealed a dreadful discovery of a great pile of bodies, stacked and burned. Flann felt ill and dizzy at the spectacle, his heart sank. Prince Tadg entered a minute later with news of a handful of survivors, women and children mostly, who had fled to the woods through a hidden underground souterrain, in the first moments of the attack. Apparently, a great host of men had sacked and burned the fort and killed all the men and took the livestock and crops with them, leaving the women and children with nothing but their lives. *This was not the work of Vikings, or the women and children would have been seized along with the livestock,* thought Flann.

King Cathal informed Flann that this fort was the domain of one of the smaller branches of the Ui Fhiachrach, a large tribe in the north of Connaught. He also added that this was one of the southernmost forts in their territory and that to get here, the force of men that committed this atrocity would have had to pass by the main strongholds of the Ui Fhiachrach clan, indicating further battlefields and loss of life yet to be discovered.

Within the hour, the army was on the move once more. Room was made on the supply wagons at the rear to carry the survivors with them. There was nothing for them here except death. The path of the host that attacked the fort a couple of days previously was easy to follow, trampled branches and the occasional remains of fires giving truth to their passage. The carrion crows that had circled above the fort had abandoned it and now followed on either side of their force of men, a sign of ill omen if there ever was one. A child could have traced the attackers' path, with the flattened undergrowth and broken branches. At dusk they stopped again to feed the men and horses and set a watch in all directions in case of an ambush, however unlikely that eventuality was. Flann was certain of what was occurring but left it unvoiced. This border since time immemorial had been fought over by the kings of Connaught and the kings of Breffni. With greater Ui Neill powers wearily circling each other in a standoff – namely Flann and Niall – there was opportunity for Breffni to expand their lands, without fear of retribution. Impossible to pin down and with their potential targets difficult to pre-empt, it was tricky for King Cathal to meet them in open battle. If he deployed his forces in one place, the Breffni would strike elsewhere. It was the same issue in fighting the Vikings, Flann found, it was like trying to catch water in your hands.

At noon the following day, the war party reached the main fort of the Ui Fhiachrach. And what they witnessed was a new level of horror that Flann had not witnessed since the siege and sack of Dumbarton Rock forty years ago, when he had joined Ivar the Boneless in breaking the ancient fortress. All the livestock had again been seized and removed. The smoke had mostly cleared, as the sack of Dun Fhiachra as the fort was known, had occurred some days ago. There were dozens of survivors here as well, mostly women, children and the elderly, ragged revenants of the fighting huddling in secluded corners. The fort had endured significant battle damage and arrows festooned the walls of all the surviving buildings. The gate had been shattered and lay in pieces on the muddied earth. Again, mounds of incinerated dead bodies were piled outside the walls. The worst was yet to come. A soldier belonging to Prince Tadg made a grisly discovery in a clearing amongst a stand of oaks a hundred yards from the walls; it was the chief of the Ui Fhiachrach himself, Aed son of Mael Patraic, hung from a sturdy branch with his entrails cut out and slopped in a bloody heap beneath him on the ground. The ravagers had not even deigned to bury him; the indignity of his death was only matched by its brutality.

Flann was sickened. In a daze he stumbled around the ruined fort. When the two lads his wife had assigned to him came to help, he shoved them away in a sorrowful rage. Everything he wished to achieve, his hopes and dreams of a unified country looked impossible in the face of such an atrocity. *How can Irishmen do this to each other?* Some hours later, amidst the camp the army had set up around the fort, Flann found himself facing one of the survivors randomly, an emaciated man with burned rags on his back and a middle distance stare that shook Flann to the core. Flann placed his hand on the man's bony shoulder,

"The two brothers of Breffni will pay for this, my friend. You have my word as High King of Ireland that there will be justice for this."

The man shook his head sadly and answered, "It wasn't just them, my King, it was the Ui Ruairc and the Ui Cathalainn too, all the tribes of Breffni. They were going to put us all to death as well, my wife and my grandchildren too, but a large man in command stopped them. He was huge and fought with two swords. Clean shaven he was with a son beside him, just as big. Devils in a fight they were, and one of them slew my son Padraig at the gate. The big man executed some of the men who tried to rape our women and girls. The big man left with his son and the Breffni only killed King Mael Patraic after that. They are too many, my King, your host is too small."

Flann could do nothing but enquire after the health of the man's grandchildren who were thankfully alive and insisted that he gather clothing from the wagons of supplies, for him and his family. The leader of the invading force had revealed himself, it could only be Niall Glundub and his son and Flann's grandson, Hector; the Kings of Breffni were secondary to them, hence the executions for any rapers and the preservation of the women and children. To Niall Glundub and his twisted code of honour, war and battle were acceptable and the lives taken in them celebrated, but civilians and the invalided were never to be dishonoured. *Small mercies at least,* Flann thought; had it been the Breffni alone no doubt the women would have been made captives and the children would be on the pyre with their fathers, but that was not Glundub's way by the grace of God. The Northern Ui Neill hated the Vikings for that very thing. Flann approached the command tent where King Cathal and his commanders sat in discussion. Every step taken hardened his mind, he knew what he must do. He swept aside the cloth entrance and stepped inside.

"I have come to a decision, King Cathal. We will march north and answer this atrocity with one of our own. Niall Glundub and his allies must learn that attacking my allies will only lead to destruction. We will march to Dromahair, the capital of the Kings of Breffni, drag the two brothers out and hang them for the traitors and murderers they are."

A cheer rose from within the tent and the King of Connaught rose in anticipation, sword in hand.

"Together," Flann continued, "the armies of Meath and Connaught will march north and put those responsible to death as an answer to this barbarism committed against your people. I will summon Donnchadh Donn my son and his army and we will force the Breffni to submit to our combined will."

The Nobles and captains of Connaught rose as one beside Cathal and shouted their thirst for vengeance to the old gods and the Christ. They wanted justice and Flann of the Shannon would give it to them.

CHAPTER 2

THE SACK OF BREFFNI
(911 AD)

Flann Sinna sat upon his horse, watching Dromahair burn. He had envisioned that he would experience a feeling of righteous justice, a sense of moral satisfaction, but all he felt was revulsion the closer his host approached the Breffni capital. With a small bodyguard of men, he overlooked the ancient fort from the ridge of the two demons, named so from the time of the old gods, but the only demons present were Irishmen from Connaught and Meath as they massacred the terrified people of Breffni. His old ally from Connaught, Cathal mac Conchobar, was also mounted on his stallion, a look of smug satisfaction carved on his face, like a Viking rune etched upon stone. The vantage point they had taken at the initiation of the dawn assault, stood on a small valley in the lee of the Sleeping Giant mountain range, comprising the three peaks Lee-an, Benbo and Keelogyboy. Their position gave them a superlative view of both the fort, the River Bonnet that skirted its eastern wall and all the land around as far as the crystalline lake that the locals called Lough Gill. King Cathal was adamant that this cleansing of the Breffni must be done to preserve his lands from the predations of Niall Glundub and his minions, but Flann could not help but regret the decision that he had made. *How has it come to this,* he questioned inwardly; *these are Irishmen under my protection in truth. A diplomatic solution should have been vigorously pursued; I was wrong to advocate violence.*

Their combined forces had marched north as the crow flies and put every village to the torch that they had encountered. Cathal had insisted that every man, woman and child should be put to death, but Flann had refused to allow it. Despite Glundub's savagery and brutal ambitions, he was no heathen monster and the northern king always refused to take the lives of the innocent or weak. Flann Sinna would reciprocate, despite the lust for vengeance the Connaught men displayed. Honour demanded it. Flann eyed up his ally, the King of Connaught. *He could never be King of Ireland,* he thought. His petty concerns of land and vengeance were unbecoming of a nobleman with ambitions to lead nationally. He was to all intents and purposes a minor chieftain who by accident of birth, had inherited the territorial rights to the fealty of similarly insignificant chieftains. To lead Ireland, a High King must look at the bigger picture, and men like Cathal mac Conchobar or even Niall Glundub, were simply incapable and ill-equipped.

It had taken three days to move the entire host to the walls of Dromahair, the capital of the two brothers, Flann and Cernachan mac Tighearnan. In terms of miles and leagues, the distance between Connaught and the capital of Breffni was not that far, but they had taken their time to rout the fighting men of various minor chieftains of the Breffni, in their path. Some had dared to give them battle, overestimating their ability to withstand a host of Flann and Cathal's size behind walls of stone, earth and wood. Other minor clans wisely fled before them, seeking refuge further north in Dromahair and beyond. With each passing fort or crannog sacked and burned, Flann's need for vengeance and justice had eroded, and before the walls of Dromahair he was certain that what they were doing was wrong.

The attack on the capital of the Breffni had begun with the first rays of sunlight hitting the eastern skies. The attacking force was split in two with the Connaught men hitting the western gate and Flann Sinna's men and the Meath tribe, the Caille Follamain, under the command of his son Donnchadh

Donn, hitting the eastern gate. Flann had sent word across the Shannon to his son, whose lands also bordered the Breffni, and Donnchadh had joined them with three hundred men in two days. The fort was relatively unprepared and had hundreds of fleeing people camped outside the walls. At the sight of the combined Meath and Connaught host, a handful of these people sprinted to the gates and began hammering on them to escape the attackers' wrath, but most scattered and wisely fled into the surrounding countryside. Perhaps one in twenty tried to stand and fight but they were quickly cut down, their bodies hacked apart. The horns had sounded an alarm in the first moments of the assault and whatever soldiery the Breffni had present at Dromahair, came to the gates and began loosing stones, arrows and short spears onto the warriors beneath them. Dozens of fighters circled away from the gate and used grapples to summit the wooden walls, while simultaneously, roughly fashioned rams were carried to the gates and used to smash the entrances to kindling. Within minutes, it was apparent from Flann's vantage point, that their host had breached the walls at various points and the sounds of fighting within the fort could easily be discerned across the valley.

Flann could scarce believe the savagery unfolding and his heart bled at the killing occurring before him. A fleeing woman, her clothes in tatters, had crawled beneath a section of the south wall and sprinted toward their position. A warrior spied her escape and chased her down. He split her from neck to groin with a single blow. Flann Sinna could not endure it any longer, Irish killing Irish; the woman's savage death was the final straw.

"Caolan, raise my standard, we are going down to the fort, NOW!" His right-hand man responded unquestioningly. Cathal mac Conchobar sputtered disbelievingly.

"My King, what is the issue? The battle is won and now our soldiers are among them!"

Flann did not deign to answer. Kicking his heels into the flanks of his mount, he galloped toward the walls. In two minutes, he was within the fortress. He commanded several of the sergeants close by to sound the horns and issue instruction for the fighting to cease. His own men, with no grudge against the

Breffni, obeyed immediately, but the Connaught men took a few minutes to come to a halt. Perhaps they were too overcome with bloodlust to comprehend the order, or maybe they thought that this command was some trick being played by the Breffni men, to buy them respite from the bloodshed, but either way their acknowledgment of Flann Sinna's command was noticeably sluggish. At the centre of the fort a brutal melee had formed where the last couple of hundred or so warriors of the Breffni surrounded a group of perhaps twice that, of women, children and the elderly, cowering in fear. The last stand of the Breffni was a harrowing thing to witness. Many of them were wounded, and most of their soldiers sported a fatalistic countenance, common to men who could see their own demise unfold on front of them. Flann galloped his horse around the fighting, shouting for his soldiers to desist and slowly but surely, the forces of Connaught and Meath extricated themselves from the circle of surviving Breffni men.

Flann Sinna screamed for peace and after a tumultuous few minutes of swearing and shouted threats, he received the respect he was due from both sides. The battle was temporarily done. Almost a thousand warriors were present with another four or five hundred whimpering innocents, in the middle of the fray. He stood on the stirrups of his horse and encouraged the animal to canter very slowly in the space between the two forces, and then he addressed them at the top of his voice.

"People of Breffni, I am Flann of the Shannon, son of Mael Seachnaill and High King of Ireland, your rightful ruler. Hear and obey me now or suffer the consequences."

He gazed piercingly into the front rank of warriors, to prove his superiority and impress his nobility upon them, in equal measure.

"For the crime of invading the lands of my ally, King Cathal mac Conchobar of Connaught, we have retaliated and brought your warriors low. I command your leaders to come forth, the sons of Tighearnan, and submit to me now and we will relent. What will it be? Submission, or massacre?"

Flann's words had the desired effect on both sides of the conflict. His own forces, despite their anger and thirst for battle, stepped back further allowing their swords to hang loosely from their fists. The Breffni men looked dejected and hung their heads defeated, some even dropped their weapons to the ground. After a moment, some movement could be discerned by Flann from amongst the northerners and a man emerged from the crowd, carrying another dead warrior before him, a broken sword jutting out from the corpse's chest. The man carefully placed the fallen fighter upon the ground and addressed Flann Sinna:

"I, Cernachan mac Tighearnan, have the right to treat with you, King Flann. My brother the King of the Breffni lies before you, killed by your men at the eastern gate. By right, I am now the Lord of the Breffni alone."

Flann acknowledged this statement of fact with a nod. The new and defeated king spoke on:

"I wish to spare the lives of my warriors and kinsmen and the many thousands of innocents who have scattered before your host. I submit to you, Flann of the Shannon, and if there is punishment to be meted out, let me be the recipient of it. There are many people in the region that owe allegiance to the Breffni tribe and their lives must be safeguarded. It is true, we attacked Connaught to reclaim lands that we feel are rightfully ours and now you have claimed your vengeance by strength of arms. The old way."

Cernachan mac Tighearnan took a knee beside his slain brother and bent his head, awaiting Flann Sinna's judgement. The wind rose and whipped around the fort, ruffling Flann's cloak. He pretended to consider the choice, but he had long decided what way this was going to go. He purely wished to project an air of indecision, just for the benefit of the King of Connaught, that to put the entire Kingdom of Breffni to the sword was a justifiable decision he was perhaps willing to make. After what he felt was an appropriate amount of time, he dismounted and offered his hand to the Breffni King. It was accepted in the warrior's grip, forearm to forearm, eye to eye.

The formalities were worked out in King Cathal's command tent and the nitty gritty of the *Borumma*, the old word for tribute, was hammered out between the nobles. The borders were returned to what they once were. Any hostages taken by either side were to be released except for two nephews of

King Cernachean being made wards of the King of Connaught, on surety of good behaviour. For a period of five years, a certain number of livestock was agreed upon that the Breffni would deliver to Cathal's seat in Rathcroghan. King Cernachean was forced to swear upon the bible of the Bishop of Connaught, that he or his kin would never march south and raise arms against the allies of Flann Sinna, the High King. They were bound by oath to remain neutral in any future conflict between the Northern and Southern branches of the Ui Neill, only allowed to take swords in hand to defend their lands or if their banners were summoned by the High King himself. With no option but to accept, Cernachean mac Tighearnan agreed to the terms and a peace was forged. Flann Sinna, against the wishes of his ally King Cathal, ordered all the men in the Connaught and Meath host to begin repairing the earthworks, gates and other fittings and fixtures that were burned, damaged or destroyed utterly in the fighting.

Local monks, clergy and even some of the women who followed the old gods were summoned to Dromahair to treat the wounded on both sides as best they could. The clergy had complained at this, being forced to tend to the invalided alongside pagan woods witches but one look from Flann withered their arguments on the vine. His patience for grovelling to the clergy had temporarily evaporated in the face of the needless slaughter of the battle. Runners were sent all through Breffni to find refugees that had fled before Flann's army and any other survivors, with news that they could return to their homes unmolested and rebuild their lives. For three nights, while repairs were being made to the capital of the Breffni, the other minor Breffni chieftains were summoned to swear the same allegiance as their over-king. Flann had to endure the presence of the King of Connaught and his son as they gloated about the victory. *Had the Breffni been ready for them, would it have been as easy?*

His son Donnchadh Donn had icily paid his respects to his father, which had broken Flann's heart, but he could not attempt to mend bridges on front of all of his subjects, lest some of them look to use the division to their advantage. His wayward eldest son had gathered his warriors on the first day after the battle and returned over the wide expanse of the River Shannon with a share of the spoils. *At least he had answered my summons,* thought Flann, although the rising power of Niall Glundub threatening the lands of the Caille Follamain themselves was the most likely reason for Donnchadh Donn's support, not any loyalty to Flann.

On the fourth day, the army retreated south after rounding up a portion of their livestock and any excess supplies, to give to the survivors of the Breffni, to shield them against starvation. Cathal mac Conchobar fumed at this, but Flann was beyond caring. They returned to Rathcroghan via the route they came. At each fort or crannog that the host had sacked, Flann ordered that they stop and make at least rudimentary repairs to any walls, ramparts or gates that were destroyed. On entering Connaught, they did the same for any forts that the Breffni had damaged or destroyed in their territorial raids, but in truth all that was left alive from these assaults were the young, the women and the elderly. The King of Connaught left armed men at each fort to help rebuild, forage, and protect the defenceless people of the land. On the sixth day since the defeat of the Breffni, the host finally returned to Rathcroghan to cheers from the crowds of people that came out to see them. There were tears as well as the army had not emerged completely unscathed in the fighting. Arrangements were made for quick funerals for the warriors that fell and Prince Tadg, who had taken a wound to the thigh, limped from home to home of the bereaved to thank them for their sacrifice and the bravery of their husbands, brothers, fathers and grandfathers. He also assured them that his father the King would take care of them all come the winter. King Cathal insisted that Flann and his retinue stay for a couple of days of celebration and feasting to commemorate the defeat of Breffni. Flann acquiesced to ease any tension that stood between them due to the mercy he had shown the Breffni, but he privately found it obscene that they could celebrate when hundreds of Irishmen had died in battle less than a week previously and hundreds of children were made orphans.

On the dawn of the next day, Flann and his forces left Rathcroghan and marched toward the Shannon. It took a day to reach the water, which infuriated Flann as it forced them to camp overnight. In his tent, he brooded, sleep evading him. He ground his teeth and smashed his old leathery fist into his palm continually as he examined every decision, every action, that led to him leading a force of men to slaughter other Irish people. *I thought these days were behind me,* he fumed inwardly. The political and military ramifications of this last month were desperately muddy and unclear to Flann. He considered Ireland and the countries across the Irish Sea as one giant spiderweb and each action reverberated across the entire structure. Would the defeat of the Breffni show Niall Glundub that his ambition and warmongering would be opposed severely and perhaps dissuade him from future battles, or would it embolden him and fuel his desire for what he believed to be his, even further? Flann would give his right arm to know his mind. At first light, Caolan mac Murchu stuck his head inside to find Flann still awake, a wine cup in his hand and staring into space, mulling and wrestling invisible problems.

The water was tumultuous, but the host still succeeded in crossing the river by noon. Within an hour, they had reached the old road, the Esker Riada, and were making good time eastwards between the forests that stood both north and south of the rocky old route across the country of Meath. A notion crossed Flann's mind when he noticed some recognisable old landmarks on the way, and he stopped on his horse and turned to face south. His man Caolan called a halt to the column and rode toward Flann, confusion writ large on his broad features. "Caolan my lad, give command to your younger brother Ruaidhri, you and I will go south and back west for a few hours. I have a wish to see the great monastery at Clonmacnoise once more and take communion with the Lord Bishop." Caolan tapped his three fingers to his head and relayed Flann's commands. In minutes he had procured enough supplies for himself and the King and a spare horse laden with tents should they be required. The column had already resumed the march when Flann and Caolan carefully walked their horses down the slope of the Esker Riada and headed southwest.

The weather was clement, and they quickly found the beaten path through the woods and the hills that covered the southwest corner of the Kingdom of Meath, the domain of the High King. They encountered a couple of farmers leading mules tied to carts coming the other way, but neither man recognised them as they passed. This pleased Flann inordinately and a wellspring of hope arose within him. Life went on and peace reigned in large parts of the country, his subjects thrived and went about their lives, unconcerned with the wider world and the threat of war and hardship. As they approached Clonmacnoise a large-browed hill with a copse of trees perched upon it, made a lump grow in Flann's throat. He had to look away from his bodyguard as tears welled unintentionally from his eyes. His memory had been eroding terribly as old age overtook him but this place, he remembered. More than thirty years ago, he and his son Donnchadh Donn had left their retainers behind and rode together to witness the beauty of Clonmacnoise, nestled in its own stunning valley with the glistening River Shannon behind it. Donnchadh Donn had been such a sweet vibrant boy, but a deal that Flann was forced to strike with Domnall mac Aed, had soured their relationship. Flann had been forced to pass the boy over in the line of succession, all for his own ambition to retake the Kingdom of Meath. He wiped his eyes, cursing himself for his own vanity, not willing to allow his man Caolan see him weep for times past.

The rode down the valley and into the bustling town that had sprung up around Clonmacnoise. The severe stone walls that enveloped the inner area with the cloisters, halls and tower of the monks, had been almost completely obscured by the wattle and daub abodes of the common folk. Fishermen, traders, blacksmiths and farriers were abundant, and hundreds of people went about their daily business without so much as a second glance at two weary travellers on horseback. Flann and Caolan dismounted at the entrance to the main hall of the monastery where they were met by a slave boy who led the animals around to the stables. They entered the hall to find a handful of tonsured monks warming themselves by the fire and taking their afternoon meal. They were deep in conversation and only acknowledged the two men's presence when Caolan cleared his throat. Several of the monks jumped to their feet in startled surprise, but the eldest of them addressed them calmly without even bothering to turn away from the fire.

"Excuse me, but this place is reserved singly for the holy brothers of Clonmacnoise. If you wish to have one of us see to your wounded or preside over a funeral or wedding, procedure dictates that you approach the chapel and speak with our brother on duty there."

Flann Sinna could only smile, the arrogance of the clergy never ceased to amaze him, he could not help but admire it.

"And what if it is the High King of Ireland coming to pay his respects to the Lord Abbot or the Lord Bishop or whatever he calls himself?"

The older monk stood up to his full height and turned to face Flann. He was about to utter a disdainful retort, when his eyes bulged open in recognition,

"By Christ it is you!" he exclaimed.

One of his subordinates tut-tutted at using the Lord's name in vain, but the Bishop exasperatedly shook his head and slapped him around the ears.

"Shut up, you waste of space, and get stools by the fire for the High King and his associate. Sit, sit, my King, take your ease."

Flann laughed and sat down beside the Bishop once a stool was provided for him. Caolan declined the invitation, excused himself and went to explore the town. The junior monks gathered food and drink for both the King and the Lord Bishop and left their presence. In the solitude of the hall, with only the crackle and pop of the fire in the hearth to shatter the silence, Flann Sinna took communion and confession. All of it, everything that was bothering him, came flooding out. The bishop, whose name was Cairpre Cromm, absolved him of each perceived sin or offence Flann deemed himself guilty of. The very end of his confession contained the details from long ago, on what had transpired between his son and him at Clonmacnoise, all to win the allegiance of Aed Findliath and how through his pact with Domnall mac Aed he had robbed his eldest son of his hopes. On hearing this part of Flann's confession, Cairpre Cromm froze. Flann noticed and quizzically raised his eyes to the clergyman's.

"My King, there is something you should know".

He shifted uncomfortably in his chair.

"We have a special guest with us here in Clonmacnoise. He has renounced all title and has taken the staff and the cross on pilgrimage. He has come here to live out his days in peace."

Flann stood up slowly, a growing sense of menace bubbled up inside him.

"Who?"

The Bishop shrank away from him slightly but answered, nevertheless.

"It is Domnall mac Aed Findliath mac Niall Caille, of the Northern Ui Neill."

Within minutes Flann appeared at the stone cloister where his former rival now dwelled. He reached up his hand to the stout door, halted and closed his fist, but then released it once more. He slowly pushed the door inward and stepped through. A man was kneeling in prayer beneath a small window, on a wooden plank before a bench. He was humbly attired and much diminished from the man Flann once knew, but there could be no mistake; it was him. Flann stood behind Domnall, lost for words. This turn of events shocked him to his core. *How could this be? Why was this man here now?* Slowly Domnall turned around and stood to face him.

"Flann of the Shannon, have you come to kill me, or join me in prayer?"

All Flann could do was stare open-mouthed, flustered at the austere appearance and the premature aging that ravaged his former geopolitical opponent. So many questions sprung to his mind, but Flann could give voice to none of them. The former Northern Ui Neill king sagged a little, a sad smile passed his face. He shuffled over to the edge of his meagre bed and sat on it and beckoned Flann to sit on a stool on the far side of the cell. Dumbfounded Flann sat mutely staring in disbelief, trying to reconcile the arrogant king he once knew with the dishevelled man he saw before him. The former king spoke first.

"I had to do it, Flann, I had no choice. The ambition of my brother Niall was uncontainable, and he has the support of all the chieftains from Breffni to the coast of the Dal nAridi. My son is dead, and I am too old to begin again. I could no longer stand in his way, Flann."

He stared back out the window as if searching for the right words.

"I was advised by my priest to take the staff and the cross and go upon a pilgrimage, and I took his advice. It was either that or go to war with my own brother."

Flann angrily retorted, "You were the King of the Northern Ui Neill, it is not just your right to rule but your responsibility. Your cowardice in the face of your brother's ambition has condemned the north to his whims."

Flann expected the Domnall of old to rise to his feet in anger, but the revenant on front of him shook his head and smiled again.

"I will not plunge my own people into civil war, and I did not have the support to face him even if I was willing. He is the greatest warrior alive, Flann Sinna, nobody can stand in his way; not the Northmen, not you, not me."

Flann answered, "Look what you have unleashed upon the borders between our lands, Domnall! Irishman fights Irishman for land, livestock and crops and the entire island suffers as a result. But if you were in charge, we would surely have come to terms by now. It is not too late, Domnall, I will back you and we can overthrow my son-in-law, your brother, together. What support you have remaining, alongside all the warriors I command, surely would be enough to depose him?"

Domnall shrunk even further back onto his cot in dejection.

"I will give you some words of warning, Flann of the Shannon, and then some words of hope, and then I beg you to leave me be." Flann nodded.

"I was forced down this path by my mighty younger brother, but my pilgrimage has softened me and surprisingly I feel it has brought me closer to God. I am content. Do I have regrets? Yes, all men do, but I swear that I am satisfied and only wish to live out my days here in Clonmacnoise. My words of warning are thus: the Viking attacks have increased in intensity and frequency in the last few years upon my former lands. Heathen warlords roughly aligned with the dreadful spawn of Ivar the Boneless plague our coastlines and have even brazenly entered Lough Neagh. I could not curtail them. But Niall Glundub was born to destroy Vikings, Flann, you know that as well as I. But he is not satisfied with just driving them out of the north, he wants the authority that Tara provides him to unite the entire country and drive the Northmen into the sea, across the entire island. When you denied the old Ui Neill pact and reneged on the passing of the crown of High Kingship to anyone but your own kin, I knew that one day both you and Glundub must go to war."

Flann could no longer contain himself.

"That was your doing, Domnall! You marched upon my lands, killing my people, and stealing what is ours."

That accusation stung the former king and the old Domnall emerged if only momentarily.

"My under-kings had forced my hand, Flann, I had no choice, it was march and fight you, or march and fight them. You would have done the same thing to nip dissention in the bud amongst your own under-kings and I name you liar if you disagree, High King or not."

Flann had no answer to that as he unabashedly concurred.

"I know you, Flann Sinna, you still wield a small bit of influence in Dublin and amongst the Ui Imair. But over time even that is eroding. They are coming, Flann. They are coming. And part of the Glundub's machinations revolves around your relationship with the Vikings. You have always pandered to them and the Glundub fears that you will fold to them when they come and perhaps even join them. He believes Ireland will never be free of them if he doesn't act and you are in the way of that, Flann of the Shannon."

Flann angrily retorted, "The Danes and Norse have been in Ireland for more than one hundred years. A hundred, Domnall! They are part of us. If or when the Ui Imair attack and attempt to exert control, I will first try to treat with them and if that fails, I will give them battle. Niall Glundub should pay me fealty as his High King and together we could smash the Vikings for good if it must be done. I don't and won't seek battle unnecessarily."

Domnall laughed and shook his head. "If you think he will ever yield to you, you are badly mistaken. He believes you might as well be half Viking yourself. Was your sister not married to the Boneless, the most monstrous heathen barbarian to ever set foot on these lands? Rumour abounds that many years ago you joined Ivar the Boneless in sacking Dumbarton Rock in the lands of the Scots, whether you admit it or not! No, Flann, you will submit to the Glundub or he will destroy you. And then he will march upon Linn, Dublin and Limerick and crucify every Scandinavian for the pagan savages they are."

Flann could envision it in his mind's eye. The Glundub was an aberrant character. Unshakeable in his core normative beliefs, but merciless to his foes or anybody who stood in his way of achieving what he deemed to be the greater good. The former king spoke again.

"I said I would leave you with hope. Muirchertach mac Niall, the warrior the men called Hector, is that hope. He is my nephew and your grandson. He is as fearsome as Niall Glundub but he possesses the same political awareness and nuance as you and I. I instructed the boy at times as did your daughter, who listened by your side, as you carved out your empire. I believe, if you relinquish the sole right of the Southern Ui Neill to claim the High Kingship, and allow Hector to be the next king, it may represent a compromise the Glundub could accept. And then a united Ireland will face down Gragabai, Garangr, Godfrith or even Ragnall himself, under the banner of Hector mac Niall Glundub mac Aed Findliath. A king of both the Southern and Northern Ui Neill. Ireland would unite under his might and smash the Vikings forever."

Flann absorbed Domnall's words and sat for long moments engrossed. At length he answered.

"I have dictated that my son Oengus will succeed me as High King after I pass, I have sworn it to the clergy of Tara. It is not just Niall Glundub, whose word is iron. My word is iron also." Domnall nodded sadly and whispered, "Then Ireland will bleed".

CHAPTER 3

THE DEBATE ON THE ORIGINS OF THE NORTHMEN (LATE 912 AD)

The wind and rain lashed around the Hill of Tara. One look outside the main door of his great hall convinced Flann Sinna mac Mael Seachnaill, to retreat to his fireside. It had been in truth a dark and stormy year, ill-omened from the beginning. The crop yields had been well down in large swathes of the country and Flann himself had to send food out to many impoverished chieftains, to keep the people alive. Ironically it was the tribute of the Munster men that kept much of the people alive around Meath, but Flann ruefully acknowledged in his own mind that should the country endure another harvest like that, many would starve.

News from abroad had been extremely worrying too, compounding matters, and the people needed to be strong for the storm when it came. War was coming, he could feel it in his ancient bones, but then this was Ireland, and violence was never far away. Aethelfled of Mercia had subjugated much of the Danelaw and held sway in the five boroughs, while her brother in Wessex brought fire and sword to Cornwallian, Welshman and Dane alike. Queen Aethelfled had continued her building spree, erecting massive stone burhs across the land of the Britons, stout keeps that her subjects could flee to in times of need. It made Flann shiver thinking about that woman's obvious ambition. Even the Norse and Norse-Gaels were wary of drawing her gaze after the massive defeat that all the major Viking warlords of the region had suffered against her at Odin's Field. *If she gazes at Tara across the sea, are we out of her reach?* Flann was not sure.

He sat on his massive chair by the fire and shifted uneasily on the furs draped across it. Rollo the Walker was firmly entrenched now in Francia and guarded the Seine and the other arteries into that land fiercely, driving all the unaligned Viking warlords to greener pastures. Charles the Simple, or more likely the advisors around him, had made a great policy decision in ceding land to a warlord like Rollo. In a single stroke they had turned a fearsome barbarian savage into their staunchest ally and lost nothing as the land they had given him had been largely depopulated due to internal warfare and Norse and Dane raiding. *If only I could do the same with Dublin,* thought Flann wistfully, *and we would have nothing to fear from Ragnall of the Ui Imair.* But that very same warlord had not been sitting idly either. Rumours had reached Flann's ears of battles fought in the Hebrides and Northumbria, as the Ui Imair grew stronger by the day. The lands directly under Flann Sinna's control had so far avoided the plundering and the raiding but the lands of the Ulaid, Dal nAridi and the Cenel nEoghain themselves, had suffered. Gragabai the Bastard with a splinter fleet of corsairs continually harried coastal villages and settlements the length and breadth of the Irish Sea and another warlord, Oitir, was operating unchecked too. Constantine mac Aed of Scotland had gone to great lengths to drive the Vikings away, but his forces were stretched too thinly. The Kingdom of Mann still operated independently from the control of Ragnall and Sihtric but Flann knew that if that island nation should fall under the sway of the Ui Imair, it would only be a matter of time before Dublin, Cork, Wexford, Waterford, Linn and perhaps Limerick, would also be absorbed. On that dreaded day, Ragnall son of Ivar, son of the Boneless one, would lord over a disparate Viking nation stretching from the Atlantic to the North Sea.

All was not as it should be in Irish politics either. Cernachan mac Duiligen of Int Airthir had risen to challenge Maol Craobh, son of the Black Fox, for the Kingship of Argialla, the central kingdom of the lands of the Northern Ui Neill. Niall Glundub had dispatched his mighty son, Flann's grandson, Hector mac Niall with a force of men and in alliance with the sons of the Black Fox they had defeated the upstarts. Cernachan mac Duiligen was put to death by beheading on the shores of Lough Erne. There was more trouble in the lands directly controlled by Niall Glundub. A malicious fire was set in the refectory of Druim Inascalainn and the superior clergyman there died in the flames. Flann's informants had expressed to him that Glundub was furious and one of the minor chieftains was almost certainly responsible for it. It was allegedly an argument over women or tribute or both that had caused it.

But all of that paled into insignificance into what was happening at home here in Tara; Mael Muire, Flann's great Queen, was desperately ill and bedridden. A heavy cough she had, which had persisted for several weeks, and only grew worse as time went by. Blood was coming up from her lungs and her skin was feverish to the touch. She had lost a huge amount of weight and her energy levels had reduced to almost nothing. She constantly abided with a great pain that wracked her fragile form throughout the day and night. When she had deteriorated further a few days ago, Flann had sent for Padraig the new Bishop Superior of Treoit to attend her. He had come and overseen her care. To Flann's surprise the Bishop had isolated his queen in her chambers, not even allowing Flann himself or any of their grandchildren to see her. The clergyman had stated caution as the reason as poisonous vapours could escape her and infect everyone in Tara if they were not meticulous and it was better to be safe than sorry. Flann had indeed recalled a chieftain in North Meath whose entire household was wiped out by a plague and his father Mael Seachnaill had stationed armed men all around the chieftain's fortress, rather than allow any sick folk to infect the countryside. *Hard policy, but fair and prudent,* Flann thought.

At that moment, a hard rap on the door alerted Flann to someone's presence. When the door opened, Caolan mac Murchu entered with a large man covered in a drenched cloak from the incessant rain outside. As the man unhooded himself Caolan announced him, but Flann recognised him straight away; it was Magnus Longtooth of Linn, the Norse-Gael trader. He was a regular visitor to Tara on his route, where he traded wine and gold from Francia for furs, iron and honey from Ireland. Flann Sinna's seneschals always purchased his wares as his quality was guaranteed and his prices were competitive. He was honourable in his dealings and always provided titbits of news from around the region. He was a surprisingly learned man for a pagan Flann felt also, and fluent in several tongues. One night while in his cups, he had confided in Flann that his mother thought he had the makings of a Gothi, one of the Norse clergymen, but his love of the high seas had overridden his mother's desires for him. He never participated in the slave trade, he had assured Flann, and he even hired non-Norse in his crew; his right-hand man was a Breton from Dumnonia. Flann beckoned the man over and signalled for a servant to take the trader's damp cloak from him and dry it. Magnus Longtooth gratefully accepted a cup of mead and plonked himself down on a chair beside Flann, giving him the three-finger tap of respect to the forehead.

"What news from the Irish Sea, Magnus my friend? How goes trade?"

The Norse-Gael sea captain stared into the fire for a moment as if considering his answer. At length he responded:

"Things are afoot, King Flann. Ragnall Ui Imair and his two brothers have taken Yorvik for their own. The man who sits the throne there is just a puppet for them and does their bidding. They tax everyone coming up the rivers there unmercifully now and they control every river in Britain from the five boroughs to Scotland. Aethelfled seems content to move east into Danish territory but everywhere north of the Mersey, is controlled by Ragnall Ui Imair."

Flann had guessed this already.

"Does it look likely that Aethelfled will move against the Ui Imair, young Magnus? Does she seek allies?"

Longtooth shook his head, my guess is that she is content to consolidate Mercia and bring East Anglia under her control. She is more likely to make her next move against the Welsh than the Norse-Gael."

This took Flann aback. He had not considered the Welsh kingdoms. An uneasy truce had held between the Saxons and the Welsh for a generation or two, but it was not that long ago since they had fought bitterly for control of the Severn River. The trader shifted uncomfortably and looked at the King.

"At some point, you must know, King Flann, that the Ui Imair must move to reclaim Dublin? Even if Ragnall did not want to do it, many of his warlords would demand it for honour's sake. It would be an insult to their Gods, the Gods I follow, if they did not seek retribution. Even my own chieftain in Linn, Gorm, pays Ragnall tribute too alongside the men of North Brega and the Dal nAridi to the north. Gorm just wants peace and trade and his people to prosper. Should Ragnall come to Ireland, I fear he will succumb to the will of the Ui Imair very quickly. Not out of any great love mind you, but out of necessity."

Flann nodded sagely. The small Viking town of Linn had sat sheltered in Carlingford Lough for almost a century, staying out of sight and always reluctant to draw the ire of the warlike Irish kings who surrounded them. Flann dimly recalled that forty years ago, when all the Viking might of the region was drawn across with the great Heathen army to make war on the Saxons, Aed Findliath father of Niall Glundub had used that opportunity to massacre all the small Viking settlements in his territory, down to the last child. It was only the fact that the ruler of Linn at the time, Gorm's grandfather, had paid tribute to the kings of Brega, that they had been spared the same fate. And now they were the most northerly surviving Viking settlement in Ireland, still in existence.

"What news from the north, Magnus? How does the Northern Ui Neill fare?"

Magnus looked at the King, and a grim look crossed his face.

"I have to be very careful when trading up there, King Flann. I usually send my Irish lads on shore to strike the deals as my kind have never been welcome. Your grandson Muirchertach, the man they call Hector, is carving out a formidable reputation as a warrior. Barely twenty and yet the victor of a dozen battles with both Viking raiders and Irish rebels. The whole of the north is firmly now under the control of Niall Glundub mac Aed Findliath.

Any supporters of the former king have either now submitted or have been put to the sword."

Flann interrupted him then, "Pray tell, young Magnus, word has reached me of severe raiding down the river systems and on the coast by Vikings. How true are these stories, my friend?"

Longtooth nodded in agreement. "To answer that, King Flann, I would say that perhaps the hatred and fear of my kind in the north is understandable. Warlords loyal to Ragnall and the Ui Imair hunt in packs like wolves up and down the Irish Sea. I am always careful to avoid them when we spot them on the horizon. Gragabai the Bastard and Oitir, and even Brunbolg Headtaker are reaving and plundering on the coast, taking slaves and goods and selling them to the Muslims and the Black men of the Aifric."

Flann was shocked at the mention of Brunbolg, "How can a man like Brunbolg Headtaker still be alive, Magnus? He is almost of an age with me and all he has done for his entire life is plague humanity with his savagery. Surely you are mistaken, and this is some nephew or bastard son of his who has adopted the same title. The Brunbolg Headtaker I know has surely fallen in battle by now?"

The trader shook his head.

"No, my King, this is the same roaring giant that has raided for generations. His hair has gone from grey to white, but he is still the same berserker I believe. How is it that you know him, King Flann? Have you faced him in battle?"

The King answered, "No, once upon a time, he and I were on the same side believe it or not, in a battle upon the banks of the River Boyne. I had joined my forces with those of Ivar the Boneless, to regain control of Meath from the Caille Follamain. That was the day that Ivar the Boneless fell and met his Gods in Valhalla. I was there that day."

Wistfully Flann stared into the fire, struggling to remember the details of the fight, but so much had been erased from his memory that it saddened him. Magnus Longtooth was visibly impressed. Even though he was a trader, the Scandinavian blood in him rang true. He grew up on stories of famous Vikings and to hear first-hand stories of battle and the fall of the legendary Ivar the Boneless, delighted him. He pressed the King for more.

"Tell me, King Flann, how did the Boneless fall? My father said he was slain in battle with the Saxons, perhaps against the Scots."

Flann smiled. "It was a long time ago, but Ivar was married to my sister. My father in his wisdom wished to make alliance with the Vikings of Dublin and bound us in blood. I helped Ivar on occasion, providing him with warriors in some of his wars across the sea. When it came down to it, he helped me reclaim my crown as the rightful King of Meath and the entire Southern Ui Neill. Ivar fell that day, pierced by an arrow through his chest by some Caille Follamain archer. For a Viking of such reputation, it makes me profoundly sad to think of it. Some anonymous rebel took the life of the mighty Ivar the Boneless son of Ragnar Lodbrok, and probably didn't even realise it."

Magnus Longtooth sat back in wonder, gulping down another mouthful of mead.

A side door opened at that moment and in strode Bishop Padraig of Treoit. He looked grave but when he saw that Magnus was there a look of anger flashed across his face. He spoke.

"My King, I didn't realise you had...eh... guests. I shall retire until a more opportune time arises."

Flann impatiently beckoned him over. "Sit, Bishop Padraig and take a cup as your predecessor Eithigen used to, don't insult my guest Magnus here."

The clergyman nervously sat down and took a cup from a servant.

"Tell me, Padraig, how fares my wife?"

The Bishop fidgeted nervously and scratched the shaven spot on the crown of his head before answering. "I have steadied her up, my King, and she rests. It is up to God now if she survives. She is inordinately tough, my King, a lady of rare strength."

Flann smiled fondly. "Indeed she is, my learned friend. She will battle to the last and endure with courage."

The three men stared at length into the fire and surprisingly it was the Bishop who posed a question to the Norse-Gael trader.

"I have heard of you, Magnus Longtooth. You are renowned for your learning and brevity despite being a pagan barbarian."

Flann shot him a warning glance at that, but the Bishop continued unabashed. *The arrogance of the clergy,* thought Flann. Longtooth just smiled affably and awaited the question.

"How is it that Vikings have plagued us for so long and how is it that your numbers are so great?"

The trader scratched his chin and pondered his answer. Flann was intrigued as well. The clergy maintained that they were all semi-demonic fiends who were sent from God to punish Christian folk for their sins, but Flann knew better than most that they were, in fact, just men. Bigger, stronger, more brutal and warlike, but not so different to the Irish in the end. The Norse-Gael trader answered,

"My father told me a tale once, of the first Vikings raids, over a century ago, and why they came to be. There may have been many famous raids and Vikings before that, but the sagas are not great at marking time. There was once a mighty Francish king, perhaps the ancestor of the current kings that rule Francia now. My father called him the Dane Slayer but you Christians would have called him Charlemagne."

Flann nodded in recognition. Charlamagne the Holy Roman Emperor had been given authority by the Pope himself to claim all of Europe for Christianity.

"The Dane Slayer was a fearsome warrior. He defeated the Berbers and Arabs of Al Andalus, he unified Italy and secured Rome. He smashed the Bulgars and the Hungarians and then he turned his attention north."

Longtooth dropped his voice low. "He marched against the Germanic tribes to the north, the Thuringians, the Saxons, long-lost cousins of the Saxons that rule the south of Britain, and the Frisians. He even marched against the Danes. When he would come upon a village or town, he would offer them a single choice, my father said: convert to Christianity or die."

The Bishop harrumphed in disdain from his seat, "My King, this pagan trader has no idea of what he is talking about. I too know of Charlamagne the Great. He was ordained by the Pope himself. He consolidated the old Holy

Roman Empire into a single cohesive force and drove out the Muslims and the barbarians of the far eastern steppe. He saved our faith and would never resort to the massacres this heathen accuses him of. He only ever used force to protect his subjects and to enforce the will of God upon the pagans. Massacre women and children, never!"

Longtooth shrugged his shoulders and continued.

"In fear for their lives, the Germanic peoples fled north, searching for protection from this Christian conqueror. Their Gods were not so different than those of the Danes and Norse and so they begged for refuge, my father insists. The problem is that the land of Denmark, Norway and the land of the Geats, is not good fertile ground and the ground that can be farmed is only workable for a short season. I have seen this with my own eyes, King Flann, in winter, the homelands of the Scandinavians are quite beautiful but bleak and inhospitable."

Flann interjected then to ask a question himself. "How is it that Charlemagne pushing north unleashed the Vikings upon the Christian world?"

The trader answered, "My father said that in the space of a few years, the population became unsustainable in Denmark and Norway. There were too many mouths to feed. The people of Denmark and Norway have always been a sea people. Fishing, trading and exploring were a way of life. But when things got bad toward the end of the Dane Slayer's reign, young men had no option but to go out and seek their fortune. With nothing to trade, and too many mouths to feed, they became the Vikings that you Irish fear. Raiders, warriors and pillagers from the sea. They had nothing to trade so they took. Nothing to offer but the edge of their axes to their foes."

Flann sat back, fascinated. He could envision it all, one nondescript event leads to another and another and on down through the years. The Bishop was unimpressed.

"This is blasphemy. Your father would suggest that it was the Christian people of Europe's own fault, that they get raided by these barbarians, their children and women slaved, their sons massacred? You are mistaken. The only people to blame are the Vikings themselves, stealing from their betters and listening to instruction from demonic entities of hell such as this Thor and Heimdall. You and your father are wrong."

The Bishop sat back in the chair with a sulk.

"I do not condone the murder and raiding of some of my predecessors, Lord Bishop. I abhor what some of my people do and have done, but it is only some of my people that turn Viking; usually young men easily swayed by the likes of Ragnall Ui Imair, looking to carve out legends for themselves or impress the Gods and some warriors who see it as an easy path to wealth. Many of us are blacksmiths, fishermen and traders like I am, not warriors. Even amongst your own people, you have raiders and warriors who fight and plunder. Was it not one of the Argiallan princes who burned down the monastery at Druim Inasclainn? No, Lord Bishop, the Irish at times can be every bit the savages that you say we are."

That shut the Bishop up and he sat back aghast. Flann had to hide his smile behind his hand. *The Bishop has not a leg to stand on,* Flann smiled inwardly.

"As the years progressed and raiders came back laden with spoils from Christian monasteries and coastal communities, this drove more and more Danes and Norse to consider piracy and the way of the Viking as a viable pathway. But tales of fertile land that people from Denmark and Norway and Geatland could only dream about, reached them too. At that point, whole communities of Danes and Norse began to move to Britain and Ireland and the Hebrides in search of a better future for their children and escape poverty. Charlamagne the Dane Slayer eventually died, and his kingdom fractured and with no centralised power to corral the Vikings, they were free to go as they will. And now a hundred odd years later, in many parts of Britain, Francia and Ireland, you would be hard pressed to tell apart Northmen from locals. I have seen it."

Longtooth addressed the Bishop then. "Lord Bishop, many of my kin in Linn have taken the cross and abandoned Thor and Odin. I believe in Dublin, many of the Norse north of the river have included the Christ god as a new member of the pantheon."

Flann knew this to be true and nodded in agreement.

"Many Norse and Danes have their blood so watered down, that they barely resemble the warriors of old who staked their claim on these lands by force, generations ago. My own brother has taken a Dal nAridi woman to wife and they have two children, both of whom are Christian. I ask you now, Bishop Padraig, would it be right for Niall Glundub and his allies to march upon Linn and crucify these children who have one Irish parent and have been christened into the faith?"

Suitably chastened, the Bishop just stared into the fire, the slight reddening of his cheeks and on the bald spot on his head, indicating his discomfort. Flann was delighted. The dogmatic world view of the highest clergy needed to be eroded and when a senior Bishop like this could be defeated in an argument on faith, history and morality, it boded well for the future. Flann knew in his bones that the Danes and Norse that called Ireland home, were now more Irish than the Irish themselves in some ways and the only way to reverse that would be through bloodshed, atrocity, and massacre. He would have no part of that. If only Niall Glundub could see that peace and prosperity could be forged with these people, rather than hostility fostered, the entire island could thrive.

The Bishop broke from his reverie and questioned Magnus once more. "These are all fine words, trader Magnus, but how can you espouse compassion and ask for Christian charity to be extended to the likes of Gragabai the Bastard, Garangr Ui Imair or Bairid mac Oitir of Mann? These men have land, they have wealth, they have almost nothing to fear militarily, coming and going upon the sea like ghosts. And yet they raid and murder at will. How would you explain their existence given all that your father has spoken of to you, and you to us? A month ago, Gragabai the Bastard entered Lough Neagh and burned a fort to the ground. He murdered every adult on sight and enslaved the children for the salt mines of the Aifric. How do you explain away that?"

Magnus Longtooth had his turn to visibly squirm. There was no answer for it, Flann knew. These warriors were generations removed from the first raiders to emerge from the north and Flann felt that it was he who should answer the bishop. "Men like Gragabai, Brunbolg and especially Ragnall, cannot be persuaded, bullied or threatened into a peaceful way of life, Lord Bishop, it is true. They take what they have the strength to keep because they can. I believe they for the most part can be bought off or traded with perhaps, as they don't want to lose their lives in unnecessary battle. I have had Sihtric, one of their senior generals, as my ward for years. Perhaps in years to come the edges of their warlords can be softened and a peace could be forged?"

Magnus nodded in agreement with him. Flann of the Shannon sat forward, hunched over and stared into the flames and spoke then in a whisper, the other two having to strain to hear him. "Ragnall of the Ui Imair though, he is a fiend and a destroyer, you are not wrong, Lord Bishop. He is a murderous berserker, the equivalent of Erik Bloodaxe, who would go out of his way to kick an old man to death. He would see the entire world burn if he was the one who got to start the fire. He must be met with force, I agree. Either I, or Constantine, or Aethelfled and her brother, perhaps even Niall Glundub may meet him on the field of battle, it doesn't matter who; but Ragnall Ui Imair must be found, cornered and sent to Valhalla with the worst of his kin, for peace to grow upon the Irish Sea."

CHAPTER 4

THE PASSING OF MAEL MUIRE INGEN CINEAD MAC ALPIN, PRINCESS OF SCOTLAND AND QUEEN OF IRELAND (913 AD)

Flann Sinna mac Mael Seachnaill, the High King of Ireland, stared down the Slige Midluachrua road toward the north. The weather was cool with the threat of rain, the sky downcast. Flocks of geese passed overhead on their way north to their spring home and great herds of cattle and sheep grazed across the plains of Meath. The Slige Midluachra ran directly toward Slane and crossed the Boyne at the fordable point there and meandered north until it reached the very tip of the lands controlled by the Ulaid. *How many warriors, how many armies have travelled upon this road to offer battle to their rivals? How many times have kings sent their soldiers from this hill to bring death to the other kingdoms of Ireland?* Flann was not looking for an army though, sweeping down from the north to sack Tara.

He was looking for just one man, but it was not just any man: it was Niall Glundub mac Aed Findliath, the King of the Northern Ui Neill. He was close,

Flann could feel it, and he knew in what manner he would arrive. A rival king or even a chieftain subject to Flann's will, would arrive with some pageantry usually, to display his power however feeble it may be, but Flann knew that that would not be how the Glundub would arrive. No doubt, he would have his retinue camped somewhere nearby, perhaps as far north as Kells, but he would never come to Tara in force. He would make a point of not doing so. Such displays of military prowess or ostentatiousness would be beneath Niall Glundub. He would come alone, by himself, and the message would be clear: *I am Niall Glundub mac Aed Findliath mac Niall Caille, lord of the Cenel nEoghain, King of the Northern Ui Neill and soon I will come to claim dominion over Tara and all Ireland.* In a way, the sheer arrogance and belief that no harm could possibly befall him was more intimidating than an army of ten thousand men. But Flann Sinna could see through him and had elected to counter him in the same fashion. Tara was a bustling town of fifteen thousand people, mostly housed in their timber and straw houses, outside of the defensive ramparts of the fort along the eastern side. Flann had refused all permission to build around the Slige Midluachra gate as he insisted upon having a clear unobstructed view of the paths to the north and what might be marching down them. Today he was ever grateful that he had made that decision. He would meet Niall Glundub on the road by himself, sword strapped to his back, unbroken by time, unbent by age, the High King of Ireland, Flann Sinna mac Mael Seachnaill, the lord the Southern Ui Neill and the High King of Ireland. And Niall Glundub would be forced to come up the hill toward him and cede the higher ground, the message clear: I am High King, not you.

Time passed by and noon came and went, but of signs of Niall Glundub, there were none. Flann's scouts swore that he was coming and would arrive today, but the Glundub was famous for never riding upon a horse and insisted that he and his captains and sergeants march with the enlisted men to share their burden and the rank and file loved him for it. Even some of Flann's veterans loved to recall the day he stood on the bridge before Tara and defended Flann Sinna from the Norse warriors belonging to Iron Knee, the former King of Dublin. That day, as a teenager, Niall Glundub had defined himself and his legend had never stopped growing since.

There was a pall of uncertainty shrouding Tara. People flitted by, eyes downcast, going about their business silently. The Glundub was a dangerous man and could inspire fear, but Flann knew in his heart and soul that it was not the reason for their uncertainty. The real reason was, his queen, Mael Muire ingen Cinead mac Alpin, was about to die. Most of the peasantry and tradesmen and their families, would not meet his eyes as he passed; furtively tapping their foreheads with the three-finger sign of respect before darting out of sight. Some of them were, Flann was sure, genuinely sorrowful at the thought of the imminent passing of their queen, but many, particularly the men, Flann felt, were more concerned with him and his advanced age and infirmity. How much longer could Flann Sinna the High King possibly last, if his queen, a much younger person, had died? He understood their concern, but it sickened him. The animosity between Donnchadh Donn and himself was common knowledge amongst the men of Meath and the ripples of that contention reverberated around not just his own lands, but the entire country. Flann had sworn before God Almighty that Oengus would inherit his title on his death, but he knew that many amongst the Caille Follamain and even his own tribe Clan Colman, harboured reservations and some would prefer Donnchadh Donn or even Conchobar, Meath's own version of the Glundub, to take over.

At length, the Glundub made his presence felt. He emerged from between the trees upon the Slige Midluachra but he wasn't alone. Flann instantly recognised who it was that accompanied him, it was Muirchertach mac Niall, Flann's grandson, and the heir to Aileach in the north. As they strode purposefully up the hill toward Flann, he could not help but take their measure. There was no doubt about it, they were two of the most impressive Irishmen that Flann Sinna had ever seen, an echo undimmed from the days of the Fir Bolg and the Tuatha De Danann. Niall Glundub sported no beard, his wind-burnt face was weathered but he possessed a jaw like an anvil. Grey hairs had invaded the brown around his temple, but his broad chest and arms spoke of the warrior he was. In his prime he was renowned for being capable of splitting men in two, not just side to side but neck to groin as well, but all men must age, Flann knew, *even one so mighty as Niall Glundub.* His son Muirchertach, though, was of a different breed. The men of the north named him Hector after the famous story the monks spoke of; the man who battled Achilles and Agamemnon before the gates of Troy, thousands of years ago. He had the build of his father if not even bigger and rangier, but he reminded Flann more of his own father, Mael Seachnaill mac Mael Ruinaid but with the same colour hair that Flann remembered Aed Findliath had sported in his prime. Hector was a throwback, a ghost of the age of heroes, not out of place striding beside the shade of Finn mac Cumhaill or even the mythical Cuchulainn. His feats in battle were already legendary. He defeated a force of Ulaidian upstarts with half the number of men under his command when he was just fifteen years of age. He had defeated two Norse champions in single combat including the known bloodthirsty reaver, Thorsten the Cruel. He had fought in the armies of his relative Constantine of Scotland against Bernicia and against the Danes of Yorvik when he was barely twenty. An astonishing example of Irish manhood.

The father and son halted before Flann and displayed the three-fingered tap to the forehead of respect and Flann reciprocated. *This is a good start,* thought Flann. Niall Glundub spoke.

"We are rivals and sometime enemies, King Flann, but there are no reasons for not being civil to each other. I am married to your daughter and my son Hector shares both of our blood. No matter what happens in the future, I know that despite our differences that we, as Ui Neill noblemen, want what is best for our people and for Ireland. On that we can surely agree. I am here to witness the passing of your wife, my mother, a sad day for Ireland. I, Niall Glundub, request safe passage beneath your walls, Flann of the Shannon, and place the lives of myself and your grandson in your hands in good faith. Do we have your leave to enter?"

Flann measured his son-in-law from head to toe. He loved him, for what he was, the epitome of what an Irish warrior should be; but he simultaneously hated him for his dissent, his unyielding, indomitable will and his willingness to use violence to solve all problems. *If only he would be my general, what worlds we would conquer together,* dreamed Flann. He answered formally at length:

"I, Flann of the Shannon, son of Mael Seachnaill, son of Mael Ruanaid, King of Meath and the Southern Ui Neill and the High King of Ireland, grant you two men passage."

Flann and Glundub approached each other and locked arms, forearm to forearm, the warrior's way. Glundub proceeded inside the walls while Flann gripped his grandson Hector in the same manner.

"Whatever about your father, you are most welcome, my grandson," he said, smiling at Hector.

The young man smiled back at him and Flann was delighted to see that in his smile, he could see much of his daughter Gormlaith and it warmed his heart.

Flann's servants ushered the Glundub and Hector into the main hall and set meat and mead upon the board for them, which they gratefully accepted. Flann joined them toward the end of their meal and made small talk, politely enquiring on the health of his daughter and his other two grandchildren, Conaing and Mael Ciaran. Conaing had tasted battle for the first time in the previous summer but the other brother was a bookish lad by Hector's account and was most likely destined for the priesthood at Armagh. The small talk dissipated after a couple of minutes and Flann could feel the tension rise again. His grandson could sense it too and decided to change the direction of the conversation back to the wellbeing of Mael Muire. Flann outlined what had occurred with his wife to his northern kin. He spoke about when Mael Muire had first become ill, all the symptoms she had displayed, and he even described the death of Padraig the young Bishop Superior of Treoit, who had fallen to the same illness and passed away a month prior. Flann had requested more help from the clergy and had sealed the Queen in her room lest the illness jump to other people. Mael Muire had consented to this. But now that her passing was imminent, her new chief carer, a monk called Diarmuid from Clonmacnoise, had decided that it was acceptable for Glundub and Flann Sinna to attend her bedside. Flann had denied access to her for their grandchildren, although Conchobar from his Clan

Colman stronghold and their two daughters in Brega, had been regular visitors.

Later in the night, the three men were summoned to the bedroom of the Queen as her death approached. Flann circled around to her left side while Niall Glundub went to her right-hand side. The monk Diarmuid dabbed at her mouth and forehead with a damp cloth, bowed to the two kings and departed, there were no more words to be said. Hector stood at the foot of her bed, his arms folded in resigned realisation that this was the end. Her emaciated frame barely made a dent in the furs and blankets that enveloped her. Her head rested on the pillow, her grey hair framing her face in a shroud. Flann could barely keep his grief at bay; he had had three wives during his lifetime, but Mael Muire was beyond the other two, she was a warrior queen, the noblest of ladies.

The barest flutter of her eyes caught the three men's attention. They had been informed that she was too ill to speak, and the pain was so brutal as to compromise her awareness of what was going on, but Flann did not believe it. Mael Muire ingen Cinead was a daughter of kings and a shieldmaiden first, death would not dissuade her from her purpose. Ever so slowly, she reached both of her hands to Flann and Glundub, both wavering like a leaf in the wind. She feebly grasped the calloused fingers of both men and gently moved her eyes to meet the gaze of both kings. One was her husband, and other was her eldest son. Flann of the Shannon met her gaze, it took all his composure, all his decades of battle courage to meet the gaze of the woman who had stood by his side as he ruled. The Queen gave each man the gentlest of squeezes which they could see required a herculean effort on her part, but the meaning was clear: the Queen on her deathbed wanted her son and husband to forge a peace, or at least an understanding. It humbled Flann that at her last, it was others that Mael Muire concerned herself with; her family, and by extension the country and her own death would not stand in the way of that. She met their eyes with her own one more time, first Niall Glundub mac Aed and then lovingly Flann Sinna mac Mael Seachnaill, and then her eyes rolled back into her head. And so passed Mael Muire ingen Cinead mac Alpin, the Princess of Scotland, High Queen of Ireland; daughter, wife and mother to the mightiest of kings, in the year of our lord 913.

The funeral was an enormous one, held a week later, and thousands thronged the Hill of Tara. She had dictated to Flann that she wished to be buried on a small patch of consecrated ground near a stream at the foot of the hill. Her remains were carried by her two sons Niall Glundub mac Aed and Conchobar mac Flann, plus Oengus mac Flann and Mael Mithig mac Flannacain the powerful young King of North Brega. The new Lord Bishop of Treoit, a Connaught man named Aonghus, led the procession from the fort and down to the secluded grave by the small sparkling stream at the foot of the hill. Flann Sinna with his daughters led the train of nobles that followed the remains as they were carried from the summit of the hill. Donnchadh Donn walked with some of his sons, the nobles of the Caille Follamain and the chieftains of Clan Colman, while Augaire mac Aililla the warlike King of Leinster walked with Flann's old ally Fogartach son of Tolarg, the King of Southern Brega. There seemed to be a void between both sets of noble men, some bone of contention lying heavy in the air, but Flann was too overcome with sorrow to pay it mind now, he would deal with it later. One of the most surprising attendees was Cumuscach son of Mael Mocheirgi, a prince of the Leth Cathail of the Ulaid. He was deep in conversation with some of the sons of the King of Connaught. But Flann had an inkling why he was here, politics and war never abated, even for the burial of a queen it would seem.

At the site of the grave Flann's guards kept all the people back except the nobility, and the new Bishop of Treoit said the final words of prayer and lament for Flann's late queen before she was finally lowered into the ground. Once it was finished, Flann held his grieving daughters close and retreated up the hill from among the silent and respectful crowds and back to the main hall. There was a feast laid on for the important people present and stalls were erected outside with mead and beer served for the common people around Tara. Mael Muire had been insistent that her life be celebrated as well as her death mourned.

The food and mead were consumed, and muted conversation echoed around Flann's main hall, but there was very little cheer present from what Flann could see from his dais that overlooked the room. The empty throne beside him washed him in a wave of regret every time he turned sideways, reminding him of Mael Muire's passing. As the hours passed and the women and children had their fill, Flann gazed around expectantly, and the only people left were the kings and princes of his realm and those of Niall Glundub's lands also. *Its time,* he sighed to himself. With a nod to his captain of the guard Caolan mac Murchu, the room was cleared apart from those same noblemen and a handful of trusted servants who discreetly secreted themselves in hidden alcoves. Flann stepped down off the dais and sat at the head of the main central bench and all the kings and princes joined him.

Two days previously, his grandson Hector mac Niall had let it slip that his father had intended for some great meeting to occur and when Flann pressed him, he had divulged only some of what he knew about what Niall Glundub and the prince of the Ulaid intended. There were two mysterious guests that Hector had mentioned that Niall Glundub had invited to Tara without Flann or even Hector's knowledge and that had intrigued Flann; all that Hector knew was that they were allies in a potential venture. There were three possible intentions harboured by Niall Glundub, he guessed: one was trade; the second was an end to northern and southern warfare, which Flann deemed unlikely despite his late queen's ambitions; the third option terrified him: it could only be an intent for an alliance to deal with the Ui Imair. *The time has come,* thought Flann. Before anyone spoke, Niall Glundub whispered in Hector's ear and his son went to the door, opened it and beckoned two men inside. Each took a seat in the middle of the bench, closer to Niall Glundub than Flann himself.

Flann spoke first. "Who are these men, King Niall, and what is it that is so important that you had to engineer a meeting with such secrecy and ambiguity within my hall?"

Niall Glundub answered, "The man to my left is Owain ap Dyfnwal, the King of Strathclyde, representing my cousin the King of all Scotland, and the man across from him is Prince Aethelstan the heir of Wessex, but also representing his aunt, Queen Aethelfled of Mercia".

Both young men stood up and bowed to Flann Sinna, who was stunned at their arrival. Owain of Strathclyde was bearded and fierce but lean as a greyhound while Aethelstan was much younger, taller and broader around the chest. He sported a jagged scar on his face which surprised Flann that a Saxon prince of such meagre years would have seen battle up close and personal, to receive such a wound. Flann did not mince his words.

"You intend to gather a force and destroy the Ui Imair, Glundub, and you want my help to do it."

Glundub nodded in agreement and shrugged his shoulders, looking across at his son Hector.

"Grandfather," the young warrior addressed him, "the raids upon the lands of the Northern Ui Neill, the Argiallans and the Ulaid have become unbearable. We must do something. Ragnall of the Ui Imair has become too powerful and soon he will plunge the entire Irish Sea into chaos. He must be stopped."

The next man to speak was Aethelstan of Wessex. "My aunt and father thought that they had destroyed Viking power in the lands of Britain forever by killing the kings of Yorvik, but Ragnall has united every Viking barbarian from Dumnonia to Iceland once more. His captains pillage the waterways at will and they slave our people. Your lands have not yet come under attack from the Norse-Gaels and allied warbands but if Ragnall intends to unite all Northmen from the Irish Sea, he must come here eventually. I beg you, King Flann, on behalf of all the Saxons, all Christian people of the Irish Sea even, to unite with us and send this demon to Valhalla."

A chorus of ayes and exclamations of agreement followed Prince Aethelstan's plea. Flann could even see some of his own kings such as Fogartach mac Tolarg and the bloodthirsty Augaire mac Aililla, nodding their heads in agreement. Conchobar and Donnchadh Donn seemed nonplussed and Oengus looked apprehensively at his father for direction. All Flann could do was ask, "What do you propose then?"

Owain of Strathclyde outlined their plan. The Scandinavian festival of *Mabon*, a midsummer's harvest celebration, would take place in twelve weeks and Ragnall would be returning from his raids and overwintering in Francia and Andalusia to oversee it from their major longfort on the Mersey. Owain had scouts and several treacherous Northmen on his payroll who had confirmed this information. He would only arrive a day or two beforehand and would be vulnerable on the sea if he only arrived with a fraction of his fleet. If the Kingdoms of the Southern and Northern Ui Neill, alongside the Scottish Bretons of Strathclyde and the Saxons, were waiting for him perhaps they could decapitate the leadership of the Ui Imair in one fell swoop. When the Scottish king finished and regained his seat Flann took a moment to consider the plan. It had its merits, but it was undoubtedly risky.

Donnchadh Donn asked a critical question. "What strength have we combined to deploy at sea? The Kingdom of the Southern Ui Neill is not a sea power, neither is Connaught or Leinster."

It was a very good question. Niall Glundub provided the answer. "The Scots of Strathclyde have thirty ships and Aethelfled has twenty to spare. The Kingdom of Ulaid have thirty-five in total. That means we can field perhaps three thousand men for this engagement."

Murmurs of excitement rippled around the table at the estimate provided by Niall Glundub. Flann could sense the belief growing exponentially among the kings and the under-kings present; it was a serious force. Flann decided that he should temper this growing resolve at least partially and douse the headlong thirst for battle.

"What if our fleet should come upon Ragnall and his brothers with their full strength? I have heard wild estimates that he possesses almost five hundred ships now and can field as many as ten thousand Vikings and other subjugated and allied people from Cumbria and the Hebrides, and even the Britons from Dumnonia. He takes tribute from many chieftains on the eastern coast of the Irish Sea. Have you considered that your intelligence could be incorrect, King Owain, and although we intend to ambush the Ui Imair, it is us that could walk into an ambush instead?"

Flann was glad to hear some grunts of acknowledgment from some of the men around the table. This venture posed massive risk. In a single battle, what little naval power the combined kingdoms of Ireland possessed could be annihilated in this one confrontation. Should that occur, the Vikings could land an army unopposed anywhere in Ireland at any time and there would be little the Irish kings could do to oppose them initially.

Prince Aethelstan responded to Donnchadh Donn's question.

"Ragnall's strength grows daily. His numbers swell with every passing season. My aunt is building burhs across Mercia and the Danelaw to reinforce our position, but a time may come soon when Ragnall leads an unopposable force south and ransacks the Saxon kingdoms, like his grandfather and great uncles of old. No, King Flann, we must take this one chance to rid ourselves of this serpent once and for all even if the intelligence King Owain obtained is false. If our combined navy comes upon Ragnall with most or all his strength, we will give him battle none the less or retreat as the leaders decide. It is still worth the risk."

Another chorus of ayes followed Aethestan's pronouncement.

"And who is going to lead this force of men, Aethelstan? Who could possibly have the ability to face Ragnall and his brothers on the open sea and hope to win?" asked Oengus.

Niall Glundub answered him. "Aethelstan will lead the Mercian force, Owain will lead the Scotsmen and the command of the Irish forces will be Conchobar mac Flann, my brother, your son and acceptable to all of us. Under him will serve Hector mac Niall my son and Prince Cumuscach of the Ulaid."

Roars of approval were bellowed on the announcement of the leadership. Even Donnchadh Donn and Oengus looked relatively impressed. Flann weighed it up. *If I refuse to help, I will be perceived as soft on the heathen barbarians, and it will undercut my position. Niall Glundub will look ever more the rightful High King upon my death. I have no option but to agree and send a portion of my strength.*

Niall Glundub stood at the end of the table. "Will you help us to destroy the Ui Imair once and for all, King Flann? Will you lend us your strength? What say you?"

The table hushed and waited for Flann to make his decision with bated breath. At length he whispered, "Meath will answer, you have my swords."

Glundub nodded while Aethelstan and Hector clapped each other on the back in excitement and joy, clearly in the belief that their gambit to gain the support of the Southern Ui Neill had paid off. A unified force of Irish, Scots and Saxons, not seen before nor probably ever to be seen again.

The kings and princes called for mead and began drinking and making boasts of how they would defeat the Ui Imair, but the joviality displayed on the day of Flann's wife's burial dismayed him and he left to go outside for some fresh air. All the potential ramifications of a military expedition like this raced through his mind, but he could not think straight. The slight screech of a hinge indicated someone had stepped out to join him. Fogartach mac Tolarg of Brega and Augaire mac Aililla approached. The King of Leinster spoke first.

"My King, I think we must consider two more things before we fully commit to the Scotsman's plan. We all three here know that the young lads reaching manhood in Dublin are joining Ragnall across the sea in numbers in search of glory and plunder. He draws them like flies to honey. I believe, King Flann, that we might have to yet again sack and burn Dublin to the ground and this time, leave no male survivors. If the battle goes ill on the Irish Sea, we cannot allow Ragnall and his brothers a friendly port to land in, to seek revenge upon all who took part in this venture. Dublin will become a base for them to lay waste to Ireland."

Flann sighed and looked to the sky for inspiration, but the stars were veiled and gave him no inkling on the proper course.

"No, my friend, I will not massacre thousands of innocents for crimes they might commit in the future."

This angered and dismayed the Leinster king, but he held his tongue. Fogartach mac Tolarg placed his hand on Flann's shoulder. At one time, he was Flann's ward here on Tara and was still close to him.

"King Flann, what of Bairid mac Oitir, the King of Mann? The traders that stop in on my shores tell me that he is still unaligned with the Ui Imair and maintains his independence. He surely must feel the threat posed by the Ui Imair too and he understands that Ragnall will come for him as well. Perhaps you could use your good standing with the Northmen to persuade the Viking Kingdom of Mann to join with us and provide their ships to our force? I would wager Bairid mac Oitir would support us, his grandfather Auisle was slain many years ago by Ivar the Boneless and Olaf the White and he bears nothing but animosity toward the Ui Imair."

Flann considered the suggestion momentarily before shaking his head.

"It is true, Bairid mac Oitir might be in favour of this attack upon Ragnall, but if any of the warriors under his control disagree with his potential alliance with us against their own kind, they could flee to Ragnall and warn him of our ambush. That would provoke Ragnall to open battle and that in turn would lead to the deaths of tens of thousands of innocents. No, my old friend, we must trust to what we have committed to now and hope it is enough. Surprise could be worth more than an extra fifty ships and warriors to man them."

The two under-kings left him after making their obeyances, but Flann could sense their displeasure. Augaire mac Aililla was a volcanic ruler and Flann briefly considered summoning him back and perhaps having Oengus threaten him into obedience. He was likely to attack Dublin himself out of spite, irrespective of Flann's instruction. But a surge of grief and exhaustion overtook Flann then. He almost fainted in the night air and gripped the wall to steady himself. He was seventy-five years old and felt every bit of it. His sons were all grown men, and his wife was dead. He had striven for control of Ireland for almost forty years all to win a peace that would unify and endure, but even now at the end of his days, there was only violence, war, and destruction. It was all futile. *Perhaps the Glundub is right, and I am not the man to lead this country.* He turned around and walked back inside to his hearth and the boasts of bloodthirsty kings.

PART 7

THE RAGE OF NIALL GLUNDUB

DRAMATIS PERSONAE:

Aed Findliath (*Aid-fin-lee-at*) – Long-deceased King of the Cenel nEoghain and the Northern Ui Neill. Son of Niall Caille and father of Niall Glundub.

Aed mac Eochuchan (*Aid-mac-ay-oh-ku-kawn*) – Ulaidian nobleman and warrior.

Aed mac Mael Ruanaid (*Aid-mac-male-ruin-ad*) – Southern Ui Neill Prince and grandson of the High King Flann Sinna.

Aethelstan (*A-thel-stan*) – Young Saxon prince and Mercian commander.

Alexander – Emperor of the Eastern Roman Empire in Byzantium.

Allacan mac Laichthecan (*Al-la-kawn-mac-like-tha-kawn*) – Young noble of the Cenel Maelchi tribe of the Ulaid.

Anastasius (*Anas-tay-sius*) – Pope of Rome, head of the Christian faith.

Augaire mac Aililla (*Ag-wear-a-mac-al-lila*) – Ferocious Leinster king and brother in law to the Ui Imair princes.

Bairid Oitirsson (*Bar-rid-oh-tier-son*) – Called Bairid mac Oitir by the Irish, distant kin to the Ui Imair as his grandfather Auisle was brother to Ivar the Boneless. Ruler of the powerful island Kingdom of Mann in the Irish Sea.

Cairpre Cromm (*Car-pray-crom*) – Bishop Superior of Clonmacnoise.

Cathal mac Conchobar (*Ca-hal-mac-con-co-bar*) – Over-king of all Connaught, subservient to the High King Flann Sinna of Meath.

Cearnachan mac Tighernain (*Kyer-na-cawn-mac-tier-nan*) – King of Breffni, under-king to the Northern Ui Neill.

Cerran mac Colman (*Ker-ran-mac-coal-man*) – Young noble of the Cenel Maelchi tribe of the Ulaid.

Colman (*Coal-man*) – Chieftain of the Cenel Maelchi, a powerful Ulaidian tribe.

Conaing mac Niall (*Co-ning-mac-niall*) – Prince of the Cenel nEoghain, son of Niall Glundub.

Conchobar mac Flann (*Con-co-bar-mac-flann*) – Youngest son of the High King Flann Sinna, and leader of Clan Colman the most powerful Southern Ui Neill tribe.

Congalach mac Garbaith (*Con-gal-ach-mac-gar-bih*) – King of the Cenel Conaille, a strong Northern Ui Neill tribe.

Cuchulainn (*Coo-cull-en*) – Mythical Irish warrior, leader of the famous Red Branch Knights.

Cumuscach son of Mael Mocheirgi (*Cum-as-scok-ma-male-mo-hergi*) – Prince of the Leth Cathail tribe of the Ulaid.

Diarmuit mac Cerbaill (*Dear-mit-mac-Ker-bal*) – Young over-king of Osraige, answerable to Flann Sinna.

Domnall mac Aed (*Donal-mac-aid*) – Deposed King of the Northern Ui Neill, older brother of Niall Glundub.

Domnall mac Cossachtach (*Dom-nal-mac-coss-ach-tach*) – Irish warrior and mercenary officer.

Donnchadh Donn mac Flann (*Dun-na-ka-dun-mac-flan-sinna*) – Powerful king of the Caille Follamain tribe in Meath, son of the High King Flann Sinna.

Edward the Elder – King of Wessex.

Erudan (*Er-roo-dan*) – Young Northern Ui Neill nobleman.

Ethelwald (*Eth-el-wald*) – Politically powerful Ealdorman in Northumbria.

Flann Sinna – High King of Ireland and over-king of Meath and the Southern Ui Neill.

Flathrue (*Flat-roo*) – Grandson of Lethlabor the chief of the Dal nAridi.

Fogartach mac Tolarg (*Fo-gar-tach-mac-tol-arg*) – King of South Brega, under-king of the Southern Ui Neill.

Giblechan (*Gib-la-kawn*) – Powerful leader of the Cenel Conaille tribe.

Godfrith Ivarsson (*God-frith-ivarson*) – Twin brother of Sihtric, the youngest sons of the former King of Dublin, Ivar Ivarsson. Commander under his brother of Ragnall.

Gormlaith ingen Flann (*Gorm-la-ingen-flan*) – Princess of the Southern Ui Neill and wife of Niall Glundub.

Gragabai the Bastard (*Grag-a-by*) – Notorious Viking raider and alleged bastard son of Harald Fairhair.

Grungni mac Conall (*Grung-knee-mac-fer-dia*) – Irish nobleman with a Norse-Gael Ui Imair mother.

Gunnar Sihtricsson – Ui Imair warlord and captain.

Harald Fairhair – King of all Norway.

Ivar the Boneless – Long-deceased former King of Dublin and a legendary son of Ragnar Lodbrok.

Laichthechan the old (*Like-tha-kawn*) – Venerable Ulaidian nobleman.

Lethlabar (*Leth-la-bar*) – Aged chieftain of the Dal nAridi, one of the strongest Ulaidian tribes.

Loingseach mac Aedo (*Ling-shock-mac-aido*) – Holy brother of Clonmacnoise monastery.

Loingseach mac Lethlabar (*Ling-shock-mac-leth-la-bar*) – Prince of the Dal nAridi.

Mael Brigte (*Male-brig-ta*) – Prince of the Cenel Connaille, a powerful Northern Ui Neill tribe.

Mael Brigte mac Tornain (*Male-brig-ta-mac-tor-nawin*) – Bishop Superior of Armagh.

Mael Ciaran mac Niall (*Male-kee-rawn*) – Prince of the Cenel nEoghain, son of Niall Glundub.

Mael Cluiche (*Male-cli-ha*) – Brother of the King of Connaught and commander in his armies.

Mael Craobh (*Male-crave*) – King of Argialla and under-king of the Northern Ui Neill, son of the Black Fox.

Mael Mithig mac Flannacain (*Male-mith-ig-mac-flan-na-cawn*) – Shrewd and charismatic King of North Brega, son-in-law to the High King.

Mael Muire (*Male-mwir-a*) – Nephew of the son of the Black fox of Argialla, serious warrior.

Mael Ruanaid mac Cumuschach (*Male-ruin-ad-mac-cum-a-cach*) – Young Ulaidian nobleman.

Mochta (*Mock-ta*) – Brutish warrior of the Dal nAridi tribe.

Muirchertach mac Niall (*Mwir-her-tach-mac-niall*) – Formidable young son of Niall Glundub and prince of the Northern Ui Neill and the Cenel nEoghain. His reputation as a warrior was such that the people of the north called him the "Hector" of Ireland.

Niall Glundub mac Aed Findliath – Ruler of the Cenel nEoghain and the Northern Ui Neill, dominant power in the North of Ireland.

Niall Noigiallach (*Niall-noi-gee-allach*) – Also known as Niall of the Nine Hostages. Semi-legendary ancestor of all Ui Neill nobility.

Oengus mac Flann (*Ong-gus-mac-flann*) – Prince of the Southern Ui Neill, son of the High King and heir designate of all Ireland.

Oitir Iarla (*Oh-tier-ee-arla*) – Also known as Oitir the Black, or Oitir the Black One. Fearsome Viking warlord.

Olaf Snorrisson – Ruler and chieftain of the Norse-Gael town of Linn.

Ragnall Ivarsson (*Rag-nal-ivarson*) – Leader of the Ui Imair.

Sean mac Piarsigh (*Shawn-mac-pierce-sig*) – Scottish mercenary commander.

Sihtric Ivarsson (*Si-tric-ivarson*) – Known as Sihtric the Scourge by the Irish. Warlord under the nominal command of his brother Ragnall.

Tadg mac Cathal (*Ty-g-mac-ca-hal*) – Prince of Connaught.

Tadg mac Ruaidhri (*Ty-g-mac-roo-ree*) – Cenel nEoghain and Northern Ui Neill warrior.

Uathmaran (*Oo-at-mar-on*) – Young Northern Ui Neill nobleman.

Uinsean (*In-shan*) – Minor Cenel nEoghain chieftain.

CHAPTER 1

THE CONFRONTATION WITH THE SEA KING RAGNALL UI IMAIR (913 AD)

Niall Glundub mac Aed Findliath stalked his son Conaing across the yard. He spun both of his swords skilfully in his hands until they became a blur before him, weaving them together in a whirligig of violence. He never fought any longer with a shield as his attack was his defence. Conaing moved to his left, his shield raised, with his practice sword pointed at a threatening angle toward his father. Glundub had seen this type of stance displayed by Conaing a thousand times and knew a thousand ways to get around it. Conaing was shaping up to be an extremely competent fighter and swordsman, perhaps not as formidable as his older brother, but a commander of men none the less. *He will make a fine captain under Hector,* he thought. Glundub moved to his left and swung his own left-hand sword at his son's head. Conaing parried the blow accurately, but Niall was already moving further left. With deft footwork he spun around and delivered a backward blow with his right-hand sword. The blow clipped the back of his son's head and Conaing dropped to the ground with a yelp of pain.

"Conaing, you must move your feet when facing an opponent like me or your brother, or you will be quickly outmanoeuvred and dispatched."

His son cursed in disgust. "But Father, if I am in the shield wall, how will I ever get exposed like that?"

Niall answered, "Because battle is not some dance, son. Every warrior has a plan until their comrade beside them is slain. You must be able to react to any scenario, Conaing, and it is important that you face the likes of me and your brother in the training yard, so when you face some better-than-average berserker on the field of battle, nothing will surprise you."

He playfully slapped his son on the rump with the flat of his sword. "Go in and get your afternoon meal, Conaing, with your mother and think upon what I have taught you."

His son solemnly tapped his three fingers to his forehead in obeisance and marched toward the main hall in Aileach in search of food and it made Niall smile, *such a serious lad*. He had called their training off, not because there was much fatigue present in either of them, but because there were several huge events to be dealt with that would happen at Aileach today, important business all. The Bishop of Armagh had arrived and had news from abroad and from the south. He had requested an audience with Glundub at one hour past noon. Secondly, his captain of the guard, Tadg mac Ruaidhri of the Cenel nEoghain, had been sent to capture Congalach son of Gairbith, the King of Conaille, who had been identified as the guilty party in the previous year's sack of Druim Inascalainn and the mastermind of the murder of many of the clergy there. The rogue under-king had interceded on behalf of a kinsman on the line of succession after the previous Bishop Superior had passed away and tried to install his own kin and allies in the deceased's' place, but he had been identified as the culprit by survivors. Tadg had sent back a rider who had reached Glundub that morning with news of their impending arrival, prisoner in hand. Allegedly, when the recalcitrant chieftain had witnessed the size of the force that Tadg had led to his fort, he had offered himself voluntarily into their custody to save his people from harm. He had admitted his guilt and peacefully surrendered, but there was no room for manoeuvre available to

Niall in this case; Congalach's head must roll, and it would be Niall himself who swung the sword. *All the lands of the north must always see me as the hand that delivers justice.*

The main event of importance this day though was not just a geopolitical matter but a personal one; the Irish part of the unified fleet that was sent to ambush the Ui Imair King, Ragnall Ivarsson, would be arriving today upon the River Foyle. Fishermen the previous day had spotted Ulaidian sails in the distance, and sent word back overland to Aileach of their impending arrival. Niall estimated that the fleet would arrive at the appointed pier on the river before the day was out. The outcome of that naval battle would alter the future of not just the lands under the sway of the Northern Ui Neill, but the entire island of Ireland, and Niall was desperate to know the result. But selfishly, in his heart of hearts, he just wanted to see his son and half-brother returned alive to him from the encounter unharmed, whatever the outcome of the battle.

Mael Brigte mac Tornain the Bishop Superior of Armagh was a sweaty little water vole of a man, Glundub felt, about as inspirational as a pile of rocks, and yet he had proved not just pious in his responsibilities, but robust in the face of heathen aggression over the years. He sat across from Niall Glundub in a wooden chair with his legs crossed and his heavy robe bundled around him.

"King Niall," he began, "I have news from both abroad and from the south. There was a battle just a week past between the men of Meath and Leinster."

Niall's eyes rose in surprise. In Ireland, the treachery of its politics was renowned, but this seemed uniquely unusual.

"Who fought who, Lord Bishop?" he asked.

"Donnchadh Donn and his Caille Follamain joined forces with his brother-in-law Mael Mithig mac Flannacain of North Brega and they marched upon an assembled host of men belonging to Fogartach mac Tolarg of South Brega and Augaire mac Aililla of Leinster. The reasons are unclear for the conflict but fighting certainly took place. Men of my brotherhood have tended many of the wounded and word has spread. Almost fifty men were killed, and many prisoners were taken. Donnchadh Donn and Mael Mithig were the victors."

Niall Glundub could barely conceal his surprise. Flann Sinna had clearly taken no part in the fighting, but Glundub knew better than to underestimate his rival. Very little happened in Flann's domain without the ancient king knowing. Most likely it was a disciplinary action that Flann Sinna sanctioned without any evidence of his desires; his will being demonstrated through puppets. Niall hated the way that Flann Sinna thought and operated. Every move calculated and measured, every piece on the board deliberated over until procrastination and ambiguity overruled all. *I would never ask any soldier to fight my battles for me and if my own kings required discipline or if censure were required, I would do it myself without the help of any pawns. Flann has a ready-made excuse should he be put to the question by angry parties, that he had sent the cream of his forces with Conchobar to chase Ragnall Ui Imair,* he mused privately.

The Lord Bishop continued, "Ethelwald of Northumbria has died, my King; thus, no strong Saxon nobleman stands in the way of Ragnall or his kin taking all of Northumbria as far as the Scottish border. Edward the Elder the King of Wessex has taken London completely from the Danes, and all Saxons and Northmen alike pay him homage there."

Niall nodded and considered these events. Constantine would now have a dangerous foreign power on his southern border as well as raiders capable of attacking his entire coastline. Edward the Elder was consolidating his power in the south and Niall could not help but wonder if perhaps Constantine was better off having Ragnall as a neighbour rather than Edward the Saxon and his banshee of a sister.

The Lord Bishop spoke on: "There is news from far afield too, King Niall. Pope Anastasius the third has succumbed to illness and died in his bed, God rest his soul."

Both the Lord Bishop and Glundub blessed themselves in his memory.

"And Alexander the Emperor of the Byzantines has died as well leaving his successor in a state of war with the Muslims in Anatolia and the Bulgar horsemen to the north."

Niall nodded although this news from far-flung places held only minor interest for him; he cared little and less for the goings-on of Bulgar savages or Muslim warlords.

A knock on the hall door interrupted the two men and a servant entered to inform Niall that his captain Tadg mac Ruaidhri had arrived from the lands of the Cenel Conaille tribe, with their prisoner in chains. Niall requested that the Lord Bishop accompany him down to the centre of the fort to deliver the last rights to the rogue under-king and to take command of the ministrations of the remains once the imminent execution took place. He would then accompany Congalach's remains back to his son and heir. When Niall came upon the prisoner, kneeling prostrate on the muddied earth, he felt little remorse or pity for him. What he did was unconscionable and sacrilegious, almost heretical, and only worthy of Viking pagan savages. The murder of clergymen to further the cause of your own kin within a monastery was despicable. Congalach had fought honourably alongside both Niall and his brother Domnall in the past, in their many wars against the heathens. He had also assisted in putting down insurrections and territorial disputes amongst the clans under the rule of the Northern Ui Neill, but all that good in Niall's eyes did not wash out the bad. And for the crime of murder, he must die, and Niall could only hope that Congalach's heir would act more honourably than his father in future. Glundub spoke to the man.

"Congalach son of Gairbith Ui Conaille, I name you murderer of some of the holy brotherhood of Druim Inasclainn. The sentence is death by beheading, by my hand. Do you have anything to say?"

The criminal king stared up at Glundub, but he elected not plead for mercy as Niall had none to offer. He was about to say something but decided against it. He shook his head and bent his head in prayer, accepting of his fate. Niall commanded that the executioner's block be brought forth and a manservant rushed to obey. The hundred or so soldiers and other retainers paused and went silent, watching intently.

"Stretch your neck, King Congalach, and die with honour, as a warrior of the Ui Neill. Die well for the honour of your kin."

The words stiffened the prisoner's resolve and he rose from his knees and walked upright and proud toward the block. He knelt once more and placed his chest upon its rough wooden surface, his neck exposed. Niall nodded to

Lord Bishop Mael Brigte and the rodent-ish clergyman droned the necessary prayers to ease the man's life into heaven and simultaneously absolve him of his sins. *God may forgive him, but I do not,* thought Niall… And he brought down his sword in a whistling arc.

Once the arrangements were made for Congalach's remains to be returned to his former lands and the care of his clan, Niall summoned his captain Tadg mac Ruaidhri and his sons Conaing and Mael Ciaran to him. Niall had learned to hate using horses as he felt that it projected an air of superiority to the world that should only be earned by someone through their honour and strength of arms; but in this case, time was a factor and he wanted to witness the return of his son and brother for himself upon the River Foyle. The place on the river where he wished to greet them was an hour away from the Cenel nEoghain's fort of Aileach, and evening was rapidly approaching. In minutes they were ready and set out from the eastern gate.

The weather was pleasant, and summer had its grip on the territory of the Northern Ui Neill. The land was covered in crops and herds of ungulates grazed calmly in the warm breeze. The trees of the wood were sheathed in greenery and the birds flitted to and fro among the branches; and yet Niall Glundub's unease and uncertainty cast a pall over his companions. Barely a word was said on the trek as each man kept his own council.

There was a small village that served as a trading port for sellers of goods wishing to access the interior of Northern Ui Neill lands and that was where they were aiming for. The river was deep at that point and a wooden pier jutted out into the water, sufficient for any boat from the largest Norse-Gael longboat to the smallest fisherman's skiff. They reached there in good time and set their horses to cropping grass. Niall sent his son Mael Ciaran to the village chieftain, a rugged old bear named Uinsean, to let them know why they were there and for how long. The sun was still two hours away from dusk and the four men took some food and water. Niall could not take his eyes off the river as it glistened and meandered its way south and his thoughts were bent on what had likely happened out on the Irish Sea. The fishermen were adamant that sails had been spotted off the shore and the word that had quickly reached

Aileach insisted the Ulaidian fleet had arrived, and now Niall Glundub mac Aed Findliath waited intently for the appearance of his son and brother.

With an hour to go before dusk, the sails they were waiting for appeared. The fleet, one by one, turned the northward bend ahead of them and began drifting toward the wooden dock where the four men stood.

"Father," Conaing exclaimed having the best sight of the four, "did you not say that the Ulaidian part of the fleet that carried our warriors was thirty-five ships strong? I only count twenty-one."

Niall could see worryingly that his middle son was correct, he had instructed the entire fleet to return to the River Foyle and not to the lands of the Ulaid and Dal nAridi, in case of pursuit. His chest tightened, thinking about first and foremost his kin, and then secondarily the battle itself. His jaw clenched in anguish; Niall stood upon the pier staring intently at the lead boat as it approached. In the deepening gloom a recognisable figure stood at the bow of the ship at the apex of the fleet. It took a moment, but with great jubilation Niall could discern that it was indeed his eldest son and heir, the mighty Muirchertach; Hector had survived. Flann could see the relief on his younger son's faces at the safe return of their brother but as the boat landed at the dock all could see that Hector sported a downcast and exhausted countenance. *Something has gone wrong,* Niall knew, *we must have been defeated.*

Hector leapt from the ship and embraced his father and brothers and grasped Tadg mac Ruaidhri the warrior's way, forearm to forearm. When they had gathered themselves, Niall asked Hector, "How fares my brother? Is he safe?"

Hector nodded to the back of the fleet but indicated that they should commandeer the chieftain Uinsean's austere little hall to speak briefly of what transpired there upon the seas, lest tales emerge from the mouths of eavesdroppers. The very last ship of twenty-one docked and Conchobar mac Flann set foot on land, and he joined his brother and nephews. Niall's heart gladdened to see him, but he too wore the bleak visage of someone who had witnessed carnage and defeat first-hand, a look Niall Glundub knew only too well. They locked eyes and said no more and retreated to the hall of the chieftain.

There were six men present around the fire once Niall Glundub had dismissed Uinsean, and all his servants and kin. Niall Glundub, his three sons, Conchobar mac Flann and Aed mac Eochucan, a prince of the Ulaid of the line of kings of Dun Padraig, a clan of Ulaidians that claimed to be able to trace their lineage to the time of the Red Branch Knights. He was not a major noble, but he was the highest ranking among the Ulaidians and Dal nAridi who had survived the battle and would have to suffice. Conchobar, when he had landed on the pier, had informed Niall that not only had their armada been put to flight by the Ui Imair, but Cumuscach mac Mael Mocheirgi had been slain when facing Oitir Iarla, one of Ragnall's chief warlords, in brutal close-quarter fighting aboard the Viking's ship. Niall spoke first.

"Conchobar my brother, tell me all of what transpired upon the sea and leave no detail unsaid, for what we do next could rule the fate of the Ui Neill, both north and south."

Conchobar stared at the great fire in the old slate hearth and began to recall events.

"Our fleet set sail from the Fort of Bangor two days before the allotted time and made good headway across the Irish Sea. We first met with the ships of King Owain of Strathclyde off a spur of rock known to both the Scots and the Dal nAridi, ten miles from the estuary of the Mersey River. We were joined half a day later by Aethelstan of Mercia. All was set and we fanned out in a crescent facing south, a mile out from the Mersey. At noon the next day, Ragnall's fleet appeared on the horizon. He had no more than thirty ships, but his flagship was a monstrous dragonboat as described from the stories we had heard from the Saxons, with two more just like it in his fleet. With the bulk of our Irish forces, we had the honour of blocking the estuary from Ragnall, denying him escape to his stronghold. Aethelstan's Saxon portion of our fleet moved to engage, due to him possessing the most experienced seamen, and he moved into arrow range to harass the Vikings, while the Scotsmen looped around to the east and then south to outflank the heathens. We outnumbered them three to one, despite their trio of giant dragon boats, and had the intention of isolating and trapping Ragnall's ship, once we had identified him, and put him and his chief lieutenants to the sword… But he did not retreat, Glundub, he attacked!"

Glundub envisioned the deployment in his mind's eye. He was no nautical captain at all, his knowledge and experience of battle was hard earned on terra firma alone, in Ireland and Scotland.

"Say on, Conchobar, how did Ragnall break the trap that we set for him?"

His brother answered, "They left perhaps five ships to fend off the Saxons and exchanged arrows, but this small group included one of their giant dragon boats. Those monstrous ships are not like any other ships. Glundub, they are remarkable feats of engineering and enormous in size, floating forts in truth. They provide their own archers with cover while the Saxons were easy targets for the Viking archers. Their remaining twenty-five ships ignored the Scotsmen, leaving maybe one or two ships with their second dragonboat to face them, and the Scots of Strathclyde faced the same problem as the Saxons; for every Viking they felled, they lost four men themselves. The remainder of Ragnall's fleet, including his flagship, went straight for us and the Ulaidians."

Niall could see his son Hector grimace at Conchobar's description. The Meath king continued:

"Ragnall's dragonboat rammed one of the Dal nAridi boats and broke it like a rotten stick. The survivors tried to leap to the deck of their neighbouring ships or onto the dragonboat itself, but they were cut down in moments or drowned. The rest of Ragnall's boats moved to engage the central ships in our fleet and hand to hand combat broke out in a dozen places. That is when Cumuschach boarded the ship of Oitir Iarla, one of Ragnall's dread captains, but he was filleted by the heathen in single combat. His head was severed from his shoulders and tossed into the sea. His gruesome death and the slaughter occurring aboard the decks broke the will of some of the Ulaidian captains, and they veered away in flight. Hector, young Aed here of Dun Padraig, and myself, rallied the rest of our forces. At that moment, further disaster ensued as the Saxons' fleet of twenty had been broken by Ragnall's rearguard and this rearguard now came upon us on our southern flank as well. The only victory however small that we achieved before our headlong disengagement and retreat, was your son Hector slaying Gunnar Sihtricsson, a cousin of Ragnall and a prince of the Ui Imair."

At this Hector's two younger brothers clapped their brother on the back but were quickly quieted by a withering look from their father.

"The death of one of their captains momentarily halted the aggression of the Northmen and we made our escape and re-joined the Scotsmen away from the fleet of the Ui Imair. One of the dragonboats with a few smaller boats harassed us with arrow salvos, but we eventually outdistanced them. Our defeat was total, Glundub."

A fury rose inside Niall Glundub and he struggled mightily to not vent it upon his sons and brother. To lose a battle to the Northmen despite outnumbering them three to one, and then to retreat like whipped curs, was anathema to him. He choked down his rage and asked his brother a question.

"How fares our combined fleet in total and how much damage did we do to Ragnall's fleet?"

Conchobar grimly answered, "We have twenty-one ships remaining of thirty-five, all the others were boarded and taken or sank. The Scottish lost three of their twenty but suffered many casualties as they were defeated in their archery battle. The Saxons, well, it is unclear, but we assume that they were destroyed or scattered south. The fate of Aethelstan is unknown, he may have survived or may be at the bottom of the Irish Sea. The Vikings lost no ships and have captured many more. Their only setback was their prince Gunnar being slain by Hector. Glundub, there is no easy way to say it, but our attack failed in every way and the Ui Imair are arguably stronger now because of our ambush. Apart from Bairid of Mann, they now own the Irish Sea completely."

Glundub faced the five men, his fists clenched in livid fury. All of them took a step back except for Conchobar mac Flann who stood his ground. Niall briefly considered breaking his brother's jaw, but decided against it, as to do that would invoke violence outside the walls amongst the survivors of their joint forces. Slowly Niall whispered his command:

"Go back to your father Conchobar and explain to him what has happened here... A truce... A truce I call, on any disputes between us, for now. I will not attack his forces directly unless they attack mine, starting from the new moon. Tell him we must regroup and begin raising and training men. If Ragnall captured any prisoners – and I am sure that he has as despite being a barbarian, he is far from stupid – he will know what we tried to do over these last few days. He will come for us all now in the seasons and years to come and even Flann's former pet savage Sihtric the Scourge, will not be able to dissuade him. The Ui Imair are coming. They will return in force to Ireland."

Conchobar departed for Meath on the hour. The surviving Ulaidian captains had agreed to ferry his men down the River Foyle as far south as they could and deposit the surviving members of the Southern Ui Neill force there, to shorten their trek to their own lands. Glundub led his forces west, away from the river in a column toward Aileach. There were injured men with them, and Niall ordered that he, his captains and sons, give up their horses to the wounded and to go on foot with the soldiery. Niall's overall fury at the defeat turned to anger at himself on the walk home. *How could I let Owain of Strathclyde and that prancing Saxon convince me that this was a good idea? We fight on land. Of course, we could never defeat the Vikings at sea.* There was no doubt in Niall's mind that Ragnall would now attack Ireland; it may take a season or a couple of years, but the gauntlet had been thrown down.

Niall was not afraid of the heathens nor anybody in combat, but he would never be able to meet them on his own terms, their mobility would ensure that they had the upper hand initially in any conflict. The obvious target was Dublin, which remained under Flann Sinna's control and paid tribute to him, but there were easier targets for Ragnall to hit all over the country. Every one of Ireland's main villages, towns and monasteries lay close to the rivers and lakes that permeated the island and none were truly out of the Ui Imair's reach. Niall shivered a little despite the summer weather; it was uncertainty that caused the involuntary reaction, not for himself or his sons who also welcomed open battle with the heathens, but for the people of Ireland. At Aileach he instructed his sons to issue orders to tend to the wounded, thank the families of the slain and feed and pay the remainder of his host. He entered the hall still lost in thought when his wife Gormlaith broke his worried reverie.

"Husband, there is a visitor here to see you. It is Cernachan mac Tighernan of Breffni. Will you speak with him?"

Glundub's first reaction was anger as here was another warrior king under his nominal rule who had suffered defeat in his name at the hands of his enemies, but when he saw the haggard and worried look upon the Breffni man's face, his anger was replaced with concern.

"Leave us, Gormlaith, and I will speak with him alone".

His wife left the room, taking the serving men and women with her, leaving just Glundub and the King of Breffni.

"Out with it, Cernachan, what would you have of me?" he asked gruffly.

The Breffni king did not obfuscate and came straight out with the problem which Niall was grateful for.

"My King, we are being attacked and two of our forts have already been burned to the ground despite the High King swearing that there would be an enduring peace between us and his allies in Connaught. Mael Cluiche, the brother of the king there, has summoned a force of men and is ravaging the land of Breffni from the coast to the Shannon. I cannot go to the King of Connaught as for all we know it was he who commanded it. The High King, we hear, has trouble in Meath as some of his kings war with the others, and who is to say who will win that fight? I cannot turn to him to enforce his promises upon his under-kings as he may not even be High King by the end of the month. If Donnchadh Donn was to win the kingship he is as likely as the King of Connaught to cleanse the entire land of the people of Breffni. He is a known berserker near as bad as the Northmen."

Niall already knew the answer as to who won the battle being referred to but did not interrupt the Breffni king.

"We need you to come and protect us, King Niall. We just do not have the manpower to defend all our forts and villages simultaneously and know not when and where the Connaught men will strike next. I know that the High King has forbidden it, but I must come to you, my King, for succour. If you do not help us, I fear Breffni will be destroyed and become vassals to Connaught or even Donnchadh Donn and the Caille Follamain, instead of the Northern Ui Neill."

Glundub felt that hot feeling he got sometimes when he was about to enter battle. Everything seemed to slow down for him and the hairs on the back of his arms and neck rose, his hands twitching in readiness for a fight. At the top of his voice, he roared for his son Hector. In seconds Hector came through the doors, a sword in hand in confusion and readiness. Niall addressed him.

"My son, sheath your weapon. Beside me stands the King of Breffni. He and his brother were ever our friends and allies. They are under attack as we speak from the Connaught men and cannot defend themselves adequately. I ask a lot of you and our main veterans, but I will rouse several more of our chieftains and their men to support us with numbers. I want you and I to go now and defend Breffni from the predations of the kin of the King of Connaught. We leave at first light, and we will accompany King Cernachan to some of our Ui Neill under-kings on the way south and gather a force that is sufficient to strike the men of Connaught such a blow of vengeance, that their ancestors will feel it."

Hector sheathed his sword as directed and stood ramrod straight.

"By your will, Father, I will lead this force myself and come down upon the Connaught men with fire and sword, you need not trouble yourself. I am not dismayed from our defeat against Ragnall and will not be defeated a second time. You can believe in me, Father."

Niall smiled at that and cupped the chin of his mighty son.

"You and I will do this together, it's about time the men of Connaught remember who we are."

Glundub turned to the King of Breffni.

"If Flann Sinna cannot keep his word, or the discipline of his under-kings, know that I will do it for him."

He briefly considered sending a message after his brother Conchobar to inform him that the peace was null and void on learning of the attack by Connaught, but then discounted it. If he did not miss his guess, he would be done with the Connaught men before the new moon and the Connaught men had acted on their own initiative. Connaught must pay, justice must be done, and peace could resume afterward. It was as valid a reason as any to bring violence to the allies of the High King and to teach Connaught a lesson; without the backing of Flann Sinna, they were as children against the Northern Ui Neill.

CHAPTER 2

THE REBELLION OF THE ULAID AND THE DAL ARAIDI (914 AD)

Tadg, son of Cathal, son of Conchobar, stood before the dais in Aileach, his arms crossed, his eyes staring vehemently in Glundub's direction. Niall could see from the corner of his own eye that his wife was a little disconcerted by the belligerent attitude displayed by the angry Connaught prince, but their son Hector clearly found it laughable; as did Glundub. *I would cut this upstart in half with one hand tied behind my back, as would my son,* imagined Niall. The western nobleman addressed him:

"I demand that you release my uncle Mael Cluiche mac Conchobar into my custody and all the other noblemen you have captured as well. They are Ui Neill nobility and deserved of your respect."

Niall Glundub stared down at this runt with an equal measure of disdain and contempt.

"You are in no position to demand anything of me, whelp. Your uncle led some of your father's men against my under-king in Breffni and burned two settlements to the ground. Be grateful that I do not drag them out here in chains before you and execute them on the spot. You and your father and all your kin are a disgrace to the name Ui Neill and I sometimes wonder about your heritage, if you are indeed descended from Niall Nogailliach at all, or just another ragged bastard of a clan, long bereft of honour."

Glundub could see the barest hint of a smile threatening the corner of his son's mouth on seeing the ruddy Connaught prince squirm under the verbal assault unleashed upon him. In fairness to Prince Tadg he displayed a modicum of courage in his response.

"It was you, King Niall, who led the Breffni down upon us two years ago without mercy and we were in the right to seek vengeance in the old way."

Niall glared at Tadg. "Flann Sinna, your master, made you all swear to a truce and your uncle reneged on it. What possible excuse have you for his actions and why at all should I simply hand back your uncle and noblemen at a whim? We smashed you in battle and now have the right to hold prisoners to ensure the good behaviour of Rathcroghan."

The Connaught prince shifted his balance from one foot to the other and tried a different approach with Glundub.

"King Niall, my uncle was perhaps… ah… misguided in his attacks upon the Breffni. My father did not sanction these raids and if you release him back into our custody, we will… ah… discipline him with… er … perhaps some time in penance across the Shannon in Clonmacnoise."

Hector snorted in humour at the suggestion. Niall did not know which statement his son thought was more farcical, that the King's brother's attack was unsanctioned or that penance in Clonmacnoise by Mael Cluiche would suffice as justice. Even still Niall gave it some thought. Flann Sinna was reaching an astonishing age and surely was not long for this earth. He had heard rumours that Donnchadh Donn once more railed against the selection of Oengus as High King upon Flann of the Shannon's demise, and even his own half-brother Conchobar held private doubts that Oengus was up to the challenge. War was coming to Ireland, and it would need a strong ruler in the years ahead. Oengus was more of a politician and a facilitator. Civil war had racked the country and even Niall's own lands had not emerged unscathed. Mael Brigte, a prince of the Cenel Connaille, had been killed fighting against men of the Ui Echach, another northern tribe over land ownership. Most of the Ulaidians and the Dal nAridi had moved to support Aed, the same Aed who had fought alongside Hector against Ragnall Ui Imair the previous year, in ruling all the lands in their combined territories. Niall Glundub had put his support behind Colman another Dal nAridi rival, but Aed and his supporters had risen in rebellion and now in the next week, Niall Glundub and his sons would be forced to march east once more, with the son of the Black Fox of Argialla, to force Aed and his myriad supporters to submit.

Even worse news had come from abroad. Ragnall Ui Imair and his brothers Sithric and Godfrith had won a battle against Bairid mac Oitir, the King of Mann. Bairid, despite being distant kin of the Ui Imair, represented one of the few remaining unaligned Viking powers in the Irish Sea, but Ragnall had come for him regardless, Viking or no. The fighting was fierce, but Sihtric the Scourge had allegedly slain Bairid upon his own walls and his warriors immediately submitted to the will of Ragnall upon the King of Mann's demise. Ragnall had split his fleet in two then, the traders said. The larger fleet descended on the Welsh kingdoms of Gwynedd and Dyfed and defeated several Welsh armies and took a prey of slaves and prisoners.

Ragnall was basically taking time to settle scores throughout the Irish Sea, with anyone who had dared oppose either him, his father Ivar or his grandfather, Ivar the Boneless. The smaller of the two Ui Imair fleets had landed in Loch da Caech in Munster, a small Norse-Gael settlement that the heathens called Waterford. The fleet was led by Oitir Iarla the Black One and Gragabai the bastard son of Harald Fairhair. *Oh what I would give to march south and put those two monsters to the sword,* thought Niall. They had already begun demanding tribute from the smaller Munster and Osraige chieftains in the region and many had submitted to them without a fight. There was no doubt in Niall's mind that this was just the beginning and was the harbinger for a full-scale invasion of Ireland.

He considered the problem of Mael Cluiche then and there with all the possible geopolitical permutations. It was a conundrum with three possible solutions: he could keep custody of these Connaught miscreants as surety of good behaviour from Cathal mac Conchobar and his annoying petitioning son; he could just as easily summarily execute them as was his right to do for breaking a truce laid down by the High King but for also attacking a kingdom loyal to the Northern Ui Neill; the third option was hard to swallow, but it was the one he, at length, elected to pursue and when he announced it, even his sons looked at him askance.

"I will release your wretched uncle, Prince Tadg, on the pledge that there will be no more fighting between Connaught and Breffni. You will also pay three years of tribute to Breffni, a *Borumma* of cattle, to compensate them for the death and suffering caused. Now leave my hall, collect your kin and begone from my presence before I change my mind and hang you all."

Prince Tadg had an antagonised look on his face like a constipated infant but with a terse nod he accepted the ruling of Niall Glundub and retreated from the hall.

When the great room at Aileach had been cleared, Hector approached Glundub.

"Father, you have let the Connaught men get away lightly I fear, we will have to fight them again before the year is out, mark my words."

Glundub slowly looked at his son. If it were another noble or someone who Glundub did not respect, he would have laid him out with a punch, but his mighty son was a different story. He would lead one day, and it was imperative that he learn why Niall made decisions as he did.

"My son, I don't profess to be as subtle or well versed in events as my cousin Constantine or even my father-in-law Flann Sinna who, for all his weaknesses, is a shrewd man; but I do have some wits about me. There is a storm coming, Hector, surely you feel it?"

He searched his son's eyes and saw the acknowledgement there. Hector was a warrior, perhaps even greater than Glundub himself but the blood of Flann Sinna also ran through his veins, the same perception.

"The raids upon the entire coastline are increasing in regularity and the Connaught men are as vulnerable to them as anybody. The Ui Imair have made landfall in Ireland within the last month, Hector."

Hector inhaled deeply, his eyes widened, and Niall could feel the anger warring with determination, rising in his son and heir as he considered the news once more of the heathen's arrival.

"They are based in Waterford in the far south. They will come north and there are many lands between them and us. We need not just the lands of our allies strong, but we need the lands of Connaught strong also, as a buffer between them and us if they come raiding upon the Shannon. To deny Connaught some of its commanders would be to weaken them sufficiently to provide no opposition to the Ui Imair savages when they come, and they would arrive unchallenged upon our doorstep. And they will come Hector, make no mistake."

Glundub could see the understanding dawning upon Hector.

"Flann Sinna has already had to quell some of the chieftains of south Connaught this year on behalf of King Cathal and he had to enter the fray himself to bring some minor chieftains in South Brega under control too. His lands are divided, and he must show strength. He has made a grave blunder I feel. He has stopped some of his under-kings from burning Dublin to the ground as he hopes to win loyalty from the Ui Imair when they arrive, as by protecting Dublin he will have demonstrated his willingness to protect the weakest of their kin. It will not suffice I fear," said Niall contemplatively.

"And now we must look to put down any rebellion within our own kingdoms to maintain unity for when the Ui Imair and their Viking allies arrive. The Breffni have time to rebuild now and produce their next crop of warriors, while the son of the Black Fox in Argialla has ever been our friend. In a few weeks hence, with our forces assembled, we must march upon the lands of the Ulaid and Dal nAridi and force their submission. If I have to, Hector, I will wipe any chieftains out who oppose my will. I will not allow enemies behind me if, and probably when, I am forced to march south."

Hector nodded in agreement and tapped his three fingers to his forehead in respect before departing the hall.

In a fortnight, they were on the road. Niall had sent his two elder sons and his captain Tadg mac Ruaidhri out into the lands of Breffni, the land of the various clans of the Northern Ui Neill, and the province of Argialla, the domain of the son of the Black Fox. The message they carried was simple: come to where the Blackwater River meets Lough Neagh, close to the borders of the territory of the Ulaid and the Dal nAridi, and there they would make camp. Niall Glundub led his elite warriors from Aileach and began the march southeast the next day. His vanguard would lead the way and announce his presence to the Ulaidians and the Dal nAridi initially. Quietly Niall hoped that the King of the North arriving with a force of men would erode any thoughts of rebellion amongst the eastern tribes, against his authority. Aed son of Eochucan was the man that the easterners wanted as the King of the Ulaid and the Dal nAridi, but Niall Glundub had disagreed. He had wanted Colman, chief of Cenel Maelchi, to be king there. Aed of the Ulaid was a warrior of significance and had proved himself to Niall on the seas against the Ui Imair, but he deemed it unlikely that he would have acted without support in rebelling against the authority of the Northern Ui Neill. *It is King Lethlobar of the Dal nAridi that has put him up to this,* thought Niall. It gave Niall hope that perhaps, just maybe, a show of force by his entire army would make Aed consider backing down in the face of Niall Glundub's military might and no battle would result. It bothered Niall that just when the clans under his rule should be showing unity, he had to deal with rebellion.

Flann Sinna was under enormous pressure in Meath, Leinster, Connaught and Osraige, trying to keep his under-kings from each other's throats. Niall Glundub had been kindling an ambition to recapture the High Kingship from the Southern Ui Neill upon the death of Flann Sinna, but to press his claim he would need the entire northern province behind him to impress his strength on all the disparate kings and clans of the south. This rebellion by the Ulaid and Dal nAridi had come at a desperately inauspicious time. If a slaughter of Irish warriors could be avoided, Niall had decided he would pursue a diplomatic solution. It was a delicate balance; in truth he was willing to withdraw his support for the Cenel Maelchi for control of the Ulaid and Dal nAraidi, but he could not just roll over politically and give them what they wanted. This was a rebellion and Niall knew that he must show strength and a willingness to use violence if required. If he just acceded to the Ulaid and allowed them to forge their own destiny, independent of his will, they would look for more and more. They would begin raiding in bordering kingdoms, maybe even demanding tribute from the Argiallans. They could even come under the sway of the men of North Brega or Flann Sinna himself.

If that came to pass, Glundub had already decided that he would raze every fort they owned to the ground and massacre them, rather than allow a Southern Ui Neill presence in the north. There was a time when the Ulaidians ruled not just the north but much of the entire island. At the time of Cuchulainn and the Red Branch knights, they demanded and accepted tribute from most of the country, even from the Eoghanachta of Munster. But as the centuries wore on, Niall Noigiallach and his descendants had conquered much of the Leath Cuinn and the Ulaid and Dal nAridi had been reduced to controlling a minor fiefdom in the northeast of Ireland. And Niall Glundub mac Aed Findliath was determined that they would not return to their former glory while he ruled the entire province.

On landing at the mouth of the Blackwater, Glundub issued orders to his elite Cenel nEoghain soldiery to begin setting up their main camp ahead of the remainder of their forces arriving. There was a reason why Niall had selected this spot – it was the same place his father used to pick when he campaigned in Ulaidian territory, as the terrain was defensively perfect. At the mouth of the Blackwater the river split in two, circumventing a block of land that jutted out into Lough Neagh. This piece of land was not quite an island but was big enough to hold a camp of significant size flanked by the fork in the river. The water was not very broad or deep but was a major hindrance to any force that wished to quickly traverse it and attack the camp. In times of trouble, it was a perfect place to retreat to also, should the need arise. As the days progressed the bulk of his forces began to arrive. Mael Craobh the son of the Black Fox arrived first with a retinue of six hundred men, killers all, and veterans of border disputes with the Caille Follamain of Meath and civil war clashes.

A day later the contingent from the Cenel Conaille arrived some four hundred strong, led by their new king, Giblechan. Hector accompanied the men of the Cenel Conaille and when they had a private moment together, he informed his father that a devastating blow had been struck to the Cenel Conaille when their extraordinary young warrior-prince Mael Brigte, the son of Gibleachan, had been slain in battle with the Ui Echach, one of the minor clans of the region. Although this news was old to Glundub's hearing, he made it his business to console his under-king on the death of his son and to thank him profusely for his support in a geopolitical venture such as this.

The Breffni arrived three days later, being the most geographically distant but their contingent only comprised two hundred men as their king, Cernachan mac Tighearnan, had perhaps only a thousand fighting men available to him due to years of warfare with the men of Connaught and the Caille Follamain. He had ceded command to Niall's young son Conaing over the soldiers he provided for Niall Glundub's campaign. The final contingent to arrive was Niall's preferred choice for king over all of Ulaid and the Dal nAridi: Colman of the Cenel Maelchi along with his son Cerran and his nephew Allacan. They had five hundred men under their command but some of them bore scars of recent fighting. *Perhaps violence will be unavoidable after all,* thought Niall.

The combined force numbered just over two thousand men and was enough to match the entire strength of the Ulaid and the factions of the Dal nAridi that supported Aed as king. Niall allowed his army to rest and feed themselves for a day, but at the break of dawn on the following day, the army began their march into the heart of Ulaidian territory along the southern shore of Lough Neagh. A token force was left to protect the camp under the command of his young son Conaing and his force of Breffni men. Niall did not want to risk the warriors of such a militarily weakened land and preferred to campaign with fresher warriors and with warbands that would not severely weaken the specific kingdoms they were from disastrously if they should fall. The first day was uneventful and the march proceeded at a steady pace through the forests and woods south of Lough Neagh. The weather was slightly cold as it was early in the autumn and the occasional squall of rain dampened spirits. The plan was to reach the River Quoile that looped around slightly to the north of Dun Padraig, the chief fort of Aed mac

Eochucan, and for the army to cut across the water at a fordable point.

Once across the water they would surround the Ulaidian pretender's stronghold until they sued for peace or offered them battle. As the day wore on, some of Niall's scouts reported being watched by warriors from high ground in the distance. *Good,* thought Glundub, *let them know I am coming.* About five miles from the banks of the River Quoile, Hector found a defensible point and made camp. It was not as formidable as their camp at Lough Neagh, but for the purposes of a temporary camp to rest the men, Glundub agreed that it would suffice. It turned out to be a mistake. Niall was awoken during the night with a rough shove from Hector. They had been ambushed in the dark and shouts and screams erupted around the entire camp. The captains including the son of the Black Fox were shouting for order and for soldiers to form up into a shield wall. Fires were quickly lit and spread to illuminate the camp which was quickly descending into chaos. In the dark, Hector scanned around and then pointed to the south,

"There!" he exclaimed.

Several dozen men painted in the traditional blue paint and spiral tattoos of the old gods were amongst some of the Argiallan soldiery, but once they were spotted, Hector was able to surround most of them with his elite force of Cenel nEoghain veterans. The Ulaidians and Dal nAridi were cut down like wheat with only a handful evading Hector's ring of steel. The fighting died down after that, but Niall could not retreat to his tent and sleep in the aftermath, and he waited for the dawn instead. They had lost almost forty men in the violence and several of their scouts had had their throats cut in the night assault which explained how the enemy were able to come upon the camp through the trees unannounced. Some of the Argiallan captains were able to recognise a handful of the slain enemies, of which there were about thirty lying dead on the ground. The chief among them was Flathrue a grandson of old King Lethlabar of the Dal nAridi. He had suffered a gruesome stomach wound and his intestines were coiled around his hips in a ghoulish heap. He had attempted to stuff them back inside himself but had died before he completed the futile task. *Such a young noble lad to die,* thought Niall, *heedless slaughter for which there is no need.*

At daybreak they once more left a rearguard, this time made up of elite warriors under the command of Hector. They were to act not just as a guard to this second camp but also to reinforce the main retinue should they be outflanked or attacked from the rear. The wounded were left with this force so as not to hinder the main advance. At midday they were surprisingly ambushed again, but this time it was the vanguard of which Niall Glundub himself was a part that was attacked by hundreds of howling Ulaidian killers, painted blue and fighting naked, some of their men with penises erect to match the strength of their swords. The old way, the Ulaidian way. The intent was clear, to wipe out the leadership of Glundub's host and decapitate the snake as it were. Niall entered the fray and eviscerated almost a dozen by himself. It felt good to fight at the front once more and the world slowed down to a crawl as he hacked the Ulaidian berserkers to pieces on front of him. By the time reinforcements got to the front, Niall Glundub and the son of the Black Fox had seen them off successfully, sending their foes howling into the trees in flight. Niall's soldiers had got the best of the fighting this time with almost twice as many dead Ulaid and Dal nAridi corpses littering the forest floor. This time it had been the turn of Loingseach of Dal nAridi, whose son had been killed just hours beforehand, who led the attack and a prisoner that was captured with a serious arm wound, was adamant that Aed son of Eochucan had been in the thick of the fighting, but Niall had doubts about the veracity of that claim. An absolute catastrophe had occurred during the skirmish though as Colman the chief of Cenel Maelchi had been severely wounded and Cerran his son and his nephew Allacan had been slain in the fight. Niall's choice for the king of all the Ulaidian tribes was terribly injured and was dying, and if he expired all the fighting would have been for nothing.

The host reached the river thirty minutes later and Niall was dismayed to see that on the far bank, with the fort of Dun Padraig visible in the distant background, the entire host of Ulaid and Dal nAridi had assembled. It was an impressive sight, Niall had to admit. The exact count eluded him, but he estimated the opposition at around thirteen hundred warriors. He himself had the support of several hundred Dal nAridi clansmen within his own ranks which highlighted the military strength of the province. The Ulaid in combination with all of their subject tribes such as the Dal nAridi and Cenel Maelchi, were the second most militarily powerful clan in the north, after the Cenel nEoghain themselves. They fought in the old way, covered in blue paint and spirals, many unclothed, and with a ferocity that would put the Northmen to shame. And now they stood on the opposite bank of the river and to cross it would mean death to Niall and the Ui Neill.

The standoff dragged on for hours. Occasionally some of Niall's men chanced the river which was waist high in depth, but they were dissuaded through arrow shot and the occasional ambitious throw of a spear. Insults were hurled from one host to the other and despite Niall's army being half again as big as the Ulaidian force, it would not matter as they would be slaughtered as they crossed the water. The long way around the water would take days and they did not have the supplies to feed their force for more than a week. It was a stalemate and there was nothing Niall or his captains and kings could do about it. All of that was to prove irrelevant though as at dusk, Colman the chief of the Cenel Maelchi died of his battle wounds and Niall had nobody legitimate apart from Laichthechan the old, father of Allacan, to put forward as king. Both armies remained camped overnight but upon the next morning, Niall Glundub sent a message of truce across the river which was accepted.

Noble hostages were exchanged on the promise of good behaviour on both sides. Niall Glundub and the son of the Black Fox crossed the river in a small boat commandeered from a local fisherman and they moved toward the tent of the leaders of the Ulaid. Sullen stares of warriors in blue met Niall Glundub as he walked through them, alongside his Argiallan under-king and ally, but it bothered him little. The idea of death in battle did not phase Glundub in the slightest and if they did attempt to harm him, not only would he cut down dozens of them before they slew him, but his sons Hector and Conaing would never rest until they reaped their vengeance. *No,* thought Niall, *they are not that stupid.* He swept the front of the tent open and stepped inside, handing his weapons to a stationed guard and the son of the Black Fox did the same. They both took their seats at a simple wooden table and faced their adversaries; old Lethlobar of the Dal nAridi and more importantly Aed mac Eochucan, the self-appointed King of the Ulaid.

"That bastard Colman is dead, eh?" asked Lethlobar.

It was a statement of fact or a rhetorical question rather than an enquiry and all Niall Glundub could do was nod slowly, never taking his eyes off the two men across from him.

"Then what on earth are we fighting for, King Niall? The man you wanted to lord over us has been slain as has his eldest son. All the rest of his children have not come of age and his brother Laichtechan is a sot, a madman and in his dotage. There is only one man for the kingship, and it is who we want; Aed mac Eochucan."

Niall steepled his fingers and began to frame a response in his mind.

"I am here plain and simple because you have defied me, King Lethlobar. You Ulaidians and Dal nAridi seem to have the opinion that you can dictate to me terms on any situation. I am the king in the north and if I say that Aed's wife will be the new ruler, you better believe it. If I say that the sky is green and the grass is blue, you better consider it as gospel."

Glundub leaned across the table then, with a menacing smile on his face to reinforce his final statement on the issue.

"The point, Lethlabar and Aed, is this; that because my son and I are so powerful in battle, even when I am wrong, I am right."

Niall sat back and folded his arms, his chin sunken into his chest awaiting their response. Lethlabar was suitably cowed, but Aed was undaunted by Glundub; he spoke next.

"We have halted your forces at the river, we can hold you off indefinitely. If we declare our independence from the Northern Ui Neill, what could you do about it? If we started raiding across the river, what could you do to stop us? If we started demanding tribute from those under-kings furthest from Aileach, do you have the power to interfere?"

It was Aed's time to sit back confidently. Niall almost laughed out loud.

"You do realise... King... Aed, that I have assembled perhaps a third of my men here to fight you? If you attempt to defy my authority in any of that fashion you describe, I will not only assemble my full strength to destroy you, I would make common cause with other leaders of the Ui Neill such as Mael Mithig of North Brega my brother-in-law, or Donnchadh Donn, the warlord of the Caille Follamain. Even Flann Sinna, whose memory is long, remembers the Ulaid causing both him, his father and even his grandfather problems. I would make a special case for you, Aed; I would make peace with my enemies, purely to create an army as large as any ever assembled in the history of Ireland, just to march east and north, to root you out of your fort and crucify you as a heathen traitor to Ireland."

Aed was taken aback, and all colour drained from his face. He attempted to stammer or stutter a response but nothing sensible emerged from his flustered brain.

Niall continued, "But do not concern yourself... King ... Aed. It is true, my choice for king in the northeast is now dead and no suitable heir is available. You fought well against the Ui Imair my son tells me, and you are a brave warrior. You also possess a fleet of ships, as do you, old King Lethlobar. It makes you useful to me. I am willing to acknowledge you as King of the Ulaid and Dal nAridi on the condition that you pay tribute to me as before and acknowledge me as over-king. What say you?"

The two men across the table whispered conspiratorially with each other. Glundub looked over to the son of the Black Fox who just shrugged his shoulders and raised his eyebrows with jaded impatience.

Aed turned back. "King Niall, your decision to attack the Ui Imair has cost us a hundred of our finest warriors, not to mention some of Lethlobar's heirs and in the last day alone you have slain another eighty warriors at least. The Ui Imair raid and harry our coastline at will and Mael Mithig of North Brega looms large on our border. We have many problems currently, some of them mutual, and we are willing to cease our rebellion and make a peace because of them; but to meet our tributorial obligations we need full control of Linn. This Norse town falls within our old borders, but Mael Mithig takes all their tribute for himself. If you help us subjugate Linn and keep Mael Mithig at bay, we will fall into line and pay you tribute and provide warriors for your campaigns both now and in the future. The Ulaid and the Dal nAridi, and all the other major allied tribes in the east of Ulster would be yours to command once more, in all things, to the end of time."

Niall Glundub considered briefly and exchanged looks with the son of the Black Fox who just shrugged again, but this time in nonchalant agreement. Glundub stood up from his chair, as did Aed.

"I accept your terms, King Aed mac Eochucan, King of the Ulaid and the Dal nAridi. For too long have the Norse-Gael of Linn sat on the fence anyway. They will abandon Mael Mithig of Brega and pay tribute to you and by extension me, or I swear that every one of them will be killed."

CHAPTER 3

THE SKIRMISH AT CROSSAKIEL
(915 AD)

A blizzard of snow whirled around the camp as Niall Glundub marched through it. Three thousand men under his command sat huddled in groups around fires that flickered feebly against the breeze. Icicles hung from the branches of trees not yet hewed for firewood and sorry bowls of stew were passed out among the men, who accepted them with eyes downcast. Niall raged inwardly at the indignity of it; again, his will was being defied by an enemy he would easily crush in open battle, who he could not get at. The Norse-Gael of Linn and their small company of mercenaries had manned the walls and wooden palisades surrounding the settlement bravely, repulsing the combined northern forces of Niall Glundub repeatedly. It was an extraordinarily well defended town in truth: a deep spike-filled trench surrounded the wooden walls on both sides of the Creggan River, the body of water that Linn straddled. A myriad of cunning traps and devices concealed in the ditch made assaulting the walls virtually impossible without huge loss.

In times of peace the town was accessible from three places: a lowerable wooden walkway that became part of the palisade once raised; on both sides of the river; and of course the river itself. The northern section of the wall was manned by men under the command of a Scottish mercenary by the name of Sean mac Piarsigh, while the southern wall was defended by his second in command, a rogue Kerryman by the name of Domnall mac Cossachtach. The river was protected and patrolled by four longboats packed with warriors and archers under the command of the son of the latest chieftain, Olaf Snorrisson. This triumvirate of veteran commanders had thwarted the forces of Niall Glundub at their ease, with almost no losses. Niall Glundub on the other hand had lost twenty men with twice as many wounded, most of whom suffered broken arms and such from rocks and missiles hurled from the walls.

Niall had decided to lay siege to the town instead of a full-frontal assault after their first attacks were repulsed, rather than risk the lives of more men, but the problem was that it would take a considerable amount of time to starve them out as the townsfolk of Linn could resupply sporadically from the sea and fish the waters. Many times, over the years, Niall had successfully laid siege to forts and encampments where his opponents yielded, but this was different. The truth was he could storm the walls with his entire force at once, but the slaughter of his men would be unimaginable and would serve no purpose. He had no qualms about ordering men to their deaths for the right cause, but to assault Linn directly he knew was folly. The whole point was to intimidate the Norse-Gael of Linn into obedience and force them to pay tribute to the Kings of Ulaid and Dal nAridi and by extension him, not massacre them or lay waste to the town. He balled his fists in anger; he was caught, and indecision plagued him. He could not just leave as his allies and enemies alike would deem him weak. To sack the town would not please anybody. Ultimately if he was to rule this country, he had to have the town of Linn under his sway as it was both a valuable source of revenue and a semi-independent Norse-Gael settlement, one of the few still out of reach of the Ui Imair or even the distant Harald Fairhair, the King of Norway. *They must pay some sort of tribute to me or burn,* he had long decided.

He retreated into his own tent with a bowl of gruel and a mug of water. He never drank mead or ale when on campaign, preferring to be fresh of mind and body always, when the threat of combat loomed. Lethlobar of the Dal nAridi had remained north with his kin, sending a bull-necked and belligerent nephew by the name of Mochta in his stead. For what he made up for in brawn he sadly lacked in cunning, and Glundub felt it was a waste of time bringing him into his councils. But his presence had provided Niall with an idea. He had elected not to take any of the main under-kings and chieftains of his domain on campaign with him. He had chosen instead to take many of the younger sons of the nobility with him of a rank with Mochta, to blood them alongside his son Hector, so they would witness first-hand his qualities; and when their sires, or even Niall Glundub himself, passed from this world, they would know Hector was the unquestionable man to follow.

Hector was camped to the south of the river but faced the same issues as Niall Glundub's own detachment. Even sending messages across the water was difficult as the accursed longboats continually patrolled the river. It was only perhaps sixty feet wide but at its centre it was almost twenty feet deep and not many of Niall's host were strong swimmers apart from the Dal nAridi and Dal Riadan contingents of his army. It was with great surprise in the evening that he learned that his son Hector had risked the river crossing and appeared in his tent with a small man beside him, wrapped up in layers of fur to defeat the winter chill.

"Father, this is Loingseach mac Aedo, a holy brother of Clonmacnoise. He has grave news for us."

Niall beckoned the two men to sit beside him before speaking. He could guess what had occurred before the young clergyman opened his mouth.

"Something has happened to my older brother."

It was not a question but a statement Glundub knew to be true. The young priest sadly nodded his head in acknowledgement.

"Yes, King Niall, he was being given his final confession and communion to ease his passing to God's arms, when my superior Cairpre Cromm the Bishop of Clonmacnoise sent me to find you. That was three weeks ago. I went to Aileach and your wife gave me a horse and I made haste to your camp. I fear that almost certainly, at this time, he has died. A man as noble and heroic as Domnall mac Aed Findliath, will surely be made welcome into God's kingdom."

The three men blessed themselves and prayed solemnly.

"Had my brother any wishes or final instructions?" Niall asked.

The young clergyman nodded slowly. "He wished to be buried in Clonmacnoise in the holy cemetery there and his remaining wealth and possessions he bequeathed to your son Muirchertach mac Niall."

Niall Glundub did not know what to feel. He was pleased that at the hour of his death, his brother had spoken no ill of Glundub and by leaving all he had to Hector, it signalled his acceptance that when Niall's time came, Hector had Domnall's blessing to rule the north.

"Brother Loingseach, go into the camp and find yourself food and fodder for your horse. Keep the animal as a token of my goodwill to Clonmacnoise and know that in less uncertain times, I myself will pilgrimage to the monastery there and pay my respects to my brother's grave and the Bishop Superior."

The clergyman bowed deeply to Niall and tapped his forehead in respect to Hector who answered with a terse nod, leaving father and son alone in the tent. Niall could sense his son staring expectantly as if waiting for some insight or nostalgic recollection to come flowing forth from him, but he had nothing to offer. There had never been a world without Domnall mac Aed for Niall; a brother he admired for years, then despised and finally pitied. All Niall could say to his son was, "May God have mercy on his soul."

A shout interrupted the moment between them, and horns of alarm pierced the snow-filled skies with discordant sound. Niall and Hector raced out of the tent, arms at the ready, and sprinted in the direction of the cacophony. The clash of weapons and the screams of the dying could be discerned in the middle distance and dozens of men reached for their weapons and rose from their fires as Niall and Hector raced past. Eventually they reached the epicentre of the violence only to be met by flame. The wagons that held their supplies on the north side of the river were afire. The culprits, although a few had been slain in the fighting, had taken the guards by surprise in the gloom of the evening, under the cover of the blizzard and destroyed their stores. The camp was set back a couple of hundred feet from the walls of Linn, but visibility was much diminished in the brutal conditions. *Sean mac Piarsigh, that Scottish bastard, if I ever encounter him in the field, I will feed him his own entrails,* fumed Niall.

He issued commands to Hector to secure what remained of their supplies and put out the flames while he gathered a hundred men and attempted to chase the violators of their camp. They reached the edge of where the ramparts met the water only to witness the last of the escaping villains being pulled onto longboats upon the river. Niall Glundub had seen how they had eluded them so quickly. The survivors of the raid had dived headfirst into the river and clasped hempen ropes floating adrift on the water, and their comrades had pulled them aboard their longboats. When the enemy had sighted Glundub and his small cohort they had unleashed a dozen arrows at them, and Niall had to call a halt to the pursuit just out of range of their archers. Niall could hear gales of laughter and cheers erupting from the wall and the two longships that sat at the throat of the river, where it flowed past both sides of the town. His men were quiet. Niall could taste their tangible dismay at events and even their fear and uncertainty at his back. It was a moderate setback but a setback none the less. He allowed the mockery of the Norse-Gael warriors to wash over him.

He turned quietly to a young Ui Neill soldier. "Give me your bow, son", he commanded.

The young man did as Niall bid tremulously, in obvious awe of his commander. Niall reached over the young soldier's back and selected an arrow from his quiver. The captain of one of the longboats had undone his breeches and had begun pissing in the direction of Glundub to howls of mirth from his compatriots. Glundub waited and watched. He did not understand Norse but the form of it that these men spoke after a century or more living amongst the Irish was a hybrid version where words spilled over into both dialects. And then he heard what he was looking for, one of the men on the wall addressing Sean mac Piarsigh by name. Glundub could pick him out, a brawny soldier with light brown hair and stubble on his chin. Glundub nocked the arrow and used his old but still incredibly powerful frame to extend the bowstring as far as he could, and he let fly. The arrow took the Scottish mercenary commander in the throat, and he toppled from the palisade to be impaled upon the stakes set at its base. The laughter died on the lips of the Norse-Gael and their mongrel band of mercenary allies on witnessing the terrible death that their commander had suffered. Niall Glundub handed back the bow to his young subordinate and stalked back to the camp, knowing every eye under his command and on the walls were watching him. Many had never fought beside him or against him before and now they knew for sure who he was, Niall Glundub mac Aed Findliath, the King of the North, and his reputation was no myth. As lethal a fighter as any that lived around the Irish Sea.

Niall's command tent was chaotic in the aftermath of the attack of the men from Linn. Some advocated launching a full-scale assault upon the walls with everything they had, especially those who had lost kin in the surprise attack. The unbelievable exhibition of assassination exhibited by Niall Glundub had lit a fire amongst the younger warriors and it took Hector several moments of barked commands for calm, to quell their bloodlust. *The steadier heads among us must prevail,* Niall thought. He explained to the senior commanders their predicament. As he saw it, they had only three options: they could launch an assault upon the town for much loss of life; they could attempt to forage for food and continue the siege until Linn broke and sued for peace; or they could cut their losses and return home. At the suggestion of the third option, anger erupted amongst the younger warriors who, for all their energy, lacked pragmatism and experience. In the end Niall decided that they would continue with the siege to bring the Norse-Gael of Linn to heel. No food was being transported into the town that the scouts could see and although their fleets had access to the sea, fishing was unreliable as a sole method of provisioning for a town of that size.

The people of Linn were suffering despite the bravado being shown by their men on the walls, Niall was sure of it. *In a week or two they will break,* thought Niall, *and despite whatever peace can be agreed, if I catch that Olaf Snorrisson beneath the walls, I will crucify the pagan on the bank of the river for all his kin to see.* At the end of the meeting, before all of Niall's captains could leave with their orders and commands, a breathless scout demanded an audience with Niall, Hector and the leadership.

"My King, a host approaches from the south to relieve the town but they are still a number of days away."

The room quieted and all stood mute at the news.

"Who are they and who leads them?" asked Niall.

"It is an army of men from Brega and they are augmented by the elite of Tara. Mael Mithig mac Flannacain has joint command with Oengus mac Flann, the son of the High King."

Instantly Niall could feel the disquiet at the announcement. Although he had not been certain if the men of Meath would respond to any calls for aid from the men of Linn, Niall had guessed that the Norse-Gael would at least try and send word by sea. They would be here in three days by the straightest route Niall guessed and the various connotations of what could occur raced through his mind. All his young captains and sergeants turned and looked to him for guidance and decisiveness. If this host from Meath hit Niall's forces beneath the walls of Linn, they would be caught between the hammer and the anvil. His men were tired and cold after three weeks of siege, the winter weather was only worsening, and half of their stores were destroyed through treachery from the Norse-Gael. Despite all these factors, Niall had a solution in mind. He cleared his throat and the room quieted further.

"This is what we will do. Hector my son will remain here and continue to invest Linn with several hundred of our best men. Nobody comes in or out."

Hector tapped his fingers against his forehead in acknowledgement.

"The remainder of our forces will go south. We will ravage the lands of North Meath and forage the land for food, using Meath's own resources against them. If we set out within the hour, we will reach the Blackwater River before this host of Meath-men and deny them passage across the water. To relieve Linn, they must cross the Blackwater and only at Kells and a few other points can they do this safely and quickly. We will leave a strong force of men at Kells and one or two of the main fording points of the river and the rest of us will gather food from the land. I will lead at Kells."

A chorus of *Ayes* and *Yes, my Kings* greeted his orders and within the hour, true to his word, the majority of the Northern Ui Neill army were marching south to oppose the men of Meath.

The going was tough and slow and the only thing that consoled Niall was the fact that the Meath-men would be slogging through the same wintery hell as his own forces. His men had been commanded to only bring what they could carry in terms of supplies, and they had left all the wagons and the few horses they had with Hector at the siege camp. Great frozen puddles constantly proved treacherous for the soldiers and intermittent sleet and snow blinded and soaked the men in equal measure. It took them the entire day, but they eventually reached the Blackwater near Kells at nightfall and made camp. The people from the lands all around had fled to Kells but Niall had no intention of besieging yet another fort, fully encircled with wooden palisades and a huge ditch; the siege of Linn was bad enough to contend with and it was not their objective here either. They skirted Kells altogether and set watch upon the river fording at the south of the town, conscious of the ever-watchful Meath folk peering out from behind their wooden walls. The night was dark and dreary, a freezing slushy sleet turning the ground into a churned muddy quagmire by morning light. Niall did not bother to send any scouts out across the Blackwater and instead had men carefully watch the far bank for troop movements, of which there was no sign.

After discussion with some of his young captains, he elected to leave half of his forces there encamped under the command of his right-hand man Tadg mac Ruaidhri, with swift runners ready to go at short notice should the men from Meath arrive. Niall did not yet trust any of the young noblemen and captains to take command fully and instead took them all with him to the west. The Blackwater only got wider and deeper to the east and more impassable at this time of the year, so Niall was confident that Mael Mithig his brother-in-law and Oengus mac Flann would have to head west to where the river was younger, to forge passage across the water.

The next fording point of any significance was at Crossakiel. In half a day, Glundub and eight hundred of his men reached Crossakiel and made camp at the ford there, choosing the firmest ground for comfort. There were no giveaway tracks or other detritus lying around that would indicate a significant body of men fording the river there and it gave hope to Glundub that perhaps they had reached the Blackwater first and would be able to deny the Meath-men passage north. They camped there for a day and a night and runners were dispatched back eastward to Kells to keep abreast of any pertinent information or visual contact with the enemy. When Tadg's runners returned, giving Niall's own messengers a breather, they informed Niall that there had been no sign of any soldiers on the far bank for twenty miles either side all day. *Perhaps they have turned back and given up Linn to northern control,* thought Niall, *or maybe the foul Irish winter weather has discouraged them?* But as night fell a sense of foreboding rose gradually in his gut. Oengus was not half the warrior that his brothers Conchobar or Donnchadh Donn were, but he was no coward either. And Mael Mithig, who was married to Niall's own half-sister was a renowned battlefield commander despite his youth. *No,* thought Niall, *they are most assuredly coming.*

On the afternoon of the third day of encampment at Crossakiel, Niall Glundub commanded several of his young captains to join him on a dual mission of both scouting further down the banks of the Blackwater to the west and also to seize grain and cattle off of any unfortunate Meath-men who worked the land nearby. His scouts had informed him that a small tributary of the Blackwater on the west side of the small settlement of Crossakiel, flowed from the north, and that was where Niall intended to lead his men. He knew from decades of battlefield experience that to understand the topography of the land was of paramount importance and that nine times out of ten, when two relatively equal forces collided, it was the side that was deployed more shrewdly that prevailed rather than strength of arms alone. The settlement of Crossakiel consisted of a small wooden and stone church and less than fifty huts and hovels dotted around it, alongside some auxiliary barns and sheds for livestock. Tilled fields radiated out from the village down toward the Blackwater where it annexed its tributary river, and the endless woods and wild lands of Ireland were at least for now kept at bay from the village.

The people had fled, where to, Niall wasn't sure, but no smoke issued from the crude chimneys and no animals were present amongst the sheds, taking shelter from the elements. Niall stopped his men from burning the village to the ground although he was well within his rights to do so; needless vandalism was distasteful to him. *They are probably gone to ground in the lands to the southwest with the Caille Follamain,* he thought. Crossakiel lay right on the border between the lands of the Caille Follamain and the lands controlled by Mael Mithig of North Brega. Due to the political situation in Meath, Niall deemed it wise to only devastate the lands of the Bregans, as to raid southwest would only antagonise the Caille Follamain and their deadly king, Donnchadh Donn. That action could serve to force the Meath-men to set aside their differences and attack him simultaneously. *This is as far south or west I will dare to go,* Niall promised himself.

While the men foraged the surrounding countryside, Niall and his captains headed down toward the nexus of the Blackwater and its tributary to survey the land. The weather was bleak, and visibility was limited. Niall looked back up the small tributary to the north and spotted that there was a hill that overlooked the surrounding countryside a half a mile distant. He indicated to the men that they should walk that way and as a body they marched parallel along the bank of the smaller river. Five hundred feet north though, Niall called for a halt and then for quiet. There were tracks upon the ground. He signalled for the men with him to duck down and conceal themselves in the brush where possible. He cursed his luck as he was now certain that some part of the strength of the Meath-men were here close by on this side of the tributary and the river, a significant body of men too, judging by the tracks. He estimated their strength at a little over two hundred. He had only one hundred accompanying him with his other seven hundred spread around the lands of Crossakiel scavenging. He sent two of his men back the way they came under cover, to quickly gather Niall's remaining forces and bring them to bear. His hundred men were composed of maybe twenty of the noble sons of the clans of the north and their bodyguards, the best fighting men being busy looting the surrounding lands or at the crossing at Kells. *Perhaps if we come upon them in force, we can break them before they realise that they have us outnumbered,* mused Niall. There was nothing he could do but quietly move toward the hill and weigh the strength of this host with his own eyes.

They edged their way forward in the freezing afternoon gloom with Niall Glundub in the vanguard. He skirted around the east side of the hill away from the river, using heavy gorse bushes as cover and keeping noise to a minimum. He had not time to issue orders and only hoped that behind him his men would have the sense to follow suit and understand the enormity of the situation. Foot by foot he slowly made his way around the hill, but at that point his plan come to naught. One of the lummoxes behind him stood on a branch and with a loud crack it shattered, and the noise thundered around the hill. Niall could hear murmurs and shouts of alarm from up ahead and four armed men sprinted around the circumference of the mound and straight into Glundub and his men.

With a roar and without a second's hesitation, Niall Glundub mac Aed Findliath was into them, thrusting his two swords into two of the men's bellies simultaneously. Their screams of death reverberated around the hill and fields of Crossakiel and instantly a grinding roar of men erupted from just out of sight. The time for subterfuge was over. More than two hundred warriors came charging around the hill and Niall's men stood forward to meet them, as there was no way out. There was no time even to form up into a shield wall; their line was staggered, and the violence was upon them whether they wished it or not. Niall had a moment to peer around the fields longingly to see if the rest of his men were about to reinforce them, but he could see nobody. *We must survive until they reach us,* he thought, and that was the last thought he had before the red mist descended and the slaughter consumed him.

Niall issued no commands, he oversaw none of the fighting, he was fully immersed in his own survival. Hack, slash, parry, and stab were the only concepts that pierced his consciousness, and he did what he had done for most of his life; he laid waste to his enemies. In minutes, that seemed to last hours, Niall Glundub could hear horns being blown and the sound of men disengaging and retreating on both sides. He was dimly aware of his own reinforcements arriving in groups of ten or twenty as both sides warily reversed from each other's swords and axes. With his wits finally about him, he shouted for a shield wall to be formed and his men obeyed quickly. Of his own party, about sixty had survived. Uathmaran, Erudan and Mael Ruaniad the young son of Cumuschach of the Ulaid, were dead on the ground. Mael Muire, the grandson of the Black Fox of Argialla was dying noisily amidst his own blood and shit, a grotesque stomach wound slowly killing him. In one skirmish Niall had suffered the loss of almost a fifth of the adult princes of the north, a grievous blow to his province. The enemy by this time had raised a banner of peace and one of them came forth looking to treat with whoever commanded Niall's forces. Glundub approached himself, looking for answers.

The two men met on the churned and bloody ground at the hill of Crossakiel under a banner of truce.

"Who are you?" commanded Niall angrily.

The young man before him did not flinch and responded sternly, "I am Aed mac Mael Ruanaid mac Flann, the grandson of the High King. And I know that you must be Niall Glundub of the Ui Neill as you bear the look of my uncle Conchobar who is your brother."

Mollified with the nobility of the young man facing him, Niall put him to the test.

"Your attack is in vain; I have a host of men encamped not a day's march from here and another sat before the walls of Linn. Summon your commanders Oengus and Mael Mithig to me and we will discuss your surrender, the exchange of hostages and your retreat as best suits you."

The young man sank a little within himself.

"King Mael Mithig is encamped a day's ride across the tributary and sent this expeditionary force to scout the land. We did not think your host would be so far south or west."

Niall wrestled with what the young man said, or what he did not say: the Meath-men had marched west themselves, many leagues to come around the Blackwater rather than having their army cut to pieces on fording the water or on the one or two humble bridges that spanned the water to the west.

Smart, thought Niall, *but also unwise in some ways as it allowed me to reach the Blackwater before them.*

"We do not know where Prince Oengus my uncle is though." The youth looked hopefully and inquisitively up at Glundub. "He was caught up in the fighting. We had hoped that you had captured him, and held him under guard?"

Grimly Niall leaned upon his sword on the ground. "We took no prisoners, young Aed, your uncle, my brother-in-law, is either with you or amongst the slain."

The two men carefully picked their way amongst the corpses on the battlefield. Already accursed crows were circling in the grey skies looking down greedily upon the feast of carcasses beneath them. Slowly and deliberately the King of the Northern Ui Neill and the grandson of the High King, searched for the familiar face of the heir designate. At length, a shout from young Aed drew Niall Glundub to him and they found the prince. He was astonishingly still alive although his back was clearly broken, and blood bubbled horribly from his mouth after every rattling gasp of breath he breathed.

The two men knelt beside the fallen prince. Niall said a quiet prayer for his enemy. Despite being on the opposite side of the field of battle this day, he was still an Ui Neill noble, a warlord and leader of men. Aed looked at Glundub pleadingly as if in an unspoken way, begging Niall to save the life of his uncle but there was nothing Niall could do, Oengus was a dead man. Glundub had seen countless wounds from the battlefield and knew instinctively that this was a mortal one, but there would be many long minutes of dreadful suffering before Oengus left this world for the next. Niall shook his head at the young man, his meaning apparent. He slid his dagger from his sheath at his hip and showed it to Prince Oengus. The heir designate held Glundub's gaze, but had not the strength to speak, only nodding in resigned agreement. Aed shouted no, but Niall placed his hand on the young man's shoulder.

"Show your nobility, Prince Aed. Would you have your uncle suffer onward for many minutes hence or pass on with dignity as a warrior of the Ui Neill? Show your men your will, shed no tears. Now is the time for courage and leadership as an Ui Neill nobleman."

Young Aed, despite his grief, wiped his eyes with his sleeve and nodded at Glundub, while simultaneously taking his uncle's hand in his own. Niall Glundub slid his dagger into the throat of Oengus mac Flann and the light died in the prince's eyes as the blood gushed forth. And so passed Oengus mac Flann mac Mael Seachnaill; a prince of the Southern Ui Neill and the heir designate of Ireland; slain in battle at Crossakiel by the forces of Niall Glundub.

Niall allowed the Meath-men to retreat over the tributary to Mael Mithig's camp, with an invitation to treat with him under a flag of temporary truce. He also sent word to his own men at their main camp at Kells, to march to Crossakiel immediately in a show of strength. The meaning, Niall hoped, would be obvious to Mael Mithig: *to try and reinforce Linn and cross any part of the river to do so, would mean massacre for the Meath-men.* They had lost. Before nightfall Niall Glundub met with Mael Mithig in a hastily erected tent with a few guards, but on the western side of the tributary; thus showing his brother-in-law how little fear he had of him. In fairness to Mael Mithig, he arrived on horseback with only one retainer, guessing rightly that Niall Glundub was incapable of treachery.

Both men took each other's measure once the few men accompanying them left the tent. Glundub was by far the bigger man and broader, but Mael Mithig was well put together and not yet thirty years of age. His career, Niall knew, was a distinguished one. The Bregan King had been fighting in the armies of Flann Sinna since he was a boy and had fought in numerous civil wars in Meath in the plethora of territorial disputes there. He had even taken part in the sack of Dublin in 902 against the Ui Imair and had fought off Viking raiders for almost fifteen years upon his coast and waterways. There was a reason that Flann Sinna chose to marry one of his precious daughters to this man. *Mael Mithig is a king amongst men indeed,* Niall acknowledged inwardly. They both took their seats and relaxed slightly. Niall spoke first:

"Brother-in-law, you have erred greatly in coming north. My under-kings demand that Linn and its incomes be returned to them in perpetuity. If you recall it was Dal nAridi land that the town was first built upon, and they feel Linn should pay them tribute by law and not you."

Mael Mithig's expressive blue eyes never left Glundub's nor even blinked as he answered,

"The Dal nAridi lost that land in battle with my father. They have not the strength to lay claim to Linn even if it didn't sit in North Bregan territory, which it does. We claimed it by the old rules and the old ways; by legal right of conquest."

Niall could understand Mael Mithig's position, the man was unshakeable and implacable. Even though it was not Niall's place to say, he had approved hugely of the match Flann Sinna had made for his half-sister at the time of her marriage to Mael Mithig. *What I could do with a man like this as general of my armies.*

"We have the town of Linn hard pressed, Mael Mithig, the length of their defiance can be measured in weeks, if not days. If we do not come to a resolution here, I can promise you that Hector, my son, will raze the town to the ground and the Ulaid are determined to see that happen rather than see its incomes go to Brega."

A slow smile gradually turned the corner of the Mael Mithig's mouth.

"You are esteemed as a general across the entire island of Ireland and Britain and the heathens hold you in high regard, but even you cannot foresee all ends. In the last couple of months, to assuage the South Bregans and the Leinstermen, Flann Sinna has placed Grungni mac Conall, a half-breed Norse-Gael, as castellan of Dublin. His mother is a sister of Ragnall Ui Imair and his father is Conall mac Finn an under-king to Augaire mac Aililla and he is acceptable to both the Irish and the Northmen. He pays tribute to all of Flann's under-kings surrounding Dublin and keeps the Norse-Gael of Dublin under control. Most importantly he has commanded his people to allow Flann the use of his ships in the direst of needs."

An ominous shiver passed through Niall Glundub and he knew what Mael Mithig was implying.

"King Niall, in secret we have sent men and food from Dublin, hence our delay in coming north. We wanted to draw you away while we reinforce the town. You are undone. Not only will Linn be resupplied, but fresh warriors will man their walls within the day, I estimate. There are twenty longboats going north, Niall, all packed with Northmen fuelled on stories, whether true or not, of the atrocities committed in your name, and your brother and father's name, upon their people. Do not bother to deny it, Glundub, your father Aed Findliath and his father before him, Niall Caille, came down upon all the Norse settlements of the north of Ireland and massacred many of the people there. You are not popular in Dublin, brother-in-law. You are defeated; you just don't know it yet."

Glundub could not believe it. He had to choke down a howl of rage and fury as it threatened to overwhelm him. He briefly considered reaching across the table and strangling his brother-in-law there and then before sense and honour stayed his hand. Mael Mithig continued before Niall could respond. The young king shifted uncomfortably and scratched his chin between thumb and forefinger.

"You have put me in a quandary though, Glundub. You have slain the heir designate and every man and his dog knows that King Flann does not want either Donnchadh Donn or Conchobar to take the High Kingship, nor will he relent and allow the Northern Ui Neill, by extension you, to take the crown by the old ways, alternating between north and south. He has been guiding me and has informally nominated me as heir should Oengus fall."

That shocked Niall, his jaw fell open in surprise.

"Donnchadh Donn will never bend the knee to you, Mael Mithig, he will rouse the Caille Follamain and march upon Tara to seize what is his and Clan Colman will most likely follow. Even those treacherous scum in Connaught will throw their lot in with him too I suspect. Flann Sinna's word is iron now, Mael Mithig, but when he dies it will mean dust. He who is the strongest will seize power, you know this as well as I. Do you possess the resolve, or the military might, to face the sons of Flann of the Shannon on the plains of Meath, for the dominion of Ireland?"

Niall could see doubt and confusion sweep across the face of his brother-in-law, and it made him respect the Bregan lord more. He was not just a mindless warlord, he was thoughtful and introspective, as well as decisive when matters required it.

"As I said, you have put me in a tight position, Niall Glundub. Oengus' death has set in motion events that can't be reversed. I must obey my High King while he is alive. I expect that when I return to my fort in Knowth, I will be summoned to Tara once word of Oengus' demise reaches there, and before the bishops I will be sworn in as heir designate of Ireland. We both know Donnchadh Donn will not stand for this. His lands are untouched by warfare, and he has several thousand warriors to command. He will march upon my lands and put my people to the sword. My wife and children, your nieces, and nephews, Niall Glundub, will have their necks stretched from the nearest tree or at best be taken captive indefinitely. You know it as well as I do. All Brega, Leinster and possibly Dublin, will back me and we will have unavoidable civil war in Meath. And in the background, the Ui Imair stir. We both know they are coming, Glundub."

Niall considered the young king's words and could find no flaw with his reasoning. Donnchadh Donn was more savage and less wise than the rest of his kin. Conchobar had always hated Flann Sinna's treatment of his oldest brother and Niall was certain that he would not allow his brother to suffer another slight like this, raising Clan Colman in support of him. Donnchadh Donn had twice before risen in rebellion against his father, but this time he would have the support to succeed and overthrow him, he guessed. And on Flann Sinna's passing, Mael Mithig would not have the means to defeat both the Caille Follamain and Clan Colman combined. And then it dawned upon him, Mael Mithig was working up the courage to moot a proposal.

"What is it exactly that you want from me, King Mael Mithig, what do you propose in return for my support?"

Mael Mithig steepled his fingers together to gather his thoughts.

"The High Kingship has never interested me, Glundub. What I want is peace. The Ui Imair are coming, every year they ravage and ransack our lands and raid our churches. I will accept Flann of the Shannon's support for now as heir designate, but remain ambiguous in my intentions. If Donnchadh Donn and Conchobar rise after his death, you must come to my aid and support me with your armies of the north. I will reinstitute the old ways then and renounce my claim in favour of you and reinstate the alternation of the High Kingship between north and south. We will restart the old festival at the Hill of Tailteann and have games and celebration to reignite our fellowship as nobles of the Ui Neill and renew all the alliances of the clans afresh. My branch of the Ui Neill is as old with honour as your own, Glundub."

Niall nodded his head slowly but put forth a serious question.

"And what if Donncadh Donn and Conchobar and the Kings of Connaught rise in rebellion against Flann Sinna before his death, on the announcement of you becoming heir designate?"

A look of disgust and anguished acceptance rolled across the young king's face,

"Then I ask that you join King Flann and me for the sake of peace. We must make a secret pact you and I, that when the time comes, together we will threaten to desert Flann Sinna unless he accepts a return to the old ways immediately and he installs you as heir designate; only then will we join forces with him to subdue his sons. Flann Sinna is above all a pragmatist and will accept these terms I believe. And Donnchadh Donn and Conchobar will back down in the face of Leinster, Tara, my own tribe, the Sil nAedo Slaine, and of course, the full power of the Northern Ui Neill and the Ulaid. Peace will resume in the land once more and, unified, we will defeat the Vikings under your overall command."

Glundub could see it all before him, every word his brother-in-law said made sense and Donnchadh Donn's predictability would make it easy to plot against every eventuality. Niall's heart rejoiced inside of him; everything he wished, for the people and the whole of Ireland, was almost within his grasp. Only one bone of contention lay before them.

"What will we do about Linn? My people are determined that Linn will pay tribute to them. These men have marched for my cause and died for me. I cannot retreat north empty-handed, or I will have civil war on my own doorstep and rebellion at every hand. May I suggest that we split the tribute down the middle between us, so nobody loses face?"

Mael Mithig pondered for a second before shaking his head.

"I will accept you receiving a third of the tribute on the grounds that most of the town is on my side of the river. It will also serve to disguise the fact that we have come to an accord you and I, so that Conchobar or Donnchadh Donn will not suspect a thing when the time comes."

A broad smile crossed Niall Glundub's face, and he stood up from his chair. He clasped Mael Mithig forearm to forearm, the warrior's way, and left the tent. When he had crossed back across the small tributary of the Blackwater, he summoned Tadg mac Ruaidhri who had arrived from Kells with his contingent.

"Tell the men to pack up, we are going home."

CHAPTER 4

THE HIGH KING
OF IRELAND –TARA
(916 AD)

Niall Glundub met the ferocious gaze of the High King Flann Sinna head-on and refused to blink. Mael Mithig mac Flannacain, on the other hand, had long since lowered his eyes, looking more like an abashed child having been caught doing something naughty, rather than a king of the Bregans and the Ui Neill. They had bluntly stated their ultimatum to Flann Sinna, once the great hall in Tara had been cleared of prying eyes and ears, and Flann Sinna had not spoken, moved, or blinked for minutes afterward. Niall could feel the waves of austere contempt washing over him from the dais where the ancient High King sat, but he was unmoved in his resolve. Glundub would not be swayed, tricked, or intimidated; the righteous disgust of an ancient king meant nothing to him, he had faced many far more dreadful situations than this. The High King would come to terms with them, or he would face his two rebellious sons without their support, one or the other. Mael Mithig on the other hand, was quailing under Flann's gaze and Niall could sense the deep uncertainty, regret, and the erosion of conviction within his brother-in-law. Before Mael Mithig could entertain second thoughts and Niall lost his advantage, he spoke first.

"What say you to our demands, Flann of the Shannon? Will you deny the return of the Ui Neill tradition and allow the country to tear itself apart for your own ambition? Or will you acquiesce to our demands? Both of your heir designates are dead and your third wishes you to make an accord with me for the sake of peace."

The High King roared in response, "YOU KILLED MY SON OENGUS IN BATTLE. YOU ARE THE CAUSE OF THIS, GLUNDUB. IRELAND, MY COUNTRY, IS ON THE BRINK OF CIVIL WAR, ALL BECAUSE YOU, MY SUBJECT; WILL NOT DO WHAT YOU ARE TOLD."

The High King wearily sank back into his chair. He shakily held his forehead in one of his gnarled hands and shook his head in despair. He spoke to the Bregan King next:

"Mael Mithig, you have betrayed me and your people. Your treason has invited the wolf through the door. Either way I choose now, Ireland will suffer. You have, at best, handed the High Kingship to my savage and unwise son Donnchadh Donn, or at worst allowed Niall Glundub to seize the throne upon my death; a warlord who is so controversial and notorious among the Norse and Danes, that he will only act as a lightning rod for battle and suffering. By betraying me you have betrayed Ireland, Mael Mithig."

The young Bregan King bowed his head ashamed, but Niall Glundub was unaffected by the High King's fury and anger.

"You have held the High Kingship for too long, Flann Sinna, it is time to relinquish your crown. You accuse me of warmongering, but it was you in your wrath that came down upon the Munster-men with fire and sword at Beallach Mughna. It was you who fought in a civil war with the Caille Follamain for the control of Meath. And do not forget that it was you, Flann Sinna, who made accord with the pagans in Dublin; a people who have ransacked our country for a century or more and now call it home. You sit there in judgement upon both me and your eldest son, and state how we are unfit to rule; yet you have never succeeded in unifying this country. You have had thirty-eight years as High King and what have you achieved? The devastation of the entire south of the island, the alienation of many of your under-kings and nobles, and the appeasement of Viking savages. And now under your watch, we have foreigners ruling the south-eastern corner of our island, paying tribute to nobody, and subjugating our people there, and you have done nothing except provoke civil war in Meath. But all that pales in comparison, Flann Sinna, with your real crime in my eyes: you were the first High King in history to defy the tradition of the alternation of the High Kingship amongst the descendants of the sons of Niall of the Nine Hostages. You betrayed us all."

It was the High King who now sat abashed and unable to meet the eyes of Niall Glundub. Flann Sinna looked ancient to Niall, like a man drawn to death like a moth to a candle. His hands were bony, and liver-spotted, and his lank white hair sat around his ears like a shroud. All his vigour and strength had deserted him since Glundub had seen him last, but when he finally raised his eyes to meet Flann Sinna and Mael Mithig once more, Niall could sense the merest flicker of the pride and ambition that still drove the High King. *It is what has made him great,* Niall acknowledged in his mind.

"Well, let us come to an accord then, Niall Glundub, and salvage something from this debacle."

Ireland was a notoriously fractious beast to tame, and rebellion and treachery went hand in hand with the internecine warfare that plagued the myriad clans who claimed dominion across the forests and fields of the countryside; it was akin to herding cats at times in attempting to rule her. Niall had been harsh with his words to the High King but the time for negotiation and procrastination had ended. They had leverage over Flann Sinna and Niall could see that the High King knew it. At length Flann spoke.

"I… accept your ultimatum if you swear your allegiance to me in the potential confrontation to come. I also demand, Niall Glundub, that you will not allow my grandson, your son, Muirchertach mac Niall to fight, as if you and I should fall in battle with the Caille Follamain and the tribes in Clan Colman who have chosen Conchobar over me along with the kings of Connaught, I say that Hector should become the High King of Ireland. Swear to this, Niall Glundub, and you, Mael Mithig, and it will be so. I will relinquish the sole right of the Southern Ui Neill to maintain the High Kingship and we will resume the old ways."

Mael Mithig looked across to Niall and nodded in excited agreement.

Niall Glundub smiled. "I agree to these terms, High King Flann Sinna. I will honour this bargain on my word as a King of the Ui Neill."

Flann Sinna nodded haggardly and shuffled down off the dais. He extended his leathery old hand and Niall took it in his grip, the warrior's way. An accord for the first time had been reached between the Northern and Southern branches of the Ui Neill, since the end of the previous century, a momentous occurrence yet laced in tragedy and violence.

"Flann, it was my brother Domnall, who is now buried in Clonmacnoise, that was the source of the friction between the clans of the Ui Neill. It was not my doing, I only wished for justice and what was right. Be comforted by the fact that I am Niall Glundub mac Aed Findliath, not my brother or father, and my word is iron. I understand your motivation for what you did back then, but now is definitively the time to renew the old accord between all the Ui Neill."

The High King nodded sagely and answered, "I believe that to cement this agreement between our clans we should initiate the sports and games of the Tailteann fair once more and allow our peoples to mingle and meet and make matches for their women, in peace. This will strengthen our pact, bolster alliances, and bring joy to Ireland."

Niall Glundub nodded in agreement. For the first time in a generation, there was a hope for a unified peace Niall felt, and all that now stood in their way were Donnchadh Donn and Conchobar mac Flann. *Conchobar can be swayed,* thought Niall, *but Donnchadh Donn will still need to be threatened with a show of force.*

Niall had camped a thousand men on the southern border of Argialla, north of the lands of the Caille Follamain and for that he was grateful. He had anticipated to an extent what way the meeting with Flann of the Shannon and Mael Mithig would go and understood very well the potential of conflict occurring; either with Flann Sinna himself or with his sons. In the aftermath of their confrontation with Flann in the hall at Tara, the three men begun to strategise, searching for the best way to bring Donnchadh Donn, Conchobar and the Kings of Connaught into the fold without instigating civil war. After several hours of debate, they agreed upon a plan. They would summon Augaire mac Aililla of Leinster, Fogartach mac Tolarg of South Brega and Aed mac Eochucan of the Ulaid and Dal nAridi, to Tara in a moon's turn, along with the large part of the strength of their own contingents, and they would march into the west of Meath in a show of force. All together they would bring two and a half thousand men to bear which they estimated would suffice in quashing dissent among the sons of Flann and help usher in the return of the old order.

By the following month, their armies were assembled and combined, although the forces dispatched by Augaire mac Aililla were disappointingly small. The captain that the Leinster king had sent in his stead had explained that the soldiers present were all that King Augaire could spare because of the running battles occurring with the Vikings of Waterford, for control of South Leinster. The Kings of Osraige were similarly indisposed. Diarmuit mac Cerbaill, their over-king, was related to Flann Sinna but they never bothered to press them for reinforcements. Both Niall and Flann knew that the warriors of Osraige were hard-pressed and faced the same foe that Augaire mac Aililla did. In fact, word had reached them that the Kingdom of Osraige was close to being overrun by the warlord Gragabai the Bastard and would need to be rescued at some point lest it fall under the sway of the heathens. Once the supplies required for their army had been gathered, they marched west toward Cill Mheasain and then deeper into Clan Colman territory; the idea being to force Conchobar to see sense and stand aside while they marched upon Donnchadh Donn. If Conchobar was swayed, Donnchadh Donn and the Connaught men would have to fall into line or risk being destroyed utterly. The going was good for the march as the late spring weather was calm and mild. At times, their scouts witnessed men on horseback looking on at their host and then galloping further west, but Flann Sinna and Niall Glundub agreed that this was a positive and suited their needs; *Perhaps the size of our host will force Conchobar to come to the table very soon.*

When the host reached the fort at Muileann gCearr on the sixth day, they finally encountered opposition, but it was such sizeable opposition that it caused Niall Glundub to briefly doubt their gambit. The host that faced them was shockingly almost as large as their own. *They had been gathering their own army for weeks now,* Niall understood instantly. A glance at Mael Mithig revealed to Niall that the Bregan King had seen what he had seen and had come to the same conclusion; that it was incredibly lucky that they had marched west when they had, or this host would be amongst the innocents of Brega and Tara already.

Niall could see from the advanced preparation apparent with the army from the West of Meath, that an invasion had been intended by the brothers to depose their father. It was only luck and timing that had ensured that he, Flann Sinna and Mael Mithig had got to them first. If Niall did not miss his guess the High King himself, on viewing this sizeable host arrayed before them, perceived this dreadful truth also. *Flann Sinna was right, these ungrateful sons are not deserving of the title High King,* thought Niall bitterly. He tried to picture himself revolting against Aed Findliath his long-dead father to seize power in his youth, but he just couldn't envision it; he considered himself immune to such disloyalty. But he then soberly recalled the events that occurred when he took power from his brother, who had been forced to take the cross, to save face. *Domnall had lost control of the north and I had to step in,* he mused, but he knew in his heart of hearts that there were even now remote corners of the north where he was still named usurper.

With the two great hosts facing off on the banks of the River Brosna, Niall Glundub instructed his men to unfurl a great white banner that indicated truce. Hostages were exchanged in the morning light and three commanders from each side rode to meet in a bare patch of grass that lay between the camps. Glundub peered at the ground all around him as he disgruntledly rode his horse alongside Mael Mithig mac Flannacain and the wizened figure of the High King Flann Sinna. It was perfect ground for fighting and the next few minutes would decide whether the earth there would be covered in grass by nightfall or the blood of young Irishmen. He hoped for the former. Three men on horses emerged from the ranks of Clan Colman, the Caille Follamain and

Connaught; they were Cathal mac Conchobar, Conchobar mac Flann and of course the fearsome general, Donnchadh Donn mac Flann Sinna mac Mael Seachnaill. The six men on horseback stared across at each other, all veteran generals, and warriors. Niall decided to wait for the High King to speak first, to reinforce the idea that this plan was the High King's decision and that his hand had not been forced by him and Mael Mithig. *It was important to prop up this illusion to maintain peace,* Niall knew, *or sooner or later I will be facing Donnchadh Donn across the battlefield once more.* The High King spoke.

"My sons, King Cathal, we are not here to negotiate, but we are not here to offer you battle either. I want peace and I have decided the terms upon which it shall be achieved."

Donnchadh Donn interrupted him, "Father, your time is done one way or the other. I will entertain what you have to say but I must warn you that if it is not acceptable to me you will have battle whether you will it or not."

Flann Sinna nodded slowly. He looked desperately tired, and it seemed to Niall that he was almost swaying in his saddle. *The excursion from Tara must have taxed him greatly,* guessed Niall, *he is in his dotage and having to subdue his sons has sapped his endurance.*

"My son, I have wronged you. In your youth, I used you as a pawn in the contest between myself and Glundub's father, Aed Findliath. The bitterness you feel was seeded when I sacrificed your birthright for my own ambition."

The High King paused for a second, hawked and spat as if having trouble swallowing. He then rubbed a temple with forefinger and thumb and winced in pain as if suffering from a headache from drinking too much mead.

"I made Mael Mithig my heir designate on the death of Oengus, but he has rejected this nomination. He wishes for the entire Ui Neill to return to the old ways of alternation of the High Kingship, and I have reluctantly agreed. This is my will. Upon my death, the Northern Ui Neill will nominate a ruler to assume the High Kingship. It may be Niall Glundub or some other, who knows, but on the death of said northern ruler, the crown will pass to you my sons, my sons-in-law and other descendants and relations in the south once more; decided by a moot on Tara."

The three men opposed to Niall, sat upon their mounts in mute shock as if the High King had named Queen Aethelfled of Mercia as heir, or one of the heathen barbarians. Before any of them could answer the High King continued.

"I want peace, my sons. The Ui Imair have tentatively returned to the south. It was our internecine warfare that has allowed them to return, and I believe it is only my life, and by extension my relationship with Sihtric Ivarsson, that holds them at bay. The Scourge cannot hold off the ambitions of his demonic brothers indefinitely."

Flann halted momentarily and felt his left arm and winced again in pain. Niall could see colour drain from the High King's face; the old man was in obvious discomfort.

"Donnchadh Donn my son, Conchobar my son, we must all of us here now heal as a country to avoid civil war. We must come to an accord. It is my wish that we return to the old ways. Who knows, if Glundub and I fall in the wars to come, the Southern Ui Neill could install you as High King despite all that I have done to you. Donnchadh, you are still young enough. When Ragnall and all his terrible warlords come – and they will, my sons – we must meet them as a unified force of Irishmen; or we will be destroyed, one, by one, by one."

The High King paused to catch his breath. Niall could see something was badly wrong with Flann Sinna, but at such a crucial and delicate time as this, he was loath to interfere. Donnchadh Donn was listening and Conchobar was clearly teetering on the verge of acceptance, moved by his father's appeal.

"What say you, my mighty sons of the Ui Neill?" Flann croaked. "Will you have peace, or will you have civil war?"

Conchobar looked to his brother. Donnchadh Donn was a hard man, dour and foreboding, as fearsome as he was bitter, but he was not without wits or pragmatism.

"We will have peace on those terms, Father, let the old ways resume and I swear the warriors of the Caille Follamain will follow you or your successors to whatever end."

Conchobar stood up on his horse and roared so that both hosts of men could hear across the potential battlefield:

"WE WILL HAVE PEACE, PEACE FOR THE CLANS OF IRELAND, PEACE FOR THE UI NEILL."

As one, a mighty roar erupted from both sides of the conflict. Men who did not know whether they would be returning to their wives and children would not now be called upon to fight against other Irishmen, and their relief was palpable. Niall turned to the High King; he had swivelled his horse around but was sagging in his saddle. As he passed Niall, the Northern King could see that one side of Flann Sinna's face had drooped grotesquely. The High King released the reins of his horse then and tumbled from the saddle in a dishevelled heap. Flann Sinna had fallen hard upon the earth at Muileann gCearr.

The procession to Tara was the most desperate journey Niall Glundub had ever taken. They needed to rush to get the seriously ill High King back to Tara but could not push the pace too hard in case he could not endure it and died. All the under-kings present had sent their armies home under able sergeants and commanders, but the kings and chieftains themselves, with their elite warriors, had formed a bodyguard around the covered tented wagon that protected the stricken High King from the elements. A rotation of priests accompanied Flann Sinna within the wagon and saw to his every need, but he took no food and could barely accept a sip of water. On the few times that Niall had entered the tent in the six-day journey to Tara, he could see that only vacant incomprehension abided within the mind of the High King. The mighty Flann of the Shannon was like a helpless infant swaddled in a bundle of furs.

Mael Mithig and Conchobar took turns in leading the vanguard of the host as it passed. Word seemed to have raced ahead of their swift passage, as at every track and fort and crannog, men and women and children stood along the route to pay their respects. The highest-ranking priest in the retinue had remarked privately to Niall Glundub that there was no way back from this affliction and this was almost certainly the last stand of Flann Sinna. He explained to Niall that he had seen this illness before where a vein had burst in the ancient king's head and destroyed his mind and bodily functions. He had made an analogy that the door of the hall was open, there was a candle in the window, but the room was bare, with nobody at home.

Donnchadh Donn sat grim upon his horse as if some great weight was heaped upon his shoulders about to crush him, and Niall recognised what the King of the Caille Follamain was feeling: it was regret, and he recognised it because he felt it himself. For so many years and decades, Niall and Flann had opposed each other politically, economically, and militarily, but for no great purpose. The only people who suffered were the Irish people themselves, caught between the anvil and the hammer. The imminent death of Flann Sinna meant that Niall Glundub would be made High King, and he had sent word with trusted men, north, south, east, and west, with news of his approaching coronation and more importantly right now, Flann Sinna's demise. It was melancholic and cynical to view it that way but there was a practicality to the situation that he could not ignore; the country could not afford a vacuum in leadership and Niall must be quickly crowned. Ireland must unite now as Flann Sinna had uttered in his final words before falling from his steed.

They reached Tara at noon on the sixth day and Flann of the Shannon still clung to life. The priests were astonished at this, the sheer resilience of the man, but Niall was not surprised; Flann would defy death to the very end just as Niall himself would. The ailing High King was carried on a bier to his main hall where servants cleared the great room of tables and chairs, and the King was placed upon a newly made bed. Conchobar mac Flann, Niall's half-brother, had sent word to all corners of Meath, Leinster and Osraige, everywhere in Ireland were Flann had close or distant kin, for them to come to Tara to pay their last respects to the High King.

Flann Sinna hung on for four more days, surrounded by grieving family, friends and grandchildren. At the break of dawn of the twenty-fifth of May 916, Flann Sinna mac Mael Seachnaill mac Mael Ruanaid; the lord or the Ui Neill and the High King of Ireland, passed into the night. The funeral was enormous, and Flann was buried beside his third and final queen, Mael Muire ingen Cinead in a last act of love and devotion, that he had instructed his bishop to oversee on the event of his death. As the Heir Designate of Ireland,

Niall Glundub was asked to speak the final words at the grave, as they sent the mighty Flann Sinna, his great rival and father-in-law, into the abyss. Niall had composed a poem and recited it before the people of Tara, knowing that forms of it would reverberate through time:

Flann, the fair of Tara, the greatest among kings, monarch of Ireland,
  fierce was his valour.
It was he that ruled our people, until placed beneath the earth's heavy
  surface.
A fount of wealth he sent amongst his people, a warrior echoing of
  ancient times,
A fine hero who subdued all, chief of the men of Tara and Ireland,
  possessed of courage.
A pillar of dignity over every head, fair chief of valour, caster of
  spears,
Sun-flash of hair, noble, pleasant, so full of honourable hospitality, the
  head of all men,
The great king, Flann of the Shannon.

The coronation of Niall as High King was delayed for another month out of respect for the deceased king. Niall had initially been impatient, but his wife Gormlaith, when she had arrived a week after her father's death, had insisted that he should respect the wishes of Flann's extended family. His brother Conchobar and his son Hector had both pointed out to him that letting almost a full month to pass before his crowning upon the Mound of Niall of the Nine Hostages, would allow many of his new under-kings and chieftains to make their way to Tara, to pledge him their fealty. The appointed day arrived, midsummers day, the longest in the year. It was an auspicious day for not just all Irish Christians, but the followers of the old gods and the Norse-Gael pantheon as well.

And so it was that upon the morning of June the twenty-first, on the year of our lord 916, Niall Glundub mac Aed Findliath mac Niall Caille, the overlord of the Ui Neill, north and south, stood upon the Liath Fail, the stone of destiny and was crowned king before tens of thousands of the people of Ireland. He was resplendent in his cloak of many colours and on his brow, he wore a slim circlet of gold. The clergy slowly intoned their prayers in a respectful circle and sprinkled holy water upon him to bless his reign with peace and bounty. But Niall knew that was an untruth, for he was not there to make peace; he was there to unite the people and defend Ireland from all comers, particularly the tyranny of the Northmen.

When the clergy retreated and all the major kings and princes from Meath, Argialla, Connaught, Leinster, Osraige and all the disparate under-kingdoms of the island stood back from him, the people quieted to hear the first words Niall Glundub would speak as High King. But long before that day, Niall had determined that he would show all his people, king and peasant alike, that he was a man of action and not words. He swept off his ceremonial cloak revealing his leather armour beneath, his shield strapped at his back and his dual swords at his side. He was a warrior first and foremost, a king of action not words and air. He slowly drew the sword at his left hip out of its scabbard with his right hand and pointed it to the sky. Silence greeted him at first with only the wind disrupting the stillness, causing banners to flap in the breeze, but from a distant corner of the enormous throng of people his name, *Glundub*, begin to stir in many throats. In moments, the tens of thousands of Irish people present were shouting "GLUNDUB, GLUNDUB, GLUNDUB" at the top of their voices.

Niall Glundub mac Aed Findliath stepped off the stone of destiny then as the undisputed and utmost power in the land.

PART 8

THE VENGEANCE OF RAGNALL

DRAMATIS PERSONAE:

Aella (*Ail-la*) – Long-dead Northumbrian King who employed Vikings to fight for his causes.

Aethelfled of Mercia (*A-thel-fled*) – Saxon Queen of Mercia and sister of the King of Wessex.

Aethelstan (*A-thel-stan*) – Young Saxon prince and Mercian commander.

Amlaib Collasson (*Am-layb-collason*) – Known by the Irish as the "Cenncaireach" or the Sinner. Vicious Viking warlord.

Amlaib Ivarsson (*Am-layb-ivarson*) – Long-deceased Ui Imair warlord, older brother to Ragnall.

Augaire mac Aililla (*Ag-wear-a-mac-al-lila*) – Ferocious young Irish warlord and bother-in-law to the Ui Imair princes.

Bairid Oitirson (*Bar-rid-oh-tier-son*) – Called Bairid mac Oitir by the Irish, distant kin to the Ui Imair as his grandfather Auisle was brother to Ivar the Boneless. Former ruler of Mann, slain in battle by Sihtric the Scourge.

Baldur – Important god in the Scandinavian pantheon.

Beollan mac Ciarmac (*Byole-on-mac-kyor-mac*) – King of South Brega, under-king of Conchobar mac Flann.

Boudicca (*Boo-dik-a*) – Long-dead, semi-legendary Celtic Iceni queen who fought the Romans.

Brunbolg Headtaker (*Brun-bulg-head-taker*) – Physically gigantic Viking warlord, subject to the influence of the Ui Imair.

Ceitl Flatnose (*Ket-tel-flatnose*) – Infamous King of Limerick and part of the Orkneys, notorious Viking raider. Now deceased.

Colla Bairidsson (*Col-a-bar-idson*) – Second eldest son of the deceased Bairid mac Oitir and King of the Viking town of Limerick.

Conchobar mac Flann (*Con-co-bar-mac-flann*) – King of Clan Colman and the Southern Ui Neill, ruler at Tara.

Constantine mac Aed – Over-king of all Scotland.

Domnall mac Constantine (*Dom-nall*) – Long-deceased King of the Scots. Known as the Dasachtach or the mad for his impulsiveness.

Donncuan mac Flannacain (*Dun-coo-an-mac-flan-na-cawn*) – Young under-king of the Northern Ui Neill.

Ealdred (*E-al-dread*) – King of Bernicia in the north of Northumbria. Related through marriage to the King of Scotland.

Edward the Elder – King of Wessex.

Erik Haraldsson – Also known as Erik Bloodaxe. Fearsome Viking marauder and raider, young son of the King of Norway.

Erik Olafsson – Ui Imair warlord and prince, cousin to Ragnall.

Fenrir – Wolfen demon of the Scandinavian pantheon of gods.

Flann Sinna – Recently deceased but legendary High King of Ireland.

Garangr Sichfridthsson (*Gar-rang-gar-sic-frith-son*) – Ui Imair prince and Viking warlord, operating in Northumbria.

Godfrith Ivarsson (*God-frith-ivarson*) – Twin brother of Sihtric, the youngest sons of the former King of Dublin, Ivar Ivarsson. Commander under his brother Ragnall.

Gorm – Prince of Denmark.

Gragabai the Bastard (*Grag-a-by*) – Notorious Viking raider and alleged bastard son of Harald Fairhair.

Grungni mac Conall (*Grung-knee-mac-fer-dia*) – Irish nobleman with a Norse Gael Ui Imair mother.

Guthfrith (*Gut-frith*) – Puppet ruler of Yorvik in Northumbria. Politically powerful Saxon-Norse eorl.

Harald Fairhair – King of all Norway.

Harthacnut (*Hartha-can-noot*) – Known as the wise, King of Denmark.

Henry the Fowler – Powerful Germanic monarch and warlord, a threat to Danish sovereignty.

Indulf mac Constantine (*In-dulf-mac-constantine*) – Prince of Scotland, youngest son of Constantine of Scotland.

Ingamundr Bairidsson (*Ing-ga-munder-ba-rid-son*) – Formidable Ui Imair warlord, slain in battle at Chester in 907.

Ivar Ivarsson – Long-deceased Ui Imair warlord and older brother of Ragnall.

Ivar the Boneless – Long-deceased former King of Dublin and a legendary son of Ragnar Lodbrok.

Liadan mac Diarmuid (*Lie-a-don-mac-dear-mid-a*) – Treacherous chieftain within the Deise tribe of Munster.

Mael Colum mac Domnall (*Male-colm-mac-dom-nal*) – Prince of Scotland, son of the long-deceased King Domnall Dasachtach.

Mael Maedoc (*Male-may-dock*) – Powerful Leinster war-leader and bishop of the province.

Mael Morda mac Muirecan (*Male-mor-da-mac-mwir-a-cawn*) – Major Leinster under-king.

Niall Glundub mac Aed Findliath – High King of Ireland and the Lord of the Northern Ui Neill.

Odin – The chief God of the Norse and Danes, also known as the Allfather.

Oitir Iarla (*Oh-tier-ee-arla*) – Also known as Oitir the Black, or Oitir the Black One. Fearsome Viking warlord.

Olaf Godfrithsson (*Olaf-god-frith-son*) – Extremely young Ui Imair prince and nephew to Ragnall.

Olga Helmsdottir – Ferocious female Viking commander, known as the Valkyrie.

Ragnall Ivarsson (*Rag-nal-ivarson*) – Leader of the Ui Imair.

Ragnar Lodbrok (*Ragnar-lod-brok*) – Long-deceased legendary Viking sea king and ravager, ancestor of multiple Viking warlords.

Rollo the Walker – Notorious Viking warlord that plagued the Francian river systems but was made a duke to encourage peace by Charles the Simple.

Sigurd Ragnarsson – Long-dead Viking warlord and Danish nobleman, known as Sigurd Snake-in-the-eye.

Sihtric Ivarsson (*Si-tric-ivarson*) – Known as Sihtric the Scourge by the Irish. Warlord under the nominal command of his brother Ragnall.

Tadg mac Faelain (*Ty-g-mac-fail-on*) – King of the Ui Cheinnselaig a major Leinster tribe.

Thor – Major deity of the Scandinavian pantheon.

Uhtred (*Ooh-tread*) – Son of the King of Bernicia and renowned warrior, sometimes known as the older.

Ulf – Ui Imair sea captain and warrior.

Wilfred – Saxon peasant and spy.

CHAPTER 1

THE LANDFALL AT WATERFORD
(917 AD)

Ragnall Ivarsson, the lord of the Ui Imair, stared out across the choppy grey seas from the docks of the longfort that served as the capital of the Isle of Mann, scanning the horizon for familiar sails. He was flanked by his younger twin brothers Godfrith and Sihtric, with Godfrith's eldest son Olaf, loitering with the Ui Imair banner behind them. Ragnall had made a point of greeting each of his sworn warlords as they came ashore. He had summoned all his captains and generals to Mann with the loose date of the Scandinavian holy feast of Walpurgisnacht, the spring equinox, as the appointed time for his army to combine. The force was being assembled for a single purpose; to take back what was rightfully theirs from the Irish. The feast of Walpurgisnacht had taken place the previous night within the halls of the capital of Mann, but so far only two hundred and fifty ships had answered his summons. Eric Olafsson his cousin would never arrive at Mann at all though, a grievous blow to Ragnall's hopes. He had been slain in battle in defence of Derby in the five Boroughs by men loyal to Aethelfled, Queen of the Mercians, and the remnants of Eric's shattered splinter fleet had limped to Mann a weak ago, much diminished from the strength Ragnall had wished for.

The Danelaw was almost completely subdued by Aethelfled now as she aggressively looked to push her Mercian borders east. She demanded tribute from Saxons, Danes and Norse alike as she progressed eastward. Ragnall controlled much of the west and centre of Northumbria and all of Cumbria, but the puppet ruler Guthfrith that he had installed and quietly supported militarily, was beginning to crack under pressure from the Bernicians and their Scottish allies to the north, and Aethelfled and her Mercians from the south. *If I ever catch that demoness Aethelfled, I swear to Odin I will feed her corpse to the ravens,* he raged inwardly.

His brother Godfrith had a legitimate claim to the kingship at Yorvik due to his marriage to the daughter of one of the three old kings slain at Odinsfield several years previously, but the delicate political situation had forced Ragnall to not only take a back seat himself, but also to keep Godfrith away from the throne as well. The people of Northumbria, although begrudgingly accepting of the indirect overlordship of the Ui Imair, were for now adamant that a Christian should rule them directly and none of the Ui Imair leadership, Ragnall knew, would ever betray the old gods. Guthfrith was half Norse and half Dane, but all Christian. It annoyed Ragnall considerably that he had to acquiesce to their wishes, but he consoled himself with the fact that if his gambit paid off in Ireland, he would not have to pander to any Christian dissent from anybody; he would have the strength to take what he wanted. Many of the people of the region were of Norse and Dane heritage, at least partially, and had somewhere along the line heretically abandoned Odin for the Christ. The reality was that although Ragnall and the Ui Imair were gathering power, wealth, and men at a furious pace, they were still stretched very thin and their vast kingdom had enemies on every side; enemies who they could ill afford to antagonise, right when they intended to invade Ireland.

Aethelfled had been at the forefront of Ragnall's mind for almost two years. Her growing power was now overshadowing her brother Edward the Elder in Wessex. In her nephew Aethelstan, she possessed a shrewd commander at her side, a foe to be reckoned with. The survivors of the battle of Derby had assured Ragnall that Aethelfled would once more turn west and not north as rumours abounded that the Welsh at Brecenanmere had dared to cross the Severn and sack and burn a handful of Aethelfled's villages and churches in revenge for some slight. To keep her bishops in line, she would have to invade Wales at least temporarily, the men suggested, and put the offenders to the sword lest she lose face with the church.

Ragnall still did not fully believe it though, nothing could be trusted where the Mercian queen was concerned. The slaughter of his kinsmen at the catastrophic battle of Chester had taught him that much at least. He elected to leave Garangr his cousin encamped upon the Mersey River, ever watchful with several thousand of Ragnall's men. If the Scots and Bernicians came south, or the men of Northumbria rebelled against Yorvik, or Aethelfled ventured north; Garangr would be there to simultaneously rush to meet them and summon Ragnall back from Ireland on a week's notice.

To bulk his own numbers, Ragnall had recruited men from the Hebrides, Francia and even Scandinavia. Constantine the Great's grip on the outer reaches of the Hebrides and the Orkneys was limited, with the Norse Gael eorls and jarls there only paying lip service to his authority. Many and more of these Norse-Gael Hebridians had flocked to Ragnall's banners rather than Constantine's, to taste the old ways of their ancestors and gain favour with the Gods. Oitir Iarla the Black One had retaken the settlement known as Lach da Cheach from the Irish in 914 and named it Waterford. It had trebled in size in three years and was intended to be a staging point for Ragnall's invasion; too far from the strength of Niall Glundub for the murderous High King to do anything about their presence, yet close enough to Dublin and Leinster to allow Ragnall to exert influence on the Irish safely and without interference. While Oitir ruled there on behalf of Ragnall, Gragabai the Bastard had been given a simple task; to set the entire southern half of Ireland on fire, a task he was singularly suited to. The southeast corner of Ireland was ripe for the conquering.

For years Ragnall had ruled the Ui Imair with an iron fist. He had assumed control in the aftermath of his cousin Ingamundr being slain at Chester in 907, when Ragnall was in his early twenties. From that point on he had devoted every single day of his waking life to protecting his people and providing them with a haven and a life worth living. He had given everything he had to them with his brothers at his side, everything, and now the shame, suffering and humiliation they had endured as a people was nearly over. In the early years he had to endure constant challenges to his authority, as despite his formidable achievements in battle, his age and his sexual proclivities drew endless challenges for leadership from more seasoned warlords. Four times he had to face rivals in single combat for leadership of the Ui Imair and four times he had slain his foes. But ever so slowly as the victories accumulated and his legend spread, the challenges to his authority dissipated. His younger twin brothers, Godfrith and Sihtric, had grown to astonishingly powerful warriors, with victories that tallied to almost match Ragnall's own. With the twins at his side, the Ui Imair had gone from strength to strength.

After the battle of Odinsfield in 910, Ragnall suddenly found himself as the foremost Viking authority in the region; and even around the known world only Igor of the Rus, Harald Fairhair of Norway and perhaps Rollo the Walker of Francia, could match him for fame and military might. As his position solidified and his wealth and power grew amongst the river systems of eastern Northumbria and Yorvik, he had recognised a sea change in his own attitudes. With his base secure, his people safe and multiplying, he no longer focused so much on protecting the people under his rule, or even expanding his power and drawing in fresh Norse-Gael men to his ranks; he had started to seek revenge upon those who had humiliated the Ui Imair over the years.

He had begun raiding Mercia and Wessex at will, plundering the settlements that lay close to the waterways. In 912, he sailed north and initiated the subjugation of the Scandinavian Hebrides; the mere fact that people of his heritage would dare bend the knee to Constantine of Scotland, the king who had defeated them in 904 and killed his brothers and father, was an affront to him. He then focused on the lands of the Northern Ui Neill and the Ulaid, sending the very worst of his reavers and warlords to harass them and it provoked the reaction he was looking for. The Drengr, Niall Glundub, had sent a fleet out to face Ragnall upon the seas and he had smashed the Irishmen and their allies off the Cumbrian coast.

The next foe to feel his wrath were the Norse-Gael of Bairid mac Oitir, who owed his allegiance to Harald Fairhair of Norway if anyone, but in truth was an independent power in his own right. Ragnall had never forgotten being turned away by that wretch when his people were fleeing from Dublin in 902. They had been turned away from Mann on pain of death right when his people needed shelter the most. Ragnall had taken great pleasure in obliterating the elite of Mann and he had wept with righteousness when his brother Sihtric the Scourge had pulled Bairid mac Oitir's entrails through his belly with his mailed fist. Justice and revenge were sometimes intertwined and now the warriors of Mann were sworn to the Ui Imair upon their arm rings.

The following year he had sent Oitir Iarla the Black One to Lach da Cheach as a vanguard force to secure a safe port in the Irish storm. Sihtric had provided the intelligence to Ragnall on how best to approach the dangerous Irish, describing the great battle at Beallach Mughna in detail and the devastation it had caused the warriors of Munster. The south of Ireland had never been as weak as it was now in Sihtric's opinion and Ragnall trusted his brother's judgement. At the same time as Oitir invaded Waterford, Ragnall had launched an assault upon the various kingdoms of Wales. For decades, the Welsh had brought nothing but pain and suffering to the Ui Imair and Ragnall had come down upon their various factions like a boulder rolling down a mountain. He had enslaved many hundreds and sold them to the Black men of the Aifric as slaves. The Islamic caliphate in Andalusia was in turmoil with civil war but the Ghanaians and the Berbers were always hungry for slaves for their salt and gold mines. And now after fifteen years of exile, the Ui Imair were returning once more to their homeland and Ragnall would sail with vengeance in his heart, at the head of all his kin.

It took the best part of a week for most of his fleet to arrive; the last two warlords of significance to dock at Mann were Olga the Valkyrie with her fleet and the mighty Brunbolg Headtaker and his twenty-five ships. There were other Viking sea kings and lords yet still to arrive who had sworn allegiance to Ragnall and the Ui Imair but he had no more time to waste waiting. They would sail to Ireland from Mann with what they had; it would have to suffice. Once combined with Oitir Iarla's men at Waterford, Ragnall estimated they would have in the region of five thousand fighting men and other allies at their disposal; perhaps the greatest army fielded by his people since the time of the Great Heathen Army, almost forty years ago. On the night before they were due to depart, Ragnall and his brothers had overseen a sacrifice each to the Gods Baldur, Thor and Odin the Allfather; for strength in battle, for fortune and health and for wisdom. On the morning of their departure, he instructed a small garrison of men to stay at Mann and should stragglers arrive, to send them onward toward Waterford. And on Easter Sunday as the Christians called it, most of the strength of the Ui Imair set sail for Ireland for the first time in fifteen years.

Sihtric had always advocated patience until the elderly king and kinsman to them, Flann Sinna, had passed away, as not only did he feel that it would be dishonourable to attack him, but he also felt that the power vacuum would initiate a civil war between the multiple Irish kingdoms rendering them blind to all else that moved. He was half right; there was civil war in Ireland, but it was very minor and occurred before Flann Sinna's death, not after. His passing regrettably had the opposite effect; it handed power to the most warlike among them – Niall Glundub mac Aed Findliath the lord of the Northern Ui Neill. The mere thought of Glundub's name sent a shiver down Ragnall's spine, and his fingers twitched in anticipation and eagerness to fight him. He would give his left arm to be the one to bury his axe in the Irish High King's face. Ragnall could not help feeling that at some point their paths would inevitably cross and when they did, finally his brothers and father could be avenged, and they would know peace in Valhalla. *I swear by Odin's missing eye that I will mount Niall Glundub's head upon a spear,* he promised himself.

The seas were calm on the passage across to Ireland. The trip was perhaps only a day and a half in length at a slow pace if the fleet succeeded in sticking together. The passage was made slightly more difficult because Ragnall had commanded the fleet to stay well out of sight of land. At least initially his presence should be left unannounced until they were fully entrenched on Irish soil, he had felt.

The mood was jovial amongst the crews of the longboats as they sailed, and in the evening, they were able to lash their boats together and feast and drink under the moonlight. Ragnall covered his head with a cloak and leapt from boat to boat anonymously to ascertain the mood of his men. Many of them were young lads, barely capable of sporting a beard but many were also veterans of the last two decades and had lived through the trials and tribulations of the Ui Imair beside Ragnall and his brothers. In these men, beneath the boasting and bravado, he sensed a nervousness and apprehension unbecoming of Viking warriors. He did not deign to question them as he felt the same way himself. For so many years, many of the famous warriors amongst the Ui Imair warbands had been too scared to show their faces in Dublin lest the Irish recognise them and exact retribution on their innocent kin within the city walls. There was still trade and commerce between Dublin and all the other Ui Imair strongholds up and down the Irish Sea; but in Dublin, Irish warriors patrolled the streets, disarmed visitors and exacted tribute from the local Norse-Gael population. Although this expedition was, in Ragnall's and his brothers' eyes, a quest for vengeance, it was also, they knew, an attempt to emancipate his people in Dublin from the strangling grip of the Ui Neill.

They resumed their sailing to the southwest on the break of day. The wind was favourable and the sails upon the longboats snapped in the breeze. As the early morning wore on, the idle chat amongst the crews grew sparse and on the cusp of land being sighted, silence ruled the seas among the longboats of the fleet. Ragnall could feel the emotion building among his entire army. Even the Vikings from Scandinavia and Frisia were subdued as they sensed the enormity of the occasion. When land was eventually sighted and the distant longfort of Waterford could be discerned upon the mouth of the Suir river, the only sounds audible were the breaking of distant waves upon the shore and the piercing cries of curious seagulls above them. A tear welled in the corner of Ragnall's eye as the many years of hurt came to the surface. He could sense his brothers on either side of him were emotional too; so much loss, so much hurt and pain, and now they were returned. Ragnall looked to his nephew young Olaf who despite his tender years, understood what was occurring. Astonishingly the boy began to sing. All on the boat turned to face him and Ragnall could see that all the crews of the boats nearby had also strained to listen. It was an old song, a beautiful song all mothers sang to their children wherever Scandinavian peoples held sway:

My mother told me, someday I would buy,
Galley with good oars, sail to distant shores,
Stand up high in the prow, noble barque I steer,
Steady course for the haven, hew many foemen,
Hew many foemen.

As the words echoed across the water, the song was picked up by every Norse, Dane and Norse-Gael warrior in the entire fleet, and the ancient song of the Vikings flowed over the water, a solemn dirge to the old gods and their ancient culture. It was haunting to Ragnall, speaking of the great longing of not just the Ui Imair, but the whole Viking world. The Mighty Ui Imair, a clan brought low, but now on the threshold of returning to greatness. A couple of hundred feet from the shoreline, all the boats drew in their sails and allowed one boat to approach the land: Ragnall's dragonboat. The entire fleet held its breath and Ragnall could feel their fear as if, somehow, they expected some divine travesty to descend upon them and they would never reach Ireland. Twenty feet from the shore, Ragnall, Godfrith and Sihtric jumped into the water and waded through the shallows. And then they had arrived. Ragnall fell to his knees and clutched great handfuls of wet sand, allowing it to flow between his fingers. His brothers just embraced in tears. Ragnall stood up once more and roared back across the water to his thousands of warriors, "FOR ODIN AND THE UI IMAIR," raising one of his axes into the air.

Every Viking throat shouted their approval in a cacophonous roar until there was only one word echoing across the Irish Sea:

"RAGNALL, RAGNALL, RAGNALL."

*

It took the best part of the day for all the longboats to be pulled up upon the shore or lashed to the docks of Waterford with sturdy ropes. Godfrith and Sihtric began to issue commands to the men on where they would be quartered and fed. The three brothers had planned this assault for years and had recited their intended actions so repeatedly that they knew their parts by rote. While Gragabai the Bastard had been plundering the midlands, Osraige and South Leinster to keep organised opposition from those provinces off balance, Oitir Iarla the Black One had been steadily subjugating the clans of South Leinster and East Munster. Some had yielded and others had been destroyed, but each had been given a choice: bend the knee and pay tribute to the Ui Imair or have your lands ravaged, your men killed, and your women and children enslaved. As Ragnall approached the main hall and peered around, he was impressed with what his commander, the Black One, had done. In three years, Oitir had built up a significant town with many buildings and the signs of commerce were everywhere.

Most Viking warriors possessed a secondary trade to accompany their skills as fighters and these men had not disappointed. Blacksmiths, fishermen, farriers, farmers, carpenters, and fine craftsmen had stalls and shops jammed along the streets. Trade had been established very quickly with subservient Irish clans of the surrounding countryside also, which inordinately pleased Ragnall. He intended to rule properly, and he had been adamant that any Irish who submitted to Oitir Iarla or Gragabai were to be treated fairly and even protected against other Irish clans who viewed them as traitors. Even rogue unaligned Northmen were driven off or killed when found to be participating in unsanctioned raiding. The only people that Ragnall wanted raided and attacked were their enemies in Osraige, Munster and Leinster.

Oitir Iarla and his most renowned warriors lined the main hall of Waterford, and as the three brothers approached with heads bowed in respect, axes smashing against shields in a steady rhythm. Ragnall clasped Oitir Iarla's hand at the foot of the dais and grasped him in a great bear hug. He drew Oitir back away from his embrace and kissed him suddenly upon the forehead. The hall burst out laughing and the powerful warlord had to look away to hide his blush as Ragnall's taste in sexual partners was well known. Ragnall jumped up to the dais and turned around to address the hall which was now crowded, as warriors followed them in:

"Men of the Ui Imair, men of Frisia, men of Britain, Ireland and Scandinavia…. I salute you all." The men as one roared in celebratory approval. He waited for the noise to dissipate before continuing:

"We have returned from exile to claim back what is rightfully ours. Our families and friends have had to endure suffering that nobody should ever have to endure, but we have emerged even stronger." More roars met his pronouncement.

"The Irish kings would have us killed, every man, woman and child. They say that we are usurpers and barbarians, but it was us the Norse, Danes and Norse-Gaels who founded their first towns. You tell me who is the barbarian here." Raucous laughter rose at that.

"Dublin, Cork, Linn, Limerick, Wexford, Longford and now Waterford are Viking towns; established where no Irishman had ever settled or lay claim to. Any land our ancestors seized was done through the right of fair conquest. The Irish say that we have no right to live here and exist upon this island, but I say to you we have the only right. And by Thor's hammer I will wage war on all Irish kingdoms until they learn this fact."

Once again, the warriors in the room cheered loudly and smashed their axes into their shields and their ale cups into the wooden benches.

"At some point, we must face their High King Niall Glundub mac Aed Findliath, and many more of the Ui Neill kings. I won't lie to you, Niall Glundub is a fearsome warrior, a *Drengr*, a great enemy. I have faced him in battle before and lost. He slaughtered our warriors fighting for his accursed cousin in Scotland. He murdered my father and two of my brothers and threw their heads at our feet. My family's bones litter the plains and hills of Scotland, and we can never recover them to honour them with proper burial."

Ragnall knew his words had sapped the hall of joy and he could sense the room filling with anger.

"Niall Glundub's father at the time of the great heathen army's conquests in England, came down upon peaceful Scandinavian settlements across his territories and he murdered thousands of our people. He massacred whole villages. He had no cause to do it, he did it because he could. And now this Glundub, his heir, will most likely attempt to do the same to our innocent kin in Dublin."

Ragnall could sense the fury building amongst the men, their righteous anger was being stoked by Ragnall's words.

"Now my brave warriors, followers of Odin, I will face this king upon the fields of Meath or Leinster, or on the walls of Dublin. And I have a simple question for you: Will you stand with me and my brothers on the field of battle? Will you fight for me and your people, or will I face this king and all his armies alone?"

The roar that erupted from the hall was almost enough to blow the roof from the tops of the walls. Many of the warriors there were in a state of frenzied berserk rage and Ragnall feared briefly that violence would spill out here and now. But as easily as it threatened to overtake the warriors, it disappeared when Ragnall ordered casks of ale to be distributed amongst them and allow the warriors to tell tales of victories to come versus the Irish and their fearsome High King.

Later the same night, the hall was cleared and all that remained were the chief captains of the Ui Imair army. Apart from the brothers and Olaf Godfrithsson, only Oitir Iarla, Brunbold Headtaker and Olga Helmsdottir the shieldmaiden known as the Valkyrie remained. Gragabai was campaigning in Leinster and several other leaders were out at sea, harrying the eastern shore of Ireland. There were two other men present, Irishmen and no ordinary Irishmen at that; they were Tadg mac Faelain the King of the Ui Cheinnselaig, and Liadan mac Diarmuid, the man who now assumed leadership of the Deise, a powerful Munster tribe who had been battling with Oitir Iarla for three years. Both men had come to pay homage to the Ui Imair. Sickened and decimated by warfare since 914, they had agreed to bend the knee to Ragnall and his brothers, for all to see. Godfrith had advocated forcing them to kneel before the entire army to swear their fealty, but Sihtric had advised against it. To humiliate them in that manner would only stir enmity.

They had effectively been defeated and had agreed to pay tribute and even fight for the Ui Imair if required, but to embarrass them in such a manner would drive them to guerrilla warfare with the Ui Imair that would never end. Both men swore upon a golden cross and a bible that the Christians seemed to show great reverence to and solemnly swore to pay tribute to Waterford and to never raise arms against the Ui Imair. When they had sworn, Ragnall had commanded them to rise as friends to the Ui Imair and he sent each of them away with a chest of silver and promises of protection against anyone who would do them harm. Tadg of the Ui Cheinnselaig seemed mollified and even offered the hand of his daughter in marriage to any one of the major chieftains, which Ragnall had graciously accepted having a young promising Dane in mind for the match.

The other king Liadan mac Diarmuid had spat the words out through gritted teeth and Ragnall could smell the treachery emanating from him. The Deise were renowned for their untrustworthiness and were detested even among the other tribes of Munster and Ragnall could see why. He elected to ignore it and allowed the wayward Deise chieftain to leave with his treasure and his head still upon his shoulders. *That could be a mistake,* he thought, as the two kings left the hall. Even later that night, after all his duties were dispensed with, Ragnall had time to walk alone outside of the walls of Waterford. With just his axes and a torch, he walked amongst the trees and listened for nocturnal creatures moving through the wilderness. No manmade sounds permeated the night, and a sense of calm overtook him. *I am home,* he thought, *the Ui Imair have come to take back what is rightfully theirs.*

CHAPTER 2

THE TRAP AT CENN FUAIT (AUGUST 917 AD)

The main hall at Limerick was crowded with men and thick with the smoke of peat being burned in the firepit; but it was mistrust and potential violence that permeated the air most. Ragnall of the Ui Imair stood brazenly before the dais of the King of Limerick, his arms crossed, utterly unmoved by the arrogance being displayed by the Norse-Gael lord on front of him. The King of Limerick was a fearsome brute of a man and a raider nearly as notorious as Ragnall himself. His name was Colla Bairidsson and he was a descendant of the famous sea king Ceitl Flatnose who ruled Limerick for nigh on fifty years throughout the previous century, through his mother's side. More importantly though, he was a son of Bairid mac Oitir of Mann who Ragnall and his brothers had destroyed in battle three years previously. Ragnall could feel the anger boiling off King Colla like a putrid smell, but he could not care less; he had a simple proposition for the belligerent ruler: join with the Ui Imair or burn.

The Limerick monarch's son stood at his father's right-hand side and glowered down at Ragnall, his axe hanging at the ready in one meaty paw. He was a fell raider in his own right and went by the name of Amlaib but the Irish,

Ragnall knew, had another name for him: Cenncaireach, which translated to sinner or the sinful one in old Norse. Amlaib Cenncaireach had ravaged the lands of Connaught and Munster for several years, capturing slaves and selling them to associates and relatives in Iceland and the Hebrides. He was a burly savage of a man, the epitome of Viking brutality but that meant little and less to Ragnall. His brother Godfrith on the other hand was visibly riled at the threatening posturing taking place before them, but Ragnall calmed his brother with a light touch on his arm. He stepped forward and addressed King Colla directly, ignoring his barbaric son.

"King Colla, I want the warriors of Limerick to join forces with me in our efforts to retake Dublin from the Irish. For too long, our people have been trodden on by the Ui Neill and their allies and I intend to free them."

The Limerick King's great bushy eyebrows rushed together like two bulls clashing and Ragnall could see him crush the arm rests on either side of his throne.

"You, Ragnall of the Ui Imair, you dare enter my hall after killing my father and taking his warriors for your own, and then have the nerve to come to Limerick three years later and ask for my help?"

Ragnall smiled. "With all due respect King Colla, I was not asking you, I was telling you. If you do not swear your allegiance to me, I will delay my assault upon Leinster and Meath just to come here and burn Limerick to the ground and sit your lungs upon your shoulders."

Dozens of warriors shouted their anger and weapons were drawn. Cenncaireach stepped toward Ragnall but before he could reach him a massive figure stepped forward into the light and intercepted him. The ancient and monstrous figure of Brunbolg Headtaker blocked his path, brandishing an axe the size of an oar from a longship. The Sinful One was a large man, but he looked like a puffed-up little child next to the Headtaker, who despite being seventy years of age stood unbowed by time at seven feet tall and more than four hundred pounds weight. The smaller man quailed and retreated to his father's side while the Headtaker emitted a huge baleful growl that could be interpreted in many ways; a threat, a laugh, or an indication that what occurred had gone the way the giant ogre had expected. When the Sinful One retreated all his other warriors and kin took a step back also, none willing to chance their luck against the Headtaker. Ragnall used this momentary respite to issue one final ultimatum to the grizzled King of Limerick.

"Your father died because he opposed my will. If you do the same, you can expect the same. I will nail your wife's corpse to the prow of my ship and use it as a decoration if you defy me. I will then sacrifice your sons to Odin to bring my brothers and I fortune in the wars to come. The choice is simple, Colla; your axes will be mine or your lives will. You have a day to choose."

With one last contemptuous glance at the king and his son, Ragnall and his chief warlords swaggered from the hall.

Ragnall did not intend to stay on land within the town of Limerick while Colla decided his own fate. He was renowned as a treacherous cur and his son had earned infamy amongst the Irish for being even worse; the possibility of attempted assassination was well within their modus operandi as the people of Limerick were widely known to venerate the trickster god Loki. Limerick was a den of scum and villainy, but their warriors would be extremely useful in the battles yet to be fought, if brought on side. In normal times, Ragnall would not have bothered to treat with the likes of Colla and would have put the leadership of Limerick to the sword outright and installed one of his own eorls as king, but time and resources had forced his hand and intimidation was the tool he had decided to employ with Colla and his kin.

He had travelled to Limerick with sixty ships and almost two thousand men, to ultimately hedge against any eventuality, but even with that number of warriors at his disposal he still felt uncomfortable. On his way back to his dragonboat while speaking to his brother, a horn sounded loudly in the dying evening light. Shouts and hurried footsteps could be heard echoing toward him from around the sides of the longships that were tied to the wooden pier on the north bank of the mighty River Shannon. A boy from one of the minor crews breathlessly ran to Ragnall and Godfrith and addressed them:

'My lords, there is a single ship approaching from the south, it bears the colours of Lord Sihtric, the raven and the sun. It has damage to it and bears signs of recent fighting."

Ragnall nodded at the boy and sent him on his way, and he and Godfrith then made haste to the closest empty spot on the pier to await the lone longship's docking. In minutes, the longship arrived and Ragnall could see that the boy was indeed correct. Parts of the ship bore signs of burning and in several parts arrows festooned its hull like barnacles. Ragnall recognised the captain at the prow, a hard-bitten warrior called Ulf. He sported a head wound that was roughly bandaged and many of his crew were likewise hurt. He had been part of the force that had gone north with Sihtric and Gragabai to Leinster, to attack the Ui Dunlainge clan, the most powerful retinue in the province. If their power could be broken, Ragnall knew, the way lay open to Dublin, overland and by sea. His heart sank at seeing the sea captain leap down gingerly from his ship to the wooden dock and he feared the worst for Sihtric.

"King Ragnall, I have grave news."

Ragnall gripped the man closely. "Tell me, Ulf, what has befallen Sihtric and Gragabai? Are they slain?"

The injured captain shook his head rapidly. "No, King Ragnall, but they are hard-pressed. Sihtric and Gragabai abandoned their boats at the Barrow River with a guard of men. They marched north in search of Augaire mac Aililla and his Ui Dunlainge fighters. They walked into an ambush at Cenn Fuait though, several miles from the river; it was an expeditionary host led by Niall Glundub in alliance with auxiliaries from Meath." *So Glundub has come south with part of his strength to meet us and gauge our ability,* thought Ragnall.

"Glundub trapped them in a valley there and then Augaire mac Aililla swept down upon them from the northeast. The fighting has been sporadic, but Sihtric and Gragabai are surrounded still, and supplies are dwindling. Their camp is strong, but they have lost many men already in skirmishes, for now the Irish kings seem content to starve them out. I was part of the guard at the river. When a few days passed, most of us went searching for our lads, not realising that they were trapped. We came upon the forces of King Augaire by accident, and we were beaten back with heavy losses. Some of their men pursued us back toward the Barrow. I was chosen to come find you or any reinforcements we could get. We stopped at Waterford to inform Oitir Iarla but he had not the manpower to help us, he sent me to you. If we don't leave now King Ragnall, I fear that in the three days it will take to sail around the country and up the Barrow, Sihtric and Gragabai will be massacred with all their men."

Ragnall had heard enough. He nodded to Godfrith who began howling at their crews to prepare to sail within the hour and instantly men leaped to obey. *Curse the Vikings of Limerick,* thought Ragnall, *they would have to wait.*

The next three days' sailing were as desperate as any Ragnall had ever endured. They burned great lamps of fire that hung from their masts and continued to sail in the dark, which was incredibly dangerous. The dozens of inlets and islands on the south coast of Ireland were riddled with razor-sharp rocks and other hazards, lethal to ships even in the daytime, never mind the depths of the Stygian darkness. By the third day, they had succeeded in reaching the mouth of the Barrow and Ragnall counted himself lucky to have only lost a single ship in their risky flight around the Island of Ireland and then north toward the Barrow estuary. On entering the estuary, Ragnall commanded the fleet to abandon sails and lower their oars into the water and they rowed in shifts throughout the day. By noon they had reached the survivors of the guards of Sihtric and Gragabai's fleet and had rowed across to the south-western side of the river, avoiding any men of Augaire mac Aililla's host. The gutted wrecks of several ships could be seen sticking out of the water on the eastern bank with bloated and mutilated corpses clogging the river close to the land.

A cold fury rose in Ragnall. He had not passed through war and suffering to have his brother and a third of his army wiped out in an ambush. He had no warning that Niall Glundub had come south, and he cursed himself for a fool for not anticipating such a move. He had sent his brother to his potential doom. He could not help but be surprised; this sort of cunning was unusual from what Ragnall knew of his enemy Glundub and he promised himself he would never make that mistake again. Augaire mac Aililla on the other hand was a betraying son of a whore. He had defected to the Saxons and allowed Athelfled's forces to hit the Ui Imair from the rear unopposed and Ragnall's cousin Ingamundr had died for it at Chester, not to mention using subterfuge to enter Dublin to sack the city and slay Ragnall's own mother. They pulled their longboats up onto the bank of the Barrow only to instantly be met with desultory arrow shot. Several of their warriors fell, pierced with arrows; some were slain outright but more were wounded.

When enough warriors landed, Ragnall formed them into a shield wall, and they marched into the trees and the lands beyond. The arrow barrage ceased and Ragnall guessed that these men had been left as a rearguard to defend the bank from the Ui Imair. They had clearly underestimated the size of Ragnall's force as they came ashore and had fled before them accordingly. Ulf had told them that Sihtric and Gragabai were holed up in a valley several miles north at a place called Cenn Fuait. The entire Ui Imair host raced north headlong into the Irish wilderness, sacrificing stealth for speed. It seemed like hours had passed before the sound of shouts and the clash of iron and steel could be heard amongst the trees, and then, breathless, Ragnall emerged from the wild and into the back of the host of Niall Glundub. The High King's huge banners bearing the red hand above the fish in blue, stood out against the forest. The fighting was brutal and hard. There was no quarter asked and none given as the forces of Ragnall and the warriors of the Ui Neill smashed together.

Ragnall was manic. He battered his way through the lines of the Irishmen and in minutes he had broken through to the other side and emerged safe amongst the warriors of his brother Sihtric. A cheer went up from the Ui Imair host as both sides reunited and the Irish were forced back west, squeezed between Sihtric's and Ragnall's host. Ragnall cupped his hands together and howled into the Irish evening like the wolf that festooned his blue and navy banners and his entire army followed suit. The ululating howls of men who were now wolves, sent the forces of Niall Glundub retreating rapidly to the west, for now driven off; the Ui Imair had possession of the battlefield and Sihtric's banner of the raven of Odin in black and white mingled with the blue wolves of Ragnall. The brothers embraced in victory. Niall Glundub had been defeated, admittedly without suffering much loss of men, but they had been driven off at Cenn Fuait; first blood to the Ui Imair.

Ragnall's men, as quickly as possible, had secured the battlefield and deployed scouts out into the countryside to ascertain the whereabouts of both Glundub's men and those of Augaire mac Aililla. The High King had retreated in good order to a defensible camp five miles to the west and was unassailable, but there was no sign of the Leinster men who had vanished into the trees and fields, as if they had never been there. Ragnall was not surprised; *The Leinstermen should know their own lands better than us I would think.* The body count was significant; Sihtric's host had lost over a hundred warriors in the sustained skirmishes over the past week since they had been caught in the snare of the Irishmen. The battle just fought had sent another fifty to Valhalla, still Ragnall counted that acceptable as his brother and another of his key men, Gragabai the Bastard, had not yet joined them.

Ragnall ordered out scavenging parties to the south and east away from the estimated whereabouts of the Leinstermen, to forage the land as well as bring up supplies from the ships. He sent several ships' worth of Sihtric's men south, back along the Barrow and toward Waterford, to resupply and return laden with food and equipment for his army. There was no going back now, he knew; the bones were cast and whoever blinked here would lose control of Leinster and the midlands. Sihtric and Ragnall both agreed that they had the upper hand despite their losses, in that they could resupply from the river and sea, while both Niall Glundub and Augaire mac Aililla had to rely on their own stores and the forage they could secure from the land. It would only be a matter of time before they would have to abandon their camps and leave. Victory was so close, Ragnall could almost touch it, all it would take was patience.

As the weeks passed, Ragnall and Sihtric's men engaged in running battles and skirmishes with parties of Niall Glundub's men who were scouring the countryside for food. Neither side was willing to launch a full-scale assault on the other's camps as they were too well defended, and the uncertainty as to the whereabouts of Augaire mac Aililla's host quenched the ambition of most of Ragnall's young captains in case they were outflanked once more. *Once bitten twice shy,* Ragnall had mused at the sea change in their collective attitudes. On one such vicious encounter, Sihtric and a company of his men came upon a group of fifty Irish foragers by accident and slaughtered them almost to a man. Included in this group were some renowned men that Sihtric had recognised, each a huge loss to Niall Glundub's leadership, the most notable being Donncuan mac Flannacain, the king of one of the subclans of the Northern Ui Neill.

On the twentieth day, since Ragnal's springing of the trap meant for Sihtric and Gragabai, Niall Glundub had no option but to retreat north in good order. Despite taking minimal casualties he had been unable to maintain his host this far south in late August. With great jubilation Sihtric and Ragnall's army then divided in half once more. There was only one destination for them now: Dublin itself. Several of Sihtric's ships were destroyed and many of his men were showing signs of great fatigue, so Ragnall ordered them to take command of the longboats on the river, while Ragnall's men, the fresher part of the host, went overland and north toward Dublin in strength.

To Ragnall's surprise, the fighting was not done despite Niall Glundub's retreat north. Not a day's march from Cenn Fuait, Augaire mac Aililla and the entire Leinster army came down upon the Ui Imair in an ambush. Ragnall and his men were hard-pressed initially, but they were the fresher force, had the numbers and possessed more discipline. Ragnall ordered Brunbolg Headtaker to form and lead the shield wall and hold the Leinster men at bay, while Ragnall and two hundred men retreated south and circumvented the entire battle. Within thirty minutes they had circled in behind the Leinster host and with one downward swipe of his axe, Ragnall had sent his warriors into the rear of the Irishmen. They massacred their foes who were caught between the shield wall and Ragnall's men. In minutes, dozens of the Irish were slain and the remainder were driven off into the hills, and then Ragnall found himself face to face with Augaire mac Aililla himself. Ragnall shouted for his men to stand aside so that the notorious Irish king could clearly see his time was up, there would be no escape for him. Augaire removed his tunic and leather armour and clasped his shield and sword tightly. Ragnall could see that although he was slightly past his prime, he still possessed a wiry strength and great spiral blue tattoos, overlain with a great Christian cross, were etched upon his skin. *He is a follower of the old Irish gods as well as the Christ,* thought Ragnall bemusedly. The Ui Imair king could not resist questioning him on it as they circled each other amidst the onlookers of the Ui Imair host.

"Your High King Niall Glundub is a follower of the Christ, whereas you follow the old gods as well as the Christ. Why bend the knee to such as Glundub and forsake your ancestors? Why not yield to me and pay us tribute as we care not whom you worship? What do you owe the Ui Neill?"

Augaire laughed and spat. "I remember you, Ragnall Ivarsson, since you were a pup, interfering still with boys, are you? It is you who should have worn a dress and married some of my kin and not your sisters. Aethelfled should have murdered the whole lot of you at Chester. It gave me great pleasure to see you savages butchered under the walls of that burh."

Ragnall was taken aback at the flurry of insults being hurled in his direction and it caused him to momentarily halt in his tracks, and that was when the Leinster king attacked. Augaire slammed his shield toward Ragnall's face, but Ragnall used his left axe head to pull the shield forward while simultaneously moving his right axe in an arc to parry the inevitable sword blow coming from the Irishman. Ragnall moved his feet carefully to Augaire's left away from his sword arm. To keep Augaire thinking, Ragnall landed thudding blows upon the Leinster king's shield. Augaire did not lack for skill as several times he switched stances and occasionally attempted spinning backhand blows and low cuts; but the dance was all too familiar to Ragnall and he evaded every blow. Slowly but surely, he reduced the Irish king's shield to kindling and he could feel his opponent weakening. Augaire threw everything he had at Ragnall in a last attack.

He threw his shattered shield at Ragnall's face and as it was parried, he swung his sword in a whistling arc at Ragnall's head. But Ragnall had seen what he intended as if it was swung in slow motion. He stepped in and caught the Irish king's blow in one hand and caught his sword arm between his own arm and his torso in a vice-like hold. In desperation Augaire swing his left fist at Ragnall's head, but Ragnall trapped that arm in a similar manner. He proceeded to smash Augaire's face with his own head and the Leinsterman's visage exploded in a slurry of teeth and blood. He then swung his right axe and buried it in Augaire's upper torso and before the Leinsterman's head could hit the earth, he smashed his second axe right through his breastbone. Augaire was dying noisily on the ground, while Ragnall called for a third axe from one of the men surrounding them witnessing the single combat. One was tossed to him, and he caught it, twirling it theatrically in one hand. He looked down at the stricken king remembering all the hurt this man had caused him: the murder of his mother, the capture of his brother by Flann Sinna and the betrayal at Chester.

"You worship other gods than the Christ, Augaire, I believe that means that you won't go to the Christian heaven. But you are a brave warrior and there is always room in Valhalla for such as you. Let me send you there so you can meet my cousin Ingamundr in person, and he can slaughter you every night for all eternity. This is your curse, you treacherous Irish bastard, good riddance."

With that he split the skull of Augaire mac Aililla straight down the middle so hard that the axe lodged in the earth beneath the slain king. He spat on his remains for good measure. And there at the battle of Cenn Fuait, fell the King of Leinster, Augaire mac Aililla Ui Dunlainge; dispatched in single combat by the sea king Ragnall of the Ui Imair.

The march to Dublin was joyous for Ragnall and his host of men sang songs of victory and glory, of battles won and lost and heroes of old. They meandered their way across the country, making their way to the coast to rendezvous with the fleet, with the intention of Sihtric and Godfrith disembarking and marching on Dublin together as brothers beside Ragnall. They passed the territories of several Leinster clans, most of whom had lost their leaders in the battle at Cenn Fuait. The people ruled by Mael Morda mac Muirecan and Mael Maedoc the Bishop of Leinster were ready with tribute, their hastily elected leaders swearing loyalty to Ragnall, to avoid slavery and butchery. The Bishop had died a most gruesome death when Brunbolg Headtaker had pulled his head off his shoulders like a chicken during the battle, but his successor was quick to bend the knee to avoid the same fate.

At the coast, five miles from Dublin, Sihtric and Godfrith joined him on land and the triumvirate of Ui Imair nobility marched at the head of their host, now swollen with numbers from Sihtric's fleet. When they reached the gates of Dublin, they were surprisingly, if not entirely unexpectedly, thrown open and a young man with a familiar cast to his features approached to greet them; it was their nephew Grungni mac Conall, a prince of both the Ui Imair and the Ui Dunlainge. He sported the attire of an Irish nobleman, but his features shouted his Norse-Gael heritage to anyone with eyes. The young man bent the knee.

"Uncles, I formally cede the city of Dublin to your control. The Irish garrison that patrolled the city on behalf of the kings of Meath and Leinster have fled north in the face of your advance. Your defeat of my relative Augaire mac Aililla has disheartened them, and they have hastily retreated north to join Conchobar mac Flann at Tara. I am the last figure of Irish authority left in the city. Dublin is yours."

He offered his sword in a sign of submission and Ragnall took it. He placed his hand under the chin of his young nephew and raised him to his feet.

"I have heard of you for some time, and it is said that you are a fair and noble administrator of this city. My brothers and I would be honoured if you would help us rule here once more and smooth the transition of leadership."

The young man tapped his three fingers to his forehead in obeisance and stood aside as the three brothers entered the city. The streets were thronged with people on either side of the main thoroughfare as they made their way toward the river and the main hall, their home for many years. Old men drew knives and axes and clasped them to their chests, heads bowed in respect. Young children stood spellbound as these three legendary characters from the Scandinavian world walked amongst them; demigods descended from near mythological heroes. A young girl, no older than two, escaped her mother's arms and ran toward Godfrith. Tenderly, he picked her up and she felt his face with her tiny hands, her blonde hair waiving in the breeze. And then they came upon the ramshackle and uninhabited old hall of their past.

On entering, the three brothers were transported back to a time in their youth: of playing amongst the benches and practising their fighting. Ragnall remembered leaving with his father for his first campaign as a boy, receiving his arm ring from him, while his older brothers Amlaib and Ivar the younger, looked on with pride. Tears welled up in his eyes, recalling the last time he had seen his mother upon the sack of Dublin in 902. He envisioned her prostrate, impaled upon the bench before the dais. The hall now was a rotting ruin, abandoned and cursed, dark and foreboding, as no people of the city had dared take it for themselves in the intervening years. A shout from Godfrith from outside brought Ragnall and Sihtric to him through a side door.

Godfrith had pushed aside an old chicken coup and reached into a concealed hole in the ground. A cloth bundle lay there and Godfrith gently picked it up. On opening it up, inside were the two Saracen swords that Ragnall had brought as gifts for his young brothers from his voyages to the Islamic caliphate of Andalusia and beyond. Godfrith had hidden the two swords from their mother as she had threatened to take them off the boys due to the roughhousing they were getting up to on the day of the sack of the city, and here they were buried for fifteen years in the earth of Dublin, lightning rods of hurtful memories. The twins took one each and slid the delicate blades inside their belts and walked back into the house to explore further. Ragnall turned around and breathed in the air, the city of Dublin and all its smells, all its sights and all its sounds, his city now.

He walked out back down the main street, still lined with people. His warriors could no longer wait, and by looking back the way they came, Ragnall could see they had begun entering the city. He could see older warriors embrace brothers, parents, children, nieces and nephews; in some cases, people they had never met before. The mute shock of the Ui Imair simply walking in and taking the city unopposed was wearing off and the people of Dublin, most of whom had at least a little Norse or Dane heritage, began to mingle with Ragnall's host.

He reached the waterfront and the port. The old abandoned slave pens were there to his right, but commerce was still bustling in the city, on both sides of the water. Several newer manoeuvrable footbridges had been constructed to help people pass from one side of Dublin to the other and it pleased him greatly. A great dirge broke out amongst the folk as the Ui Imair reunited with their long-lost kin and subjects, a song that Ragnall remembered from his

youth called *Havamal,* and he let it wash over him and it lingered in the air of
Dublin across the Liffey from thousands of throats:

At every doorway, ere one enters, one should spy round, for uncertain
   is the witting
that there be no foeman sitting,
within, before one on the floor

Hail, ye Givers!
a guest is come;
say! where shall he sit within?
Much pressed is he who fain on the hearth
would seek for warmth and weal.

He hath need of fire,
who now is come,
numbed with cold to the knee;
food and clothing the wanderer craves
who has fared o'er the rimy fell.

He craves for water,
who comes for refreshment,
drying and friendly bidding,
marks of good will,
fair fame if 'tis won,
and welcome once and again.

He hath need of his wits who wanders wide,
aught simple will serve at home;
but a gazing-stock is the fool who sits
mid the wise, and nothing knows.

Let no man glory in the greatness of his mind,
but rather keep watch o'er his wits.
Cautious and silent let him enter a dwelling;
to the heedful comes seldom harm,
for none can find a more faithful friend
than the wealth of mother wit.

It was an ancient hymn on the treatment of a guest, and it echoed around the city as the people threw off Irish oppression and welcomed back the founders of their city and the long-lost protectors of their way of life. A jolt of excitement past through Ragnall at the realisation of what he and his brothers had achieved. They had taken back their birthright from their mighty Irish foes, the only home they had ever really known. And now Ragnall Ivarsson of the Ui Imair, the descendant of Ivar the Boneless, Ragnar Lodbrok and Odin himself, was the King of Dublin and all the foreigners in Ireland.

CHAPTER 3

THE SUBMISSION OF
BABENBURG
(918 AD)

Ragnall emerged from under the canvas that protected the entire length of his dragonship from the elements and made his way to the prow. His huge vessel smashed its way through the waves at the head of a section of his fleet, his hold laden with gold, spices and wine. His stay at Dublin had chafed at him and the sea had beckoned him into her embrace. He had decided to happily cede the rule of Dublin to his younger brother Sihtric, who was more at home among the Irish, more accustomed to being tied to the land. Ragnall was ever restless, ever searching for some intangible goal that he could not fathom. He had spent his time in Dublin reinforcing the fortifications of the north of the city, raising the walls to an imperious height, and making it impervious to attack from the various Irish kings who assailed it.

In the beginning of resumption of Ui Imair rule in the city, he had led sorties into South Brega and into the heart of Meath and was successful in pushing back the new King of South Brega Beollan mac Ciarmac further north with his great fortress at Lagore being the southernmost stronghold of that king's territory. All the Irish people between Lagore and Dublin, now paid tribute to the Ui Imair. Sporadic conflicts with the King of Tara and Clan Colman, Conchobar mac Flann, had erupted over the following months but the Ui Imair had held their own without any significant loss. As for the south of the city, most of Leinster paid tribute now to Ragnall and a lot of the land of Osraige had fallen under his sway too. Several recalcitrant chieftains still defied the Ui Imair but they were reduced to employing guerrilla warfare among the forests and mountains of the land.

The drudgery of rulership bothered Ragnall very quickly though and when word reached him of a village belonging to the Ui Imair in western Northumbria being levelled by forces from Mercia, he decided there and then to delegate the rulership of the foreigners of Ireland to his most serious brother Sihtric. The Scourge as the Irish called him had even taken an Osraigan princess to wife and already she was heavily pregnant with their first child. Ragnall approved as it strengthened the bonds between Dublin and their subject kingdoms to some degree and tied their fates closer. Many other significant marriages were made between his key men and the daughters of his more noteworthy warriors with noble men and women from Munster, Leinster and Osraige; to such an extent that Ragnall half suspected that these aligned minor Irish clans were as likely to fight for the Ui Imair as Niall Glundub, should the Northern Ui Neill march south once more.

Before Ragnall had set everything in order in Dublin, another worrying report had arrived at his hall. Garangr, his cousin and able lieutenant in Britain, had been wounded in Northumbria and in the space of a month, he had suffered three notable defeats there; once to the Bernicians of north-eastern Northumbria and twice to men from Mercia, who just happened to be perfectly positioned to ambush columns of Ui Imair and aligned Viking and Saxon warriors as they patrolled the land. Garangr had been forced to move most of his men to Yorvik to garrison the town and to deploy the rest closer to the west coast, to protect the Ui Imair settlements there, chiefly Liuerpul on the Mersey River. Ragnall knew that Garangr was a trustworthy commander, but he did not have the numbers to effectively control the regions of Northumbria under their sway currently and protect it from both north and south. He would have to make his presence felt and it gave him an adequate excuse to sail the Irish Sea once more.

He had his suspicions about what was occurring in Northumbria but kept his own council until he could meet with Garangr and confirm them. He decided to take Oitir Iarla, Gragabai and his brother Godfrith into the Irish Sea with him, leaving the Valkyrie and the Headtaker with Sihtric. His intention was simple: he needed to raise money to strengthen his position in Northumbria. To do this he intended to attack Anglesea in Wales and raid them for slaves, sell those slaves at Cordoba, and use that wealth to solidify his position with the Norse and Dane eorls and the Saxon thegns and ealdormen of Northumbria. Then he would march on Babenburg to put old King Ealdred and his retainers to the sword if necessary. It would send a simple message to both Constantine of Scotland and Aethelfled of Mercia that the rule of Northumbria was his and no other's. Gwynedd had been weakened by internecine civil war and had also been defeated in battle with some Mercian noblemen in the intervening years. They simply did not have the strength remaining, Ragnall guessed, to defy two thousand warriors of the Ui Imair descending upon Anglesea unannounced. And he was right.

The sons and grandson of the famous King Rhodri the Great were a feeble and degenerate bunch and on the fifth of May, 918, Ragnall Ui Imair assaulted the Kingdom of Gwynedd like a tidal wave and smashed their pitiful armies. They took more than a thousand slaves and obliterated a dozen small villages and towns down the entire coast of Wales in less than a week. He sent a portion of the new stock over to Dublin to rebuild the slave trade which had been disbanded there by order of Flann Sinna, but the rest he personally accompanied down to the slavers' pens of Cordoba, the capital of the Islamic Caliphate of Al Andalus. The Muslim empires were always thirsty for the blood of pale-skinned slaves for their armies, mines, and harems. The profits they earned were astronomical, but Ragnall cared little for wealth, it was only a tool to be used to attain power. He distributed most of it to his men, setting some of them up for life in the process. The rest, he held as tribute to disperse amongst the Norse, Dane and Saxon nobility of Northumbria and even though it galled him, he also set aside some for several of the notable Christian bishops of the region whose support, or at least apathy, he required to maintain the peace.

When the fleet reached Liuerpul on the Mersey, Ragnall gave orders for the men to disembark. With a small bodyguard of men, he entered the main hall and was greeted by Garangr's wife.

"King Ragnall, Garangr is sitting outside our quarters. Will you join him?"

Ragnall agreed and ordered his guards to remain in the hall with her, while he made his own way to the rear. When he found Garangr he was sitting on a wooden bench staring up at the hills and trees outside the wooden palisades that surrounded the settlement at Liuerpol. His left arm was in a sling, and he had a linen bandage wrapped around his torso, showing his most recent wounds that he had suffered in the skirmishes with the Mercians. Ragnall sat down beside him.

"What has been happening, Garangr? One hundred men killed and much of the countryside revolting against the authority of Yorvik? How has this come to pass?"

Garangr moved slightly and winced with pain before answering. "It just seems that that witch in Tamworth is anticipating every move we make. Whatever I try, wherever we go, we are ambushed. It's like Loki himself is whispering in her ear to spite us."

Ragnall had an idea what was going on and was frankly surprised that it had not occurred to Garangr. *I was right to give more power to Sihtric and Godfrith and not Garangr, he is showing his limitations here,* thought Ragnall.

"Have you considered that we do have someone whispering in Aethelfled's and Ealdred's ears, but that it isn't Loki, but someone more... mortal?"

Garangr sat up.

"Who could possibly do this? I would swear on my life that every one of the men underneath the Ui Imair banners is loyal to our cause."

Ragnall nodded. "And where is it that you decided all of your strategies and campaigns for the last year, Garangr?"

With a puzzled expression Garangr responded, "In Yorvik of course, in Eorl Guthfrith's hall."

Garangr stopped and looked inquisitively at Ragnall. "You think Guthfrith has betrayed us? Why would he do that, Ragnall? We were the ones who installed him in the first place, why would he jeopardise his own position? Without our support he could not possibly hope to hold all the disparate Saxon, Norse and Dane rulers together under his rule."

Ragnall was glad that Garangr had finally grasped at least the possibility of treachery.

"Because, Garangr, Aethelfled and Ealdred and maybe even Constantine have made him promises you would imagine that allow him to keep his power without our influence and all he would have to do is bend the knee to one of them."

Ragnall could see Garangr's face twitch in furious understanding as if the veil had lifted to reveal the skulduggery. Despite his wounds he rose unsteadily to his feet. "Injured or not, Ragnall, I want to accompany you to Yorvik. I am going to rip off that traitor's testicles and make his wife and children eat them."

Ragnall nodded solemnly. *But not before I have my way with him first.*

Ragnall allowed his men another week of rest and recovery in the halls of Liuerpol which also afforded Garangr more time to recover. He more than anyone had a right to be there to see Guthfrith dealt with. On the appointed day, the host set out on foot, with supplies for a full campaign loaded on wagons to the rear of their column. Two thousand warriors of the Ui Imair accompanied Ragnall, almost a third of the entire strength of the men directly under his command around the Irish Sea, every one of them a proven killer. The going was slow as the hilly midlands of Northumbria were tough to traverse and the boggy land was difficult for the wagons to navigate through.

After a few days they successfully crossed the most awkward of the terrain and approached the woods close to Yorvik. All the minor settlements there paid respect to the host as they passed and some even offered food and ale to Ragnall and his captains. Ragnall was pleased to see that the Ui Imair still held sway at least this close to Yorvik. When they approached the huge walled town itself, Ragnall could see that the men who manned the walls were a combination of all of the different races and nationalities that inhabited

Northumbria and it brought it home to Ragnall that the thegns, ealdormen and eorls of this particular region didn't really care who ruled and demanded tribute from them or where they came from or what their heritage was; the most important requisite for rulership was the ability to keep their people safe and prosperous. The gates were thrown open and the host entered in a long column of Norse-Gael might.

Yorvik itself was a large walled town with almost thirty thousand people; after Dublin it was probably the largest Norse-Gael or Scandinavian-controlled town this side of Denmark. The streets were paved in ancient cobble, a piece of infrastructure left behind by the mighty Roman empire that ruled here centuries before. The Britons, Saxons and Norse who took over the town adopted this infrastructure into their own vision of the town and built around it or expanded upon it. The Saxons had called the town Eoforwic but the men of the Great Heathen Army who first captured it more than fifty years ago had renamed it Yorvik. Ragnall, Garangr, Oitir Iarla, Gragabai and Godfrith wasted no time once their men were sequestered within the barracks of the town and outside of the walls in camps; they made their way to the hall in the centre of the town. Ragnall dismissed the guards at the door while sending Gragabai and Oitir Iarla to the two side entrances. On entering Ragnall cleared the hall instantly. Guthfrith sat in shocked surprise upon his throne on the dais. He was a weaselish man, well past his prime with a large belly and a ridiculous beard. To Ragnall, an expert on spotting fear in others, the puppet ruler of Yorvik reeked of it upon witnessing their arrival.

The intimidated runt stammered out small talk in an attempt to defuse the situation.

"God's blessings upon you, Ragnall of the Ui Imair, and you too, Garangr and young Godfrith. Do you know, Godfrith, we are almost of the same name, curious that isn't it?"

The three men fanned out around the throne, unmoved by his words. The eorl changed tack.

"Why do you come to me in such a threatening manner? I have ruled here justly. You have no cause for anger. Remember, all the Christians of Saxon,

Dane and Norse heritage will follow me, you need me. If I take my men and leave, the Ui Imair could not possibly hold Yorvik. Whatever this is, you need to step back and explain yourselves."

Ragnall smiled, stepping up the dais toward the frightened eorl. "I am going to give you one chance for wisdom here, Eorl Guthfrith. You are going to come clean with us and tell us everything that has transpired. Who you are in league with, and why?"

Ragnall slowly slid from his belt a dagger, razor-sharp and gleaming in the light of the fire that burned in the hearth. The eorl's pale flabby flesh became even paler as Ragnall pointed his dagger at the eorl's throat and the other two Ui Imair warlords closed in from either side. Ragnall whispered to him quietly.

"It is said in the sagas that Odin, my ancestor and chief god of our people, sacrificed an eye to gain all the knowledge in the world. I think you should have the same advantage."

The three men reached for the eorl who bucked and screamed wildly for them to release him. It was no contest as the three massive Viking warlords overwhelmed one past-his-prime administrator. Ragnall used his dagger to gouge out Guthfrith's eye. Blood spattered Ragnall's leather armour as he undertook this gruesome act and the eorl's screams reverberated around his hall. After that all resistance fled from Guthfrith as he completely divulged the facts. He had indeed been in league with Aethelfled and Ealdred, but separately. Both wished to consume and annex central Northumbria for different reasons and Guthfrith had been playing one off against the other for greater gain. He admitted to disclosing the route Garangr's men had taken on campaign on several occasions which cost him three fingers of his right hand by Garangr's axe: one for each ambush. Aethelfled had spies in Yorvik, he admitted, and Ragnall forced Guthfrith to divulge their names so they could be dealt with, but Ragnall guessed that these men and women would have fled south on the first sign of major Ui Imair forces arriving at Yorvik.

At the end of their inquisition, Guthfrith was a bloodied and broken man and Ragnall believed that he had spoken true throughout the ordeal. Ragnall decided that they would not kill him and would show him a modicum of mercy.

He would be banished from the town with his family and whatever wealth he could carry, which disappointed Garangr who was hugely aggrieved by the eorl's betrayal. Ragnall's reasons were twofold: firstly, Guthfrith would serve as a warning that anyone who betrayed the Ui Imair could expect retribution which would intimidate the lesser chieftains, eorls and thegns into compliance. They must answer to Yorvik and not Tamworth or Babenburg. Secondly, as a Christian man, Guthfrith was shown mercy and his family were spared despite their treason, thus showing that although not Christian, the Ui Imair could be merciful and show some Christian-like forgiveness. This would ingratiate them with some of the bishops and Christian thegns and ealdormen. Within the day, the mutilated former puppet ruler was thrown from the city gates with three or four servants and his family, and they took the route north toward Cumbria and then on to the Britons of Strathclyde, vassals of the Scots.

Ragnall and his captains ruled Yorvik in peace for several weeks then and a state of normalcy resumed around the town. Ragnall had wanted to capture at least one of Athelfled's spies to feed her false information, just to give her forces a taste of their own medicine, but they had all fled at the first sign of trouble, to the best of Ragnall's knowledge. Trade picked up from the river systems east and west, north and south, and the roads between the North Sea and the Irish Sea were opened and garrisoned. Weeks stretched to months and then the peace they had thought they had earned through taking Yorvik completely, was shattered. A scout had come racing into Yorvik on horseback with frightening tidings. Ealdred of Babenburg and his brother-in-law, Constantine of Scotland, had joined forces and were marching south to sack Yorvik and drive the Ui Imair from Northumbria once and for all. Their strength was estimated at around two thousand warriors, and they would soon march or were moving south already on foot from Babenburg.

Ragnall summoned his chief captains to the hall immediately and informed them of the grave news. They discussed then what they would do in the face of this existential threat to their power in Britain. Garangr and Oitir Iarla advocated staying where they were and manning the walls of Yorvik for a siege, secure in the knowledge that they could repulse any attacker. Gragabai, the ruthless barbarian that he was, stated that the best plan was to sail their entire force north toward Babenburg and burn it to the ground, thereby forcing the joint Bernician and Scottish army to turn and face them, or else have their people massacred and enslaved behind them.

In the end, Ragnall went with Godfrith's suggestion; that they would march in four distinct columns of five hundred men each and create a net where somewhere upon the route, one of the columns would encounter this army. Whatever column it was would try and halt and delay it and send riders on horseback to the other four columns to reinforce them and flank their enemies, catching them in a pincer movement. The plan was risky as for a time, whatever column encountered this army first would be outnumbered three to one or more. But Gragabai and Oitir Iarla scoffed at those odds, with the Bastard stating that he would murder ten Scotsmen to get to a decent fight and he had been raiding Bernicia since he was a boy. Ragnall laughed with the rest at that brazen boast, but he secretly knew that it was likely that some of the men in this hall would never return to Yorvik or Dublin again.

Within a day the four columns of the army of the Ui Imair were on the march, heading north with roughly ten miles between each detachment: five hundred or more men apiece. Garangr, with his wounds still healing from his battles with the Mercians, was left to man the walls of Yorvik and should the battle go ill, he was to hold the city and send word to Sihtric in Dublin for reinforcements. The column furthest east was led by Oitir Iarla the Black One, the next one by Gragabai the Bastard, the next by Godfrith Ivarsson and the last and furthest west by Ragnall himself, with a contingent of his fiercest warriors, berserkers, and shieldmaidens. The reasoning being that if he could swing around behind the Scots and Bernicians, it would be his men who would do the most damage, and also in the worst-case scenario, his men would be closer to Yorvik in case the other columns failed to hold.

Ragnall's contingent quickly left the other columns behind within hours of leaving the walled town of Yorvik. The weather was sublime, and his men made good time. They were spoiling for a fight having not seen action since battling against the men of Meath in skirmishes after the recapture of Dublin. Many of

Garangr's contingent were with them also and Ragnall could sense the berserk need for vengeance emanating from them like a mist. Ragnall's plan was to hug the eastern side of the Pennines mountains, the range that formed the topographical spine of the entire island of Britain. It was very unlikely that the Bernicians and Scotsmen would risk the mountains, with a force as large as the scouts reported; Ragnall believed a direct route would most likely be taken by their host, straight south and then east. The Kielder Forest stood between the old Northumbrian Kingdom of Bernicia and Deira but there were pathways through it for an army to pass unnoticed. Ragnall suspected though that the forces of Constantine and Ealdred would skirt the forest to the east and live off the rich farmland all around there, and that would lead them inevitably to the banks of the River Tyne. *It would be decided there,* guessed Ragnall.

They camped at a small settlement sworn to Yorvik called Reeth on the first night having made great time. There was a squall of rain overnight, but it did little to dampen the spirits of his men. At the break of dawn, the column was on the move again. Ragnall had sent out scouts on horseback during the night to ascertain the whereabouts of his three other columns with Gragabai's column being the node through which all communications would flow. Those horsemen returned after midday to report that there had been no sign of the enemy and each column was marching north unmolested and unopposed.

The second day brought further squalls of rain down upon Ragnall's column and the men did their best to cover their supplies from the elements. Twice they had to seek cover from the deluge under the canopy of the trees, but luckily, they were only temporarily delayed from their course. They reached the ancient fort at Consett which paid tribute to Yorvik on the boundary between the old Northumbrian kingdoms of Bernicia and Deira. Ragnall forbade his men to forage the land or interfere with peasantry from the surrounding region as the entire purpose of this campaign was to win control of them unconditionally from the Bernicians and the Scots. To plunder their meagre holdings now would drive them into the arms of Ragnall's enemies.

He sent out riders once again to ascertain the whereabouts of the other three columns and when they returned during the night, he was informed that

Oitir had reached the banks of the River Weir, Gragabai was ten miles inland but five miles further back, having had to traverse trickier terrain. Godfrith was camped at the old fort at Durham some twelve miles to the east of Consett. The four columns were in ideal position to detect and counteract any invading host moving from the north. But still no sign of the northern army had been witnessed. *They have not reached the old Roman wall, or the Tyne,* thought Ragnall, *we have been strangely fortunate.*

The third day brought a subdued mood to Ragnall's cohort as the combination of damp weather, reduced energy from the trek north and the realisation of impending battle weighed heavy on the minds of his warriors. Ragnall led his forces west with the intention of sacking the church at Hexham before crossing the Tyne and progressing north. They would attempt to meet the Scots and Bernicians as they crossed through the Kielder Forest and made their way to the river. With luck they would catch their enemies in a vice and envelope them, allowing them no retreat. It was all to go terribly wrong though for Ragnall at roughly midday. A ragged rider approached from the east with dreadful news. Because Ragnall had veered slightly off course to sack the church at Hexham, his column had been delayed in crossing the river. All three of the other columns had crossed the river ahead of his own. The rider had breathlessly informed him that Oitir Iarla's column had encountered the entire northern army thirty miles to the east and had been quickly routed and destroyed. More than half of Oitir Iarla's warriors had fled west to join with Gragabai's host, but the Black One's head now adorned a Scottish spear. The forces of Constantine and Ealdred were in pursuit and within an hour, they would be upon Gragabai and his column next. Godfrith had elected to deploy his own column at the small defensible village at Corbridge ten miles to the east of Ragnall, but on the other side of the river, and Gragabai had sworn to sacrifice himself to slow the northern army, to allow Ragnall time to reinforce his brother.

Instantly Ragnall had commanded his men to abandon the march east to the church they intended to sack, and they crossed the river haphazardly, the water being only waist high where they were closest to the Tyne. It had taken ten minutes to move the entire five hundred men and the fifteen horses they had across the water, and they simply abandoned their stores. The battle would be decided today and either they would survive and retrieve these stores, or they would die and enter Valhalla, and it would not matter anyway. On crossing the river, Ragnall sent fifteen of his most ferocious berserkers with the horses they had on ahead toward Godfrith to reinforce him; every single body would count in the fighting to come, with the knowledge that Godfrith had to hold until Ragnall arrived, or it would all be in vain. He privately accepted that Gragabai would be supping in Valhalla long before they were able to reach him. It would be decided at Corbridge, Ragnall knew.

The bastard son of Harald Fairhair was a savage in a fight and despite only possessing between five and seven hundred men, Ragnall knew he would sell his life dearly and give their foes a bloody nose they would never forget. Ragnall's warriors then broke out into a run. Ragnall decided to take them slightly north toward the fort at Sandhoe and then wait there. Once Godfrith was engaged, they would come upon the Scotsmen and Bernicians and smash them from the rear. It took four hours for Ragnall's column to reach the old fort which had been completely abandoned on the rumour of the Ui Imair host's approach from the south. The run had been harrowing as every minute of the trek Ragnall could not help but dwell on the fate of his brother, facing a force that at the minimum would be twice as large as his own.

He sent his scouts a couple of miles to the south with strict instructions to stay out of sight. If Godfrith had not yet been engaged, they were to approach his camp and inform him of Ragnall's plan, and if he had been engaged already, they were to race back unseen and inform Ragnall that fighting was underway. The third option was left unspoken; if Godfrith's column had been destroyed already, Ragnall would come upon the rear of the northern army as they crossed the Tyne and break them there and then as they crossed the river or perish in the attempt.

Nervously Ragnall waited with his captains and minor chieftains for what seemed like hours. All the worst-case scenarios alternated through his brain and the fear for his younger brother caused him palpitations in his chest. So many of his kin had been slain in battle over the years that he would do anything to avoid further loss. They were ensconced a few miles away to purposefully avoid being spotted by potential scouts from the enemy and he hoped that sound did not carry across the trees, hedgerows and fields that lay between his force and Godfrith's camp upon the river. His men were silent now too, preparing themselves for the fight to come. One way or the other, they would do battle with the Scots and Bernician Northumbrians for control of Yorvik. The victor would rule almost a quarter of the island of Britain, the loser's bones would litter the ground for the scavengers to consume. Before the afternoon had passed, Ragnall's scouts returned breathless with news to report. The chief among them spoke.

"King Ragnall, we succeeded in reaching Eorl Godfrith before the Scots and Bernicians fell upon him. They are still some two miles off and approach from the east along the banks of the Tyne."

Ragnall answered, "What of the Black One? What of Garangr? Do they fight with us still or have they left us for Valhalla?"

The scout looked downcast upon the ground. "The Black One was slain earlier this morning far to the east, while Garangr's fate is unknown as he led a rearguard of fifty men to hold the enemy while the last few hundred of his warriors escaped to reinforce Godfrith. Everybody assumes that Garangr is either slain or captured."

Ragnall gripped the haft of his axes in blunted rage; the loss of two warriors of such repute weakened him severely. The men around him listening in to the conversation removed their helms and nodded in sombre acceptance of the news, some whispering prayers to the Allfather and his Valkyries to treat the warriors slain today with reverence and respect.

"Your brother agrees with your plan. He says that you should move shortly as by the time you get there the fight would have begun but do so out of sight so that the Scots and Bernicians never see you coming until it is too late."

Ragnall summoned his men to the base of the stone wall of the abandoned fort and addressed them.

"My warriors, my brave sons of Odin, my brother is besieged and Oitir Iarla and Garangr are most likely dead. The Scotsmen and Bernicians wish to take what is rightfully yours, your lands, your women, and your children. If we do not stop them here and now, Northumbria is lost."

The men roared in unison, slamming axes to shields. A jolt of worry raced through his mind at the noise of his men banging weapons together, but he elected to say nothing that would dampen their fervour.

"I ask you now to pick up your axes and swords, come down upon your foemen and slay them all for Odin and the Viking way of life."

More roars of excitement met his words. Ragnall stepped down from the wall and amongst his men. He raised his axes and pointed at many men in turn, coaxing their Viking spirit.

"These enemies outnumber us and some or all of us may never make it back to Yorvik or Dublin alive. All I can give you is death in battle. I ask you all, now, as Viking warriors, will you join me in battle and slay these Christians? Or will you hesitate so that the Gods in Valhalla turn their faces away in shame at you?"

Ragnall looked around at them, the berserkers among them were terrifying to behold, their eyes rolling around into the back of their skulls, drops of saliva dripping from their chins in rictuses of undiluted anger and violence. Ragnall knew he had them then.

"I run now, to relieve my brother and save our people from subjugation and murder. Who among you will join me?"

The response was deafening and when Ragnall turned to run, he did not feel just five hundred of his most ferocious Viking warriors with him, but the Gods as well.

At approximately two hours before sunset, Ragnall of the Ui Imair came down upon the rearguard of the combined army of the Scottish and Bernician Northumbrians. Ragnall's enemies had no inkling of Ragnall's approach, and they were smashed against the shield wall of Godfrith on the outskirts of the village of Corbridge. With nowhere to run or retreat to, almost half of the invading army were massacred in a matter of minutes. Ragnall had given the order to take no prisoners, and the command was clear: slaughter everybody who was not them. The battle finally broke apart when the ragged survivors of the Scots and Bernicians were able to rally around the banner of the Lord of Babenburg and under the cover of archers, they successfully formed up the semblance of a shield wall. Ragnall's men had not come away completely unscathed as more than a hundred slain Vikings lay beside their Bernician and Scottish foemen. At length, a banner of truce was erected, and four men approached under the rippling cloth to the blood-soaked centre of the battlefield. Ragnall and Godfrith walked to meet them as representatives of the Ui Imair, kicking the squawking scavenger birds out of their path who had already begun to feast upon the fallen.

From the armour and colouring the four men wore, Ragnall could see that there were two Scots and two Bernicians present. The two Scottish leaders were surprisingly young with the two Bernicians being obviously father and son. It was one of the Scots who spoke first.

"I am told you Ui Imair all speak our tongue. My name is Mael Colum mac Domnall, Prince of Scotland and this is Indulf mac Constantine my kinsman and son of the King. We speak with the authority of the High King of Scotland. To my right is Ealdred of Babenburg King of the Bernicians, and his son Uhtred the Older. We accept defeat here at Corbridge and do not wish to see any further loss of life. We seek fair terms or else violence will resume. It is true that we would not win as you have killed many of our men, but if you try us, I can guarantee you that most of the Ui Imair here will not see Yorvik."

Ragnall smirked at the young Scottish prince. He had heard of this Mael Colum, a son of Domnall Dasachtach the former King of the Scots. Word of several notable victories achieved over Norse raiding parties by the young prince had even reached Dublin. Ragnall strutted forward, sure in his superiority.

"Do you know, Prince Mael Colum, that as a young man I was there when Harald Fairhair my grandfather and my uncle Erik Bloodaxe slaughtered your father and his vanguard? I still possess trophies from that day aboard my ship with my treasure hoard."

Godfrith smiled at that while the faces of the four noblemen before him darkened.

"But I agree, I believe there is no need for further fighting. You are defeated. I will allow you to leave with your remaining men on three conditions. Firstly, no armed man from Scotland will ever cross the border into Northumbria without my express permission. Secondly, Babenburg will pay tribute to me now, you will acknowledge me as overlord of all of Northumbria. Bernicia will pay taxes to Yorvik and provide soldiers to me in the wars to come, should I require them."

The young Bernician Uhtred bristled at this, but his father shot a warning look to him for calm.

"And thirdly, one of you four will become my hostage for a period of two years in Yorvik on the promise of good behaviour and the holding of your two kingdoms' oaths. You have a moment to decide before we resume the battle. And I promise you this, my men have been given orders to slay everybody, there will be no prisoners. But if I catch you four alive, by Odin's beard I will blood-eagle the four of you and hang your flayed remains from the trees as an offering to the Gods."

Young Uhtred hawked and spat in Ragnall's direction but none the less turned to converse with his three other cowed associates. In moments, shoulders slumped and with a defeated cast to their features, they each formally accepted Ragnall's terms. The young nobleman Uhtred disarmed himself and handed his sword and daggers to his father and walked forward; he was to be the noble hostage. There was a familiar cast to him Ragnall decided and despite the boy's belligerence and arrogance, he could not help but like the young pup.

"Are you adopted, young Uhtred?" Ragnall enquired, "or have you Viking heritage?"

Uhtred answered, "My mother, Father's first wife, was a Dane."

This gets better and better, thought Ragnall as he made his way back to his warriors with his young hostage and Godfrith beside him. *Northumbria is a mad interwoven place.*

With Uhtred having been forced to swear both on Thor's hammer and the Christian bible to remain in captivity and not try to escape, he was permitted freedom of their camp and given food and drink. Ragnall and Godfrith inspected the camp then and what they saw worried them. Of the two thousand that they had set out from Yorvik with, they had perhaps twelve hundred remaining. The retreating Scots and Bernicians had even less but they did not have the Mercians sitting right on their borders. Many of the men and women who had survived the battle sported terrible wounds, and the journey alone back to Yorvik would kill many, Ragnall knew. He had witnessed over his entire military career that if wounds were not treated with boiling mead or wine and dressed properly, they could suppurate and kill a man as easily as a blow from an axe to the skull. The groans and the gasps of the wounded and dying eventually sickened Ragnall and he retreated to one of the simple abandoned houses of the people of Corbridge. Godfrith came with him but only when the two brothers were out of earshot of the rest of the warriors did they risk speaking openly. Godfrith looked haggard. He sported a cut across his temple, and he carried his right arm low.

"How are you, brother?" Ragnall enquired earnestly. "How badly are you injured?"

Godfrith slowly swung his shoulder around in a wide ark until an audible pop echoed around the room.

"Some little goblin of a man landed a glancing blow with a hammer to my shoulder before I took his head from his shoulders and I was a little slow in avoiding a slash from some Bernician. My wife will find the scar irresistible."

Ragnall laughed at that. Slowly the echoes of the battle began to fade in his mind and his heart was beating normally now. Godfrith turned to him and spoke.

"We have lost a lot of our best fighting men and women out there, Ragnall. What kind of victory is it when you lose the bulk of your own strength?"

Ragnall had no answer for that. He hugged his brother and went outside while Godfrith went in search of stitching for his cut. *If Aethelfled comes north for us, we will not have the strength to oppose her,* thought Ragnall. *Perhaps it is time for a new strategy,* he mused. He stared out across the small wall that surrounded the abandoned house. He could barely make out the last remnants of the Scottish and Bernician host retreating over the horizon. *We have defeated our foemen at the battle of Corbridge, but have the Ui Imair ultimately lost the war?*

CHAPTER 4

THE ASSASSINATION UPON
WATLING STREET
(918 AD)

The great hall in Yorvik was crowded, heaving with dignitaries, traders, artificers and affiliated Saxon and Viking warriors. The weather was abysmal outside, and snow and sleet had turned the streets into rivers of mud and detritus; treacherous to even the most sure-footed mule. Ragnall sat on the dais staring out at the eclectic crowd that packed the room and mused on how such disparate people from disparate places could mingle amicably without violence. There were Britons and Angles negotiating over furs and timber. There were Frisians, Norse, Danes and Saxons bargaining over the price of spices from Al Andalus. There were Francian wine merchants peddling their wares to the local Northumbrian ealdormen and their representatives. There were even Irishmen and Welshmen looking for buyers for honey and mead left over from the autumn harvest. And of every major deal, the Ui Imair took a piece of the action, swelling their coffers exponentially.

Since the battle of Corbridge, Ragnall had focused on consolidating his strength, building ties with the nobility of Northumbria while occasionally launching raids upon Strathclyde and Scotland to keep them guessing. As trade in the region gathered momentum under his steady governance, he began to look to attract warriors from around the Viking world. Ragnall had no interest in accumulating wealth; only prestige, respect and the success of his people concerned him. Any wealth he accrued was distributed out to his captains and senior men, and they loved him for it. Under his cousin Garangr, Ragnall had formed a multinational militia that patrolled his southern border with Mercia and the old Danelaw. Men from Bernicia, Deira and Cumbria rallied to join the ranks as word was spread of Ragnall's generosity and although the quality of warrior was not quite there from before the battle of Corbridge, their numbers had swollen back up to a similar amount.

Ragnall, and by extension the Ui Imair tribe of Norse-Gaels, were as powerful as they ever had been in their history. The Ui Imair sat above all the other factions within Ragnall's armies, and he himself sat above them all in turn. It was truly an international force assembling as the fame of Ragnall and his brother grew. He was under no illusions though: should he suffer several significant defeats, the Ui Imair would find themselves in dire straits once more, like they had after being expelled from Dublin all those years ago. There had been very little warfare to contend with since the defeat of the Scots and the Bernicians at Corbridge and any fighting done was instigated by the Ui Imair for their own purposes, with no defensive action required. Their hostage from Babenburg, Uhtred the Older, had also proved to be extremely useful.

Once Ragnall was able to impress upon the lad that he intended for Northumbria to be prosperous and independent of all kingdoms, save the nominal rulership of Yorvik itself, the Northumbrian nobleman became less surly and belligerent and chose to be reasonable and amenable. Ragnall had even appointed him as a captain of the guards employed directly by the town of Yorvik to keep the peace. He had toyed with the idea of sending him raiding with his brother Godfrith at one point but had declined in the end in case his alliances were put to the test, and they were forced to kill him.

Uhtred was proving useful though and long conversations into the night with the lad had revealed to Ragnall that he had no love for the Saxons of Wessex and Mercia either. He had disclosed that both his father and King

Constantine of Scotland had launched an assault upon Yorvik purely to defend the north from Edward the Elder and his accursed sister, as they didn't believe that the Ui Imair were strong enough to be a stable buffer between the south and north. Uhtred, despite his tender years, already had a son in Babenburg who was also called Uhtred and Ragnall had offered to accommodate his young family moving to stay with him in Yorvik; but Uhtred had declined on the grounds that despite their warming friendship, he was still a hostage. He insisted that his father would never allow it either, to protect the line of the Kings of Bernicia. Ragnall knew that if he were honest with himself, he would have taken the same course as Ealdred; to lose one heir even temporarily was bad enough, but a second would be impossible to accept.

As the night wore on, guests and traders drifted out in ones and twos and by the early hours there were only a handful remaining, with the most drunk being picked up by the armpits and flung from the hall by Ragnall's guards. When there were only Ragnall's four personal guards, his brother Godfrith and two other guests who had bedded down near the fire for the night, a hooded man emerged from the darkest shadows of the furthest corner of the hall. He wore a wolfskin cloak, thick and furry, but it did little to disguise the size of him or his warrior frame as he approached the centre of the hall. Ragnall's guards turned as one and reached for the axes at their belts, each sensing the threat the man posed, but a hand signal from Ragnall stayed their intent.

"Reveal yourself," Ragnall commanded, "and show us who you are?"

Slowly the man shrugged off his cloak and threw it to a faraway bench. Ragnall and Godfrith gasped as one. The man bore a stunning resemblance to their fearsome older brother, the long-dead Amlaib who had died in battle beside their father and other brother Ivar, against Niall Glundub and Constantine the Scot in 904. It was as if their brother had stepped back from Valhalla's halls and re-emerged into the land of the living. He could not be more than his mid-twenties and more than likely was younger, and so common sense ruled out any supernatural possibility in Ragnall's mind. He bore the famous genetic heirloom of the Ui Imair though, of a single white stripe in his hair, his growing diagonally from left temple to right ear; a true scion of the line of Ragnar Lodbrok. He stood there, axe at his hip in total surety, as if Yorvik belonged to him in its entirety. Godfrith spoke, entranced by this figure:

"Are you of the Ui Imair, young man? Perhaps some long-lost son of Ingamundr or our father Ivar?"

The powerful young man smiled at that and answered, "No, Eorl Godfrith, I am not of the Ui Imair, but I am distant kin to them. My name is Gorm. I am the son of the King of Denmark, Harthacnut the Wise."

Ragnall fitted the pieces together and spoke:

"And Harthacnut is of course the son of Sigurd Snake-In-The-Eye, the brother of our grandsire, Ivar the Boneless. We are all here descended from not just Ragnar Lodbrok, but from Odin the Allfather himself."

The man nodded in humbled respect and spoke again:

"King Ragnall, I come on behalf of my father, risking the autumn storms for one purpose; we wish for you to aid us in the name of the blood we share."

Ragnall shifted in his seat and questioned Gorm, "What befalls Denmark that you need the assistance of the Ui Imair? Surely your father possesses thousands of warriors at his disposal. I couldn't think of a king who should be more secure in his power than Harthacnut the Wise."

Gorm's shoulders slumped despairingly at Ragnall's statements.

"My father is hard-pressed to keep his borders intact. He is surrounded by a sea of enemies. To the north Erik Bloodaxe and the Norse launch raids into our territories. Even in his dotage Harald Fairhair seems not content to just control Norway and the Hebrides, but he wants Denmark too. In Denmark itself, various eorls and minor sea kings constantly rise in rebellion against my father's rule. But that is not the worst of it, King Ragnall. To the south and east, the Carolingian's who used to control East Francia have ceded their territory there to a powerful German warrior called Henry the Fowler. Unlike the Carolingians, he is determined to further his reach into our lands. He is a legendary fighter and commander who has defeated everybody who has stood before him. He has crushed the Magyar steppe nomads in battle many times and commands tens of thousands of Thuringians, Germans and mercenaries. In the autumn of next year or the year after, my father expects that the Fowler will come north and force all the Danish eorls and kings to submit or be banished or murdered. King Ragnall, our way of life, the historic lands of our shared forefathers, are under threat as never before." The young prince of Denmark then knelt before Ragnall. "Will you join us with your fleet, if we call upon you in your kinsmen's direst hour?"

Ragnall was moved by Gorm's appeal. He could see the lad was sincere and by the scars he already bore, Ragnall could tell that he could handle himself in a fight. For a nobleman of such lineage to humble himself before Ragnall in this manner would have been humiliating and it also shouted the great fear that Harthacnut clearly had of this Germanic king to the southeast. There were many things to consider though. Although Ragnar Lodbrok was a Dane, the Ui Imair were almost a distinct people now. Ivar the Boneless had married an Irish princess. His own father then had married a princess of Norway, a daughter of Harald Fairhair. Although these Danes could stake a claim to Ragnall's loyalty through their mighty forefathers, Sigurd and Ivar, the Norse through Erik Bloodaxe and Harald Fairhair had equal claim to the Ui Imair's allegiance, through his mother. To side with the Danes against the Norse or the Norse versus the Danes, could result in retribution for his own territories should he pick the losing faction.

There was something else that Ragnall had to consider too: if he remembered the tales correctly from his father's knee, Sigurd Snake-In-The-Eye, had fought as a mercenary almost seventy years ago beside Ragnar Lodbrok on behalf of King Aella, a long-dead Deiran-Northumbrian king, in the Saxon civil wars at the time. His prize for service had been... the hand of Aella's daughter. That made this Gorm very distant kin to many of the nobility of Northumbria itself. Ragnall quickly shuffled the many permutations involved and came to a decision.

"Prince Gorm, I agree to assist both you and your father in the potential wars to come in Denmark, but only subject to several conditions."

The young prince rose from the floor, sporting a broad optimistic grin.

"Firstly, I will not join with your father against the Norse. They are as much kin to me as you and your father are. If further fighting between Norway and Denmark occurs, my men and I will stay neutral. Secondly, we will not interfere in any internal dispute in Denmark. Civil wars are for Danes alone and although I command many Danish and Danish-Saxons among my warriors, I will be commanding them to remain here. Thirdly, I will join you purely in defence of Denmark against the threat of this Henry the Fowler. Should he march north to destroy you, we will invade his river systems and set the Germanic kingdoms and East Francia on fire. All loot and plunder are ours solely to claim should this come to pass. In exchange for our assistance, we may at a future time also call upon you to assist us in a similar manner, should the need arise; we expect Harthacnut the Wise to answer. The final condition is this: my kingdom is also hard beset by foes north, south, east and west. Irishmen, Scots, Bretons and Mercians plague my lands. Because of this I will only deploy a portion of my strength to your aid when required, but do not despair, young Gorm, this portion I assure you is enough to lay whole nations low and level cities. Do you accept these terms, Prince Gorm, on behalf of your father King Harthacnut?"

The prince was less happy than he had been moments before Ragnall had laid out his conditions, but still seemed reasonably satisfied. He approached Ragnall, and the two men grasped forearms the warrior's way to seal the alliance. At that moment, the doors burst inward amidst a flurry of snow. Three men had another struggling man by the arms and neck, and they flung him on the floor in the middle of the hall. Two other men gently led a sobbing woman who was dressed poorly for the weather, who had clearly been pulled from her home with three terrified children, two boys and a girl. The leader of the men was Uhtred the Older of Babenburg. With a nod Ragnall sent Godfrith out a side door to another adjoining building to continue to negotiate the finer points of their new alliance with Prince Gorm. On the way out he woke the two guests by the fire abruptly and demanded they leave the hall at once. When the four men had left the room, Ragnall addressed Uhtred:

"What is the meaning of this, Uhtred? Why have you dragged a family to my hall in the depths of an autumn night?"

Uhtred kicked the prostrate man once more before answering.,

"King Ragnall, this is Wilfred the smith. He approached an associate of mine looking for information on military deployments, thinking incorrectly that all Saxon, Jute and Anglian people in Northumbria would be allied to Wessex and Mercia rather than Yorvik or Babenburg. He thought wrong. My friend was able to maintain the charade and gain this traitor's confidence before coming to me. I raided his home and brought him directly to you. What is to be done with him and his family, my lord?"

Ragnall considered the situation carefully. When he first took Yorvik directly from the puppet ruler that he had installed, he was under the impression that all Aethelfled's spies had fled south to evade him. The fact that raids from Mercia had completely stopped had given credence to this theory; but here on front of him was evidence contrary to that view. He addressed the spy directly.

"Wilfred the smith, why would you betray your Northumbrian countrymen in this manner? Have you anything to say for yourself?"

The man looked up and grovelled, hands clasped in prayer as if Ragnall himself were some statue of a Christian saint.

"Please, lord, I had to do it. One of Queen Aethelfled's ealdormen has my brother and father in captivity on the charge of trading with the Danish rebels, making weapons for them and shoeing their horses. They bade me come as far north as Yorvik with my family and gather intelligence for them or their lives were forfeit. I had no choice, lord."

Ragnall was unmoved by the man's desperate pleading having seen it so many times before.

"Just like all slaves or any kind of conquered people, you do have a choice. It is just a choice that you are too cowardly and weak to make. That is to fight and die for your freedom. You get exactly what you deserve."

The man began to wail which annoyed Ragnall. He nodded to Uhtred who struck the man a backhanded blow which enforced a stunned silence from him. Ragnall spoke again.

"Now Wilfred, you are going to do a favour for your Northumbrian countrymen and by extension the Ui Imair and be a central piece in a plan that I have had in mind for some time; a chance at redemption. Until now I had not the opportunity, but you, my Saxon friend, have just made it possible."

The man let loose a sob and interrupted Ragnall.

"Please, my lord, if Queen Aethelfled finds out I trucked with you and the Ui Imair, she will kill my family."

Ragnall reached down and sharply forced the man's eyes to meet his own. "Cretin, I will kill you and your family long before Aethelfled even knows that you have been caught. Don't worry about what she thinks, you have more pressing concerns."

The man shuddered and began sobbing freely now but another blow from Uhtred of Babenburg silenced him.

"On the morrow, Wilfred the smith, we are going to set out from Yorvik. I happen to know that even this close to the winter, Queen Aethelfled is still campaigning in the Five Boroughs of the Danelaw. What we are going to do is prepare an ambush for that witch and rid us all of her ambitions."

Ragnall turned to Uhtred.

"Did anyone see you raid this man's house and bring his family here to the hall?"

The captive Bernician shook his head.

"Good. Now, Wilfred, we are going to leave on fresh horses by a circuitous route to avoid being seen by anyone who would hinder us. Somewhere on the old Roman road of Watling Street, we will lie in wait with a small but deadly force of Vikings and you, my little friend, are going to send word to Aethelfled that you have intelligence of such import that it would only be appropriate for Queen Aethelfled herself to witness. If she presses you, you will tell her that one of the chief warlords of the Ui Imair is in hiding there and wishes to swear allegiance to her cause and convert to Christianity. Tell her that he insists that he must do it in secret lest he be seen, and he would only swear to her himself in private. That should suffice to draw that wretched harpy to us. Her greed and hunger for power will overcome her caution."

Ragnall ran through his plan in his mind, and it all seemed sound. He commanded Uhtred to inform Garangr and Godfrith to gather a hundred of their most seasoned killers and some of their berserkers too and be ready to move at the break of dawn with the swiftest horses in Yorvik. He turned back to Wilfred the smith.

"Wilfred, you do realise what I will do to your family here if you betray me?"

Tears streamed down the man's face, and he nodded. Ragnall chuckled darkly.

"I have decided I will tell you anyway. If I do not come back to Yorvik in one piece, I will leave instruction for the following to occur. Your sons will be shipped down to Seville or Cordoba to be castrated to become eunuch slave soldiers in the Umayyad Caliph's army. Your daughter will be shipped further down the coast of the Aifric to the Ghanaians, the Fir Gorm, as the Irish call them. There she will begin life as a salt miner and if she survives that ordeal she might end up in some barbarian's harem if she is lucky. Most likely she will be thrown on a mound of slave corpses for the jackals to devour. Your wife though, I will make a gift of her to one of my captain's ships as a whore to be used by the crew for the rest of her days or until they grow tired of her and throw her into the sea as an offering to Njord or Thor. Do you understand the enormity of the situation?"

Urine was pooling beneath the man's knees at Ragnall's description of the fate of his family should he fail in his task. Ragnall commanded the man and his family to be kept under custody in the hall with no petitioners allowed in or out until his force had gone south.

At dawn, the next day all was in readiness and the small host, hooded and cloaked, exited Yorvik in a column. There was no rain, but the grim bleak midlands autumn weather had an iron grip on the land. In a day they had crossed the Humber River on the way south, careful to stay off the beaten track. There was nothing overly unusual about a party of Norse or Danes moving around or across the countryside but Ragnall, Godfrith and Garangr had agreed that secrecy was of paramount importance for what they intended. The most northerly of the five boroughs was the small semi-independent Kingdom of Lincoln and despite not yet having submitted fully to Saxon rule, Ragnall instinctively knew that Aethelfled would have eyes and ears there ever watchful, reporting to her any pertinent information. A column of hardened Norse-Gael-led warriors could potentially draw semi-ambivalent attention this far south.

They skirted the walled town there far to the west and made camp in the wilderness. They then spent several days skirting the lands north of Nottingham and Derby, two more of the Five Boroughs who had already capitulated to Aethelfled's advance east from Mercia, to avoid detection. It infuriated Ragnall that the eorls and nobles of these boroughs would choose Aethelfled as their ruler just for the sake of economics; Yorvik really should have had their allegiance and not the Saxons. On the sixth day they risked heading south amidst the woods and forests of Mercia but chose to widely circumnavigate Repton, a large Saxon town.

They selected an isolated spot to carefully traverse the Trent River, using scouts to cover their passage and ensure no eyes witnessed their crossing into the territory close to Tamworth. On the seventh day they reached the ancient road of Watling Street, the giant Roman road that dissected the country. The ancient Celtic Iceni queen, Boudicca, had marched one hundred thousand men and their families up Watling Street in pursuit of the last remaining Roman legions here nine centuries before and they had ended up being massacred down to the last child. Ragnall felt that that was a good omen for what they intended; another famous queen would hopefully meet her end soon upon Watling Street.

Ragnall's warband made camp about ten miles east of Queen Aethelfled's capital at Tamworth, extremely careful to lose his party in the wilderness. To be discovered now would mean an ignominious death for them all. Once they were defensively set, Ragnall sent scouts out to ascertain the goings-on in the land. He had heard through many traders' mouths in Yorvik, that Aethelfled had invested Leicester with a siege, looking to bring yet another of the Five Boroughs under her direct control. There was only thirty miles between Leicester and Tamworth and Ragnall sent riders on Watling Street going both ways. Single travellers on horseback, even if they were not local, would draw no enquiry, Ragnall felt. Within a day they each returned with a report. Leicester had just submitted to Aethelfled in the last three weeks, and she was busy fortifying the town to her own designs and delegating the administration of the surrounding borough to her ealdormen, loyal Danish eorls and thegns. It was only a few weeks from Christmas and Ragnall knew that her forces would be on the move back west for that Christian festival; they had to act swiftly.

And then it was time. They had found an old abandoned and dilapidated crofter's hut in the wilderness a few miles off Watling Street and that was where they would set their ambush. Wilfred the smith was sent on his way with the direst of threats to his family resounding in his ears. They would get one shot at this as Aethelfled would never be so vulnerable again: her own intelligence network for once betraying her. Should the smith divulge their position and judge his brother and father more important to him than his young family, Ragnall's men were prepared to fight to the death.

A pair of horses had been hidden away a mile north of there for Garangr and Godfrith to escape alone, as Ragnall had taken responsibility upon himself to offer the Saxons battle should it come to that. The Ui Imair leadership in Yorvik must endure. All that was left was to wait and pray to Odin that the smith would be convincing enough to entice Aethelfled to this bleak place. The day passed slowly, and a film of snow began to cover the trees, ditches, and the crofter's hovel. All the men were sequestered away. Many of them were armed with bows too as it was imperative that Aethelfled's bodyguard were annihilated in the first moments of the fighting, if she arrived. Her personal guard would be the cream of Mercian soldiery, veteran huscarls, and individually would probably be a match for any of Ragnall's berserkers.

Ragnall himself of course fancied that he could down any amount of them one by one, but if they attempted to break out in a fist in his direction to save their queen, he was humble enough to realise that he may well be Valhalla-bound in that scenario; but it was all worth the risk. He knew her death would reverberate around the entire island and would have massive political connotations. Would the Mercians accept another Wessexian as their lord or would their witan elect a Mercian ealdorman in her place? Her daughter was unproven, and her nephew Aethelstan was a son of the King of Wessex.

Would there be civil war in all the Saxon lands if Edward the Elder installed his own puppet ruler in Mercia? Ragnall practically salivated at the thought of that. Should that occur, he would await a victor emerging and then come down upon them like the Hammer of Thor and shatter the Saxon kingdoms forever. He was broken from his reverie by the sound of hooves clattering and branches and twigs being snapped two hundred yards away. He signalled for all his men to lie flat in their hiding places and to be still and quiet. By sound alone, Ragnall could hear that the force coming was not overly large which delighted him. *Could this Wilfred have pulled it off?* he pondered. He heard the distinctive voice of Wilfred then as the small contingent trotted toward them:

"Over here, my lady, Garangr of the Ui Imair is willing to swear his allegiance to you in that hut in the clearing over there. He is concealed within for fear of discovery from his heathen kind."

Garangr was hidden beside Ragnall and Ragnall devilishly looked in his cousin's direction with a smirk. Garangr muttered under his breath, cursing the Saxon for being named as the member of the Ui Imair elite that he had chosen as a potential traitor. Ragnall would have laughed but for the impending fight to come. The Queen rode into sight and she had twenty men with her on horseback with the smith riding beside her. It was indeed the elite of Mercian soldiery that accompanied her, each covered from head to toe with the finest mail and helms, with shields strapped to their backs. Aethelfled, although in her mid-forties, still carried herself like the warrior queen that she was. She was heavily mailed also and had a sword in a scabbard by her hip. She swung down off the horse athletically with three of her men and the smith in tow. Ragnall waited until they approached the doorway and then gave the nod to Garangr. The whole world held its breath.

Garangr raised his horn to his lips and released an unmerciful blast that reverberated through the woods and ditches and fields; and Ragnall's concealed archers let fly. Five of the warriors on horseback were flattened to the ground as arrows punched them from their saddles. The remainder dismounted and instantly moved to surround their queen in a protective ring of steel. The great lady of Mercia drew her sword and without a word removed the head off the shoulders of the smith; *Clever girl,* thought Ragnall, *she knows now what is happening but it's too late.* She entered her circle of warriors and placed a helm upon her head ready to sell her life dearly. Ragnall slowly emerged from the trees and his warriors moved to join them. He drew his two axes and broke into a jog and then a run and then a sprint, and the Ui Imair fell upon the Queen and her bodyguard like the great hound Fenrir was destined to do upon the forces of the Aesir, when Ragnarök began.

The fight was short, brutal and one-sided. None of the Saxons survived save the Queen herself, but the Ui Imair had taken some losses also. Aethelfled had had most of her teeth knocked out with a mailed fist and her face was drained through blood loss, having had her sword hand removed from her arm by Garangr. Ragnall approached her and his men parted to allow him close. Even now she spat defiance.

"You heathen bastard, I should have slain you and your brother in my hall all those years ago. I should have never listened to that worm smith and now I am going to pay the price. What is it to be then, Ragnall Ivarsson? Ransom and concession, or death?"

Ragnall said one word, "Death."

Solemnly the Queen nodded and with her one remaining hand shakily grasped a dagger strapped to her calf and prepared herself to fight Ragnall of the Ui Imair, who dwarfed her in size and weight. Ragnall clasped both of his axes tightly and told all his warriors to stand back out of the way. Only Godfrith and Garangr remained where they were, standing stone-faced with arms folded across their brawny chests. Ragnall could sense the emotions rolling off both of his kin on seeing this queen in the flesh and at their mercy. Ragnall spoke to her loudly for all his warriors to hear.

"Aethelfled of Mercia, for decades you have wished nothing but ill upon my people. You have slaughtered many of Scandinavian heritage, burned our villages and towns to the ground and put our close kin and friends to the sword. For these atrocities, I, Ragnall of the Ui Imair, sentence you to die. Have you any last words, witch, before I bury my axe in your chest and rip out your beating heart?"

The Queen nodded slowly, pain and blood loss hampering her movements.

"My death will be traced to you and your dreadful kin. My nephew and brother will hunt you down to the end of the earth and destroy you all for this. I have no more to say to a heathen savage like you, Ragnall. Come then, barbarian, and try my dagger. I have heard you go with men, perhaps I can help with your attractiveness to them, by gelding you."

Ragnall knew that she was trying to goad him into giving her a quick death, but it would not work. Not this time. Ice rolled through his veins, not fire. Vengeance for the Ui Imair had come. Slowly he walked toward her.

Hours later, the horrified vanguard of the Mercian army returning victorious from Leicester came upon a loan female figure, crucified, in the middle of Watling Street. Her torso had been chopped open and her innards lay slopped on the ground in a grizzly mess beneath her corpse. Her hands and feet were nailed to the timber and a sword was rammed through her side. Ravens quorked raucously on her shoulders, feeding on her dead flesh. Her heart had been removed from her chest. And so it was, there on the old Roman Road of Watling Street, ten miles from her capital of Tamworth, that Aethelfled, Queen of the Mercians, was ambushed, slain and crucified by Ragnall Ivarsson the Lord of the Ui Imair, on the fifteenth of October, 918.

*

A Saxon Lament for Aethelfled

> *Courage is best for those that oft must endure profound misery. Think deep on their torment. Their Lady's death when it comes, woven by fate's decree, they shall grieve with sorrowing soul, knowing their kind treasure giver is hidden in earth.*
> *Our Lady, leader of warriors, the best of those between the seas, to God's judgement, staff of the weary, from worldly joy and loving kin, in glory has gone to seek that dwelling-place on high.*

Now her portion of earth, a broken bone-house, is a house inhabited with death's-rest, and that wondrous portion of body has in God's light sought the glorious reward, to partake with the peaceful host of that well-spring of bliss.

PART 9

THE BATTLE OF ISLANDBRIDGE

DRAMATIS PERSONAE:

Aed mac Eochuchan (*Aid-mac-ao-chu-cawn*) – Head of the Dal nAridi and all of the other Ulaidian tribes, answerable to Niall Glundub and the Northern Ui Neill.

Aethelfled of Mercia (*A-thel-fled*) – Saxon Queen of Mercia who was assassinated on Watling Street.

Albann Godfrithsson – Young Ui Imair prince and warrior.

Amlaib Collasson (*Am-layb-collason*) – Known to the Irish as the "Cenncaireach" or the Sinner. Vicious Viking warlord.

Amlaib Cuaran (*Am-layb-cuor-on*) – Infant son of Sihtric the Scourge.

Beollan mac Ciarmac (*Byole-on-mac-kyor-mac)* – King of South Brega, under-king of Conchobar mac Flann.

Brian of Kells – Young Bregan warrior and scout.

Brunbolg Headtaker (*Brun-bulg-head-taker*) – Physically gigantic Viking warlord, subject to the influence of the Ui Imair.

Cathal mac Conchobar (*Ca-hal-mac-con-co-bar*) – Over-king of all Connaught.

Ceallach mac Fogarteach (*Kyal-ach-mac-fog-ar-tach*) – Heir designate of South Brega.

Cearnachan mac Tighernain (*Kyer-na-cawn-mac-tier-nan*) – King of Breffni, under-king to the Northern Ui Neill.

Conchobar mac Flann (*Con-co-bar-mac-flann*) – King of Clan Colman and the Southern Ui Neill, ruler at Tara.

Constantine mac Aed – Over-king of all Scotland.

Domnall mac Cossachtach (*Dom-nal-mac-coss-ach-tach*) – Irish warrior and mercenary officer.

Domnall mac Donnchadh (*Dom-nall-mac-don-na-ca*) – Known as Domnall Donn after his father, prince of the Caille Follamain and Southern Ui Neill.

Donnchadh Donn mac Flann (*Dun-na-ka-dun-mac-flan-sinna*) – Powerful King of the Caille Follamain tribe in Meath.

Eiremon mac Cendetigh (*Air-a-mon-mac-cen-de-tig*) – Ruler of the Cenel Maine tribe and under-king of the Northern Ui Neill.

Erik Haraldsson – Also known as Erik Bloodaxe. Fearsome Viking marauder and raider, young son of the King of Norway.

Flaibhertach mac Domnall (*Fla-her-tach-mac-dom-nal*) – Head of the Cenel Conaille tribe and under-king of the Northern Ui Neill.

Flann Sinna – Recently deceased but legendary High King of Ireland.

Godfrith Ivarsson (*God-frith-ivarson*) – Twin brother of Sihtric, the youngest sons of the former King of Dublin, Ivar Ivarsson. Commander under his brother Ragnall.

Gotrek – Norse Gael businessman of Dublin.

Gragabai the Bastard (*Grag-a-by*) – Notorious Viking raider and alleged bastard son of Harald Fairhair, slain in battle at Corbridge by the Scots and Bernician Saxons.

Grainne ingen Muiredach (*Graw-nya-ingen-mwir-e-dach*) – Osraigan Irish princess, married to Sihtric the Scourge.

Grungni mac Conall (*Grung-knee-mac-fer-dia*) – Irish nobleman with a Norse-Gael Ui Imair mother.

Hywel nDa (*Hugh-wil-da*) – Powerful Welsh warrior-king.

Loki – Significant deity in the Scandinavian pantheon.

Mael Craobh (*Male-crave*) – King of Argialla and under-king of the Northern Ui Neill, son of the Black Fox.

Mael Mithig mac Flannacain (*Male-mith-ig-mac-flan-na-cawn*) – Shrewd and charismatic King of North Brega.

Magnus Magnusson – Known as the Longtooth. Norse-Gael trader of Linn and advisor to Eorl Olaf.

Muirchertach mac Niall (*Mwir-her-tach-mac-niall*) – Formidable young son of Niall Glundub and prince of the Northern Ui Neill and the Cenel nEoghain. His reputation as a warrior was such that the people of the north called him the "Hector" of Ireland.

Niall Glundub mac Aed Findliath – High King of Ireland and the Lord of the Northern Ui Neill.

Odin – The chief God of the Norse and Danes, also known as the Allfather.

Oitir Iarla (*Oh-tier-ee-arla*) – Also known as Oitir the Black, or Oitir the Black One. Fearsome Viking warlord, slain in battle at Corbridge versus the Scots and Bernician Saxons.

Olaf Godfrithsson (*Olaf-god-frith-son*) – Extremely young Ui Imair prince and nephew to Ragnall.

Olaf Snorrisson – Ruler and chieftain of the Norse-Gael town of Linn.

Olga Helmsdottir – Ferocious female Viking war-leader, known as the Valkyrie.

Ragnall Ivarsson (*Rag-nal-ivarson*) – Leader of the Ui Imair.

Rhodri the Great (*Rod-ree*) – Long-deceased famous Welsh king, who made his name fighting both Vikings and Saxons.

Sihtric Ivarsson (*Si-tric-ivarson*) – Known as Sihtric the Scourge by the Irish. Warlord under the nominal command of his brother Ragnall and ruler of Dublin.

Sven Olafsson – Norse Gael nobleman, son of the Eorl of Linn. Occasionally known as Ironfist.

Tadg mac Cathal (*Ty-g-mac-ca-hal*) – Prince of Connaught.

Tadg mac Ruaidhri (*Ty-g-mac-roo-ree*) – Standard bearer of the Irish and warrior of the Northern Ui Neill.

Thor – Major deity of the Scandinavian pantheon.

Ulf Francslayer – Long-dead Viking warlord and reaver.

CHAPTER 1

THE LEATH CUINN ALLIANCE (919 AD)

Niall Glundub mac Aed Findliath passed his cache of weapons to the guards on the door of the longfort at Linn. He entered alone and unafraid, ready to confront any of the Norse and Norse-Gael warriors present, meeting each eyeball to eyeball, daunting them with his presence. In truth it was only the largest berserkers who could match him for size and even at forty-nine years of age, he was sure that there were none here who could take him in single combat. The longfort was long and possessed a musty smell, hinting at great age. *It indicates how long the Northmen have had a presence in Ireland,* Glundub thought to himself ruefully; although he wisely elected not to voice his conclusion, lest it offended the denizens of the place. He was here to offer an ultimatum after all. Great shields and spears were hung decoratively from the rafters hinting at the martial pride of the people here despite their relative civility compared to the rest of their savage kin in the region. Glundub understood well that trade and not raiding was the modus operandi of the Norse-Gael of Linn but he had no doubt that if their... *traders*... even now, came upon a weakly defended village on a river system in Ireland, Wales or Francia, they would most certainly take, rather than buy or trade.

He strode right up to the dais where the Eorl of Linn sat upon a throne draped with wolf pelts. The eorl's name was Olaf Snorrisson and he had ruled here for almost a decade. His hands and neck were bedecked with jewellery, and he wore a circlet of gold upon his head. It mystified Niall how a man like this, who was perhaps only two generations removed from absolute barbarism, could have accumulated such wealth, much less kept it from the more powerful heathen warlords of the region. To still maintain a modicum of independence from not just the Ui Imair, but the Irish kingdoms that surrounded it, spoke to the political guile that Eorl Olaf wielded. Glundub could not recall a single time where the forces of Linn fought, that was not purely in defence of their town. There were three men at the foot of the dais, two to the right of the eorl and one to his left, whom Niall recognised. The rest of the occupants, guards and petitioners stood back from both Niall and the eorl and his chief men and waited for the inevitable heated exchange to begin. Niall hated pleasantries and spoke bluntly.

"Eorl Olaf, I am here for a single purpose: to demand your allegiance in the battle to come with the Ui Imair. I am the High King of Ireland and Northman or no, your land is on my island and only by my authority are you even allowed to exist. Many of my predecessors would have thrown you back into the sea. You defied me once successfully, that is true, but now I command the armies of Meath and Connaught as well as the north. If you don't submit to me here and now and agree to aid me in the destruction of Viking Dublin, I will send every warrior that I have under my command against your walls until Linn is subdued and you are crucified on the shoreline, as a warning to all of your kind."

Niall could feel the blistering anger all around him as proud Norse, Norse-Gael and allied mercenaries of the eorl took affront to Niall's threatening directness, but Glundub cared not a fig. He had come too far to be cowed by such as these and saw the eorl as having little option but to join him or die.

Before the eorl could answer, the man to the left of the dais addressed Niall. The man bowed low before speaking.

"Greetings, High King Niall Glundub, my name is Magnus Magnusson, but

I am known in many ports around Ireland as Longtooth. I am a simple trader and lead Eorl Olaf's mercantile fleet. I know that I speak for the Eorl when I say that we have no intention of standing in your way and would never oppose you militarily unless it was in our own defence. I also trade with the Ui Imair in Dublin admittedly, but we have very few ties to them apart from economic ones. Although we are all descended at least partially from Northmen, we pay no homage to Sihtric the Scourge. And yet, should you demand this of us and some of the Ui Imair survive, I fear it would go ill for our town. They would come down upon Linn and sack it, putting the entire population in chains. Surely in your wisdom, King Niall, you can see our predicament and why it would be my lord's preference to remain neutral in any conflict between the Ui Neill and the Ui Imair?"

Niall was unmoved. He disliked this man and the oozing words spilling out of his mouth. He looked every bit the rugged Norse trader but spoke like a Saxon courtier; effeminate and obsequious.

"Trader Magnus, I did not come here to negotiate or pander to the quandary that Linn finds itself in. I came to command. Let me repeat, and this time, the eorl can speak for himself; you will join us in two weeks' time at the yet to be decided appointed place with your warriors, or I will level this town."

The eorl stood up from his chair, veins bulging from his neck in fury and shouted at Niall, "YOU DARE COMMAND ME IN MY OWN HALL? WE ARE INDEPENDENT AND PAY FAIR TRIBUTE TO THE KINGS AROUND US, WHO ALL SUBSEQUENTLY PAY TRIBUTE TO YOU. YOU HAVE NO REASON TO THREATEN US WITH DESTRUCTION, NONE AT ALL."

Niall almost laughed at the outburst and interrupted the eorl immediately.

"Sit yourself down, eorl and comport yourself calmly. I will say and do anything to anybody at any time… for my country… and if it means rousting some greedy eorl from his town, so be it. Now consider your position and be quick about it. Are you with us or are you against us? There is no middle ground here for you to inhabit for once, Eorl Olaf."

The two men to the eorl's right were livid with rage. Niall recognised both on entering the hall. One was the eorl's nephew, a tall, broad, and blond brute of a man, while the other was the mercenary captain, Domnall mac Cossachtach of Munster.

Niall stared at the Irishman and smiled. "Domnall mac Cossachtach, mercenary commander, I seem to remember putting an arrow through the neck of your friend several years ago. Maybe it was you whom I should have slain instead as here you are defying and betraying your countrymen once more."

The Munsterman hawked and spat on the ground in front of Niall and rasped a response. "My whole family – father, uncles, brothers and cousins – were all slain at Beallach Mughna, by your Southern Ui Neill kin. It may not have been you that day, but men under your command now were present. The entire Ui Neill clan can hang for all I care. You, Donnchadh Donn, Conchobar mac Flann, Mael Mithig, you are all the same; warlords near as bad as the Ui Imair. If you are not fighting the Vikings, you are fighting each other. The eorl wants peace for his people and you will not give it to them. You claim to be their High King, but all you do is bring them death. Either we defy you and die in a siege, or we die in two months when Sihtric the Scourge comes for us if you lose, or his brothers come if you win. Where is the justice in that, High King?"

A chorus of ayes and yesses echoed around the hall at the mercenary captain's pronouncement. Niall Glundub had not been at Beallach Mughna but he knew that thousands of the best fighting men of Munster had been wiped out in a single day and this man's family was obviously among them. And despite this, and the prevailing sentiment in the hall, he still could not care less. The concerns of petty kingdoms and mercenary captains were beneath him. They would obey or they would hang.

"Eorl Olaf, silence your minions. I will repeat my demand one more time and give you a chance to answer. There will not be another. If I do not like what I hear I will march outside of these walls and invest you in a siege immediately. Should you lose your collective minds and attempt to take me captive here and now, my half-brother Conchobar and my son Hector have orders to reduce this place to ruins even at the cost of the loss of my life. And you see that is the difference between you and me, Eorl Olaf. I am High King and with that title comes responsibility. Regularly I must make grave decisions that can cost the lives of not just my warriors and my people, but my own life as well. And I am willing to do so in a heartbeat. The country of Ireland is worth infinitely more than one nobleman's life, even my own. While I rule, I will not allow my people to suffer under the tyranny of the Ui Imair. I have fought them over the last couple of years since they have returned, and I believe I have their measure.

"For three seasons I have instructed all my under-kings to begin to store supplies and train men for this day, and they have. The Northmen of Dublin are not as strong as they suppose. The brothers of the Scourge are locked in battle with the Scots and the Saxons and they cannot come to Dublin's aid. I deem the time ripe to march upon Dublin and do what my famous predecessor Flann of the Shannon failed to do, and put Dublin to the Sword. I look around this hall, Eorl Olaf, and I see many warriors both native and paid for. It is obvious to me that you also have built up your military strength as we have. You knew this day was coming as much as we have, you cannot fool me. So will you join us, Eorl Olaf, with as much strength as you can spare, or will you sit behind your walls and await a victor? I assure you, if it is us, and I believe it will be, you will not long survive the Ui Imair. I will leave now to my command tent far outside your walls and I will say no more. Decide!"

On his final words, Niall Glundub turned and strode from the hall, unconcerned with any threat of assault from the men assembled. At the threshold he snatched his weapons from the guard there, who stood in mute surprise, and he armed himself once more. The sunlight was beaming down upon the streets of Linn and Niall allowed the warmth to wash over him. It felt good to have a decisive plan in place. Every kingdom of the Leath Cuinn had provided warriors for his assault upon Dublin; Linn were the last holdouts.

He hated the subtleties of politics, preferring the honesty of the sword. Briefly the hope that the eorl would defy him crossed his mind, but he quickly dismissed the idea; to do that would be paramount to suicide and the eorl was clearly a shrewd man. Niall Glundub already had eight thousand warriors under his command outside his walls and more were arriving every day. As he purposefully marched toward the front gates on the south side of the river, he memorised the layout of the streets of Linn on the off chance that the worst-case scenario occurred. *If they defy us, this place is doomed,* he knew.

When he reached the gate a whole squadron of Norse-Gael warriors stared at him sullenly as he slipped through the wooden gates of the palisade, but it was about as threatening to Niall as the sunshine itself. *They will stand beside me on the field of battle on the fortnight or they would litter the ground as corpses by the end of the day.* In his command tent, several of his under-kings awaited him, all standing around a map drawn on calfskin across a makeshift table.

Glundub wasted no time, addressing his mighty brother, the King of Tara, Conchobar mac Flann: "Tell me, brother, what of our dispositions? Will we be ready to march on the fortnight?"

Conchobar, who was leaning on the map examining it carefully, stood up straight and met the gaze of his older brother, being almost of a height with him.

"Yes, brother. I have brought a thousand from Tara and another two thousand from Clan Colman and the Cenel Maine, under the command of Eiremon mac Cendetigh, the husband of my eldest daughter. Donnchadh Donn has arrived in the last couple of hours and is overseeing the setup of his camp with the Caille Follamain. His eldest son Domnall Donn, my nephew, is here. They have fifteen hundred men."

Glundub nodded at the young lad and grasped him forearm to forearm the warrior's way. Niall could see him swell with pride. This sort of awestruck deference was something that he was accustomed to when meeting green warriors on campaign, but it did not bother him as it was good to command such respect from the men under him.

Conchobar continued, "You yourself have brought your entire host of six thousand men south with only a few hundred left behind to defend the north against attack. The northerners are obviously under the command of both you and the men here in the tent."

Niall looked around; the son of the Black Fox from Argialla was there, Flaibhertach mac Domnall of the Cenel Connaille, Cernachan mac Tighernan and a powerful young man from the Ui Ruairc too. The Dal nAridi and the other Ulaidian tribes were under the overall command of Aed mac Eochuchan who stood proud beside the table.

"What of the men of Connaught and Brega, Conchobar?" Niall asked.

"Beollan mac Ciarmac and his nephew and heir designate, Ceallach mac Fogarteach, are leaving it to the last moment to join us, but when we approach the Liffey, they will come. Mael Mithig mac Flannacain awaits us in Kells with fifteen hundred men and scouts as far south as the River Liffey for us. The Connaught men are some two days out, Cathal mac Conchobar and his son Tadg lead a force of some twelve hundred mostly made up from the Ui Briuin clans of Sil Muiredaig and the Sil Cathail."

Conchobar stood up straighter and spoke excitedly. "Brother, when our host is fully assembled, we will have in the region of twelve thousand warriors under your command."

Niall exulted inside. This was arguably the greatest force of Irishmen ever assembled in one place for a single purpose. And yet he wanted more. "What of the word we have sent across the sea, brother? Is there help from foreign sources? What word from Leinster, Osraige and Munster? Will any come or will this army be purely composed of us from the Leath Cuinn, the northern half of Ireland?"

At these questions, Conchobar's confidence deflated a little.

"We sent messages to Constantine our cousin, but he replied by letter saying that he has recently suffered terrible losses at the hands of the Ui Imair in Northumbria last year. All he can do is think of us in his prayers. He says that should the battle go ill, to send as many of the noble children of the Ui Neill to him as his wards to protect them from heathen retribution. He has some good news though, both Oitir Iarla the Black One and the bastard of Norway, Gragabai, were both slain in battle against Constantine's young nephew Mael Colum."

Murmurs of satisfaction broke out amongst the kings present at that news, but a glance from Conchobar silenced them.

"Continue, brother," said Niall.

"There is civil war in Wales among the surviving sons and grandsons of Rhodri the Great. The old king, Hywel nDa, looks the likely victor, but no help will come from that quarter. Aethelfled of Mercia was slain, allegedly by a Viking warband on Watling Street, and her brother is busy subduing Mercia to annex it on her demise. He intends to unite the crowns upon his own head and has taken Aethelfled's daughter captive. The Munster men and Osraigans have been ravaged by the Northmen and are reduced to minor skirmishes and Guerrilla warfare. They have no help to offer. The most grievous blow to our hopes in the Leath Mogha is that some of the Ui Imair nobility have married some of the princesses of Leinster and vice versa. It is likely when we attack Dublin, we will face Irishmen on the field of battle as well as the Northmen."

That sent a shocked ripple amongst the men in the tent. Niall had suspected as much, that the Ui Imair would have subdued the lands around Dublin and their other longforts and would have demanded not just tribute, but warriors as well. Irishmen who likely would have little love for the Ui Neill either.

To distract the men more than anything from the fact that they would face Irishmen in the field, he asked his brother about the enemy.

"What do we know of the Ui Imair and what they can likely field, Conchobar?"

The King of Tara and Clan Colman scratched his chin and shrugged before answering. "Well, I estimate their strength at any one time at between three thousand warriors and seven thousand. At this time of the year, I hope that many longboats will be at sea and if we hit them hard and fast, they will be of no use. They have the allegiance of roughly twenty to thirty warbands that operate around the Irish Sea, Britain and Francia, but they are not a cohesive force of men and are never settled at one port for long. Ragnall Ivarsson's Kingdom of Northumbria is in constant turmoil and the fighting is endless there, my bishops tell me. I must believe that this is a constant drain on his men and resources. He will not be able to provide much help to his brother when we come. Sihtric the Scourge himself will lead the Ui Imair. His four main commanders based here in Ireland are firstly, Brunbolg Headtaker who is almost seventy-five and in his dotage, although admittedly still deadly. The second is a woman who is deep in his councils, by the name of Olga. They call her the Valkyrie and she has as many women under her command as men, with many of them rumoured to sharpen their teeth and eat the flesh of the vanquished."

Niall shuddered in disgust at her description but allowed his brother to continue.

"The young son of Godfrith Ivarsson, despite being only fourteen years of age, is the third. He is gathering repute and has been trusted with command on several raids into Brega. And the final man of renown that we know of, who will be fighting at their side is the warlord Amlaib the Sinner. He leads a contingent of berserkers from Limerick, on behalf of his father. As for the rest, who knows. At any one time there could be warriors from Norway, Francia, Frisia, Denmark or the Rus but there is no way to know, and it is up to God to decide if we are fortunate or not."

Glundub nodded, his jaw clenched in determination. 'It doesn't matter, whatever they have, it won't be enough. Dublin, we know, is defended well from the north. And because of that I have decided upon our plan of action. We will cross the Liffey River at Islandbridge and hit them from the rear where their walls are lower and more difficult to defend. If we break into the city in any strength, the day is won. Domnall mac Donnchadh, you with some of your father's men and the Connaught men when they arrive, will invest the northern wall of the city and throw the occasional feint at them. That way, they will have to man the walls properly on the northern side and even if they discover us, by the time we cross the river it will be too late."

At that moment, a horn could be discerned from the babble of the warriors camped around the tent. In moments one of the guards let through a large man, Norse-Gael, helmed and fierce. Niall recognised him; it was Sven the nephew of the Eorl of Linn.

"What say you, Sven?" asked Niall. "What says the Eorl of Linn?"

The Norse-Gael warrior removed his helmet and placed it under his arm, staring at Glundub and Conchobar both. "We fight for you, Niall Glundub."

"We fight."

CHAPTER 2

THE STORM OVER DUBLIN
(919 AD)

Seagulls floated on the breeze and the salt sea air of the Liffey estuary washed over Sihtric Ivarsson. Great Drummonds, galleys, broad fat-bellied trading vessels and of course Viking longships, were clustered on the docks like flies on a carcass. The city was bustling, and trade was thriving. He always made it his business to walk around the city at around midday, every day, to allow the people to see him. His unmistakable spiked helmet was ever strapped at his waist, letting the people know who it was that walked among them, but at six feet four and two hundred and fifty pounds, and being possessed of the heirloom stripe of white hair upon his black-haired head, he could not really be mistaken for anybody except Ui Imair nobility. He carried his infamous scourge-flail weapon on his back alongside his shield. At his hip, he carried a Francian sword and of course, his Saracen sword, the twin of which his brother Godfrith carried by his side in Northumbria. He had knives and throwing axes strapped to various parts of his anatomy, a veritable arsenal of human death.

On the streets there were Danes, Norse, Norse-Gaels of varying heritage, Irish, Welsh, Bretons, Francians and even the occasional Arab, Berber or black man, the *Fir Gorm* of the Aifric, amongst the throng. Anything that was for sale in the whole of humanity, Sihtric surmised, could be purchased in some far-flung corner of Dublin. Since they had retaken the city in 917, they had fortified it and begun building up the infrastructure. Two bridges now spanned the Liffey further up its course, one wide enough even for two carts to be drawn across simultaneously. They even built several smaller bridges further up the river outside the city walls to help all the lands under their control, both economically and militarily, in their ever-expanding kingdom.

He stopped briefly at the stall of a Norse-Gael man named Gotrek that sold ale and purchased a beverage, taking time to take in the sights and sounds of the city and listening in to several conversations taking place around him. Some men leaning against the left edge of the stall were angrily discussing the recent submission by the Eorl of Bedford to Edward the Elder and how the Saxon king had placed a tariff upon all goods coming into the town; all of them were out of pocket because of it. On a small upright table that Gotrek had set up out on front of his business, several Vikings were excitedly talking about the price of slaves rising ever higher as the Fatimids and Abbasids lost thousands of soldiers in their wars against each other. Representatives of these two caliphates could be found in every Viking port from Kiev to Limerick looking for likely young lads to make eunuch slave soldiers out of, and these Vikings looked to Sihtric like they would be most pleased to meet demand with supply.

A fascinating conversation was breaking out close by between several Danes about a Mercian ealdormen looking to hire mercenaries to rebel against Wessex and Sihtric was about to eavesdrop when he felt someone grab his arm. It was his young nephew Albann Godfrithsson. The young lad was long and thin but at thirteen years of age he was already showing promise with axe and sword.

"Uncle, there is a man at your hall who wishes to speak to you urgently and he insisted that it cannot wait. The Valkyrie sent me to find you."

Sihtric frowned but left his ale and walked swiftly down toward the nearest of the two bridges to get to the south side of the city with his nephew. With his long strides, he reached the main hall of Dublin in minutes. His guards moved from his path at the entrance to his hall, showing obeisance. He ordered one of them to check on his wife Grainne ingen Muiredach, the sister of the King of Leinster, and their young son Amlaib Cuaran, after a shiver of apprehensive precognition raced down his spine. *The news I am going to hear will be bad,* he thought.

There was no fire lit in the hearth due to the warm autumn weather, but a single man stood by it, in the centre of the hall none the less. Sihtric approached him.

"Who are you and what do you wish to tell me?"

The man was tall and lean and dark of skin, yet clearly Irish. He had calloused hands and a litany of scars that spoke of a history of violence. He was weather-beaten and his leather clothes were shabby, but his weapons gleamed in the daylight and were maintained in exquisite condition. *He is a man who can handle himself,* thought Sihtric.

"Greetings, Eorl Sihtric. My name is Domnall mac Cossachtach and I bring grave tidings involving Niall Glundub mac Aed Findliath. The Ui Neill are coming in force. I can tell you where and when they will strike but it will cost you a bag of silver for me to divulge details as it were. Me and my men have taken a great risk coming to Dublin like this and we expect recompense."

Sihtric waved his hand impatiently. "Yes, yes, now tell me where and when they are coming, Domnall, and tell me why you have come to me with this information. Are you allied to the King of Leinster, or do you care for peace in the region like one of your Christian saints?"

The man snorted in derision at that.

"I sell my sword for a living, Eorl Sihtric, ever since the Ui Neill came down upon the Munster army that I fought in in 908 and destroyed it. My lads are some of the last survivors of that battle, the cream of Munster. We escaped on some ships down the river with some of your Viking friends and ever since, I have been working in Linn for pay, for the eorl there."

Sihtric deemed it wise not to mention the fact that he himself had fought on behalf of the Ui Neill that day.

"I hate the Ui Neill and what they have done to this country. I do not particularly like you lot, the Ui Imair, either, or any heathens really, but at least your people are honest. I do not care who wins this fight to come and my lads will take no part. We can still profit from it though, through you."

At that moment, the Valkyrie entered the hall and beside her strode the massive form of the Headtaker, Brunbolg the mighty. Each tapped their chest in respect to Sihtric and then turned to face the Irish mercenary in a semi-circle with the Dublin eorl.

"Say on, Domnall mac Cossachtach, and you will have your bag of silver," said Sihtric.

The Irishman shrugged his shoulders and laid out the entire story to the three Viking leaders. He spoke of Niall Glundub preparing for this assault for more than a year, waiting for an opportune time to strike. He spoke of how the High King threatened his now former employer, Eorl Olaf, with destruction if he did not fight beside the Ui Neill. He talked at length tactically of Niall Glundub's intention to march in the coming week and how he would send a convincing feint toward the northside of Dublin, but in secret, send the bulk of his army across the river at Islandbridge, miles to the west, and hit the city from the south. He angrily relayed what had occurred when he had argued against helping the Ui Neill against Dublin with Eorl Olaf and how he suggested that they should stay behind the walls of Linn to await the outcome and throw the Ui Neill back if they attacked; but that the eorl had overruled him on the advice of his nephew Sven Ironfist, and his key man, Magnus Magnusson the Longtooth. He and his hundred warriors had deserted that very night and absconded by boat, heading down the coast to Dublin.

When he finished, it was the Headtaker who asked the most pertinent questions of all: "Which kingdoms have allied themselves to the High King? Do we face the Northern Ui Neill, the Argiallans and maybe the Ulaid? Who do we face, little Irishman?"

The man answered his question very simply: "Every king from the Leath Cuinn."

Sihtric felt dizzy and the Valkyrie looked even paler than she usually did, her forked tongue nervously licking the tips of her pointed teeth. The Headtaker had not seemed to grasp the enormity of the horde that faced them. "And how many is that, little Irishman?".

Domnall cleared his throat. "Between ten and fourteen thousand fighting men, lord." The Headtaker's eyes went wide.

"Oh," is all the ancient and giant Viking could utter.

Sihtric sent the man on his way with his promised bag of silver. He was well within his rights to throw the man in a stockade or sell him to the nearest Ghanaian, but he did not want it said that the Ui Imair were not generous with those who shared pertinent information. To harm this man would send out the message to any future agents and purveyors of good intelligence that the Ui Imair were not to be trusted. In truth, Sihtric felt as if the Gods had smiled upon them really; at least now they had a little time to prepare. He had suspected for years that it would be a matter of when, not if, Niall Glundub would march upon Dublin. The very first actions that Sihtric undertook were to send scouts into the land to ascertain the veracity of the mercenary's statement, while simultaneously summoning his major captains and generals to a *thing* to discuss what to do next.

When his two dozen or so senior men were gathered, he laid it bare, what faced them: "My eorls, chieftains and captains, news has reached us of a dreadful threat that approaches." The room quieted on hearing his words.

"Niall Glundub the High King of the Irish has summoned his banners and within the week will march upon Dublin. He intends to throw a feint to the north and attempt to deceive is into putting our best fighters on those northern palisades, when really he will bring most of his army to the south of Dublin over the river. He will cross at Islandbridge and march east and attack the city from the rear."

Shouts and jeers broke out equally amongst the leadership present before a warning grumble from the Headtaker and a sinister hiss from the Valkyrie, quieted them.

Sihtric's nephew Olaf asked a question: "Which of the Irish kings lead them apart from Glundub himself and how many men do they have?"

Sihtric answered them honestly. "All of the northern kings, all of the kings of Meath and Connaught and even our kin from Linn will take the field against us."

The room went deathly quiet, so much so that Sihtric swore that he could hear a mouse scuttling in the corner of the hall.

"They will have somewhere between ten and fourteen thousand men, we estimate."

Sihtric had been present in dozens of halls were battleplans were discussed and orders given on the eve of a campaign or fight, and usually they were met with boisterous shouting and jovial boasts, but this pronouncement was met with a silence that froze his soul. None of his captains moved and none spoke. Sihtric's men knew what this host of Irishmen meant, and they were smart enough to grasp what this single battle would mean if they lost, the end of Viking Dublin and perhaps their way of life upon the island of Ireland. Many of them had faced Niall Glundub and his brother Conchobar before and there was a healthy respect in the hall for their prowess. The Valkyrie's own father had been slain thirty years or more ago in single combat by Niall Glundub and Sihtric's own father had been sent to Valhalla by the Irish warlord as well. He spoke again, not just to ease the tension, but to lay out the plan that he, the Headtaker and the Valkyrie had decided upon.

"This is what we are going to do. We have already sent out scouts as far as north Meath to ascertain the whereabouts of this host. There is a slight chance that the information we have received is spurious, but I think not. I have spoken to our seer and the runes portend violence. Glundub is coming with all his strength. I will send out ships to search for allies as we have a week or more before the Irish arrive. We may be in luck, Loki may be with us and we may be able to entice many warbands to our cause, but the trickster god may also abandon us, and we may have to face the Irish by ourselves. Ragnall my brother has no strength to spare although I may be able to gather perhaps five hundred warriors from Cumbria or Northumbria in time, but I deem that unlikely. We will send word to our Irish client kings in Leinster and Munster and to Limerick, Waterford, Wexford, Cork and Longford, for reinforcement. We have almost four thousand men in Dublin amongst our warbands. And not just any four thousand, but the fighting pride of the Viking people of the Irish Sea!"

He raised his voice on the last few words looking to kindle hope in his captains, and he could see it had worked. A couple rolled their necks around their shoulders, emitting audible pops, as if readying themselves for a fight right now. Others nodded solemnly at each other in agreement.

Sihtric continued, "We will leave just a token force of shieldmaidens and greybeards on the northern palisades to bluff the Irish into thinking we have taken the bait. Who knows, they may attack there too. My nephew Albann Godfrithsson will take command of this northern defence, his first as a Viking captain."

Shouts of encouragement were hurled in his direction and many a grizzled veteran clapped him on his thin shoulders and grasped him in great bearhugs. *Another Ui Imair prince takes the field,* Sihtric thought proudly.

"The main bulk of Glundub's forces are going to cross the river at Islandbridge and it is here that we will meet them. The water is not that deep at this point and there are two small islands on this part of the river along with a simple wooden bridge. The land either side has two hills on both sides of the river that act as a natural corridor for people and animals to cross the Liffey. I have a certain plan in mind but in general we are going to allow a portion of this host to cross the river, then cut them apart through the middle, upon the water. We will then surround both halves of Glundub's army, trapping them in with their backs against the river and fighting up hill. Our archers will rain hell upon them from the higher ground and we will form shield walls on both north and south. With no room to manoeuver, we hope their numbers will mean nothing and we will butcher them all."

A confident buzz grew in volume on the announcement of Sihtric's plan. It was simply laid out and he could sense that all in the hall understood it. The tangible confidence growing that this could be done was unmistakable, the belief rising exponentially amongst his captains. *This is a fight that they believe they can win,* Sihtric exulted.

He thought then that it would be wise to temper their optimism with some reality. "Should we fail, we will have to evacuate as many people from the city as possible. Our fleet of longboat's usefulness is limited in this engagement, so we will use them here in Dublin to protect the people. Make no mistake, if Glundub takes the city, he himself as a Drengr may show mercy in certain quarters, but he has savage tribesmen in his host too such as the Ulaid and the Caille Follamain, who will not hesitate to rape and murder anybody they find. Should our shield wall be breached at Islandbridge, our surviving warriors are to retreat to Wexford and in that dreadful scenario we will await Ragnall's command, but put that thought out of your mind. Send word out to the city of what approaches. Speak with no fear. Tell the people to be calm but to be prepared. We are Viking, and if this is to be our end, we will make it such an end, that the Gods will have no choice but to welcome us to Valhalla with open arms. WE FIGHT FOR ODIN; WE FIGHT FOR DUBLIN AND THE UI IMAIR!!!"

He roared the final war cry and raised his sword to the ceiling and his warlords bellowed their own war cries in response. They were ready.

Sihtric elected to bring word out to the city alongside the other leaders in person. He had learned at the side of the great Flann Sinna on the nuances of leadership, and he felt it was important to show that despite the pending existential threat to their entire way of life, he was unfazed and not burdened with fear and by extension the people should be confident also. The people would draw belief directly from their leader. *It is what Flann Sinna would have done*, Sihtric knew innately. He deliberately stopped to talk to all and sundry who wished to speak with him. He assuaged their fears as best he could and outlined the failsafe plans in case of disaster in a simple and calm manner. Young warriors trained with wooden swords, shields and axes on the street and wherever he found them he stopped and praised their skill and strength and gave advice.

Many young warriors would get their first taste of pitched battle at Islandbridge and Sihtric could sense that each was trying to show outwardly no sign of nerves or fear; but Sihtric knew their hearts. He had once been where they were, albeit fighting for an Irish king. Several asked him directly on how best to face a warrior with a long reach and who fought with two swords simultaneously, the same style as Niall Glundub. No doubt word of the Irish king's prowess had reached every young warrior in Dublin and each of these young Norse-Gael Vikings dreamed that most likely, at some point in the battle to come, it would be they who would face the formidable Irish king and slay him. Sihtric did not bother to try and diminish their excitement or describe the unlikelihood of encountering one individual amidst twelve thousand.

He nodded his head and advised them the best methods in his view, to beat a man like Niall Glundub mac Aed Findliath. The thought of single combat worried him though with Glundub. The Irish High King had earned the name Drengr as a young man and that term carried weight in the Viking world. It had many meanings in the different dialects of the various Scandinavian kingdoms, but it usually meant honoured enemy or great opponent. If Glundub demanded single combat against Sihtric or any of their warlords, they would have to answer, one by one; the Gods would demand it. Reputation was everything in the Viking world and Glundub's reputation was all-encompassing. The man who took down the High King would be remembered forever. So prized would his head be, that Sihtric half suspected that his own captains and champions would fight each other to the death, just to be the one to face Glundub and defeat him. It meant immortality.

After a couple of hours of calmly briefing his people, Sihtric found himself down beside the docks and the slave pens on the south side of the river, enjoying the sounds of the city. It gladdened him that his people had accepted the news of an impending army of enraged Irishmen with nonchalant ease and had gone about their business regardless. They believed in Sihtric and his captains and despite the doubts that Sihtric harboured, he felt his own confidence growing by the minute as well. A shout broke him from his thoughts, and he looked toward the sea; it was his nephew Albann once more. The boy was out of breath from sprinting, but he spat out his news without pause.

"Uncle, there is a fleet of ships some thirty strong anchored offshore to the south. Their lead dragonboat is approaching by itself."

Curiously Sihtric questioned Albann on his report.

"What colour are the sails, Albann? Are there runes or motifs upon them to be marked and identified?"

The lad nodded. "It is a black sail with a great red weapon emblazoned upon it."

A slow smile of recognition danced its way across Sihtric's face. He knew exactly who had come to Dublin and at such an opportune time. *The Gods must have had a hand in this. Thirty ships mean almost twelve hundred Viking warriors or more.* Sihtric gripped young Albann by the shoulders.

"Run, lad, and fetch your brother Olaf, Ceanncearach of Limerick, the Valkyrie and the Headtaker. Tell them to come to the docks immediately to greet a new arrival."

Sihtric looked back out to sea and there sure enough in the distance, visible in the evening's last light, was a black sail standing on an enormous dragonboat. There was a red weapon upon the black background as his nephew had described, but it was not just any weapon, it was specifically a red axe. With a grin on his face Sihtric turned to his nephew with one last command.

"Tell them all that my uncle, Erik Haraldsson, is here."

His nephew's eyes widened at the news, but he obediently sprinted away about his business. Sihtric peered at the sails once more as they drew ever closer to the port. *With the Bloodaxe on our side, victory is not just possible, it is well-nigh assured.*

CHAPTER 3

THE BLOOD IN THE WATER (MORNING OF 14TH SEPTEMBER, 919 AD)

The weather was unseasonably warm for an Irish September, yet Niall Glundub shivered in the morning breeze. Despite having more than ten thousand men marching at his back, and another two thousand marching three miles east to the northern barricades of Dublin, the land seemed disturbingly quiet. He led his warriors as he had all his life, at the head of his vanguard, the tip of the spear. Niall Glundub mac Aed Findliath would never send men where he dared not go himself. That was the only way he knew, into the fire first and the rest would follow; and the men loved him for it. He could feel the eyes of thousands of young green boys and grizzled veterans alike upon his back. He could hear the hushed whispers, even above the thunder of the marching footfalls and the rumble of the bodhran drums.

"There is a king I could follow," one man said, and another he heard saying, *"We will fight beside the High King today."*

The army marched almost a hundred abreast and a hundred deep with each under-king marching within his own faction. Glundub was only joined at the front by one man, his captain of the guard: Tadg mac Ruaidhri. The big man held aloft a massive standard that Niall had commanded the women of Aileach to prepare. It did not show the colours and insignias of any of the Ui Neill clans, not even his own. It was emerald green and sea blue and, in the centre, sat a golden harp and above it the Christian cross. The message was clear: this battle was not like any typical battle or territorial skirmish. This battle was for control of all Ireland against a heathen foe. All Irishmen excluding any traitors amidst the Northmen, today, had set aside their petty differences temporarily to march as one, to free their country forever from Viking oppression.

The land around the very south of Meath and the border of the territory controlled by Viking Dublin directly, was heavily forested. There was one main arterial route through the trees that was wide enough for a body of men to traverse unhindered toward the river, and that was the way Niall Glundub had chosen to march. They were committed now and the time for subterfuge and intrigue was nigh over. Niall could not care less if the Scourge and his warriors knew they were coming at this point as it was too late to turn back; the men of the Leath Cuinn were here. Some two miles from the fording point at Islandbridge, one of Niall's scouts surprisingly came galloping into view from the muddy thoroughfare through the forest. Niall raised his hand and Tadg mac Ruaidhri blew one blast of his horn for the host to come to a halt. The scout rode up, a young man from Cill Mheasain by the name of Brian Breathnach, and spoke to Niall directly: "King Niall, there is smoke on both sides of the river at Islandbridge and it obscures the way. A haze has descended. I also saw furtive movements in the trees. I think we are undone, lord; I think at least some of the Northmen know we are coming."

Glundub paused for a second and weighed up his options. His son Hector and brother-in-law Donnchadh Donn emerged from the ranks toward him, to see what was going on.

"What is happening, Father?" asked Hector. "Why have you called a halt to the march?"

Niall peered into the pregnant grey skies, and despite the warm weather he could feel that there was a storm coming.

"It appears the element of surprise is either partially or fully lost, my son.

The scout has reported movement on both sides of the river and reports heavy smoke obscuring the Liffey and the hills and forest around Islandbridge."

Donnchadh Donn harrumphed.

"We have thousands of men, Glundub. Even if they do wish to meet us on the river, we will break through their shield wall and destroy them. They cannot hold us no matter what ambush they prepare, surely."

Niall frowned at the lack of title the King of the Caille Follomain used when addressing him, highlighting the temporary nature of the alliance. *His hatred of Dublin outweighs his suspicion of me,* Niall thought, but he couldn't deny that he had a point. *How many men could the Ui Imair possibly field?* he wondered. After a moment Niall made up his mind.

"Tell the men, we press on through the smoke, trees, water and their shield wall if need be. If they set us an ambush, we will break through it."

Tadg mac Ruaidhri blew two blasts from his horn and the army was on the march once more through the trees.

The land sloped gently and then sharply down toward the river. The clearing through the forest there was two hundred yards wide, and a muddy track dissected the trees to the east and west. Niall could see the wooden crossing in the distance. It was composed of two bridges that linked a fifty-feet wide island in the middle of the river with both banks, so men would traverse one bridge, cross the little island, and then cross the other bridge to the southern shore of the Liffey. There was another smaller island, that was perhaps half the size of the larger island, about seventy feet further west along the course of the river, but to get to that one the water would have to be waded through and in some parts of this broad expanse of the river it reached depths of twelve to fifteen feet deep; enough to drown a man in heavy armour or one who could not swim. The dense and looming oak and ash trees that dominated the land here held an eerie menace and Niall could feel eyes upon him. *We are being watched.* The fires his scout had reported were visible now everywhere on both sides of the river, obviously deliberately lit, and a thick smoke hazily enveloped the army's path and across the land. When they reached the river, Niall looked up and down its course, there was no sign of ships, but the river meandered a few hundred feet out of sight in both directions. *There could be a Viking fleet hidden past the bends and I would never even see it coming.* The bridge was a simple one, made of thin timbers but could fit six men abreast, Niall estimated.

With a raised hand, Niall signalled for the bodhrans to begin beating and the percussive sound of the ancient Irish war drums echoed across the river. With one last look into the pregnant grey skies, Niall Glundub crossed the Liffey, the first to set foot on the bridge. His men followed six at a time. Niall and his standard bearer waited on the island in the middle and watched their forces go by. Conchobar mac Flann was in the vanguard as was Flaibhertach mac Domnall, the Ui Neill under-king. Instructions had been given hours before to the commanders of the army, that on crossing the narrow bridge, the men were to form up into a cohesive formation once more on the other side of the Liffey and Niall could see his younger brother, Conchobar the King of Meath, was following the plan closely on the flat earth between the two forested and smoke-ridden hills.

In ten minutes almost four thousand men had crossed in a cohesive manner, but something felt off to Niall. He did not know if it was a change in the shadows beneath the trees or perhaps a slight movement in his peripheral vision. The first raindrops of the threatened storm started to patter off his shield then, and a flash of lightning lit up the gloom momentarily. It was closely followed by the rumble of its accompanying thunder. One piercing, almost endless note blown from a single horn, echoing across the trees, hills and river, was met with the howls of thousands of wolves, reverberating through the air. Some shouts for order began to emerge from amidst Niall's army. The entire host stopped and began searching for the source of the howls, but none could discern exactly from which direction they came. Niall knew why: *It is from all directions. We are surrounded.*

Another flash of lightning hit the north side of the river and finally the Vikings of Dublin made their presence felt. At the top of the upward sloping ground on front of the vanguard of Niall's army, hundreds if not thousands of Viking warriors emerged from the gloom and formed a shield wall, tightly packed and menacing. The smoke-filled pall made it hard to gauge their numbers accurately but the fact that there was a disturbing amount of them was dismaying to say the least. Tadg mac Ruaidhri tapped Niall's shoulder and pointed back the way they had come and there too at the top of the broad way through the trees to the north, another force of Vikings had formed a second shield wall behind Niall's army, of even greater size and threat. Niall scanned the summit of the four hills surrounding Islandbridge and there, hundreds of Vikings stood ready. Niall was concerned to see that most of them carried bows, their plan obvious and apparent. Niall started bellowing orders immediately, as did the commanders of the army, roaring at the enormous body of Irish fighters to form up into cohesive formation against the multiple threats they faced. They were surrounded and to some extent cut off, but Niall's hope was yet undimmed as they had a much larger force than the Northmen still.

Quickly he summoned a young lad to his side. "Boy, you need to work your way through the trees back the way we have come. Stay low and out of sight and go fast. Get to the camp of Cathal mac Conchobar three miles to the east and tell him he must come immediately. Gather three of your friends with the same message to ensure that word gets through and make sure to take different routes to avoid capture. In two hours, I want the Connaught men and the other half of the Caille Follomain hitting the Vikings in the rear. Do you understand what I have told you, boy?"

The boy's eyes were wide with nervousness, but he nodded furiously and blurted a "Yes, my lord," before scampering back over the bridge to the north side of the river.

The Vikings were not advancing; they stood in their shield walls, both north and south, and Niall could hear their massed whispered prayers to their heathen Gods. The Irish army on both sides of the river braced in two massive shield walls of their own, with the warriors in the middle placing their shields upon their heads, bracing for the inevitable deluge of arrows yet to come. Niall had no real control of the battle from his vantage point upon the river and he knew that he had to rely on his under-kings and regional commanders to decide the direction of the fighting to come. His influence would be minimal, he was just one man after all. He was glad to see that each king had elected to wait and see what the Vikings intended, instead of just charging maniacally into a set force with the higher ground. But all the commanders of his army were veterans to a man, and it was clear that for now the Vikings had the ground and by extension the upper hand. One way or the other, many Irishmen would die this day; there was no escaping that.

The rain was now pouring down in the warmth, even putting out some of the fires lit amongst the trees, but the smoke kept billowing across the river none the less. A distant swoosh from the water drew Niall's gaze in the direction of Dublin. There were two Viking longboats of significant size bearing down upon them, some two hundred feet away. Momentarily puzzled, all Niall could do was stare at the two ships until it dawned on him what was happening. Frantically he began roaring at the warriors that still packed the bridge.

"CLEAR THE WAY! CLEAR THE WAY!"

It dawned on the warriors as well on what was about to occur and they began to push and shove and jostle their way to either the island, or both banks of the river; but many were blocked by the bodies in front and behind them. As the longboats approached, Niall could see that their prows were in fact massive rams and dozens of men were rowing furiously, building up a tremendous amount of speed. Both boats were packed with berserkers and Niall feared the worst. Simultaneously both ships smashed the bridge to kindling on both sides of the island, isolating Niall and around fifty warriors on the island, but most importantly they had successfully cut one half of his army away from the other. The longboats powered through the remains of the bridge and several dozen Irish warriors were flung into the water, who were too slow to get out of the way. As the longships passed by, they used torches to skilfully set fire to the remains of the wooden bridge to further destroy the structure and drive the Irishmen into the backs of their comrades who stood in formation upon the land.

Niall could sense an air of panic beginning to fester within his force. Once more an enormous flash of lightning lit the sky and both armies held their breath one last time before the plunge. The thunder erupted seconds later and then all hell was unleashed. Both Viking armies methodically marched down upon the Irish and the Irish charged uphill to meet them. Arrows rained down from the four hills into the rear ranks of the Irishmen, but Niall's stranded group of fifty warriors were out of range and all he could do was watch on in isolated frustration as two separate conflicts occurred on either side of the river. The battle of Islandbridge had begun in earnest, the great fight of the age for control of Ireland was here.

The slaughter was biblical on both sides of the river and Niall desperately tried to make up his mind where and how he should go to make his presence felt. Hundreds died in the first minutes of the violence. He commanded all his men to divest themselves of armour if they had any and ready themselves to either swim to either shore or jump toward the remnants of the bridge and pull themselves toward the shoreline to reinforce either army. An abrupt shout erupted from the men at his back on the island at that moment. When Niall turned, he saw what had caused such alarm in his men. Both longboats had begun to reverse after smashing both sides of the bridge to pieces and were pulling up to the island. Each disgorged dozens of Viking warriors on land. One berserker stood head and shoulders above the rest. He wore his hair in a great crimson crest, standing tall like a giant rooster, and he wielded a colossal stone-headed axe in two meaty hands.

Niall recognised him at once; he had faced him before after all on the plains before Dunnottar in Scotland; Erik Haraldsson the Bloodaxe had come to Ireland. Niall Glundub stepped on front of the Irish warriors by his side to meet the threat head on and show his men that he was unafraid, his two swords whistling through the air with intent. The giant Norse barbarian beckoned his forty or so men to fan out and step aside to allow him to lead. He uttered something at Glundub in guttural Norse, but Niall could not comprehend its meaning. Seeing that Niall did not understand, in broken Gaelic the colossal berserker roared, "DRENGR, GLUNDUB. COME. DIE NOW."

And then the Northmen charged toward the fifty or so Irishmen packed on the small island, a microcosm of the enormous battles occurring either side of the river. Niall had no more time to think about the fights north or south of him – only the fight right here, right now, mattered. The Bloodaxe went straight for Niall. He led with an unusual trust with the butt of his axe which was capped with an iron spike and some hooks. When Niall parried it, the huge Norse berserker flipped his axe forward, turning it into an overhead blow that furiously descended at Niall's head. Glundub parried that blow too, but the Bloodaxe was already twirling his axe in an arc, swinging a massive lateral blow toward Niall's left-hand side. Niall had to keep retreating in the face of the Bloodaxe's ferocity. One attack led into another and another.

Moments into the fight Niall knew how he would slay this beast, by allowing him to spend his energy in the initial flurries and he would then cut the Norse prince down as he tired. On the occasion that Glundub parried with something significant and bought time to counter, his sword glanced off the thick chainmail the Viking prince wore on his person. Eventually a scrum of bodies got in the way of the two enemies and the wider battle broke them apart. Immediately Niall decapitated a crazed berserker who looked to do the same to him and so the small battle went on, but Niall could not reach the Bloodaxe. In minutes it was over. The Vikings, with the Bloodaxe among them, had fled the confrontation after losing around twenty of their number. Niall and his men had defeated them and driven them off for a similar loss. The fleeing Northmen quickly pushed their longboats out into the water, much depopulated with warriors, and looked to row back west away from the rear of the trapped Irish armies. Their retreat gave Niall time to assess the situation once more. And what he witnessed was terrifying to behold.

There were piles of slain Irishmen everywhere. With nowhere to retreat to, barring they chance the river, the half of the army on the north of the River Liffey were effectively trapped. They were fighting uphill against a brutally efficient and organised Viking shield wall and the rain of arrows from the hill had not yet relented. Death rained upon them, as when the Viking archers aimed at the centre of the Irish formation, it was like shooting fish in a barrel. They could not miss. The Norse and Norse-Gael archers on both sides of the water were taking a dreadful toll upon the Irish forces. Many men from both conflicts were running into the river to escape the wrath of the warriors of Dublin; some were drowning, and more were being picked off from the hills. A familiar voice reached Niall from the north side of the river upon the edge of the destroyed section of the bridge there – it was Niall's son Hector. He looked bloodied and bedraggled but determined still.

"Father," he shouted to Niall across the broken section of the bridge to the island, "we are in disarray. Your brother Conchobar has been slain and the son of the Black Fox has been run through by the Headtaker. We must go now; we need to buy time to retreat. What say you, Father?"

Niall turned around and tried to take a panoramic all-encompassing view of the entire battlefield, as if some clear insight would occur to him, some hint of a strategy which he could use to free his men from the horrendous slaughter being inflicted upon them. There was no doubt in his mind that they were defeated. The Scourge had won this battle, but how bad a defeat was it going to be? How many Irish lives could be saved?

"Hector, begin an orderly retreat across the river. A rearguard must be left behind on the bank to stop pursuit of our men. Get as many of our men to try and cross the river or leap from the furthest part of the destroyed bridge into the water and look for safety. I have sent word to the Connaught men and the son of Donnchadh Donn to relieve our forces on the north of the river. When they arrive, we will break the trap and we will be free to retreat. We cannot defeat the Vikings on the south side of the river, Hector."

His son answered with a shouted question in the cacophony of battle: "What will we do to draw Sihtric away from our retreating warriors? What can we do to get their attention while our men chance the river to escape? What is your plan, Father?"

Glundub peered up into the angry sky and breathed deep, shutting the terrible din of battle out of his mind. He cleared his thoughts of the smoke, the fire, the death of thousands of his men and clarity came along with resolve. His choices quickly narrowed from many, to a few, to one. Solemnly he gave command to his surviving warriors to fight beside his son. He asked for three spears from his warriors and strapped his other weapons to his body. He walked toward the bridge at the edge of the island and spoke to his son, man to man, in a steady voice.

"Hector, the north is yours. With Conchobar slain, tell Donnchadh Donn he will get his wish; he will take the High Kingship and protect Ireland as long as he can. If he is slain, his eldest son will take that honour, or whomever the Southern Ui Neill sees fit. I will challenge the leaders of the Northmen to single combat on the smaller of the two islands in the river for all to see. I will plant our standard. My name carries weight in their world, they will have no choice but to face me or risk the displeasure of their heathen demonic gods. There will be a slackening of the Norse-Gael's attack as none will want to miss my end if I know my enemies' hearts. And I do, Hector, after almost thirty-five years of fighting them. I know my enemies."

Hector was visibly upset. "Father, there must be another way? You should not have to sacrifice yourself like this? There must be another way?"

Glundub sadly shook his head with a smile breaking slowly across his face.

"He who presumes to lead the people of Ireland must be willing to sacrifice himself to save them too. Remember me, boy, comfort your mother when I go down fighting. Save as many as you can, Hector. Who knows, son, one by one I may kill them all!" He laughed.

With a last farewell to his tearful son, Niall Glundub picked up his weaponry, and divested himself of all his armour that could weigh him down in the water. All of his men punched their fist to their chests in respect as they passed him, and they ran toward Hector. They leaped into the water, looking to grasp some of the structure of the bridge and pull themselves across the stream by its base, or scramble up onto its surface to reinforce Hector.

Niall Glundub picked up the giant banner that his man Tadg mac Ruaidhri had planted in the ground before the skirmish with the Bloodaxe and his gang of fiends. There he found his man lying beside the standard, an axe buried in his chest and yet even in death, his captain had one hand still clasped around the standard. Gently Niall removed Tadg's arm from the banner and picked it up. *I will see you soon, my friend,* he whispered. He ran toward the bank closest to the second island seventy feet away and hurled the banner perfectly through the air like a spear. It landed with a few feet to spare on the sand of the far island. Taking the three spears in his hand and a horn from around the throat of a dead heathen, he waded out into the Liffey. The water deepened sharply but, in a minute, he was able to paddle his way to the island without issue. Wringing wet, he took the banner of Ireland and planted it in the sand and scrub at the island's centre. He stood his three spears beside the banner vertically, ready for use. With one last regretful look around the enormous battle occurring on either bank of the river, he raised the Viking horn to his lips and blew a cacophonous and ominous blast through it that echoed across the water. The sky itself answered with a fearsome lance of lightning and a booming peal of thunder. Niall Glundub had issued the challenge, his last challenge to his ocean of foes, and he considered briefly that the old Norse gods had perhaps seen him. And through the thunder and the lightning, perhaps they had answered.

CHAPTER 4

THE FIRE IN THE SKY (AFTERNOON OF 14TH SEPTEMBER, 919 AD)

Sihtric Ivarsson stood tall on the easterly hill overlooking the battlefield and revelled at the sight. Thor was beating his hammer against his celestial anvil in delight at the violence, the lightning radiating out across the Irish skies being proof of it. The archers on all four of the high hills that stood sentinel over the River Liffey had finally spent their store of arrows and now those hundreds of warriors were sprinting down to join their brothers in arms in the shield wall. The Irish were in disarray and many thousands of them had already been put to the sword on both sides of the river. In his arrogance, Niall Glundub and his commanders had marched their entire force into a catastrophic ambush. Sihtric was frankly astonished that despite the Irish kings being no doubt aware that they would meet opposition crossing the river, they had cockily believed that through strength of numbers alone, they would smash their way through. *Hubris,* thought Sihtric, *and now thousands of young Irish warriors have paid the ultimate price.*

To Sihtric's right stood Olaf Godfrithsson his nephew, in a mute trance, mesmerised at the slaughter occurring before them. To Sihtric's left stood the chief Gothi of Dublin, his eyes rolling back in his sunken eye sockets, in deep communion with the Gods. That very morning, all the Gothi in Dublin had held a private ceremony with Sihtric and his commanders and they had unanimously concluded that the omens favoured victory. Sihtric had secretly vowed that if they were wrong their heads would adorn spears.. Their forces on the north of the Liffey were led by the Valkyrie and now, Erik Bloodaxe, who had earlier committed to a skirmish upon an island in the river before rowing back to the north shore to join the shield wall there.

On the south side of the river, Brunbolg Headtaker led the shield wall and spearheaded the inexorable Viking advance into the Irish host, driving them into the river. The ground of the battlefield had devolved into a treacherous quagmire formed of slimy mud and human entrails and the Irish upon the slopes leading away from the river were finding it almost impossible to keep their feet. The army of Dublin on both sides of the Liffey were fighting downhill and using their collective weight to force their opponents backward. But there was nowhere to run for the Irish, nowhere to retreat to. The choice was simple for them: death by the axes of the Norse-Gael and their allies, or chance the inexorable current of the river. Sihtric could see from his vantage point that many Irishmen, scared witless at their inevitable fate, had chosen the latter and the result was that hundreds of corpses now floated on down lazily toward the city of Dublin itself, drowned or pierced with arrows.

A boy approached him running up the hill as fast as his little legs could carry him. It was yet another nephew of Sihtric's, Ragnall Godfrithsson. Sihtric had assigned him as a runner to his nephew Grungni mac Conall, who commanded the Irishmen under Sihtric's control.

"Uncle, I have news from the battlefield from cousin Grungni. He has witnessed the death of several notable leaders of the Irish," the boy excitedly informed him.

"Who has been slain?"

"Conchobar mac Flann the King of Meath is dead. Cellach mac Fogartach of Brega tried to flee but was cut down. The King of Argialla has been killed as has the leader of the Ulaid."

Sihtric gripped his sword tightly. These names were the names of fearsome kings and princes, each, men of renown capable of commanding a thousand men or more in their own right, even without the aid of Niall Glundub.

"What of the High King Niall? What of Hector mac Niall his son? What of Mael Mithig of North Brega or the savage, Donnchadh Donn?"

The boy shrugged his shoulders. "Perhaps they fight on the far side of the river, uncle?"

Sihtric thought about that suggestion but then deemed it unlikely. Niall Glundub mac Aed Findliath would never be in the rear. He would be either in the centre directing the fight or in the vanguard.

"Good boy, Ragnall. Tell Amlaib the Sinner and the Headtaker to begin the final attack. Drive the Irish into the river and tell them to take no prisoners for ransom. Today they all die."

The young boy nodded and sprinted down the hill toward the back of the gigantic battle occurring several hundred feet away. It was impossible to make out any individual in the chaos from the distance from the top of Sihtric's hill to the southern battlefield, and the maelstrom across the river was just a heaving blurry mass. In Sihtric's mind the battle, to all intents and purposes, was done. He had a small bodyguard beside him, and he could sense that each man and the one shieldmaiden amongst them, fervently wished to enter the fray. Sihtric understood the emotion, he felt it himself; but it was his duty to direct the battle as best he could, and his bodyguard had a responsibility to him. Each carried an oversized horn that when blown in concert would be heard around the battlefield, even amidst the thick of the fighting. One blast indicated that the forces south of the river should retreat and form up into a shield wall around the easternmost hill. Two blasts indicated the same for his warriors on the other side of the river. Three blasts indicated that the two thousand men that Glundub had sent at the walls of Dublin were arriving imminently to reinforce their beleaguered countrymen and the Vikings on the north bank were to retreat away from them and form up on the hill furthest west, lest they become outflanked.

He had men secreted at various locations between Islandbridge and the city walls of Dublin and when the Connaught men were within a mile of the battle, they were to light a beacon fire that would be visible to Sihtric on his hill and only then would the three blasts be blown by his bodyguard. He had given clear and concise instructions to all his commanders, eorls and captains that at some point during the battle, one or all these blasts would be blown consecutively and to be ready to deploy accordingly. For this reason alone, he and his nephew and his small bodyguard had to remain upon the brow of the hill, to give that order. There would be many more battles to fight for these young warriors, thought Sihtric, and if the Irish by some trick of Loki prevailed, no doubt they would see action in Dublin itself.

A rough shove on his shoulder from his nephew Olaf drew Sihtric's attention away from scanning the far bank of the river and discerning any sign of the signal fire indicating that the Connaught men were coming west. He turned in the direction of Olaf's stare to witness a strange sight. Hundreds of feet away, without any orders to do so, some of the forces of Dublin had simply stopped fighting. The Irish in that part of the line were now retreating away and wading into the river unmolested. They were clambering across the ruins of the destroyed bridge or paddling and struggling back across the water toward the large island in the centre and then on, toward the north bank. It was about as orderly a withdrawal as could be hoped for by the Irish. Sihtric furiously turned to his nephew.

"WHAT IN ODIN'S NAME ARE THEY DOING? THEY ARE ALLOWING THEM TO ESCAPE. IF THESE MEN REACH THE OTHER BANK IN FORCE, THEY COULD TIP THE SCALES IN THE IRISHMEN'S FAVOUR."

The frail old Gothi pointed a gnarled old finger toward the river, over the main island and toward the smaller island further west.

"Look, lord", the old priest croaked.

Sihtric peered through the smoky haze to where the Gothi was pointing and there he could see the giant green and blue banner that he had earlier witnessed being held aloft in the vanguard of the Irish before the ambush had been sprung. Beside it stood one man and despite being more than half a mile away, Sihtric knew that only one human would have the audacity to challenge an entire Viking army to single combat.

"The Irish High King stands alone, Lord Sihtric," the Gothi rasped. "Look to the skies and see Thor's will. He is a Drengr and he offers a challenge to our greatest warriors. The Gods have seen him and demand that his request be granted, his challenge accepted. Look at your men, lord, they sense it too, that is why they stop and stare."

The old man closed his eyes and clenched his staff, shaking the holy objects attached to its top.

"Niall Glundub must be faced, or we risk offending the Gods, lord."

Sihtric was aghast. His entire southern force had unanimously stopped fighting now and the remaining thousands of Irish warriors were escaping across the river. Several hundred were washed away in the current, but many more were succeeding in their flight. In minutes, they would join forces with the Irish on the north side of the river and the Irish then would outnumber Sihtric's men almost four to one there. He would have to sound the horn to preserve the lives of his men. He gritted his teeth in livid angst, helpless against the three spinners of fate. *This is the work of Lok,i* he fumed, *the Gods have betrayed me.*

With a roar of frustration, he gave the order for the three blasts of his bodyguard's horns to be unleashed, even though the forces of the King of Connaught had not been sighted. Whether the Irish king was coming or not was irrelevant, he needed the men on the north of the river to move west and allow the Irish to pass and retreat, rather than risking the slaughter of half of his army. The echoing dirge from the giant horns almost blasted the eardrums from Sihtric's head, and even the half-deaf Gothi winced and covered his ears with his old, withered hands. The fighting had completely stopped on the south side of the river by this point and Sihtric could see from his vantage point that the Viking line on the other side of the river had thankfully begun to curl north and west, allowing thousands of fleeing Irishmen to race north away to safety. The survivors of the slaughter on the south bank had almost all made it now toward the north bank and were clambering, bedraggled, onto the bank; each were then joining the ranks facing the Viking line, or fleeing north away from the wrath of the Bloodaxe and the Valkyrie. Sihtric turned to his nephew Olaf Godfrithsson.

"Run to the river and take five hundred men from the rear of the line. Make for Dublin to reinforce your brother Albann in case the Irish double back and attack Dublin directly. It is unlikely, but we should not take the risk."

The young Norse-Gael noble nodded and jogged down the hill toward the victorious army at the bank. The battle of Islandbridge had concluded mostly satisfactorily, Sihtric felt, but for one thing: Niall Glundub stood undaunted and unchallenged in the river. *And he must be faced,* thought Sihtric, *but perhaps not by me.*

The rain that had plagued the early part of the battle had abated but the booming thunder and the sporadic lightning that accompanied the downpour were still rampaging across the sky. If anything, the weather had compounded in its intensity. The amount of lightning in combination with billowing smoke imparted a reddish fiery tinge to the upper atmosphere, hinting at the Gods' desire for more blood this day. There was only one more Irish life to take though, the towering king upon his island in the river. It took Sihtric a couple of minutes to reach the men below at the southern riverbank. He was angered to see that his nephew was still there, having not yet gathered his men to march back to Dublin and the city's defence.

"Olaf, I gave you an order, what delays you?"

"The men will not leave. They demand to see the combat to come, to say that they must witness the leaders of our host face the Drengr in the river."

Sihtric fumed inwardly, but the words of the Gothi still rang true in his mind. The Gods were here and now, in this place, looking on; and they would judge. Sihtric marched down further to the edge of the water and stared across at the Irish king who stood proudly, staring down belligerently at Sihtric's entire army. He could feel the respect for the Irish king growing amongst the ranks of his warriors, who stood back in awe, unsure of what to do. The sheer courage and insane arrogance to dare defy the entire Ui Imair army and their allies by himself was intimidating in its own way.

Single combat like this with a beaten king was what the sagas were made of. The death of the Irish king was assured, and in its way served as a sort of honourable execution; but Sihtric was under no illusions as to the High King's intentions; he had purely offered this challenge to buy time for his warriors to escape. He had sacrificed himself knowing that Viking custom would take over and give his forces the chance to flee. If it took all four thousand-odd surviving Viking warriors, each would take their turn to face Niall Glundub and one of them would surely land the killing blow. It was the honour of the great lords to step forward first though and try the High King; the rank-and-file warriors understood this and stood back.

Sihtric was at a loss as to what to do. He did not fear Niall Glundub personally, but he did respect his abilities. He had taken the High King's measure many years ago in the hall of Flann Sinna and had always felt that he could win; the High King was nigh on fifty at this stage and Sihtric was in his prime. But single combat sometimes came down to a sliver of fortune. A slip on the grass, or a gust of wind in your eye, could seal your doom. If he was to fall to the Irish High King, he would no doubt feast in Valhalla, but he feared Olaf and his brothers would be too young to keep control of the multitude of factions in Dublin and the entire Norse-Gael army could tear itself apart despite the victory. *No doubt that is what Niall Glundub desires* Sihtric acknowledged.

Erik Bloodaxe posed a problem. Should Sihtric fall to the Irish king's dual swords, the Norse prince could claim Dublin for his father in the power vacuum that would form upon Sihtric's death. That would force his brother Ragnall to declare war on the Norse and a circle of violence would consume the entire Viking world. The Ui Imair would never survive such an encounter.

At that moment, his quandary was temporarily solved. A familiar figure waded into the river from the north. It was the shieldmaiden, Olga the Valkyrie. She had stripped herself of her armour to make the swim across and just carried her shield and weapons on her back. She went bare-breasted, showing her heavily scarred and tattooed torso rippling with muscle. The entire army on both sides of the river hushed. Sihtric could not believe that thousands of men could remain silent for this length of time but quieten they did. In a minute, the Valkyrie, a savage Viking raider near as notorious as her father, the dreaded Ulf Francslayer, reached the small island in the river.

She unslung her shield and moved to the centre of the island, drawing a short sword along with her shield. Sithric could see from a distance that words were being exchanged between the Irish High King and the ferocious pirate-queen, but the distance was too great to carry the words. No doubt the Glundub was chastising the Valkyrie for being a woman and daring to face him, but Sihtric knew that to underestimate this shieldmaiden usually meant death for her foes. Niall Glundub unsheathed both of his swords and swirled them menacingly in front of himself, beckoning the Valkyrie forward. And come forward she did, with a spine-shivering war-cry.

The fight was disappointingly one-sided. Despite the Valkyrie's speed, she lacked the reach and power to trouble the Glundub. Her main attribute usually was the fact that her opponents were stunned at her skills despite being female and were momentarily caught by surprise. In that moment, their lives were forfeit. Niall Glundub was a veteran of a hundred battles though and had probably killed dozens of shieldmaidens and was not perturbed by anything. Killing a woman would mean nothing to him. Without her armour, the powerful Viking woman found herself taking wounds to her chest and torso that slowly weakened her. Her speed took her out of killing range in the early exchanges, but Sihtric downheartedly acknowledged the inevitable; that her time on this earth would be measured in moments. A half a minute later it was proved true, when the exhausted Valkyrie had her shield battered down, missed her own right-handed stroke, and was cleaved from jaw to sternum by a dreadful blow from Niall Glundub. With her head half hacked off her shoulders, she slumped to the grass in a lifeless heap, killed instantly.

The Irish High King dragged her body across the grass beside his giant banner and gently clasped her sword and shield upon her chest. Sithric could see many warriors nod their head in respectful acknowledgment, not just for the dead warrioress going out the warrior's way, but the honourable manner the Irish High King had treated his vanquished opponent, respectful of Viking traditions, sending the Valkyrie to Valhalla with a weapon in hand. It did not surprise Sihtric in the slightest that the Irish High King was aware of their customs; the Ui Neill lord had been fighting warriors from all parts of the Viking world throughout his entire adult life.

The Irish king used a piece of cloth then to clean his sword and stared contemptuously at both banks of the river, daring with his eyes the next foeman to enter the water to face him. Thunder and lightning broke the sky open above the battlefield and Sihtric could feel the hair rise on his arms in response. The Gods were here, of that he was certain. He half expected Thor or Heimdall to emerge from the lines of his warriors and wade into the river themselves to face Glundub. A quick glance at the north bank told Sihtric that the remainder of the Irish army had now fully retreated, and the northern half of his army now mirrored the southern portion of his forces, in looking on quietly at the combat in the Liffey.

A disturbance some hundred feet away from Sihtric's vantage point on the bank drew his attention. The warriors there were brushed aside en masse by some great force, and he was not far wrong. The next mighty challenger was emerging to take on the Irish High King in single combat; Brunbolg Headtaker, all seven feet and four hundred pounds of ancient anger and might. He contemptuously smashed his way through his own warriors and stepped into the Liffey. He did not remove his armour; he just strode into the water. The river quickly reached his loins, then his naval, then his chest and shoulders. Ever so briefly it reached his nose and eyes but the giant Viking implacably marched forward. The river's current made no difference to his course, and he trudged forward as relentless as an avalanche in human form. Near the island, the depth of the water diminished, and he lumbered up the slope toward the Irish High King.

This time there was no talking, no insults and no taking the measure of each other. The Headtaker fought with a great axe in one hand and a crude barbarous club in the other. The club was made with a lump of obsidian meshed to an axe handle and tied with steel wire, as blunt and savage as the man who wielded it. Brunbolg fought as he always fought, with no regard for his own defence. Thick plates of iron and rings of steel covered every part of him, and his pure size allowed him to endure terrible blows that would fell a normal man. His fearsome helm had a single horn at its centre adding another foot to his prodigious height. He swung wide scything blows with both of his enormous weapons, wielding them as if they were dainty short swords.

Niall Glundub though, despite giving ground to his colossal foe, seemed unperturbed to Sihtric. He parried and ducked each blow and moved toward the Headtaker's left-hand side, willing to back his speed against the club rather than deal with the Headtaker's axe. After a minute, the Irish king darted away and reached for one of three spears that were planted in the ground beside the great Irish banner and almost immediately the tables turned. He proceeded to jab the spear at Brunbolg's faceguard, blinding the giant Viking to his movements and exceeding Brunbolg's vaunted reach. The Headtaker swung desperately to swat the spear away so he could see and keep the faster Irish warrior at bay. Glundub at that moment changed tactics. He jabbed with the spear, but at the last second turned it into a feint. He simultaneously ducked a loose blow from the Headtaker's club and twirled around with the butt of his spear and smashed the Viking's helm from his head.

The almost bucket-sized helm landed in the grass and Sihtric could see even from this distance that the Headtaker was almost done. Rivulets of sweat and now blood were running down his old and haggard face and the blow had clearly dazed him and in the face of a relentless warrior like Glundub, it spelled doom. Sihtric could see the first tell-tale signs of doubt just by the Headtaker's body language as well. For the first time in Brunbolg's life he faced a foeman who was beyond his abilities and unfazed by his freakish physical attributes. Again, Brunbolg pressed forward though, his warlike if small brain only knowing one way. Glundub's speed, reach and movement were proving far too much and in one moment, the Irish king danced away putting twenty feet between the combatants and launched his spear with a mighty throw.

The tip took Brunbolg square in the chest and lodged almost a foot deep into his armour and flesh. The look of shocked surprise in the giant Viking's face hinted to Sihtric that something vital had been hit and moments later a rush of blood erupted from the Headtaker's mouth. He toppled to the ground like a poleaxed horse shortly afterward, his death being met with a titanic bolt of lightning in the sky. Brunbolg Headtaker, the bane of Francia, Scotland and Ireland, had been put to the sword by Niall Glundub the High King of Ireland.

Sihtric looked around him. The warriors were staring at him in mute expectation. He half hoped that Erik Bloodaxe would wade into the water and challenge Glundub himself, but he could not allow that to come to pass either. It would be said then that it was the son of the King of Norway who vanquished the Irish High King and not the Ui Imair, and in the Viking world, reputation was everything. Without a word to any of his bodyguards, Sihtric moved down the bank of the River Liffey in front of his warriors. One berserker beat his axe against his shield as he passed, and then another and then ten more. In moments, thousands of Viking warriors were beating their weapons against their shields or against their chests if they did not carry a shield; all in a slow rhythmic beat. Sihtric could feel the Gods stirring in his soul, they were with him as he walked, crowding around him.

One of the longboats that had been used to smash the bridge to kindling at the beginning of the battle had docked upon the southern shore. Sihtric indicated to the men aboard that they should bring him across to the island. As he stepped aboard, he turned and saluted his warriors for perhaps the last time. He did not say anything to any of them, not even Olaf his nephew, for there was nothing left to say. He would stand or fall on the island; the Gods would decide. Another crack of jagged lightning lit up the gloom as the longboat was steered expertly by the warriors aboard and slowly, they rowed to the smaller of the two islands. He leapt into the shallow water before the island and waded onto the shore, fully armed and armoured. He strode into the middle of the island and stopped ten feet from the enormous Irish banner that fluttered in the breeze.

And there facing him, weapons drawn, was Niall Glundub mac Aed Findliath mac Niall Caille, the High King of Ireland, and the most legendary fighter of the age. The Irish king was clean-shaven with brown hair flecked with grey and white. He had aged very well since Sihtric had seem him first across the hall at Tara many years ago. His arms were powerful and well-knit with sinewy muscle, his reach was long. His leather armour was scarred and scratched but robust-looking and his weapons were in tremendous condition. Sihtric briefly wondered how many Viking warlords had fallen to those blades before he chided himself for allowing his mind to wander; he needed to focus.

Glundub then spoke. "I remember you, pup, from the halls of Tara. I knew it was a mistake by Flann Sinna to allow a heathen mongrel like you to learn at his side. You should have been slain with all your kin that were captured at the fall of Viking Dublin. The power of the line of Ivar the Boneless should have been broken that day."

A smile flickered across Sihtric's face. He was a veteran warrior in his own right and was not capable of being goaded into rash action.

"You are defeated, Niall Glundub. Your dreams of conquest are over, your army is shattered, and your kin are slain. Dublin is safe from your predations and malcontent. Conchobar mac Flann was slaughtered by the Headtaker. And now you will die as well by my hand."

It was Glundub's turn to laugh, a great gale of laughter, before he retorted, "You are the lesser son of mightier men. For all your pageantry and your ridiculous spiked helm and unusual weaponry, you are just another Ui Imair savage to be cut down like the dogs you are. Your father and older brothers were no match for me, nor your two captains that lie here dead beside us. What makes you believe that you can take me? It is true that my armies are defeated, but only temporarily. My son is… mighty. Donnchadh Donn is as ferocious a warlord as any within your own ranks and the men of Connaught are almost untouched by the fighting this day. Ireland will never accept or endure the oppression of the Ui Imair. We will rise, again and again until you are banished from the land or destroyed. We will never accept a foreign ruler, and if it takes a thousand years we will keep coming and coming forever."

As if to emphasise his point the Glundub twirled his paired swords in his hands so rapidly that they became a blur of movement. Sihtric had no more left to say. He removed his infamous spiked helm from the belt at his waist and placed it on his head. He then removed his gruesome weapon, his infamous scourge, from his back, untangling the coils until its nasty collection of razor-sharp hooks and brutal mace heads fell to the ground. He left his shield strapped to his back and drew one of his swords. He took a deep breath and then summoned himself. The Irish king merely beckoned him forward.

"Come then, barbarian, and die."

The fight that took place next was one for the ages, a blurring whirligig of savagery met with skill, as the greatest Irish warrior, perhaps of all time, faced the Lord of Dublin, a Viking so formidable that armies had been known to break and flee in terror upon the sight of his unique helm and what it portended. Sihtric had the better of the early exchanges, driving the Irish king back with his scourge weapon, but as the Glundub repeatedly parried it, the weapon was eventually decapitated of all its killing paraphernalia. Sihtric then drew his shield to accompany his sword, discarding his ruined scourge, and it was the turn of Niall Glundub to assume the upper hand. In minutes he had reduced Sihtric's shield to kindling and he had to discard it and draw his hand axe to accompany his notched sword.

The two men went toe to toe. Glundub was the taller with the longer reach, but Sihtric was the physically stronger and broader and was right in his prime. After ten minutes of exhausting and dreadful combat, it was Sihtric who landed the killing stroke, when Glundub brought up his guard a fraction too slowly and the lord of the Ui Imair buried his axe in his chest. The Irish king fell to his knees, dropping his swords to the grass. Sihtric drew out his axe from his stricken foe and was about to strike the final blow when something in his defeated opponent made him halt. The High King, amidst a fountain of blood erupting from his mouth, wheezed the discernible word, "Waaaiitttt."

Sihtric understood. The High King of Ireland was not asking for mercy, never that. He was asking to die on his feet. In an astonishing feat of courage and bravery, Niall Glundub staggered to his feet and nodded once to Sihtric. He weakly blessed himself in the Christian way.

"Strike," he whispered.

Sihtric pierced him through the heart, to the clashing of Viking weapons upon shields and Thor's hammer beating his anvil in the skies.

And so fell Niall Glundub mac Aed Findliath mac Niall Caille; the lord of the Ui Neill and the High King; slain in single combat by the Lord of Dublin,

Sihtric the Scourge of all Ireland. Sihtric raised his weapons to the sky and roared his victory to the Gods, and the Gods answered. The Ui Imair had crushed the Irish at Islandbridge, September 14th, 919.

In the aftermath, spoken long in the halls of all Irishmen and even in the strongholds of all Norse-Gael Vikings, the following was recited:

Mournful today is virginal Ireland,
Without their mighty king in command of hostages,
To see the heavens and not see the sun,
Is to behold Niall's land without Niall.
It has no mirth, no possessions of real worth,
It has no peace nor pleasure in a throng,
It is powerless to enjoy itself at a fair,
Since the Scourge who brings tears of sorrow has cast it down.
Sad indeed, are the yellowing plains of Brega,
O lovely desirable land,
That you have parted from your lordly king,
That glorious deadly Niall has left you.
Where now are the princes of the western world,
Where now the horror of every clang of arms,
Since valiant Niall Glundub of Aileach,
Has brought desolation with his fall?

PART 10

THE IRON FIST
OF SIHTRIC THE
SCOURGE

DRAMATIS PERSONAE:

Aethelstan (*A-thel-stan*) – Young Saxon prince and commander.

Aethelwold (*A-thel-wold*) – Long-dead Saxon prince and contender for the throne of Wessex.

Ailche's son (*All-che-s-son*) – Brutal Norse-Gael warlord operational in Ireland.

Albann Godfrithsson – Young Ui Imair prince and warrior.

Alwin – Ambitious Mercian ealdorman.

Amlaib Collasson (*Am-layb-collason*) – Known by the Irish as the "Cenncaireach" or the Sinner. Vicious Viking warlord.

Amlaib Cuaran (*Am-layb-cuor-on*) – Young son of Sihtric the Scourge.

Aralt Sihtricsson (*Ar-rawlt-sih-tric-son*) – Infant son of Sihtric the Scourge.

Arne – Norse Gael Gothi/priest of the Scandinavian pantheon.

Aufer Karlsson (*Off-er-karlson*) – Hebridian Viking warlord.

Auisle Ragnarsson (*Owsh-le-ragnarson*) – Long-deceased brother of the leaders of the Great Heathen Army and partial ruler of Dublin at one time.

Auisle Sihtricsson (*Owsh-la-sit-tric-son*) – Very young son of Sihtric the Scourge.

Beollan mac Ciarmac (*Byole-on-mac-kyor-mac*) – King of South Brega, under-king of Conchobar mac Flann.

Blacaire Godfrithsson (*Blac-care-a-god-frith-son*) – Young warlike Ui Imair warlord, operational upon the Irish Sea.

Cadlinar Rollosdottir (*Cad-lin-ar-rollos-dottir*) – Scandinavian noblewoman of West Francia, wife of a minor Irish king.

Cathal mac Conchobar (*Ca-hal-mac-con-co-bar*) – Over-king of all Connaught.

Charlemagne (*Sharl-a-main*) – Deceased leader of the Holy Roman Empire, which encompassed most of the land between the Danube and the Atlantic in Europe.

Charles the Simple – The King of West Francia, descendant of Charlemagne.

Congalach mac Mael Mithig (*Cong-ga-lach-mac-male-mith-ig*) – Powerful and warlike young King of North Brega and the Southern Ui Neill.

Constantine mac Aed – High King of Scotland.

Cormac mac Airt – Semi-legendary High King of Ireland.

Crom Bjornson (*Crom-b-yorn-son*) – Ui Imair warrior.

Donnchadh Donn mac Flann (*Dun-na-ka-dun-mac-flan*) – Powerful King of the Caille Follamain tribe in Meath.

Dubgall mac Aed (*Dub-gal-mac-aid*) – King of the Ulaid in the north of Ireland.

Eadgifu – Saxon princess and Queen of West Francia.

Ealdred (*E-al-dread*) – King of Bernicia in the north of Northumbria. Related through marriage to the King of Scotland.

Eorl Piotr (*Eorl-pee-ot-ir*) – Minor Dano-Saxon nobleman in Northumbria.

Eorl Thurkytel (*Eorl-Thurk-e-tel*) – Scandinavian Powerbroker in the Five Boroughs in Britain.

Edith – Saxon princess.

Edward the Elder – King of Mercia and Wessex.

Eiremon mac Cenditigh (*Air-e-mon-mac-ken-da-tig*) – Northern Ui Neill under-king, slain at Islandbridge.

Elward – Saxon prince.

Fergus mac Duilgen (*Fer-gus-mac-dil-gen*) – Opportunistic chieftain of the Breffni clan.

Flann Sinna – Deceased High King of Ireland and over-king of Meath and the Southern Ui Neill.

Freya – Deity of the Scandinavian pantheon.

Frigga – Deity of the Scandinavian pantheon.

Garangr Sichfridthsson (*Gar-rang-gar-sic-frith-son*) – Ui Imair prince and Viking warlord, operating in Northumbria.

Godfrith Ivarsson (*God-frith-ivarson*) – Twin brother of Sihtric, the youngest sons of the former King of Dublin, Ivar Ivarsson. Commander under his brother Ragnall.

Gorm – Prince of Denmark.

Grungni mac Conall (*Grung-knee-mac-cone-nal*) – Irish nobleman with a Norse-Gael Ui Imair mother.

Haakon Haraldsson (*Hack-on-haraldson*) – Known as Haakon the Good due to his Christian piety. Norse prince who dwelt at the court of Aethelstan.

Hagrold the Bold (*Hag-rold-the-bold*) – Notorious Viking warlord, operational in the Francian river systems.

Halfdan Birgersson (*Half-dan-burg-er-son*) – Formidable Ui Imair warrior and bodyguard.

Harald Fairhair – King of all Norway.

Henry the Fowler – Powerful Germanic Monarch and warlord, a threat to Danish Sovereignty.

Hywel nDa (*Hugh-wil-da*) – Powerful Welsh warrior-king.

Ivar the Boneless – Long-deceased former King of Dublin and a legendary son of Ragnar Lodbrok.

King Ordono – Spanish king who controlled some of the Spanish peninsula.

Liadan mac Diarmuid (*Lie-a-don-mac-dear-mid*) – Treacherous chieftain within the Deise tribe of Munster.

Louis – West Francian prince and nephew to King Aethelstan.

Mael Craobh (*Male-crave*) – King of Argialla and under-king of the Northern Ui Neill, son of the Black Fox.

Mael Duin mac Aed (*Male-du-in-mac-aid*) – Ulaidian nobleman.

Mael mac Dui (*Male-mac-do-wee*) – Minor Irish nobleman.

Mael Mithig mac Flannacain (*Male-mith-ig-mac-flan-na-cawn*) – Shrewd and charismatic King of North Brega who was slain at the Battle of Islandbridge.

Mael Ruanaid mac Conchobar (*Male-ruin-ad-mac-con-co-bar*) – Strong young Southern Ui Neill warlord in Meath.

Magnus – Ui Imair captain and reaver operational in Northumbria and Ireland.

Magnus Magnusson – Known as the Longtooth. Norse-Gael trader of Linn and advisor to Eorl Olaf.

Muirchertach mac Niall (*Mwir-her-tach-mac-niall*) – King of the Northern Ui Neill on the death of his father, Niall Glundub.

Njord (*Ne-yord*) – Sea God of the Scandinavian pantheon.

Nydhogg (*Nid-hog*) – Demon of the Scandinavian pantheon.

Odger the Swollen – Influential Norse-Gael chieftain, ruling part of Northumbria.

Odin – The chief God of the Norse and Danes, also known as the Allfather.

Oitir Iarla (*Oh-tier-ee-arla*) – Also known as Oitir the Black, or Oitir the Black One. Deceased Viking warlord who was killed at the Battle of Corbridge.

Olaf Godfrithsson (*Olaf-god-frith-son*) – Young Ui Imair prince and nephew to Ragnall.

Ragnall Ivarsson (*Rag-nal-ivarson*) – Leader of the Ui Imair.

Ragnar Lodbrok (*Ragnar-lod-brok*) – Long-deceased legendary Viking sea king and ravager, ancestor of multiple Viking warlords and kings.

Robert the First – Pretender to the throne of West Francia.

Rollo the Walker – Monstrous Viking warlord that plagued the Francian river systems, but was made a Duke to encourage peace by Charles the Simple.

Rolt the Wrong – Axe-Hebridean Viking warlord.

Sancho of Pamplona – Spanish king who controlled part of the Spanish peninsula.

Sihtric Ivarsson (*Si-tric-ivarson*) – Known as Sihtric the Scourge by the Irish. General under the nominal command of his brother Ragnall and ruler of Dublin.

Skarde Hardman (*Skard-a-hard-man*) – Ui Imair warrior and bodyguard.

Sven Olafsson – Leader of Linn, the Norse-Gael town on the east coast of Ireland.

Sytrigga (*Sih-trig-a*) – Danish sword-thegn, installed by the Ui Imair as ruler of Liuerpul.

Uathmaran Uathmaransson (*Uath-mar-an-uath-mar-an-son*) – Grandson of the deceased King of Mann, Bairid mac Oitir.

Uhtred (*Ooh-tread*) – Son of the King of Bernicia and renowned warrior, sometimes known as the Older.

CHAPTER 1

THE KING OF YORVIK
(LATE 920 AD)

Sihtric Ivarsson, the lord of Dublin and all the foreigners in Ireland, glowered down at his bedraggled nephew Albann. The young man was bloody and sore and his senior men standing behind him were equally dishevelled and battered-looking. Sihtric wanted to roar and shout and bawl at them all, but he successfully swallowed his apoplectic rage and choked out a simple demure question of his nephew: "How?"

He had sent his nephew with more than three hundred men north to Knowth in North Brega, to exact tribute from the new king, Congalach mac Mael Mithig, who held sway in the region. The young under-king had bent the knee to Sihtric and swore to pay tribute to the Ui Imair after the catastrophic defeat of the Irish at Islandbridge, the year previously. Mael Mithig, Congalach's father, had been killed in the fighting and he had been anointed the chieftain of the Sil nAedo Slaine there and then by default, the King of North Brega. When the second agreed-upon caravan of tribute did not appear on the appointed day, Sihtric had sent his nephew Albann north to put the recalcitrant Meath king to the question and exact what was due from him. Slowly the young Ui Imair noble raised his eyes to meet his uncle's and answered Sihtric:

"Uncle, we marched north from the river to the fort at Knowth and as you know, it is well defended by stone and timber walls and a deep ditch. All the countryside fled before us and retreated into the fort. We surrounded the walls and demanded entry to speak to Congalach and we threatened him with fire and massacre if he did not submit. He answered us with insult and arrow shot from the ramparts. We camped there overnight, but on the morning, we were ambushed. Donnchadh Donn and the men of Tara came upon our rear and smashed us. We could not form the shield wall and were desperately fighting for our lives. Then Congalach emerged from his stronghold and hit us from the back as well."

The young Ui Imair prince's eyes dropped more.

Sihtric spat out the words, *"How... many... men... Albann?"*

The boy answered, "Thirty slain and the same taken captive."

Sihtric could bear it no longer, he charged down off his dais and struck Albann with a closed fist, dropping him like a sack of grain upon the ground. Albann was not quite unconscious but looked severely stunned from the punch. Sihtric did not care.

"YOU MARCHED YOUR MEN INTO AN AMBUSH WITHOUT SCOUTING THE LAND AND WITHOUT ANY SUSPICION THAT THE IRISH WOULD NOT ATTEMPT SOME SORT OF TREACHERY? DO YOU THINK DONNCHADH DONN IS SOME NOVICE WARRIOR, SOME GREEN IDIOT LIKE YOU, ALBANN?"

All the boy could do was look abashed from the floor and shake his head, blood running down his chin. Sihtric calmed himself and as the anger receded, he reached down his hand to his nephew and pulled him to his feet.

"I shouldn't have struck you, nephew, and perhaps the fault was mine. I should have sent your brother Olaf in your stead, for even those few men we could ill afford to lose."

His brother Ragnall's kingdom was surrounded by enemies and untrustworthy allies, and every minor defeat or loss of men was a potentially disastrous blow for the Ui Imair. The new High King of Tara, Donnchadh Donn, was a thorn in Sihtric's side. The son of the late Flann Sinna had successfully rallied the remnants of the kingdoms of Meath and the Northern Ui Neill under his banner and regularly came out on top in the various skirmishes with Dublin that had occurred since the Battle of Islandbridge. Sihtric had all but given up trying to enforce his will upon any of the clans that lay more than forty miles north of Dublin and had resorted to raiding and pillaging to keep the Meathmen in check. He had sent crews of Vikings north by sea also to sew confusion and fear amongst the Irish tribes along the coast.

His nephew wiped his bloodied face with his sleeve, waiting for Sihtric to issue a command. *We must respond,* Sihtric thought, *this treachery and violence must be repaid ten-fold or else word will get out that the Ui Imair can be opposed without retribution and our enemies will multiply.* He mulled the varying retaliations that he could muster in the face of Donnchadh Donn's aggression and a plan that he had been formulating for some time came to the forefront of his mind. It tasted right and felt proportionate.

"Nephew, rest and recover and tell your men to do the same. In a week we will respond in kind to the High King and the men of Meath will learn to not cross the Ui Imair."

Puzzled, Albann questioned his uncle: "What do you intend?"

Sihtric rubbed his chin between forefinger and thumb. "We will sail down the River Blackwater with a force of our men and sack the town of Kells."

A renewed vigour grew in his nephew, and he seemed to stand a little straighter and taller, as did his warriors present in the hall; the opportunity for vengeance was being presented to them by Sihtric. The boy spoke before retreating:

"We won't let you down again, uncle."

Sihtric nodded. *Congalach and Donnchadh Donn can employ guerrilla warfare, or retreat or hide behind their walls all they want, but they cannot hide Kells from me. Their armies are fluid, but Kells most assuredly is not,* Sihtric thought, *and we will have our tithe of food, gold and slaves; one way or the other.*

Within a week Sihtric and Albann had assembled four hundred of the most hardened killers in Dublin and launched fifteen longboats secretly at night. They sailed by the moonlight, miles out to sea before turning north out of sight of land. Sihtric guessed that, always, Donnchadh Donn had eyes and ears both within the city and without, ready to report military movements back to him. Because of this, Sihtric had left his nephew Olaf in charge of Dublin in his temporary absence and the welfare of his wife and two young boys, Amlaib Cuaran and Auisle. He had also issued instruction that as a feint, Olaf should send out a war party west along the north of the Liffey and draw the eyes of Donnchadh Donn and his minor chieftains away from his intended target. With one last look at his city, Sihtric himself boarded his dragonboat. He had named it Nydhogg, after the fabled dragon of the Norse underworld, and it was as fearsome as any vessel that patrolled the Irish Sea. The passage was smooth and after sailing out for ten miles in the darkness, the small fleet changed course with little drama as the winds were favourable. Dawn's light found them just south of the estuary of the River Boyne.

Sihtric's fearsome dragonboat led the way. It was not long before the many small settlements upon the banks of the river became aware of the fleet's presence, and the predictable screams and shouts of alarm were raised all along the Boyne valley in response. Bells were rung from the stone and wood belfries at the sight of Sihtric's small but deadly fleet and confused and frightened farmers and villagers formed together in ramshackle militias to oppose the Viking warband upon the patches of the riverbank that each settlement controlled. But they need not have worried; Sihtric was not here for them, just for the town of Kells.

At the small town of Slane, one of Sihtric's men, Crom Bjornson, pointed into the middle distance as terrified townsfolk scattered to the hills or to the walls of the local petty chieftain's fort. He had spotted men on horseback riding hard to the south, toward Tara. *No doubt Donnchadh Donn will be informed of our presence within half a day,* Sihtric thought. But it did not matter, Kells would have no warning, the river was the quickest route. Within an hour, the fleet had reached the fort known as *An Uaimh* in Gaelic, which translated to *The Cave* in old Norse. Here the River Boyne forked with the Blackwater which meandered to the north, while the Boyne flowed from the southwest. The town of Kells sat fifteen miles further upriver on the Blackwater, Sihtric had been there many times as a lad. Between An Uaimh and Kells, several small settlements straddled the river, but all the villagers fled in fear before the Dublin fleet.

Within the hour, the fifteen longships arrived before the ancient town of Kells and disembarked unopposed. Sihtric had listened to the stories about this storied town at the side of Flann Sinna as a young boy. He remembered being told that it had been founded by the famous High King of Ireland, Cormac mac Airt, and as Christianity had flourished in this part of Meath, it had become one of the biggest settlements of Brega, all built around a monastic fortress. As they landed, bells and the terrified screams of women and children could be discerned in the still afternoon air. Sihtric commanded his men to fan out in a semi-circle but to attack from the far side of the fort to hopefully drive people to the river if they fled. Some would inevitably escape but if things went predictably, the holds of his fleet would be full of booty and slaves to sell to the Arabs, Berbers and Ghanaians by the end of the day.

The town itself was composed of several hundred small houses, shacks, sheds and hovels, with many pens for animals; all built like barnacles on a hull, against the wall of the monastery within. Its stone tower was visible from the water lording the skies for miles around, and Sihtric did not doubt for one second that the clergymen were busy escaping into it, leaving the townspeople to their fate. A shout from Crom Bjornson drew Sihtric's attention once more as he emerged from the trees. A small militia of somewhere between sixty and eighty men had emerged from the town to face them. Sihtric almost smiled, it had been so long since he had had a proper fight, and he positively welcomed the chance for violence. As one, the entire force of Ui Imair Viking warriors emerged from the trees and into the clearing on front of the town. Sihtric raised his infamous scourge in the air.

"FOR ODIN, DUBLIN AND THE UI IMAIR!!" he shouted.

On his word, the four hundred-strong warband charged as one.

The fighting was savage, bloody, and brief. In minutes, the defenders of Kells had been murdered or incapacitated. Two minutes after that, the walls of the monastery itself had been scaled. Although many of the townspeople had managed to escape, almost a hundred slaves had been captured very quickly: old men, strong women and young girls and boys, most submitting without a fight. When, finally, the defensive tower at the centre of the monastery was also scaled and entered through a doorway twenty feet up in the air, Sihtric's men discovered that all the monks except the abbot himself, had fled through a concealed subterrain at the foot of the structure. They had no time to carry off all their gold and wealth and had to leave some of it behind for Sihtric's warband. Many delicate and beautiful chalices and religious totems were seized and Sihtric gladly shared out most of the plunder with his warriors.

Any grown men found were killed or gelded and dozens of women and children were tied in long chains with sturdy rope. Sihtric did not care. Within the fortnight they would be packed like fish in an Arab trader's hold on their way to the Levant. Dublin would make a profit. Many of his fighters had kin that were killed in the ambush set by Donnchadh Donn at Knowth, and this prize would assuage their anger. *Let this be a lesson to the men of Meath,* thought Sihtric, *that to defy the will of the Ui Imair is to bring suffering and death down upon themselves.*

Sihtric considered briefly that he had been too merciful with these Christian peasants. Had it been Ragnall or Garangr in his place here today, the entire town would have been massacred and burnt to the ground in vengeance. Sihtric was glad though that many had escaped as word would spread of the sack of Kells and the men who committed this atrocity; it suited his purpose. *Let them seek revenge upon me and mine and I will break them all on the walls of Dublin.* Before they left with sacks full of loot and chained lines of sobbing captives, Sihtric had one more blow to strike. He dragged the abbot to the altar of the Christian church in the monastery and had him sacrificed to Odin upon it, daubing the church walls with ancient runes dedicated to the Norse pantheon. With a last lingering look at the town on his way down to his waiting fleet, he issued a command to Crom and his nephew Albann:

"Burn all the houses down outside the walls but leave the monastic compound. I want them to find the abbot."

He spat on the ground and boarded Nydhogg without a backward glance, his men moving to obey. Once upon the water again, they rowed for more than an hour. All the villages that they had passed on their way toward Kells remained empty, all residents having fled or remaining in hiding. Even at the large settlement of An Uaimh, not a single Irishman stirred, with only a clutch of chickens left to disturb the peace.

At Slane though, on the south side of the Boyne, there stood Donnchadh Donn himself on the riverbank with hundreds of men behind him; but with no way to reach Sihtric or his fleet, all the High King and his men could do was shout and curse at them. There were many archers amongst their number, but with so many captives aboard to use as shields and with every Norse-Gael warrior armed with a shield, the Irish king did not even bother to give the order to nock or loose. Sihtric stood on the edge of the boat with one hand on the prow staring at the Irish king, goading him into some sort of foolish action, but all Donnchadh Donn could do was stare back and accept that Kells, one of the principal towns of Brega, had been sacked in a single day by Sihtric the Scourge of Ireland; and the Lord of Dublin had not lost a single man.

It took the rest of the evening to row out of the Boyne estuary and then sail down the coast toward Dublin. Without any need for subterfuge, they sailed a direct route south and made good time. On arriving at his hall at dusk, Sihtric could sense that something was wrong innately. He entered directly through the front door and recognised a familiar face; his twin brother had come. Without any words they embraced, and being twins it was as if they had never left each other's sides despite not having laid eyes upon each other in more than a year. On releasing Godfrith, Sihtric spoke.

"Come back to my quarters, brother, and meet my sons. They would love to meet you. Your own lads are in fine fettle and all three have been blooded in battle now beside me. Albann even accompanied me this day."

His brother grinned but there was a hint of grief and worry behind his eyes.

Godfrith answered, "All in good time, brother. There are important matters to discuss. Can we speak privately?"

For something to spook his twin this badly, a veteran of fifty or more battles, raids, and skirmishes, Sihtric knew the news would be suitably dreadful. With a few sharp words he cleared his great hall of all servants, slaves, and guards. He poured his brother a drink and beckoned to him to sit by the fire. His brother accepted the drink and with one last furtive look over his shoulder, he began his tale.

"Brother, Ragnall has been mortally wounded and Garangr has been slain in battle."

Sihtric could not believe what he had just heard. "How could this happen? Has Yorvik been sacked? Have we lost Northumbria?"

Godfrith shook his head. "Ragnall struck a deal with Gorm, Prince of Denmark, to fight for him for pay. They fought side by side at the town of Utrecht in Frisia against the army of Henry the Fowler, the King of Germania and East Francia. Ragnall barely escaped with his life, but he took a terrible wound in the side. Garangr was slain. The weapon that wounded Ragnall must have been covered in poison or shit because he has not healed at all and has deteriorated terminally. The Valkyries are near, Sihtric, he will soon be taken to Odin's hall."

A rage grew in Sihtric and he balled his fists, outraged at his famous brother's imminent demise.

"You and I, brother, should gather our men next battle season and raid down the rivers of East Francia. We will massacre everybody. Every German or Francian we find dies, everybody. We will beard this Henry the Fowler in his castle and feed his children to him feet first."

Sihtric was contorted with rage but his brother calmed him, placing his hand on his forearm and spoke softly.

"I hear you, brother, and believe me I feel the same, but we have larger concerns. Ragnall is feverish and I fear his mind wanders in the pain of his coming death. He speaks in riddles and has agreed to several pacts with King Edward the Elder of Wessex that you won't like, in his illness-induced madness."

Sihtric's eyes went wide in shock. "What has he agreed to, Godfrith, when he isn't in sound mind? Are we beholden to Edward the Elder?"

Godfrith looked away in despair, and whispered, "Yes."

Sihtric shook his head in disbelief. "Why?"

In low tones Godfrith explained what had occurred in the previous four months since the Danish defeat by Henry the Fowler in Frisia.

"Despite not losing too many men in Utrecht, the terrible wound Ragnall had suffered has made him paranoid and unpredictable, even fearful. The Saxons sent a small army north and Aethelstan, the King's son, forced Ragnall to recognise that Northumbria would now be subject to Wessex and that Yorvik would have to pay tribute. Ragnall had refused at first but when Ealdred and his son Uhtred of Babenburg had bent the knee, and then we heard that the Welsh kingdoms had done the same, he began to waiver in the face of Aethelstan's demands. Word then reached Yorvik that Eorl Thurkytel, a powerful warlord in the Danelaw, had fled to Francia with his retainers. Ragnall had seen no option other than to accept the title of 'Sub-Regulus' under King Edward's patronage.

"I advised him to reconsider. We still have the strength to defy the Saxons if they come north, with the option of calling on Mann, Dublin and the Hebrides for support should it come to battle; but Ragnall refused. He has withdrawn to his bed and has not risen since. He barely speaks, only to issue the most basic commands, for drink and food and has delegated away all tasks to lesser more cowardly men, more sympathetic to the Saxon cause. Me and the other eorls loyal to the Ui Imair are concerned, Sihtric. The vultures are circling and soon we will have revolt from certain ealdormen, and some of the Danish chieftains. You must come and take Ragnall's place. Only you can unite or intimidate all the other rulers of the region to obey the rule of Yorvik."

Sihtric absorbed all of what his brother had said and sat back in stunned amazement. His mighty brother Ragnall Ivarsson, the terror of the Irish seas, wounded near unto death, and now Yorvik subjugated by the Saxons. It beggared belief. The brothers then spoke long into the night on the vast array of problems the huge and unwieldy kingdom controlled by the Ui Imair now faced and it took until dawn's light to agree on how they should proceed; Sihtric must come to Yorvik and take command.

It took two weeks for Sihtric to organise the retinue he deemed fit as suitable for the journey to Yorvik. He settled on six hundred warriors in twenty ships; enough to intimidate the lords of Northumbria as they witnessed his arrival, but not enough to severely weaken Dublin from potential Irish attack. He left his Irish capital in the joint command of his nephews Grungni mac Conall and Olaf Godfrithsson; with Grungni to administrate the city and Olaf to ensure its safety. His brother Godfrith had travelled with only a single ship and a loyal crew composed of just his bodyguards as his rushed mission to gather support from Sihtric was intended to be done in secret. Even now he suspected that the Deiran, Bernician and Cumbrian lords were feverishly waiting upon Ragnall's death to occur and the void that would emerge, before taking power for themselves and expelling the Ui Imair from Yorvik completely.

The sail across the Irish Sea was rough. The autumn storms had arrived with a vengeance and the swell of the water undulated like mobile mountain ranges. It was usually barely a day's sailing to get to the coast of Northumbria, but this trip took two in the inclement conditions. One longship almost capsized in the night and was so several damaged that it had to be towed toward land using ropes and hooks. By the grace of Njord, the God of the sea, they did not lose a single ship in the passage east and the fleet struggled into Liuerpul on the Mersey River.

Every foot closer they came to Yorvik compounded Sihtric's sense of doom and anger as he thought on the fate of Ragnall, and sleep evaded him that night. He and Godfrith had decided that their warband would rest for a night in Liuerpol and they also commanded that repairs be made to any of the longboats that were damaged in the crossing. Sihtric barely spoke a word to his brother or his men, utterly consumed in the possibilities and options available to him in Yorvik. The next morning on the cusp of their imminent departure into the interior, Sihtric spoke to his brother.

"Godfrith, we can't just arrive and be shouted down by the eorls and ealdormen. Yet we can't just slay them all, as these are the men that we mean to rule even upon the death of Ragnall. We need to force their hand, brother. We need them to have no option but for them to look to our strength for succour."

Godfrith looked curiously at him. "What do you intend, brother?".

Sihtric had made his decision close to the dawn.

"We will enter the north of Mercia and sack one of the settlements there.

That way we wreck any peace that Ragnall in his illness may have agreed with Aethelstan or his father. The Saxons will have to treat the entirety of Northumbria as hostile, not knowing who to trust or who is allied with whom. The ealdormen and thegns of Northumbria will have no option but to back us, as they no more want civil war than we do, nor have they any love for Edward of Wessex. In their minds the Ui Imair will be the lesser of two evils, I believe."

Godfrith looked away for a moment. Sihtric had to admire his brother; perhaps he was not as considered or practical as he was – having grown up as a Viking raider in comparison with Sihtric, who grew up in a royal hall – but neither was he a savage and retaliatory in his thinking as Ragnall or their deceased cousin Garangr. Sihtric had used his time instructing Godfrith's sons in his care about what it was to lead, half remembered lessons from a long-dead Irish king; always impressing upon them the need to observe the larger picture. At length Godfrith spoke.

"It is a good plan, Sihtric. Where do you intend to strike?"

Sihtric pointed away to the east and across the river.

"Davenport, brother. And we will leave just enough of them alive to let the Mercians and Wessex know that I am in charge now, not Ragnall. And no peace can be agreed without my say-so."

The sack of Davenport was brutal. Sihtric unleashed his berserkers upon the settlement and the atrocity committed startled him to some degree. Women and men both were slaughtered on the spot, and the young children had their heads bashed in against the walls. Old men and women were bludgeoned to death with bare fists and the minor nobleman who presumed to lead the town was strung up between two sapling tries that had been tied to the ground and then both were released, ripping the man asunder in a rain of gore. Sihtric had to step in on several occasions as the bloodthirsty massacre became too much even for him to endure.

Some fifty inhabitants managed to hide in a stone keep in the centre of the town and several hundred more escaped south, *with word of the fractured peace,* Sihtric thought, satisfied. They did not bother with slaves as they had neither the time, nor the space to transport them. All in all, it took less than an hour for the substantial Mercian village of Davenport to be sacked and effectively levelled. Before noon, Sihtric's forces were on their way once more, a message firmly sent southward written in fear and stories of devastation and murder.

They had moored their longboats at an Ui Imair settlement further up the Mersey later that day and began the trek overland toward Yorvik. The going was reasonable and by nightfall they had reached the small town of Loidis and made camp around its stone walls. It was a Northumbrian town ruled by a Danish eorl named Piotr and he hosted Sihtric and Godfrith in his hall. He told them of all the news that he had heard both locally and from guests passing through. He spoke to them of an emissary on his way north to Scotland that had stopped to rest here a week previously. He had been a Christian monk from the Kingdom of Leon, looking for good Christian men to join the forces of King Ordono and Sancho of Pamplona, in their wars against the Emir of Cordoba. They had suffered a significant defeat recently and were desperate to recruit warriors for whom they would pay.

News had reached Eorl Piotr too of Hwyel nDa the strongest King of Wales, unifying two of the minor kingdoms there, to create the new Kingdom of Deheubarth. Despite this unification, he assured the two brothers that Hywel nDa had still bent the knee to Edward the Elder, rather than risk open war with the Saxons. It was all a sham and Edward could not care less what Hywel nDa did in his own lands if he paid tribute to Wessex. The most curious piece of news he imparted to the two brothers was that a dark-skinned slaver from the chief kingdom of the Ghanaians had been sending word throughout Britain that they were looking for girl slaves to be brought back to Wagadou, the chief province of that far kingdom of the Afraic.

Sihtric had briefly sent a prayer to Odin to send this trader to Dublin where they had just come into some fine Irish stock from the sack of Kells. The next morning, the force of Ui Imair Vikings were marching once more throughout the wild and untamed Northumbrian countryside. The wind was bitter, and the occasional sheet of rain washed over the warband, but Sihtric had no time to waste hiding from the elements under trees. It took them the entire day, but they eventually reached Yorvik. The town was busy with traders and people going about their business, but their warriors were met with suspicion as they walked under the newly installed Francian portcullis that guarded the front of the inner town.

The brothers gave orders for their men to disperse and spend some free time in the town amongst the alehouses and the whorehouses, but to be vigilant in case they were required for bloodshed. Sihtric and Godfrith hurried onward toward the main hall. Their way was blocked by two Saxon warriors at the front entrance and that gave Sihtric momentary pause. *Why were Ui Imair warriors or at least Vikings not guarding Ragnall?* A fawning, preening Saxon chamberlain emerged to meet them, his eyes widening slightly at the sight of the two formidable Ui Imair warlords. No doubt the hereditary white stripe on both of their heads gave him pause and an inkling of whom he faced.

"My lords," he began obsequiously, "King Ragnall is not well as you know and has relinquished all duties to Ealdormen Cuthbert and Edgar. The priests of Yorvik watch over King Ragnall now. Would you like to await the ealdormen inside once they have discharged their other duties?" he asked noxiously.

Sihtric was furious. The gall of this fop to ask the lords of the Ui Imair to await anyone made him want to vomit and cut the man's slimy tongue from his head. But it was his brother who answered first.

"Move aside, worm. We will see our brother now. I will allow you to live after offering us this insult for one purpose. You will run along now and clear the Christian priests from our brother's deathbed, or we will kill them on sight."

The two guards on the door moved to interject but one look at Sihtric's face made both think twice about blocking the way. On seeing the guards' courage evaporate away, the effeminate seneschal fled before them, no doubt doing what he was told and to save the lives of some Christian priests.

Sihtric and Godfrith marched straight through the empty hall and into Ragnall's extensive chambers at the back. A door closed ahead of them, indicating that all the priests had been hurriedly ushered from the room due to Godfrith's promise of violence. Sihtric entered Ragnall's room first and what he saw devastated him. Ragnall was a skeleton lying prone upon a sodden cot, his sheets covered in urine stains and vomit. His wound was yellow and purple with the hint of movement within, indicating maggots moving beneath his flesh. His eyes were open but pus-filled and vacant. *He has already gone then,* thought Sihtric sadly. He turned to his brother who shook his head once, his mouth downturned.

"He has depreciated further, Sihtric, since I came for you."

A tear came to Sihtric's eye unbidden.

"No, brother", he answered softly. "He is already in Valhalla."

To see his mighty brother laid low hollowed out Sihtric's heart. Ragnall Ivarsson had saved their people. At their lowest point he had brought them out of the darkness and into prosperity once more, magnifying their reputation ten-fold on the journey. The names of Ragnar Lodbrok, Ivar the Boneless and all the heroes and descendants of the Ui Imair, and even those yet come, would ascend through time due to Ragnall the fierce sea king, the bane of every Christian kingdom from Iceland to Byzantium. Here he was decrepit, rotten, and emaciated with his wits scattered. He was no more able to negotiate a treaty with the Saxons in this state than he was to sail around the world. He was done. Sihtric slowly drew a dagger from his belt and looked to his twin. Godfrith stared back unblinkingly for a full minute before tentatively nodding in the affirmative. Sihtric turned to their mighty older brother, their notorious, outrageous, and formidable brother, looking for some recognition. But all he saw was emptiness, pain, and vacant madness. Sihtric slid his dagger home between the emaciated ribs. And so passed Ragnall Ivarsson, Lord of the Ui Imair and King of Northumbria; put out of his misery by the hand of his own brother.

Sihtric turned to Godfrith, his fury and thirst for vengeance spilling out of him.

He whispered, "Summon the eorls and ealdormen now to the hall. We will settle all, right now within the hour."

His twin obeyed and by nightfall all the senior men present in Yorvik had answered the summons from Sihtric. Once they were gathered in one place, Sihtric stepped forward into the light in the centre of the hall. He placed his iconic spiked helm upon his head and threw a sword upon the ground. He informed the lords there and then that Ragnall Ivarsson had passed to Valhalla and then drew his other weapons. He informed the witan that he would now assume the mantle of King of Northumbria and his brother Godfrith would rule in Dublin and that any who disputed his claim to Yorvik were welcome to challenge him in fair single combat. Unsurprisingly, no Dane, Saxon or Norse summoned the courage to step forward. On the next day he was crowned, unopposed, Sihtric Ivarsson of the Ui Imair, the new King of Northumbria.

CHAPTER 2

THE BATTLE OF SOISSONS
(923 AD)

Sihtric wrestled on the ground with his four young boys on the floor of his hall in Yorvik. The youngest, Aralt, simply watched on gurgling in amused fascination, being far too young to participate in the rough and tumble. Aralt was only five months old, but Sihtric could see his dead wife's features in his face even at this stage of extreme youth and it saddened him. She had been a princess of Osraige, staunchly Christian, but Sihtric had never cared about that, even judging it as a positive in controlling some of the Irish petty kingdoms under Ui Imair rule. He had hundreds of thousands of Christian subjects under his indirect rule across Britain and Ireland and had grown up in a tolerant Christian court in Tara beside Flann Sinna and his sons. All his sons bore the hereditary white stripes or intermittent patches at least of white hair, proving their lineage from the Ui Imair bloodlines, but in their lineage there was Norse, Dane and Irish Christian blood too. His oldest boy, Amlaib Cuaran, was already showing interest in the ways of the axe and the sword, and Sihtric had commissioned one of the local carpenters in the city of Yorvik to carve some toy swords and axes in preparation for his training. *I had held a wooden sword in my hand at four,* recalled Sihtric.

A booming thump on the doors of his hall stopped their play immediately. It was one of his powerful young bodyguards, Halfdan Birgerson or Skarde Hardman, announcing a petitioner of some sort. He summoned a female servant and ordered her to take his children from the hall and back to his living quarters at the rear.

"COME IN," he shouted while taking a cup of water from a nearby table and moving to his seat on the dais.

Two men were permitted to enter the hall, both unmistakably Norse-Gael Viking warriors, but they had been disarmed in Sihtric's presence none the less. He had insisted upon the disarmament of all guests in his hall after a botched assassination attempt the year before by a Saxon spy. Normally he would welcome anybody to try their hand against him in full confidence in his Gods-given abilities, but his priorities had changed considerably in the last few years. He had a country to rule, and he had young sons to raise. As the two men approached the dais, he recognised one as Olaf Godfrithsson his nephew and the second man also had a familiar caste to him although he had never met him before. Sihtric stepped off his dais and embraced his nephew.

"Olaf, what news from Ireland? Please take your ease and have some food and drink."

Olaf nodded respectfully and then introduced his companion.

"Uncle, this is Uathmaran Uathmaransson, the grandson of Bairid mac Oitir."

Sihtric took a step back, reaching behind his back to a dagger he had secreted there. Bairid mac Oitir had been the Norse-Gael ruler of the Isle of Mann, but Sihtric had slain him on the walls of his fort, winning all his men to Ragnall's cause. Uathmaran spoke calmly, his palms raised in placation.

"King Sihtric, I know that you are the one who slew my grandfather and as such have cause to doubt me. But I accept that it was done in honourable battle when my grandfather refused to support you in reconquering Dublin. I have no desire for vengeance and only wish to serve you, your brother in Dublin and the Ui Imair. I am after all the great-grandson of Auisle, the brother of Ivar the Boneless."

Olaf spoke next. "My father had to put down an insurrection in the Isle of Mann a month ago, as the warriors there will follow no single lord. Uathmaran is Father's choice to rule Mann on behalf of the Ui Imair but he wished to send the matter, and Uathmaran, to you for your judgement and blessing. Uathmaran, although young, has done great service for us in our wars with the Irish."

Sihtric turned to the young warlord, grandson of Bairid. He was tall, powerful, and supple. Judging by the runes tattooed on his flesh, he was clearly a follower of Odin and not the Christ although Sihtric knew that many Norse, Dane and Norse-Gael had integrated the Christ into the Norse Pantheon as another deity. Uathmaran's name had in fact reached Sihtric's ears in the last year or two and his exploits were to be respected if true. But Sihtric wanted to gauge if these deeds were correct and not just rumour. *I will hear them from the lad's own mouth.*

He urged the two young warriors to sit beside him at his hearth and had a servant bring the three of them mead.

"Now tell me, young Uathmaran, of the battles you have fought against the Irish. I want to know you before I give my blessing to Godfrith's appointment of you as ruler of Mann, in your grandfather's old seat."

The lad looked unflustered and began regaling Sihtric with his exploits; and Sihtric had to admit, they were substantial. He had found service under Oitir Iarla the Black One in Waterford after his grandfather had been defeated in battle. He had fought in the wars with the Leinster men in 917 and was there when the Ui Imair had taken back Dublin. His lord Oitir had deemed him too young to travel to Britain to fight against Constantine of Scotland and Ealdred of Bernicia, so he had remained in Waterford fighting in the small conflicts there against the treacherous Liadan mac Diarmuida of the Deise and the chieftains of Munster and Osraige. In 919, he had fought at the battle of Islandbridge and he had been on the south side of the river that day. He claimed that it was he that killed the King of the Cenel Maine, Eiremon mac Cendetigh, and the legendary son of the Black Fox of Argialla. Sihtric was impressed. He could not help but be by this young man. The year after the battle of Islandbridge Uathmaran had begun gathering young warriors together in his own band, using plunder earned from the various battlefields to purchase his own ship from a Danish shipwright based in Wexford. He then joined the service of Amlaib the Sinner, his cousin, who had resumed raiding upon the River Shannon.

In the following two years, they successfully sacked Clonmacnoise twice and went as far as Lough Ree, ravaging the countryside there. The Kings of Connaught had reached out to the High King Donnchadh Donn mac Flann and together they marched south toward Ennis, to rid themselves of the Sinner. But Uathmaran had fought and helped the Sinner to victory, even killing Mael son of Dui, the King of Aidne, in single combat. His wealth grew as did his reputation. Eventually the son of the King of Limerick, his own cousin, banished him, concerned that the young warlord was garnering too much power and prestige at his expense. The Sinner had favoured another warlord simply known as Ailche's son, a raider from the Hebrides. Uathmaran had to flee Limerick with his fifty warriors and two longboats and the plunder that he had won. He went to Dublin then after successful raids in Dumnonia and Wales and swore his allegiance to Godfrith, Sihtric's brother, directly. He participated in wildly successful sanctioned raids on behalf of Eorl Godfrith. He joined forces with several other warlords, and they sacked Lann Leire, For Rois and the monastery at Armagh. They razed the settlement at Fir Arda, in North Brega, to the ground, taking many slaves to be sold to the men of the Afraic. Cell Shleibe, Snam Aigneach and much of the territories of the Ulaid were devastated by them too. Godfrith had bestowed honours upon both Uathmaran and his own sons Olaf and Albann, and they had become sworn friends. And in the last month, trouble had arisen in Mann and Godfrith had turned to Uathmaran to solve it.

Sihtric took it all in and sat back thoughtfully. The line of Auisle had ruled the Isle of Mann and some of the Hebrides since the middle of the last century, and it was only their defiance of Ragnall's will that had brought about their downfall. Had Bairid mac Oitir agreed to bend the knee, he would rule Mann still and this Uathmaran would have come to his throne in time anyway. Sihtric had ripped open his father's belly and pulled out his entrails in a bloody end, but if the boy held any desire for vengeance, Sihtric could not detect it. There could be no denying it though, this warrior was a true scion of the line of Ragnar Lodbrok, his fame and prowess would no doubt spread. He would make a superb eorl under his and Godfrith's rule… but could he be trusted? Sihtric was not sure. Many of the warriors of Mann that came under the sway of Ragnall in 914, would probably wish to side with the son of their own lord. A vacuum of leadership was never a good thing in the Viking world though, as it always resulted in a rapid descent into anarchy and violence with every warlord and captain working for himself. Uathmaran would bind many warriors together under the nominal command of the Ui Imair and there was an undeniable stink of destiny about him. But who was to say that in five or ten years' time, he would not throw off the Ui Imair and go independent, paying no tribute to Dublin or Yorvik? Sihtric would rather execute this warrior on the spot in his hall here, rather than allow that to come to pass. It all boiled down to trust. At length he turned to the two men.

"In principle, I am not opposed to you, Uathmaran, becoming the Eorl of Mann. Your deeds are spectacular, you are a true Viking, and I have no doubt there is more to come from you. I will need time to decide and to think on an appropriate way that you can prove yourself to me. How many ships and warriors do you two have here in Yorvik?"

Puzzled, Olaf responded, "We have eight ships with us, lightly crewed though with only a hundred men to make space for cargo."

Sihtric nodded thoughtfully.

"I want you two and your warriors to stay with me here in Yorvik for a few weeks as you have come at an auspicious time. I wish to speak to my Gothi and my advisors about what to do about this Uathmaran and have them cast the runes. I am inclined to allow you to proceed as eorl, but I want to know more about you; what kind of man you are, and if I can trust you thoroughly."

Sihtric thought he saw a slight glimmer of resentment briefly in the depths of the young Viking warlord's eyes, but not enough to suggest outright defiance. For another hour, the three men spoke together of politics and war and future raids that the two young men intended to initiate upon the lands of the Ui Neill and the Welsh kingdoms. Close to dusk, Sihtric made his excuses and retired from the hall to see his sons once more. All night, he tossed and turned in his bed, rolling the problem of Uathmaran in his mind. He was clearly made of the right stuff and to bring him onboard would be the safest option; but to allow a ferocious warlord whose star was waxing, the access to men, ships, and resources, could undercut the line of Ivar the Boneless. This young Viking was of the line of the legendary Ragnar Lodbrok as well, his name would carry weight. Toward the dawn, the solution presented itself to Sihtric. In the autumn, some weeks away, he had an obligation to fulfil with a powerful Norse lord in Francia and he decided that Sihtric and his nephew would accompany him with their eight ships. *If Uathmaran proves himself loyal, resourceful, and brave, I will give him the title of Eorl of Mann. If he proves otherwise, I will slit his throat and throw him overboard into the sea.*

The next morning, he summoned his captains and senior men to his hall, and his nephew with Uathmaran. He stood from his seat and raised his hand for silence; three thumps of Skalde Hardman's axe handle into the wooden dais quietened them quickly.

"My lords and captains; as some of you know, Rollo the Walker, the most powerful Norse warlord of Francia, has requested my assistance in his battle to come with the usurper, Robert the First. Charles the Simple is the staunch ally of Duke Rollo and has been ousted from his seat as King of West Francia. He is raising a force to recapture his throne and Rollo and King Charles have decided to offer Robert battle. Robert's armies are currently camped at Soissons on one of the tributaries of the Seine. The plan is simple; Charles will march upon Robert, but in secret a small deadly force of Vikings under both myself and Rollo the Walker will sail behind Robert's forces once the battle commences and hit them from the rear. Duke Rollo believes that Robert will command from the rear and be vulnerable to ambush from the river. We will slay him and end this rebellion."

Murmurs of excited talk erupted from amongst the men in the hall. One of the Saxon nobles stepped forward and asked a pertinent question:

"King Sihtric, why are we sending men to Francia to fight on this... Rollo's behalf, have we not enough trouble maintaining our independence from Wessex to the south, and becoming a part of Edward the Elder's England? What do we owe him or Charles the Simple? Surely we have enough problems at home without spending our strength in some foreign war?"

A ripple of ayes and grunts of agreement reverberated throughout the hall but another belt of Skalde's axe handle silenced them again. Sihtric answered:

"We have been in negotiation with Rollo the Walker for a time now. He has delivered us gold and slaves in abundance in exchange for two promises; gold and slaves I might add, that can be used to buy us allies and attract more warriors to our cause. Firstly, in Ireland, we are to leave the lands of South Brega in peace. His daughter Cadlinar has married the king there, Beollan mac Cormac, and Rollo desires peace between the Ui Imair and his new son-in-law. Both my brother Godfrith and I have agreed to this request. He secondly asks that we aid him in this assault against Robert the Usurper and has offered us all the spoils of battle should we win. His lordship and lands were given to him by Charles the Simple and if Robert should win, Rollo may be next for conquering."

More buzzing conversation abounded in the room on his pronouncement. Sihtric could tell that the Norse and Dane senior thegns and eorls in the room were enthused by the plan, but simultaneously the Saxons were not. Those who still followed the pantheon of the Scandinavians accepted that death in battle, even if in defeat, was a pathway to Valhalla, so effectively this chance to fight in Francia was a win-win situation. Victory gave them wealth and fame; death brought them a seat at the table of the Gods. For the Christians it was not such an easy choice. He spoke again:

"The appointed day is on the next full moon. We will meet with Rollo and his chief lieutenant, Hagrold the Bold, at his fortress in Rouen and join our fleet to his. I have committed to twenty-five ships, and I want Olaf my nephew and his companion Uathmaran, to join us with their eight. That will give us eight hundred men, the quota that I have agreed with Rollo."

Some of the men looked around at Uathmaran and Olaf, not knowing who they were, but nobody voiced objection.

"I will select the men going, the rest of you will remain here and protect Yorvik and the rest of Northumbria."

With one last scan around the room he roared, "Prepare yourselves and your retinues and be ready to sail at the end of the month."

Many in the room raised their drinks or weapons in the air in celebration at the news; many others, mostly Saxons, said nothing with arms folded. But Sihtric only had eyes for Uathmaran and his expression was unreadable and ambiguous.

Three days before the full moon, their fleet was ready to depart upon the morning tide. Sihtric elected to sail with young Uathmaran to see how he handled himself and the men under his command. He proved to be exactly as Sihtric expected. He was already a veteran sailor and balanced on the deck like a raven on a branch. His men loved and feared him in equal measure and carried out every order meticulously and rapidly. When they reached the mouth of the Seine, Sihtric himself volunteered to take an oar to fight against the current into the estuary and he was pleasantly surprised when he saw that Uathmaran chose to do the same. When they approached Rouen itself some seventy miles from the mouth of the Seine, Sihtric abandoned his constant appraisal of his newest potential eorl, just to take in the view of the town.

It was massive; an incredible fortress with a towering stone circuit wall surrounding it. It made Dublin and Yorvik, and perhaps every town in Ireland or Britain, look primitive in comparison. Although he knew the story of how Rollo the Walker had acquired the town and all the lands that owed the seat their fealty, it still beggared belief. Charles the Simple had forged a peace with Rollo, honouring him with the title of Duke. Rollo had led warbands throughout the river systems of Francia for a decade, a constant menace to Francian trade; but in the face of internecine warfare, the King of West Francia had considered him a minor threat. In the end, the King had decided to make Rollo and his key men landholders and nobles, purely to bring them onside to fight his battles against rebels and usurpers, and to protect the northwest of his lands against others of Rollo's kind. Ragnall, Sihtric's brother, had chanced the Seine on multiple occasions and ran into Rollo's warriors. Each time his brother had backed down in the face of Rollo's power. *The Gods are strange,* Sihtric mused, *Rollo and the Ui Imair are now sometime allies.*

Rollo's throne room was cavernous. Huge drapes covered the windows and massive tapestries hung from corner to corner to corner. Francian courtiers stood around the room, but jumped back horrified at the vision of Sihtric, Olaf and Uathmaran, approaching under guard. Sihtric thought their reaction was amusing, as the sight of Rollo himself and his close allies revealed that they were still every bit the barbarians that he and the two young men at his side were, despite the titles they had earned. *Better the devil you know,* Sihtric thought. Rollo was an enormous Viking and whatever honours the deposed Francian king bestowed upon him; his heritage was unmistakable. Beneath the silk robes he wore, Sihtric could see a salt-stained leather jerkin and the impression of a dagger beneath the material of his cape. A well-maintained heavy axe lay within easy reach beside his winecup.

He was well past his prime but still looked formidable despite his grey hair and rounding midriff. To his right stood a true son of the Viking code. The courtiers gave him as much of a wide berth as they did Sihtric and his two companions. The rank Rollo had earned had diluted their fear and disgust at the sight of his Viking heritage, but for this warrior there could be no such reprieve. He had plaited hair and was tattooed from neck to temple. A long tail of hair hung to his knees at the back and weapons were strapped everywhere across him. Sihtric recognised him as Hagrold the Bold. Rollo the giant Viking warlord, and now Francian nobleman, spoke first.

"Welcome, Sihtric of the Ui Imair. You are a man of your word and Hagrold told me that you have delivered on what you promised me."

Sihtric nodded. "Duke Rollo, I am happy to deliver upon my word as the King of the Ui Imair and all of Northumbria and the foreigners in Ireland and the Irish Sea. I have received the gold and slaves that were due to me, and I am content to fight for you. I must however question you on behalf of my brother, the Eorl of Dublin. If the Bregans attack Dublin, do you accept that Beollan mac Cormac's life is forfeit? Godfrith swears upon his arm ring that your daughter will be spared and brought back to you safely and any sons from the union will be installed by us as Kings of Brega under our protection in that event."

Rollo rumbled menacingly before answering. "Not one hair on Beollan's head is to be touched. Woe betide the Viking who plants an axe in my son-in-law's face, Ui Imair or no. I will ensure that Beollan makes no move to threaten Dublin while the Ui Imair rule."

Olaf bristled slightly but Sihtric raised his hands palm out in acceptance as he had no desire to provoke the powerful Franco-Viking warlord; they were allies in this endeavour after all.

"We accept the terms, Duke Rollo. When do we set sail?"

It was the warlord Hagrold who answered. "We sail in three days' time. Prepare your men."

Sihtric used the three days constructively. He was astonished at the complexity of the buildings in Rouen and its impregnable defences. He brought several of the carpenters on the fleet with him to inspect the walls, the crenelations, the buttresses and the towers that dominated the skyline. It was so far in advance of the structures in Dublin, that it was laughable comparing the two cities and only the old remnants of the Roman infrastructure of Yorvik bore any similarity. He determined there and then that he would bring as much of this building technology home that his masons and carpenters could understand to improve his defences in the towns, forts, and burhs under his control. The Saxons for years had been reinforcing their burhs in Mercia and Wessex, small fortresses within which fleeing populations could hide and await reinforcement; and they had proved difficult to break into when the Ui Imair raided south.

He brought Olaf and Uathmaran with him to inspect the walls and inner castle too on occasion, hoping that they would learn something; but he could tell that both only wished for battle and to mingle with their comrades, each only feigning interest out of respect for Sihtric. But Sihtric was riveted. *If I could build… fortresses… like this, we would fear no Saxon, Scot, Breton or Irishman. The Ui Imair would rule for all time,* he mused frequently.

On the morning of the third day, the fleet departed from Rouen and rowed into the interior. After two hours they reached the nexus point where the River Oise joined the mighty Seine. It was a significant river and in mid-autumn it swelled up to a breadth that could comfortably take four longboats abreast. Rollo and Hagrold's ships led the way, but all ships showed the colours of Robert the First, Blue and Red with a white cross. According to Rollo's information, or at least the information he had provided to Sihtric, the battle between the usurpers and loyalists was already underway and that secrecy was of paramount importance lest some of Robert's forces were diverted from the battlefield to the river. In another hour they turned further north on the River Aisne, an even smaller tributary that could only take two longboats parallel upon the water. Sihtric had transferred himself from Uathmaran's ship to his own dragonboat for this final leg of the journey, as when the signal came, he would need to be ready with his own men.

A mile out from the town of Soissons, a noise began growing in the evening calm of the countryside. It was a din that was familiar, a rising gut-wrenching cacophony that signalled the death of men. Sihtric gazed around at his warriors and as one they began to abandon oars and reach for weapons. Rollo was visible at the helm of his ship. He raised his axe in the air and blew one booming blast from his horn. Sihtric took his spiked helm from his side and placed it on his head and all his warriors, and those of the other boats, gathered themselves, knowing that if their general was readying himself, they should follow suit. Rollo signalled for the entire force to pull their longboats up upon the north bank of the river, half a mile out from Soissons and the plain around it.

There were no roars of encouragement or shouting, just an osmosis of stoic determination rippling out from the combined host. Rollo and Hagrold commanded a hundred of their warriors to remain with the boats, all armed with bows. In case of disaster, they would cover the retreat of the host to the river. With almost three thousand men, almost eight hundred of whom were the Ui Imair, Rollo the Walker the legendary Viking warlord and lately Francian noble, marched his warriors into the rear of the massive army of Robert the First on behalf of the deposed West Francian King, Charles the Simple.

Hours later in his dragonboat, Sihtric sat exhausted against the prow. He sported an arm wound and a dislocated finger. All around him, his fleet had mostly come through unscathed with a minimal loss of men, but Rollo's forces had lost perhaps a fifth of theirs. The rearguard of archers had served its purpose upon their retreat and bought Rollo's army time at the cost of some of their lives. Sihtric looked over to his nephew who met his gaze, wide-eyed and breathing heavily. A burst of laughter erupted from his mouth and Sihtric could not contain himself either and a loud guffaw escaped his at the absurdity of what had just occurred. The laughter was infectious and men from all the longboats were soon laughing too. And Sihtric knew why: despite succeeding in their goal of catching the command of Robert the First completely by surprise and slaying them to the last man, the armies of Charles the Simple had been destroyed, the deposed king himself had been captured, making their whole enterprise moot. Upon emerging from the wilderness and onto the battlefield, it was instantly apparent that the rebels had won or were just about to; Rollo's army had arrived too late to Soissons.

Sihtric had asked Rollo if they should retreat there and then, but in a cold fury, the Walker had urged his men forward; not out of any tactical nuance, or even political gain, but from what Sihtric could tell, just vitriolic volcanic spite. Robert, the first of his name, had positioned himself on a hill overlooking the broad plain where the battle was taking place, surrounded by a few hundred retainers and bodyguards. The Viking army had fallen upon them and the Francs were quickly routed. Sihtric had witnessed Robert being cut down by Uathmaran of Mann, the Norse-Gael prince. In response, a battalion of what Rollo had described as "Heavy Cavalry" had extricated themselves from the battle below and charged back toward the Viking host. Sihtric and his men had never seen anything like it before. They were men on horseback in heavy armour and carrying lances and spears, and even the horses themselves were armoured. To face them in a shield wall with no spears of their own, Sihtric had known there and then that many in Rollo's army would simply be ridden down and flattened in the charge. He had never seen such outrageous mechanisms of death as this before – men and horse alike, sheathed in metal plate, like the centaurs of old he had learned about from the Christian monks in Flann Sinna's court.

For long moments Rollo stood still and his army, including Sihtric and his contingent, waited for his command. With a few hundred yards before the heavy cavalry reached them Rollo uttered one word: "Run".

The entire Viking army sprinted through the trees and toward the river as fast as their legs could carry them. The thunder of the hooves of the heavy cavalry echoed ever closer, their speed almost twice that of the Vikings on foot. As they reached the boats, men splashed into the water and clambered aboard their longboats for a half mile stretch down the river while the rearguard unleashed a storm of arrows which finally put a stop to the gallop of the Francian heavy cavalry. In minutes, much of their army had cast off and were rowing furiously away from the vengeful Francian rebels. Despite putting Robert the First to the sword, Rollo the Walker had been on the losing side; his liege lord captured or slain. He would now retreat to his capital in Rouen, Sihtric presumed, and await the coming storm. *No doubt he will forge some new unholy alliance with some other Francian nobles,* thought Sihtric. He looked across then to the longboat that had rowed up to join his own, where the river became broader; it was Uathmaran's ship, and the proud young Viking warrior stood bloodied but unbent at the prow. Sihtric could sense the respect that had been kindled in all the warriors around him for the young sword-thegn. He smiled to himself; *Uathmaran grandson of Bairid mac Oitir, my new Eorl of Mann indeed.*

CHAPTER 3

THE VAGARIES OF FATE
(924 AD)

The woods around the fortress at Thelwell were thick and close and Sihtric's small host of men were able to move unseen through them. The fortified burh itself was ruled over by an ambitious young Mercian ealdorman named Alwin. He had been installed there by Edward the Elder in 921 as a bulwark against Northumbrian and Viking raids into Mercian territory, across the River Mersey. Today the fortress would host a secretive meeting between the ealdorman, who spoke for several of his peers in North Mercia and stood as chief among them, and himself, Sihtric of Northumbria. They would discuss the aftermath and fallout of the death of that same king, for Edward the Elder had fallen ill and died on campaign not twenty miles from where they stood. On the news reaching Yorvik of Edward's demise, Sihtric had immediately begun formulating plans on how best to exploit the situation for his own benefit. The old King of Wessex had ruled undisputed for twenty-four years, but his death allowed Sihtric a small chance to influence events to the benefit of the Ui Imair and Northumbria as a whole.

When Edward had taken over on the death of his father Alfred the Great, there had been a civil war amongst the Saxons for control of Wessex and the recently deceased king had emerged triumphant, despite losing the Battle of Holme against his cousin Aethelwold. Many Norse and Danes had pledged their support to Aethelwold against Edward fearing his ambition to conquer all lands in creating his vision of a unified "England", and they had helped crush the Wessexian Fyrd; only to have their candidate for kingship killed in the fighting. Edward had by default assumed the kingship then and twenty-four years later had succeeded in uniting three of the major old kingdoms into one, under his rule: Wessex, East Anglia and Mercia.

Sihtric was aware that there were at least two other candidates eligible for kingship currently and if he played his cards right, a lesser scion of the house of Alfred would succeed; better yet, there was a slim chance that with the right influence Sihtric could help break up the formerly unified Saxon kingdoms, nipping Edward the Elder's idea of a unified England in the bud. Whatever came to pass, Sihtric fervently wished for Aethelstan to not win the crown, as he was the most like his father and grandfather in both ambition and temperament. He had learned from his aunt Aethelfled just as he himself had learned from the side of the legendary Irish king Flann Sinna and Sihtric feared that he would become an even more powerful monarch than his father. He had summoned his chief Gothi in Yorvik, a man named Arne, and explained what he intended to do, and asked him to cast the runes on its potential outcome.

What he intended was precarious at best and the Gods would have to be firmly on his side. Any miscalculation now would backfire spectacularly upon the Ui Imair. But after long deliberation, the Gothi had ambiguously phrased that the Gods favoured such political moves, and that the God Loki in particular, was impressed with the scheme. And so armed with the blessing of one of the God's representatives on Midgard, Sihtric had ridden south hours later under cover of darkness, with a hundred warriors and sacks full of silver.

He had sent several envoys, Saxons of noble birth who were loyal to him, with much of the silver and a little bit of gold, to butter up the unaligned Mercian lords and make them amenable to suggestion and open to a meeting toward common goals. With the remainder of his column, he had descended south toward the Danelaw, and the two towns of Nottingham and Lincoln.

Lincoln was the furthest north and Sihtric and his warriors, after some negotiation, were allowed through its walls. He had immediately taken that as a good sign, as a month previously when Edward the Elder was alive, the Danish rulers of the town would not have allowed an Ui Imair warlord, jarl or eorl as notorious as Sihtric, to set foot within its walls. The fact that they did allow him in, and grant him an audience with Eorl Thurkytel, newly returned from Francia after paying tribute to Wessex, was proof of Lincoln's uncertainty about the future.

It took mere hours, and a combination of persuasion, bribery, and threat, to bring Lincoln onside and into open defiance of Wessex. *Flann Sinna would have appreciated my dealings with them,* Sihtric thought fondly. They would now pay tribute to Yorvik, at least temporarily, and await the victor in the coming election of the new English king. A day later, they reached Nottingham, and it took even less effort to sway the lords there to renege on their oaths of fealty to Wessex. These Danish eorls, although mostly Christian now, only respected strength and with the death of Edward the Elder, there was a definitive void in power; one which Sihtric was very happy to fill – or at least have it filled – with someone less competent or more pliable to his whims.

On leaving Nottingham, Sihtric had led his column of warriors north through central Mercia, but off the old Roman road of Watling Street, to avoid prying eyes. A hundred-strong Viking warband in times as contentious as these could bring the local fyrd down on top of them and Sihtric was here primarily to negotiate; he would only fight if provoked. About two days' ride north, his envoys had returned to him with superb news: several senior Mercian ealdormen were willing to listen to what he had to say. All wished for Mercian independence, and one even put himself forward as a candidate for King of Mercia and that was young ealdorman Alwin.

They had each assured Sihtric's envoys that with the support of Northumbria, they would throw off the yolk of Wessexian control and declare independence from whomever succeeded Edward the Elder. Ealdorman Alwin was the ealdorman that they were going to meet in the burh of Thelwell and all the other ealdormen had agreed that he would negotiate on behalf of them all. He had been promoted to leadership by King Edward after the rebellion of the fortified town of Chester the previous year, in which a dissatisfied ealdorman who had been allied to Edward's sister Aethelfled before her death, had raised his standard in open rebellion against Wessex. Edward had marched north and besieged Chester successfully, having the recalcitrant ealdorman burned at the stake as a heretic and usurper. The ambitious young Ealdorman of Thelwell, Alwin, had then been promoted to the leader of both the estate of Chester and Thelwell. *Clearly his ambition has outgrown even that,* guessed Sihtric.

He did not trust any of the ealdormen of Mercia nor any of the eorls of the Danelaw; they were each as treacherous as they were greedy. The eorls of the Danelaw would only follow strength, and if no king was able to bribe, intimidate, or bully them, they would continue to pay tribute to nobody and act independently. The ealdormen of Mercia had warred with the Ui Imair for almost twenty years, each using tit for tat acts of terrorism and plundering to weaken the other on either side of their shared border; the Mercians called the Northumbrians and those of Scandinavian heritage barbarians, but Sihtric had witnessed them behaving in equally as savage a manner. He had brought one hundred warriors with him in case one of these conniving nobles, Saxon or Dane, thought that it would be more profitable to capture Sihtric for ransom or to produce him as a gift to whomever came out on top in the succession to ingratiate themselves with the next administration rather than parley with him. He prayed to Odin that their greed for power or independence would outweigh their hatred toward him for once. He wanted them to be treacherous, just not treacherous toward him.

On entering the stone and timber walls of the burh at Thelwell, he left half of his men outside the walls, half in the outer perimeter between the outer walls and the stone keep, and only brought his two trusted men inside with him to meet the ealdorman. Halfdan and Skarde his bodyguards were much displeased when Alwin's men disarmed them, but Sihtric knew that both carried secreted weapons on their persons in case of emergency, as did he. Should any skulduggery occur, Sihtric had no lack of faith in his men both inside and outside the fort to murder everybody within five miles of the burh in retaliation.

On entering Lord Alwin's chambers, Sihtric was pleased to see that there were no guards and that Alwin himself wore the leather jerkin of a warrior and not the robes of a pampered noble. He wanted his allies made of steel not wool. *This boy has confidence,* Sihtric smiled inwardly. He possessed curly wavy brown hair and a face that no doubt many a peasant girl fawned over, but Sihtric had to admit that he moved with cat-like grace, which spoke of at least some experience earned on campaign. As they took their seats, Sihtric spoke first, being fluent in the tongue of the Saxons.

"Are you a warrior, Lord Alwin? Have you skill with the blade?"

Sihtric wanted to gain further insight into the man by judging his response to what was a blunt question.

Alwin smiled affably and answered, "I have some skill with the blade, lord. I have fought against the Welsh on behalf of King Edward and when I was a lad, I had the honour of carrying the Mercian standard beside Lord Aethelstan and Queen Aethelfled. But I assure you, King Sihtric, I am no match for a warrior of your repute."

The last comment soured Sihtric a little. Faux flattery did not work on him, nor any efforts by anybody to ingratiate themselves with him. Flann Sinna had shown him how to see through such chicanery. Although he did not doubt that the Saxons, including this one, saw him as a Viking savage with perhaps a few more golden arm rings and better weapons than the average barbarian, he had learned at the side of Flann Sinna and had honed his mind in political intrigue.

"Don't pander to me, boy. I come here to negotiate firstly a truce between your lands and the eorls and ealdormen that border your lands in Northumbria. Secondly, I want to discuss two potential plans depending upon an alliance between us."

The ealdorman nodded his head gravely and Sihtric could see that Alwin understood the enormity of what was at stake and that Sihtric was not some mindless savage to be condescended to. Young lords and warriors from whatever background tended to think politics and war as a sort of game; but the opposite was true, and that reality usually hit when their friends were being slaughtered beside them on the battlefield.

"Say on then, King Sihtric, and let us see if we can come to an accord," said Alwin.

Sihtric outlined his plan. The peace between Northern Mercia and Southern Northumbria was an easy accord to come to. Sihtric swore upon Thor's hammer that if any of his ealdormen, jarls, chieftains, warlords, sword-thegns or eorls broke the peace first, he would personally put them to the death. Alwin assured Sihtric that he and his other three allies would do the same south of the border. Secondly Sihtric floated the idea of sending his gold and silver south with the four ealdormen bound by this alliance, to try and foment opposition to Aethelstan's succession.

Although Aethelstan was the eldest son of Edward the Elder, he had been sent to Mercia after the King had remarried a Kentish princess. She had borne him other children and these heirs were preferred by the nobles of the south of Edward's England. Sihtric had pressed Alwin for further information on the political situation in Wessex and Mercia. The young noble had explained that the men of Kent and Essex, two of the minor sub-kingdoms of Wessex, preferred an aetheling, or prince, called Elward. He was an unimpressive man to say the least, but he had grown up around his father's court, whereas Aethelstan had grown up in Central Mercia battling Danes and Welshmen, out of sight and out of mind. The minor lords would always prefer a king more sympathetic to their various causes. Sihtric stated that Alwin and his allies should use the gold to strip Aethelstan of his supporters and bring people to the side of the lesser aetheling. Ealdorman Alwin concurred. Finally, the two men agreed that no matter who won the kingship, Mercia would raise the fyrd against Wessex and Sihtric swore that he would provide warriors, harry the Wessex coastline, and force the eorls of the Danelaw to back them. At the end of the meeting, once the minutiae were agreed, Sihtric swore upon his arm rings and the young ealdorman swore upon a silver cross, to be true to their joint endeavour.

On leaving the burh at Thelwell, Sihtric led his small warband across the

River Mersey, employing a local ferryman to carry them over. He could have just confiscated the boats required but his new oaths to his sometime Mercian ally prevented him from taking what he wanted by force. It took them several hours, but all landed safely on the Northumbrian side of the river, horses and all. Sihtric then headed west with his warriors and this time he cared not who witnessed them in his own lands, and he stayed upon the beaten track. They were heading for Liuerpul. Before nightfall they arrived and Sihtric was pleased to see that the ramparts had been extended on the longfort and the settlement was quickly evolving into a massive trading town with thousands of inhabitants. He gave permission to his men to take their leisure in the drinking halls and amongst the women of Liuerpul as he had business to attend to.

The men had been on the road for almost a week and were well deserving of rest and recuperation, despite having seen no fighting. The thegn who ruled there was called Sytrigga, a variant of his own name, with a Danish slant. He had originated from the Danelaw, but Sihtric and his brother had recognised his ability as a leader and given him the responsibility of ruling Liuerpul on their behalf. He had their blessing to make judgements on the law in local disputes, to defend it from attackers and to charge taxes on the traders who frequented the settlement, kicking back a large portion to Sihtric in Yorvik. When he entered the main hall, he was surprised to see his nephew Albann Godfrithsson present beside the fire with Sytrigga and both wore worried expressions. Sihtric did not waste any time.

"What has happened?"

It was Albann who answered,

"Uncle, it is fortunate that you have arrived here and saved me a couple of days' travel to Yorvik. There is bad news from Ireland."

Sihtric balled his fists.

"Has Hector mac Niall struck again? I swear by Odin's missing eye that I will collect that man's head as I did his father's and no more will he plague us."

Hector mac Niall, the son of the former High King, had inflicted several spectacular defeats upon the forces of Dublin and their allied warbands across the north of the island over the past year. It was coming to a point where Sihtric and Godfrith would have to join forces and destroy the Northern Ui Neill once and for all. As it turned out, it was not the case this time. It was not the Ui Neill who troubled them. As with all things in Ireland, it involved treachery.

"Uncle, the old eorl in Limerick has died and now Amlaib Cenncairech and a warlord called Ailche's son are joint eorls there. They have declared their independence from Ui Imair rule and have smashed some of our Irish allies in battle. The Dal gCais from the Burren, who pay us tribute, were soundly defeated."

That cold familiar fury rose inside Sihtric. It exasperated him. Every time it looked like the politics of Britain and Ireland were going his way, some wayward king or warlord would defy him. The endless treachery drained him and simultaneously made him livid with anger. Just when he needed to consolidate his strength, with war on the horizon in Mercia or Wessex, this issue had come to distract him and bleed resources from his cause. In a voice laced with venom he spoke: "Sytrigga, send word to Yorvik to send Magnus and Odger the Swollen to come to Liuerpul with five hundred men. With the hundred I have here, we will sail to Dublin, march with Godfrith and root this raider Ailche's son out of Limerick and quarter him as a traitor. As for Amlaib the Sinner, we will make a present of him to the Irish, they have a few scores to settle with him."

*

A month later to the day, Sihtric sat by that same fire, staring into it, mystified at the dreadful turn of events. The sword-thegn Sytrygga was minutes away from meeting with him as he had to attend to some messengers at the front gates of the enormous longfort. The excursion across the Irish Sea had been an unmitigated disaster. On the way over they had lost a longboat and all hands aboard due to foul weather and their fleet had limped into Dublin, battered. They had gathered a force of three thousand warriors and elected to march over land toward Limerick and avoid the rough seas but when they arrived, they found the city barricaded and bristling with spearmen. They had initiated a few attempts to storm the walls but had taken minor losses for no gain. They settled down then for a siege but without ships to hem the Limerick Vikings in, they were simply able to resupply from sea. After two weeks they were forced to abandon the siege as the land around was devoid of forage, having long been picked clean by Ailche's son. Limerick had successfully defied the Ui Imair, and the several thousand warriors under the command of Ailche's son and the Sinner were no longer Sihtric's or Godfrith's to command. The only consolation was that the Vikings of Limerick only had eyes for ravaging the lands of Meath, Connaught and Breffni upon the Shannon; all of whom were enemies of the Ui Imair as well.

Licking their wounds, the Ui Imair had retreated to the northeast, where they were ambushed by an under-king allied to Donnchadh Donn. They managed to drive these bandit raiders off with little loss of life, but not before suffering the destruction of their remaining stores. That had served to make their trek back to Dublin, cold, hungry and miserable. After a week recuperating in Dublin, Sihtric had his men prepared to set sail back to Northumbria, but intelligence had come indicating that one of Hector mac Niall's under-kings, the King of the Ulaid, was currently residing with some kinsmen on the shores of Lough Neagh, deep in Northern Ui Neill territory. The trader from Linn who had divulged this information had sworn on his arm rings that King Dubgall mac Aed of the Ulaidians would be there with fewer than fifty bodyguards and kinsmen. To lose such a competent commander would severely weaken Hector mac Niall, Sihtric knew.

Ruefully looking back, Sihtric considered that perhaps he should have organised an assassination rather than a full-on assault, or maybe even ignored the information entirely; but with the defeat to Limerick fuelling his rage at the time, he had commanded his fleet north, looking to salvage something from the expedition. It took them two days to reach Lough Neagh in worsening weather, with even the water of the River Bann proving turbulent to navigate. When they reached the fort alluded to by the trader from Linn, they had jumped ship and attacked it from all sides, storming the walls. They were met with fierce resistance from around fifty Ulaidian warriors, but within a half hour they had killed them all. Of the King there was no sign, but Sihtric did personally execute King Dubgall's brother, Mael Duin son of Aed. They took almost forty slaves and distributed them amongst the longboats, but on the way back across Lough Neagh toward the River Bann, a dreadful storm arose and sent another of his ships to the bottom. He lost almost twenty men and a dozen of the slaves they had just taken – all for the gain of one executed minor Irish nobleman and fifty or sixty of his retainers.

The miserable losses incurred in the last month distracted Sihtric so badly that he did not realise that the chieftain Sytrygga had returned to the hall.

"King Sihtric, I have some news of import from the south that you must hear immediately."

Sihtric could sense that the news would be bad and he could feel his vitriol rise.

"WHAT NOW?" he shouted.

Taken aback, Sytrygga took a moment to compose himself before answering:

"Aethelstan employed a team of Danish berserkers to intervene on his behalf a month ago upon the death of his father. They succeeded in their task and murdered his half-brother Elward, who has been buried beside his father at Farndon in Mercia. All Elward's supporters have now sworn fealty to Aethelstan with none having the courage to call him out for a kin-slayer. He has been crowned king."

Sihtric flung his cup against the far wall where it shattered. He exhaled his fury, attempting to calm himself, and questioned Sytrygga further.

"What of the Danelaw and the Mercian ealdormen that I bribed and encouraged to strike for independence?"

Sytrygga elected to take a step backward away from his king before responding.

"Both Nottingham and Lincoln have sent envoys to Wessex to convey their submission. They have reneged on their promises to you, lord. The ealdormen of Mercia who swore to join you have been brought back into the fold also. All except young Lord Alwin, who has been crucified as a traitor alongside his family. A new ealdorman has been installed in both Thelwell and Chester."

Sihtric stood up to his full height. With merely a whisper he commanded the thegn of Liuerpul to issue commands for his men to gather immediately for Yorvik and that they would leave upon the hour. Despite being a Viking warrior to the bone, Sytrygga fled from Sihtric's presence.

The ride home across central Northumbria was every bit as abysmal for the men as the march from Limerick to Dublin was, with the only caveat being that they were unlikely to be attacked. Sihtric half expected a force of Scotsmen or Saxons to come down upon him though, consistent with the luck that he had endured. He cheered slightly on reaching Yorvik and he commanded his men to go back to their families with their plunder and enjoy themselves. *By Odin's beard, they deserve it,* he secretly acknowledged. Sihtric was exhausted himself and he had not seen his children in more than a month. He was desperate to see if his four sons had grown any. But he had one more task to complete and it would not wait. He unstrapped his fearsome scourge from his back and made his way to the hall where the Gothi of the Scandinavian faith in Yorvik made their home. Ironically, their hall was built opposite to the main Christian church in the town, but Sihtric would have it no other way; thus, forcing his people to mingle and meet no matter their creed, diluting enmity.

He jumped the last two steps and kicked in the wooden doors. Startled, the four Gothi present turned to face him. They were mid-ceremony, overseeing some animal sacrifice, perhaps even to divine the future which only served to enrage Sihtric further. He reached forward and gripped the chief Gothi by the collar of his robe and dragged him kicking and screaming into the centre of Yorvik. The man pissed himself and tried to scratch his arm to get Sihtric to release him, but with one clubbing blow to the head with the butt of his scourge, the Gothi seer was quietened into a stupefied semi-unconsciousness. His three acolytes wailed and begged for his release, but Sihtric ignored them. A crowd quickly formed around Sihtric and the stricken Gothi, wondering what was going on, and then he spoke:

"This Gothi has betrayed Yorvik, Northumbria and the Ui Imair by casting the runes and informing us that our mission south would be a success and that the Gods favoured us. He was wrong and now children go without fathers, wives without husbands and fathers without sons." *I go without warriors,* Sihtric hissed in his mind. "Northumbria is… unsafe… now because of his words."

Sihtric stood back a step and began to lash the Gothi. His screams were otherworldly and primal as the razors and maces attached to the chains of Sihtric's infamous weapon ripped flesh from the Gothi's torso, arms and legs. Sihtric was deliberately careful to avoid the man's head. One of the other Gothi stepped forward and pleaded haltingly, "Please stop, King Sihtric, Gothi Arne communes with the Gods, he casts the runes and divines the will of the Gods. Please spare him."

Sihtric turned to face the terrified acolyte.

"If he was so good at predicting the future then how come he didn't see this coming?"

He turned once more to the maimed Gothi, removed his axe from his back, and severed the man's head from his shoulders. Sihtric spat on his corpse. Without even turning around he shouted to the surviving acolytes, "One of you other Gothi take over, I care not who, but if you send me down the wrong path once more, I will blood-eagle the lot of you."

He strode to his hall with not a single glance backward.

CHAPTER 4

THE THREAT OF ENGLAND
(LATE 926 AD)

Snow fell gently on Sihtric's hair and face and for a moment he dreamed peacefully that he was back in the ancient homeland of his mother's people in central Norway; a land he had never set foot in. He quickly shook himself from his reverie and readjusted his rump in the saddle of his horse, lest any lapse of concentration send him plummeting to the ground. Everything had to go to plan and the projection of power, strength, poise, and confidence was more important than anything else. He led a party of five hundred warriors and another fifty retainers and servants south to Tamworth for the most ignominious of tasks: to negotiate a peace with Aethelstan the King of England. It was a necessary pact, of that Sihtric was convinced. He had no choice but to approach the Saxons to sue for peace, as geopolitical events had forced his hand. Trouble plagued the kingdoms of the Ui Imair, the only consolation being a recent non-aggression pact signed with Constantine of Scotland, which at least partially secured his northern border.

In Northumbria, rebel ealdormen stirred trouble in the old Kingdom of Bernicia and twice he had to march to quell it. On neither occasion did it come to violence as the show of force was enough to intimidate those rogues, but it was only a matter of time, Sihtric felt, before he would have to act with decisiveness to bring the rebels into line. It was either that or as sure as day, lose control of Yorvik and the rest of Northumbria.

The news from Ireland was …. tumultuous… at best. Civil war had erupted in Connaught between the sons of King Cathal mac Conchobar, who had died suddenly. In Meath, Godfrith his brother and Beollan mac Cormaic the King of South Brega, had backed a grandson of Flann Sinna, Mael Ruanaid mac Conchobar, against the High King, the fearsome Donnchadh Donn. Minor skirmishes were erupting with regularity on the fertile plains of Meath as a result. This disruption in normal times would usually mean good news for the Scandinavians of Ireland and anyone with Norse or Dane heritage, as the disunity left the Irish vulnerable; but this was not normal times. Albann mac Godfrith, Sihtric's nephew had set up a permanent camp in Loch Cuan in the north and had been attempting to subdue the Irish under-kings and chieftains nearby. Fierce fighting had erupted across the north of the island proceeding this. Albann had sacked Dun Sobairche, a fort belonging to the Dal nAridi, but then was ambushed at Snam Aigneach by Muirchertach mac Niall, the warlord known as the Hector of Ireland, with the loss of two hundred men. One of the few minor northern Irish kings to throw their lot in with Godfrith and his sons, Fergus mac Duiligen, was also ambushed in Breffni and his whole warband was wiped out to a man.

It descended even further into chaos though when Albann mac Godfrith, in his arrogance, made an alliance with Sven Olafsson of Linn and marched against Hector of the Ui Neill. The Ui Imair were betrayed by the men of Linn who sided with the Ui Neill on the eve of battle and Albann's small army was destroyed at a place known as the Meadow of the Priest. Albann was cut down in the fighting with a curse on his lips and an axe in his hand, the Ui Imair way. Allegedly it was a son of Hector who killed Albann along with two eorls from the Hebrides: Aufer Karlson and Rolt the Wrong-Axe. The ragged band of survivors fled to their camp on Loch Cuan, pursued by the Northern Ui Neill and the Ulaidians. They made a desperate last stand there and were eventually rescued by Godfrith himself, who landed in force and put Hector mac Niall to flight. In the last fortnight, some minor positive news was reported to Sihtric when he heard that his nephew Blacaire, the second from youngest son of Godfrith, had sacked Cill Dara, breaking the last of the defiance of Leinster in the process. Leinster, Osraige and East Munster were firmly now under the control of the Ui Imair and paying tribute to Waterford and Dublin.

This latest piece of good news just was not enough to convince Sihtric that the move he was making was the wrong one. Aethelstan was now the prominent power on the island of Britain, and it was inevitable that his gaze would turn north eventually. And as news filtered north and time flitted away, Sihtric could not help but feel that by making a sort of alliance with Aethelstan now, before his power waxed, was prudent. Even serving as sub-regulus in Aethelstan's England was preferable to invasion and eventual conquering, expulsion, or death. The sad demise of his nephew Albann, who had learned at his side, had brought it home to Sihtric that no matter how mighty the Ui Imair may seem, they were only ever one defeat from disaster. The idea that Aethelstan and his father had promoted, that of a united England, was a clever one. It seemed like a multinational idea with Britons, Welsh, Angles, Jutes, Danes, Norse and of course Saxons, welded together and all with a say, but there could be no mistake; the Saxons would be first among equals in terms of power. Even calling it after the Angles, the least of the tribes, was duplicitous, thought Sihtric, as it cleverly deflected scrutiny from the fact that it would be the Saxons who dominated. He hoped that it had not yet occurred to Aethelstan, that even without being fully consolidated south of Northumbria, he could probably march north and take it if he so wished. *I hope he overestimates my strength and would rather have me inside the tent pissing out rather than on the outside pissing in,* Sihtric mused.

Upon reaching Tamworth, Sihtric gave orders to his commanders to set up camp a half mile from the town. The last thing he wanted to do was antagonise the English king, but it was simultaneously important to show that despite offering the hand of friendship and even partial submission, the axe was always close at hand; in this case five hundred killers. The Saxon leaders in his force were happy that Sihtric had elected to make this peace with Aethelstan as with this agreement, war was unlikely. Christian did not like killing Christian. Some even argued that making an alliance, whatever form it may take with the King of England, would intimidate other powers in the North Sea such as Norway, Denmark and the Scots, into leaving them alone in the medium to long term. The Danes and particularly the Norse and Norse-Gaels were less accepting of the deal that he was about to make. Many hated the idea of bending the knee to a Saxon ruler having grown accustomed to being the elite of Northumbria, Ireland and around the Irish Sea. Sihtric could see their point, but he was all out of both options and time.

He marched into Tamworth like he owned the place, accompanied by just his two loyal guards, Halfdan Birgerson and Skarde the Hardman. Despite only bringing two warriors, Sihtric went fully armed and even wore his notorious helm upon his head, to distinguish himself from the average Viking warriors in his warband. The guards warily allowed them in and once inside, the people of the town gave them a wide berth. Both Sihtric and his two bodyguards were well over six feet tall, and a lifetime of sailing and battle had forged them into ferocious paragons of violence.

The town, which served as the capital of Mercia, was bustling. The influx of the considerable retinue of King Aethelstan had every stall and ale sink rammed with people. Sihtric had insisted on meeting here at Tamworth as a sort of semi-bluff; firstly, to show his sincerity at wanting a peace, but also to show he was unafraid of Aethelstan and would happily enter Tamworth unconcerned about being captured or killed.

Before the main hall, a contingent of guards descended upon Sihtric and his two men. These were no ordinary guards, but murderers to the bone, the elite huscarls of the Saxon army. They were heavily armed and armoured and eyed the three Norse-Gael warriors with deep suspicion and contempt. Sihtric did not even wait for their command and began disarming himself before them. To carry a weapon before Aethelstan, even being the King of Northumbria, meant death.

While his two guards waited outside, Sihtric entered Tamworth's main hall. His brothers Ragnall and Godfrith had been here before once when treating with the long-dead Queen Aethelfled, but the description each had relayed to him did not do it justice. It was cavernous and clearly built on the astonishing Roman ruins that were here before the coming of the Saxons. Great banners and glorious tapestries had been hung from one end of the room to the other. Francian-made stained-glass windows showered the room with light and the throne on the dais itself was gilded in pure gold. For a moment Sihtric briefly pondered sacking this place in the future, taking its ostentatious wealth for himself, but then thought better of it. The combined fyrd of Mercia was rumoured to be close to ten thousand strong once fully assembled, and that was a force that Sihtric could not match currently or without serious preparation.

From a side door, Aethelstan emerged into the room. He wore a simple tunic with a dagger at his hip. He was a fit man with the rounded shoulders of a warrior, but the thin waist of a man with agility. A great scar ran down his right cheek and the memory of Ragnall brazenly wounding the young lord after the battle of Odinsfield came flooding back to Sihtric. *The balls on my brother,* he chuckled darkly in his mind, fondly remembering the outrageousness of Ragnall Ivarsson. The King at once noticed Sihtric's gaze and guessed what he was staring at, but he did not respond with anger.

"I see, King Sihtric, that you are admiring my scar. I have your brother to thank for that," Aethelstan said.

Sihtric said nothing and allowed Aethelstan to show his hand.

"You know I must thank you for your efforts in Francia several years ago. Your actions and those of Rollo the Walker saved the life of my nephew Louis and my sister Eadgifu. They now reside here with me, for if Robert the First and his legion of usurpers had taken them, they would have been put to death gruesomely, or sold into slavery."

Aethelstan paused momentarily as if considering something. Sihtric was surprised, the last thing he expected was to be thanked by his potential enemy. He deemed it prudent to not mention that he did not know at the time that Charles the Simple was even married, never mind possessed of an heir related to the King of Wessex. He had fought beside Rollo purely for gold, slaves and goodwill that could lead to a future potential alliance. But on considering the man before him, he guessed that Aethelstan already knew all of it. *I must not underestimate this man*, vowed Sihtric, *he is more than he seems.* Aethelstan took a seat then and offered a chair on the far side of the hall's central bench that had been laid for them and Sihtric took his ease.

"You see, King Sihtric, my point is that there is no need for us to be at odds with each other. I see this not as any sort of concession on either of our parts, but as an opportunity."

Aethelstan paused and placed his hand on the table and stared at Sihtric,

"Of course, you will have to sign a charter acknowledging that Northumbria would be subservient to Wessex and my vision of England, and to all intents and purposes you would be a sub-regulus under my patronage. I assume you understand this reality, King Sihtric… of Northumbria… and the Ui Imair."

Aethelstan's eyes never left Sihtric's own, and the Ui Imair King could not help but be impressed. Sihtric did not say anything for a long minute. He quickly deduced that this Saxon king had the political clout of his father with the pure steel of his aunt. And Sihtric was never surer that if he did not come to terms here and now, his life would be taken before he reached his warriors. He rolled the permutations around his head. Aethelstan was clearly very well informed and if he was anything like his dreaded Valkyrie of an aunt, he likely had placed spies in Yorvik and quite possibly Dublin too. He surmised that the only reason that Northumbria was not already invaded was because there were still a few minor nobles to be brought into line and subdued further south and west in Wales. At length, Sihtric leaned over the table and smiled his most wolfish smile.

"Let's begin negotiations then, King Aethelstan."

The treaty dragged into the night and onward into the early morning, and at noon the next day, Sihtric emerged shattered into the daylight. His two men were waiting for him. The elite guards belonging to Aethelstan handed back their arsenal of weapons and the three warriors left on foot toward the gates of Tamworth. Within twenty minutes they had reached their camp and Sihtric sent his two men to summon the ealdormen, thegns and eorls who had accompanied him. He intended to tell them what had occurred truthfully and, more importantly, what he had agreed to. Once assembled, he spoke loudly and clearly to the lords of Northumbria.

"I have come to an accord with the King of the Saxons," he began. A solemn hush fell upon the lords there as he spoke. "King Aethelstan and I, Sihtric of the Ui Imair, have agreed that Northumbria will remain nominally independent and pay no tribute, but that I must accept the title of Sub-Regulus."

Some men clapped; others shouted in outrage.

"To seal this union, I have agreed to take Aethelstan's sister Edith to wife as I currently have no wives of my own."

That was met with laughter in some parts of the tent, and curiosity in others. Sihtric knew that a Saxon king marrying his sister to what amounted to a pagan warlord was unheard of; whatever about the Scots, Welsh or Irish allowing such a match to take place, the Saxon lords, all viewed themselves as inheritors of Alfred the Great's or even Charlemagne's great pedigree and above marriages with pagan savages, no matter how powerful they may be.

"Aethelstan has told me that as part of the agreement to pacify the Mercian ealdormen, he has agreed to stay unwed. In place of children, he has taken on many wards to tutor from many kingdoms, including a son of the King of Brittany, his nephew the rightful heir to West Francia, and even the youngest son of the Norse King, Harald Fairhair. I believe that boy's name is Haakon."

Sounds of shocked surprise echoed around the tent with even the Norse and Danes stunned at Sihtric's disclosure; but he had three more conditions to speak of. He continued:

"Princess Edith is probably too old to bear children, but should it come to pass, I am bound to send the firstborn to Aethlestan's court –" uproar washed over Sihtric, but he hadn't yet finished and ploughed on: "– for a Christian education."

Shocked astonishment warred with fury around the tent and a Danish eorl and a Saxon nobleman had to be broken up as their opposing views on the news evolved into a fist fight. Three thumps from Halfdan's axe handle on a table silenced them; there was more to say.

"I have signed an agreement of military support also. Should we require military assistance, Aethelstan will answer, and we will reciprocate."

The final point of the agreement was the hardest for Sihtric to say to his men. It made him nauseous, but he had seen in Aethelstan's hall that there was no other way. He was lucky even to get an extension of time from the Saxon king but had spouted some pious nonsense to assuage him and the time had been granted. There was a lump in his throat as he spoke:

"I have been forced, by Christian Easter-time next year, to be baptised in Tamworth in the Christian faith itself. If I do not do this, Aethelstan has stated that he cannot trust the word of a pagan and all agreements are null in void. And he will invade us at once."

Chaos descended in the tent then. His two bodyguards had to draw weapons to calm some of the lords down. One Norse-Gael warlord threatened to leave, but one look from the Hardman made him reconsider. One of them plucked up the courage to ask Sihtric, if he meant to follow through with this, or was it just a bluff to buy time to raise an army. Sihtric had no answer because he truthfully did not know himself.

The marriage was a simple private ceremony only attended by a few noble lords, and Sihtric got it out of the way as quickly as he could. The mass was held in Latin, and he did not understand a single word. His wife was unveiled to him at the end of the ceremony and Sihtric could see that she was as deeply unhappy about the match as he was. She was clearly a pious woman and Sihtric could understand that for her to be married to a barbarian savage like him, king or not, would feel like a betrayal by her brother. Women were pawns and expendable in British politics, Sihtric knew. In Scandinavian culture, they were afforded far more freedoms, and could even captain ships and fight in battles; but in the lands of the Saxons, a woman like Queen Aethelfled only came around once a century. And this woman was no Aethelfled.

The way home to Yorvik was uncomfortable and awkward. Sihtric decided to ride with his men rather than travel accompanying his new wife, who was sheltered away in a wagon with a handful of servants and maids. Sihtric had tried to gift her two young girl slaves to try and ingratiate himself with her, but the minute he turned his back she set them free and told them to flee to

Mercia and freedom. Amongst some of his men, Sihtric could feel the cold metallic taste of betrayal worryingly. Many of them were followers of Odin to the bone and the rest had accepted the Christ as perhaps a minor member of the pantheon to be included on the edge of prayers; not an entity to be bound to before all others. Sihtric was not a pious man *per se* but he did respect the Gods and every way he tried to justify his decision to himself felt like betrayal of his people and his heritage.

It took three days to get to Yorvik and when they arrived, Sihtric appointed rooms separate to his own for his new queen. And so began four months of absolute avoidance from both parties. Sihtric had little time for women anyway, the job of ruling a kingdom and raising four sons swallowed all his attention, while the new Queen of Northumbria only ventured to the church and back to her quarters.

Two months after Christmas and still a month before Sihtric was due to travel south and be baptised, a strange visitor appeared in his court. He introduced himself as Magnus Longtooth, a trader from the Kingdom of Linn. Sihtric considered having him arrested for the betrayal that Linn had shown in siding with Hector mac Niall against his nephew Albann some months before, but then curiosity won out and he commanded the trader to speak. Irish politics was famous for this type of betrayal, the Ui Imair were masters at it after all.

"King Sihtric, I come as an envoy of Eorl Sven of Linn. He wishes to serve you as the Irish have proved untrustworthy and dishonourable."

Sihtric had to laugh at the irony of that.

"He understands that there has been betrayal and violence between Linn and the Ui Imair, but he wishes to move past that and is willing to swear his allegiance to you, upon his arm rings. He was forced to betray Albann by Hector mac Niall as the Lord of the Northern Ui Neill had hostages of import."

Sihtric scowled. "Why does he not come himself?"

The trader answered, "My lord has lost a leg in the fighting and is feverish from sickness due to the wound. He requests that you come to him to accept his oath of fealty. He commands eight hundred warriors and half again as many mercenaries and he has kin in Limerick who may be willing to betray the Sinner and Ailche's son to you too. He also offers a chest of silver which I have left in the corner of the hall."

He nodded over at a wooden case. One of Sihtric's guards went over to it, flicked open the lid, and turned to Sihtric, eyebrows raised in surprise, and nodded. Sihtric rubbed his chin with forefinger and thumb. The betrayal was sickening and made him dreadfully wary of the Norse-Gael of Linn, but twelve hundred seasoned warriors coming to his side was too good to refuse. The endless political tightrope that he walked was chafing him, becoming unbearable. He was a warrior and a general first and foremost and he suddenly decided, there and then, that he had enough of ambiguity and subterfuge. He had been seriously considering abandoning the Saxon deal for months and this influx of warriors perhaps was the sign from the Gods that he was looking for. Summoning a servant, he sent for his lady wife, and the ealdormen, eorls and thegns in Yorvik, to come to the hall. In an hour, they were all present with many and more normal folk crowding into the hall, expectant of some news of import from their king. And then he spoke:

"As you all know, I have promised to ride south at Easter to accept Christ as my chief God in exchange for peace with Aethelstan and the Saxons. I summon you now, my warriors, my lords, my kin, to say that I have decided to renege on this deal. No son of the Ui Imair will ever accept the Christian God above Odin. And I am no different."

Sihtric could see his Danish and Norse warriors beating their hands against their chests and the shafts of their weapons upon the tables, each of them appreciating this turn of events. Even those of Scandinavian heritage who had taken the Christ and accepted him fully or as part of the pantheon, nodded in acceptance. They understood honour. Some of the Saxon lords bore shocked expressions, some showing fear and others, disgust, but a significant and satisfactory amount of them nodded their heads in agreement with Sihtric's sentiment too. They no more wanted to be placed under the thumb of a southern ruler than Sihtric did. He then looked down at his wife and her servants from the dais.

"To you, my Lady Queen, we were never married under the eyes of Freya and Frygga and our marriage is a sham according to my beliefs. Remove yourself from Yorvik before daybreak or your life and those of your servants are forfeit."

She did not need to be asked twice and fled from the hall with her small train of courtesans. Sihtric bore her no ill will in truth and although the right thing to do would be to take her hostage, he felt that that would be a dishonourable course and probably would have no effect on the ruthless Saxon king anyway. Sihtric thought it likely that Aethelstan would sacrifice a dozen sisters just to be called king of the entirety of Britain.

"This decision I make, does not come lightly. I hope you all understand that it means war. I will sail now to Ireland and raise many allies to face the Saxons, including our hopeful new allies of Linn." He nodded at the trader, who nodded back, arms folded.

"We will meet Aethelstan in the field and face him, the Ui Imair way. The Viking way. Even if he defeats us and forces us to submit, we will decimate his armies and water the ground of Northumbria in English blood." He did not wait for the roar of approval of his lords, but left the hall immediately. There were preparations to make.

Within a day, Sihtric had his sons readied to travel alongside a bodyguard of two hundred and fifty warriors to take with him to Ireland. He commanded his ealdormen to summon the Northumbrian Fyrd and his own eorls, who were not accompanying him, to remain in Yorvik and prepare for war; or parabellum as the Christian priests called it. He sent word to Constantine of Scotland in hope of an alliance too, but the answer to that request would not be known to him until he came back in three weeks. It was imperative that if he were to go to war with Aethelstan over the control of Northumbria, that he should remove his sons from harm's way. *They will be safe in Dublin with my brother and nephews*, Sihtric thought. He left one of his trusted men, Halfdan Birgeson, with joint command of the warriors of Northumbria alongside a stoic and trustworthy Saxon ealdorman named Kenneth, from the southern marches. They had strict instructions on what to do should Aethelstan get wind of Sihtric's refusal to comply and attempt an invasion. He made a solemn vow to the men he left in charge minutes before his column departed for the west:

"Know this; If Aethelstan invades and Northumbria falls before I return, my brother and I will burn Britain to the ground in the fires of vengeance. For every single man of yours whose life Aethelstan takes, Godfrith and I will take ten."

He half expected that within the hour, Aethelstan's spies would be aware of his movements and policy decisions, and before the week was out, the news would reach Tamworth. He hoped the threat of reinforcement from Ireland would carry alongside the information of his movements and it would make Aethelstan reconsider an invasion. The trip west was uneventful and Sihtric and his warriors did not stop regularly on the route, with time being of the essence. He brought several servants to take care of his four boys to keep them occupied and as comfortable as possible on the trip. It took them four days, but they reached Liuerpul safely and Sihtric immediately ordered the fleet there to take his retinue across.

The late winter and early spring seas were mercurial at best and hard to predict, but he chose to travel with fifteen ships, which reduced the risk of disaster. He even elected to split his four sons onto two different vessels, while he himself sailed upon his dragonboat, to hedge his bets. After two hours' sailing across the Irish Sea, Sihtric sent word to all but three boats of his small fleet that they should sail west for Dublin. The three boats that carried him and his most hardened warriors veered slightly north and headed for Linn. There was a fourth boat with them, which was captained by the trader Magnus, the envoy from Eorl Sven. No less than ten miles from the estuary of the Creggan River, astonishingly their four ships were attacked, out of the blue. Sihtric immediately looked over to the ship belonging to Magnus Longtooth, suspecting yet more treachery, but the trader looked just as surprised to be coming under attack upon the Irish Sea as Sihtric was. These waters were Viking waters and had been for a century or more; to be attacked upon them was outrageous.

Longtooth, Sihtric could see, was quickly organising his men, getting them to abandon oars and sails and take up shields, axes and bows. This was no treachery, at least not by them. The sails were unfamiliar to Sihtric, but Magnus shouted across the water that they were in fact Dal nAridi sails. *The Irish have a fleet once more,* Sihtric fumed, *how has this intelligence escaped me?* The last time anybody had challenged Ui Imair power upon the Irish Sea had been more than a dozen years ago and Ragnall his brother had smashed the joint Irish, Scottish and Saxon fleet off the Cumbrian coast. Of all the days he wished for a battle upon the open sea, this was not one of them, time was of the essence. The four ships – Sihtric's three and the one captained by Magnus Longtooth – flung ropes with hooks to each other and lashed the ships together. There were six Irish boats in total bearing down upon them and when they hit Sihtric's flotilla it sounded like a rock breaking. Sihtric placed his spiked helm upon his head and drew his weapons. There was no more time to think, only to fight, as he had been doing all his life.

On the 24th of February 927, Sihtric Ivarsson of the Ui Imair fought in his last ever battle at the head of his men. Although soundly defeating a small Dal nAridi ambushing fleet upon the Irish Sea, he took an arrow to the chest as his grandfather Ivar the Boneless had done fifty years before him. As the remnants of the Irish fleet withdrew, Skarde Hardman took command of Sihtric's dragonboat and raced to Dublin as fast as he could; but an hour before reaching the city in the dark of the evening, his king drowned in his own blood and died in Skarde's arms, Valhalla-bound.

And so passed Sihtric Ivarsson of the Ui Imair, descendant of Odin, Great Grandson of Ragnar Lodbrok and Grandson of Ivar the Boneless. On his death, he was the King of Northumbria, the entire Irish Sea and all the light and dark foreigners in Ireland; one of the mightiest Viking warlords of all time.

PART 11

THE LAST STAND OF CONSTANTINE THE GREAT

DRAMATIS PERSONAE:

Aed Findliath (*Aid-fin-lee-at*) – Long-deceased King of the Cenel nEoghain and the Northern Ui Neill. Son of Niall Caille and father of Niall Glundub.

Aethelfled of Mercia (*A-thel-fled*) – Saxon Queen of Mercia who was assassinated on Watling Street.

Aethelstan (*A-thel-stan*) – King of the English.

Ailche's son (*All-che-s-son*) – Brutal Norse warlord operational in Ireland. Properly known as Tomrair Ailcheson.

Aileen ingen Constantine – Scottish princess.

Alfred – Defiant Saxon ealdorman.

Allison ingen Constantine – Scottish princess.

Amlaib Collason (*Am-layb-collason*) – Known by the Irish as the "Cenncaireach" or the Sinner. Vicious Viking warlord.

Amlaib Cuaran (*Am-layb-coo-ar-rawn*) – Ui Imair prince and Viking raider, barely in his teens and already notorious.

Arnkel – One Jarl of the triumvirate of Norse-Gael warlords who rule the Hebrides.

Attila the Hun – Ancient nomadic steppe warrior whose hordes once threatened Rome.

Beollan mac Cormaic (*Byole-on-mac-cormac*) – King of South Brega, son in law of Rollo the Walker and sometime ally of the Ui Imair.

Blacaire Godfrithsson (*Blac-care-a-god-frith-son*) – Young warlike Ui Imair warlord, operational upon the Irish Sea.

Cathal mac Timo – (*Ca-hal-timo*) – Highland prince and guerrilla fighter.

Ceallach mac Constantine (*Kyal-ach-mac-constantine*) – Scottish prince and general.

Ceangalach mac Cathalainn (*Kyan-ga-lach-mac-cath-hal-an*) – King of Breffni and under-king to Hector mac Niall.

Cinead mac Alpin (*Kin-aid-mac-alpin*) – Long-deceased King of Scotland.

Conaing mac Muirchertach (*Co-ning-mac-mwir-her-tach*) – Prince of the Northern Ui Neill.

Congalach mac Mael Mithig (*Cong-ga-lach-mac-male-mith-ig*) – Barbaric Southern Ui Neill King and High King of Ireland.

Conmal (*Con-mal*) – Loyal Dal nAridi under-king to Hector mac Niall.

Conrad the First – Heir to the throne of Burgundy.

Constantine mac Aed – Over-king of all Scotland.

Domnall mac Constantine (*Dom-nall*) – Long-deceased King of the Scots. Known as the Dasachtach or the mad for his impulsiveness.

Domnall mac Muirchertach (*Dom-nall-mac-mwir-her-tach*) – Prince and commander of the Cenel nEoghain tribe and the Northern Ui Neill clan.

Donnchadh Donn mac Flann (*Dun-na-ka-dun-mac-flan*) – Deceased High King of Ireland and King of the Caille Follamain tribe in Meath.

Donnchadh mac Ceallaig (*Dun-na-ca-mac-Kyal-ig*) – King of Osraige who pays tribute to the Ui Imair.

Dungaill mac Giric (*Dung-gal-mac-gir-rick*) – King of Fortriu and under-king of the King of Scotland.

Eadred of Wessex – Powerful Saxon Ealdorman.

Eadwulf (*A-ad-wolf*) – Long-deceased Bernician King, father of Ealdred.

Ealdred (*E-al-dread*) – King of Bernicia in the north of Northumbria. Related through marriage to the King of Scotland.

Edmund – Murdered King of the Saxons.

Einar Iron Knee (*Eye-nar-iron-knee*) – Brutal Viking warlord who held some sway in Dublin. Long-deceased.

Erik Haraldsson – Also known as Erik Bloodaxe. Fearsome Viking marauder and raider, son of the King of Norway.

Erland – One Jarl of the triumvirate of Norse-Gael warlords who rule the Hebrides.

Faelen mac Muiredeag (*Fail-on-mac-mwir-a-deg*) – King of Leinster who pays tribute to the Ui Imair.

Fergal (*Fer-gal*) – Rebellious chieftain belonging to the Ui Loingsigh tribe of the Ulaid.

Fergal mac Domnall – Rebellious Ulaidian chieftain.

Flaithbertach mac Muirchertach (*Fla-her-tach-mac-mwir-her-tach*) – Prince of the Cenel nEoghain and Northern Ui Neill.

Flann Sinna – Deceased High King of Ireland and over-king of Meath and the Southern Ui Neill.

Fogarteach mac Donnegan (*Fog-ar-tach-mac-don-egg-gan*) – King of Argialla and under-king to Hector mac Niall.

Geabachan (*Gyab-a-cawn*) – Powerful Viking Jarl and rival to the three brothers who rule the Hebrides.

Godfrith Ivarsson (*God-frith-ivarson*) – King of the Ui Imair on the death of his twin brother.

Gormlaith ingen Flann (*Gorm-la-ingen-flan*) – Princess of the Southern Ui Neill and wife of Niall Glundub.

Haakon Haraldsson (*Hack-on-haraldson*) – Known as Haakon the Good due to his piety. Norse prince who dwelt at the court of Aethelstan.

Harald Fairhair – King of all Norway.

Hywel nDa (*Hugh-wil-da*) – Retired Welsh warrior-king, and advisor to his son Owain.

Indulf mac Constantine (*In-dulf-mac-constantine*) – Scottish prince and general.

Ivar the Boneless – Long-deceased former King of Dublin and a legendary son of Ragnar Lodbrok.

Lyot Thorfinnsson – Hebridean Norse-Gael warrior and nobleman.

Maible ingen Timo (*Mable-ingen-timo*) – Pictish princess and daughter of regional warlord, Timo.

Mael Coluim mac Domnall (*Male-col-lum-mac-dom-nal*) – Scottish prince and heir designate to Constantine mac Aed.

Mael Muire ingen Cinneide (*Male-mwir-a-ingen-cin-aida*) – Long-deceased princess of Scotland and Queen of Ireland, wife of Flann Sinna and Aed Findliath, aunt to Constantine, mother of deceased High King Niall Glundub.

Maelgarb (*Male-garb*) – Loyal Dal nAridi under-kings to Hector mac Niall.

Matudan (*Mat-tu-dawn*) – Rebellious chieftain belonging to the Ui Loinsigh tribe of the Ulaid. Resentful of Ui Neill rule.

Mildred of Bernicia – Saxon noblewoman and Scottish queen.

Morgan Mwynfawr (*Mor-gan-mwin-for*) – Politically astute and ancient Welsh king. Sometimes called Morgan the Old, subject to the will of Aethelstan.

Muirchertach mac Niall (*Mwir-her-tach-mac-niall*) – King of the Northern Ui Neill on the death of his father, Niall Glundub.

Muireann ingen Constantine – Scottish princess.

Niall Glundub mac Aed Findliath – Deceased High King of Ireland and the Lord of the Northern Ui Neill.

Odin – The chief God of the Norse and Danes, also known as the Allfather.

Oisle Amlaibson (*Oosh-le-am-layb-son*) – Viking warrior from Limerick.

Olaf Godfrithsson (*Olaf-god-frith-son*) – Ruler of Dublin and the Ui Imair on the death of his father.

Olaf Haraldsson – Slain Norwegian prince.

Osulf of Bernicia – Minor Northumbrian King and only surviving son of Ealdred.

Owain ap Dyfnwal (*Oh-wane-ap-dyf-n-wal*) – King of Strathclyde and under-king to Constantine. Cousin of the Scottish king also.

Owain ap Hywel nDa (*Oh-wane-ap-hugh-wel-n-da*) – Politically powerful Welsh king.

Ragnall Ivarsson (*Rag-nal-ivarson*) – Deceased ruler of the Ui Imair.

Rhodri the Great (*Rod-ree*) – Famous long-deceased Welsh king, who made his name fighting both Vikings and Saxons.

Rorek Haraldsson – Norwegian Viking lord.

Ruaidri ua Canannain (*Roo-ree-mac-can-nan-nawn*) – Formidable young Irish leader within the Northern Ui Neill and Cenel Connaille tribe.

Sichtfrith Amlaibson (*Sicth-frith-am-layb-son*) – Viking warrior from Limerick.

Sifrith Uathmaransson (*Sif-frith-uath-maran-son*) – Brother to the ruler of Mann.

Sigurd the Destroyer – Norwegian prince.

Sihtric Ivarsson (*Si-tric-ivarson*) – Known as Sihtric the Scourge by the Irish. Ui Imair King, killed in a skirmish on the Irish Sea.

Sinead – Wife of the Pictish warlord Timo, mother to Maible, Cathal and Uilliam.

Skathi Svarti (*Scat-tee-sf-arty*) – Norse-Gael chieftain of the Scottish west coast, loyal to Constantine.

Skulli Thorfinnsson – Hebridean Viking warrior and nobleman.

Thorfinn Skull-Splitter – One Jarl of the triumvirate of Norse-Gael warlords who rule the Hebrides.

Timo mac Duibhne – (*Timo-mac-doov-ne*) – Gaelic-Pictish Highland leader. Ally of Constantine and enemy of the Saxons.

Torulb (*Tor-ulb*) – Hebridean Viking raider.

Uathmaran Uathmaransson (*Uath-mar-an-uath-mar-an-son*) – Ruler of Mann, subject to the Ui Imair.

Uhtred (*Ooh-tread*) – Son of the King of Bernicia and renowned warrior, sometimes known as the Older.

Uilliam mac Timo (*William-mac-Timo*) – Pictish prince and fearsome guerrilla fighter.

CHAPTER 1

THE KING OF ENGLAND
(927 AD)

Constantine mac Aed mac Cinead came screaming awake in his bedroom, deep within his fortress at Dunkeld. His ever-patient wife had shaken him awake in the pre-dawn light, with a look of deep concern etched upon her ageing features. His nightdress was drenched with sweat, and his heart hammered in his chest with the last lingering memories of warriors coming for him, receding from his mind. His wife, Princess Mildred of Bernicia, was a sister of old King Eadwulf and Constantine had married her within a year of assuming the Kingship of Scotland from his long-dead cousin Domnall Dasachtach. Arranged marriages of the royal kind seldom resulted in happiness for either party, but Mildred had captured his heart. She dutifully bore his children, two strong male heirs in Ceallach and Indulf, and three daughters in Allison, Muireann and his youngest Aileen. It was impossible to hide his.... mental affliction... from his wife, but she had loyally and stoically endured his ravings and demons and kept his secrets.

In the early years of their marriage, his queen had made discreet enquiries among the wise and learned and they had suggested to her that he may be suffering from some sort of battle-shock, that men-at-arms sometimes suffered from and that it was nothing overly unusual. Constantine had agreed that this may be so, judging this scenario far more likely than demonic spirits tormenting his mind, as the Bishop of Dunkeld suggested; but he had sworn his wife to secrecy along with that same bishop as there was nothing that could be done. *Besides,* he thought, *the common warrior would lose respect for me and that would be intolerable not to mention dangerous.* That bishop had died, and his wife had never uttered a word to anybody else on his affliction. She placed a hand upon his arm, bringing him back to the present.

"Husband, the terrors were bad this time?"

Constantine frowned amusedly at the rhetorical question.

"No, wife, they were as pleasant as a walk in a spring rain."

She smiled awkwardly at that, patted him once more on the shoulder and rose from their bed. Constantine appreciated her for not pressing him for details. He never liked revisiting or verbalising the horrors of his past, deeply fearing perhaps passing on these visions to his spouse. He could endure them, but he could not endure inflicting them upon another if that were even possible. He swung his legs out of bed and called for a servant to appear. He dressed in his most regal clothing as he was hosting many nobles, chieftains, and under-kings this day; all of whom were nominally under his overlordship. He had received a summons from the south, from Aethelstan the King of all the Saxons, and he knew that he had no option but to answer. The trick would be, unpalatable as it was, to make the court believe that they had a collective choice but that his solution was the right one. In truth, he had already decided exactly what he would do on behalf of all Scotland, but he always tried to give his lords the illusion of choice. To not do so, was to invite dissent and rebellion; Flann Sinna and Niall Glundub endured years of internal warfare that boiled down to this simple truism; Constantine was sure of it. The two most important guests due to arrive were his cousin Owain ap Dyfnwal the King of Strathclyde, and his own younger son, Indulf mac Constantine, who now ruled Caithness in the far north of his lands, on his behalf.

The summons from Aethelstan had arrived a month ago, when Christian clergy had appeared in not just Constantine's hall, but in the halls of three of his strongest under-kings: Owain of Strathclyde, Dungaill mac Giric of Fortriu and in that of his son Indulf of Caithness. The Norse-Gaels of the Hebrides and the west coast had been entirely ignored, despite being in cases, at least nominally sworn to Constantine also, and the Highlanders were not mentioned either in the letters, seemingly beneath the notice of the Saxons. Constantine had sent messages by horseback to the most powerful chieftains of the Norse-Gael and the Highlanders on what had occurred, whilst also summoning the three other Scottish kings to convene a council.

Constantine wanted all the factions under him to be at least singing the same tune when they arrived upon the full moon at the small settlement of Dacore in Cumbria, the surprising location selected by Aethelstan. Indulf's invitation was puzzling though. To all intents and purposes, he was only the fourth most powerful of the line of Cinead after Constantine himself, his oldest son Ceallach and the son of Constantine's predecessor and cousin, Mael Coluim mac Domnall, his sworn heir. There was a reason Aethelstan did this, but the purpose eluded him for now. Aethelstan was as shrewd as he was powerful in Constantine's opinion, and he did everything for a reason. For the last number of years, Constantine suspected the Saxons of having spies in the courts of all their rivals in the region and he had no reason to believe that his court would be immune to infiltration.

Aethelfled the deceased Mercian queen had been famous for this tactic and as Aethelstan had served at her court, Constantine could think of no reason at all why he would not have adopted the very same practice once he came into his power. Indulf though was still a strange one and it bothered him. Four years ago, Constantine had arranged a marriage on his son's behalf with a daughter of one of the three Norse-Gael rulers of the Orkneys. She was a daughter of Eorl Erlend, the most reasonable of the three rulers there. The other two Viking brothers, Arnkel and Thorfinn Torf-Einarsson, the Skull-Splitter, had no daughters between them. Constantine was glad of that as Arnkel was an enemy of multiple friendly Irish kings, and Thorfinn the Skull-Splitter was nearly as notorious and barbaric as Erik Bloodaxe himself. Constantine suspected that it would shine a bad light internationally on Dunkeld to be seen to be marrying daughters of the two more savage brothers of the three. Their triumvirate-ruled kingdom sat just north of Caithness in the North Sea and by uniting their blood with his own, he had harnessed a supremely powerful ally in the region. Because of this marriage, Caithness was now immune to Viking raiding as the lands there, as part of the agreement and marriage dowry, directed a third of their tribute to the Orkneys and two thirds to Dunkeld; no reaver or pirate would dare raid or defy the brothers. And so Caithness, one of the largest provinces in Constantine's realm, was now ruled by his son and a Norse-Gael princess.

Constantine took his breakfast in a room behind his great hall, usually his last period of solitude before appearing on the dais and ruling his kingdom. Today he was not even afforded that. A huge, shocked gasp shattered his peace, and he had no choice but to emerge into the main hall, his boiled eggs lying uneaten. There were several nobles present there already, breaking their own fast. His cousin's son and his own heir, Mael Coluim, stood in the centre of the hall having dropped his bowl of gruel and he sported a shocked look of bemusement. Constantine's own son Ceallach cursed under his breath, also staring at the apparition at the entrance. Constantine at first could not see who had caused the commotion but once he parted the nobles and strode forward, he could see for himself; his youngest son Indulf had arrived early. He looked from head to toe, every bit the Viking warrior and not a Scottish noble. His blond hair was set in a braid down his back, he carried both sword and axe, and even his leather armour sported vague effigies of the Norse religion. Constantine was stunned. His son was unrecognisable from the young fresh-faced Scottish noble that he had left in charge in Caithness. With one look at Mael Coluim, the young Scottish prince on Constantine's behalf, cleared the hall of all but the four men of the line of Cinead. *Now I know why Aethelstan wanted Indulf to attend the gathering in Cumbria,* Constantine thought ruefully, *he seeks to embarrass me and undermine my authority in front of the other kingdoms of the Island. He is better informed about my own kingdom than I am.*

Constantine could see that Mael Coluim was furious as was his son Ceallach. As of late those two princes had been arguing continually over policy direction and the rulership of Scotland, as Constantine had delegated more and more responsibility to them. Each ruled their own fort now and each had married, but ever since the debacle at Corbridge where Ragnall of the Ui Imair had put them to flight, they had not seen eye to eye, each blaming the other for that defeat; but both were united in abhorrence on witnessing Indulf's appearance. Constantine had sworn before the clergy at Saint Andrews the great Scottish monastery, that upon his death, Mael Coluim would succeed him as heir, and Ceallach would succeed Mael Coluim after that, so the succession itself was not the issue. If it was an issue on Ceallach's part, he hid it well from his father. Indulf spoke first:

"I am here, Father, as commanded in both yours and King Aethelstan's letters. When do we depart to meet with the Saxon king?"

Constantine had to shake himself into action, still stunned at his son's appearance.

"Indulf, you look like… a Viking. Have you taken leave of your senses? Tell us the truth, do you still observe the Christian faith at least?"

Both Mael Coluim and Ceallach both leaned in to hear the answer. Indulf stared each of his kin in the eye before answering.

"I do observe the Christian faith… But I also give respect to the Allfather too, the faith of my wife and her people."

Ceallach turned away in disgust and spat and Mael Coluim slammed his fist against a table in the hall. Both were about to begin shouting at the young prince, but before they could open their mouths, Constantine held up his hand for silence.

"You do realise, son, that Aethelstan has learned of this before me and whatever he intends in this great meeting to come, he will use you as a political pawn? That is why he demands your presence. He is a devout Christian as are many of his under-kings and he will use this to alienate Scotland from every other potential ally we would wish for. Don't you realise what is at stake here, son? Our independence and even our way of life. One look at you and Aethelstan's sworn ealdormen and kings will accuse you of being a heretic and accuse me of trucking with heathens. They will advocate invasion, and he will agree. All he is looking for is a reason to invade and you may have given it to him."

Indulf looked abashed, and cast his head downward, but then sharply raised it to face his father.

"I did not consider that it should be so large an issue. I apologise, Father, I did not consider my actions geopolitically. But if I am only third in line and my wife's people are pagan, what difference does it make if I am partly pagan too?"

Exasperated, Constantine could only shake his head, feeling the beginnings of a panic attack overwhelming him. Thankfully Ceallach answered, allowing Constantine to quietly calm himself.

"Because, you dolt of a brother, should Athelstan require a reason to rally all the kingdoms south of us to march north, he has a ready-made excuse now in that we, the royal line of Cinead, have at least partially abandoned Christ. He will suggest to our own under-kings and chieftains that he as a Christian king would be a better choice to lead Scotland than the line of Cinead, and some perhaps will listen."

Constantine nodded having subdued the panic attack momentarily, pleased that at least one of his trusted men could see the wood from the trees.

"Gather yourselves," Constantine croaked shakily, "King Owain our cousin is due in with his retinue today, and I will explain what I wish to happen when we meet Aethelstan."

By the time King Owain arrived with his bodyguard, all the key eorls and warlords of the west coast still under Constantine's control, had arrived also; but they had to wait into the night for King Dungaill of Fortriu and Timo mac Duibhne, the most powerful chieftain of all the Highlanders, to get there. Once the main hall of Dunkeld was furnished and food and drink put up for his guests, Constantine had his son Ceallach expel everyone else from the hall. When all the great leaders of Scotland were hushed, Constantine addressed them, laying it bare, the delicate situation that Scotland found itself in.

"My Lords, thank you all for coming. As you know, Aethelstan has summoned myself, Dungaill, Owain and my son Indulf to a meeting in Cumbria. For those of you whom he has not, I immediately sent word to you of what was occurring as I would never partake in something critical to all your lands without informing you. We are in great peril whether you believe it or not, and Aethelstan is central to this impending doom."

A murmur grew amongst the men present on Constantine's pronouncement, but he ploughed on regardless. He did not intend to be bogged down in endless questions.

"With the death of Sihtric the Scourge in battle with the Irish, Aethelstan has seized Yorvik and now controls most of Northumbria. Godfrith of Dublin was unable to deny him and Aethelstan has taken pledges of loyalty from many ealdormen, eorls and thegns, whilst expelling the Ui Imair leadership directly. All they now hold is several longforts along the coast of the Irish Sea. And even those warlords pay tribute and heavy taxes to Aethelstan. I believe that my wife's kin in Babenburg have also been summoned to this meeting in Cumbria. And although it has not been stated in any letters that I or those of you who received them, possess, this moot in Cumbria has but one purpose: an ultimatum that Aethelstan has designed for us." The room grew hushed.

"Aethelstan will offer us a simple choice. He will require all the remaining independent kings of this entire island to bend the knee. And if we decline, he will march north and destroy us one by one and subjugate our people."

A furious uproar erupted from the nobility present. The din painfully roused an instant headache in Constantine's brain and for a second, he could taste blood at the back of his throat, the same sensation he endured when he suffered from the very worst of his nightmares. He took a drink of mead from his cup to dull the torture while the men settled, waiting to hear more from their overking.

"In a week, those of us who were invited, will ride south and west to Dacore on the River Eamont, and there we will meet with the King of the Saxons. I will, with some concessions, only for now, agree to a peace and submit to what I suspect he will demand: that I accept the title of Sub-Regulus on behalf of all of you."

Howls of derision and rage washed over him, but all Constantine could do was close his eyes and try and rub the pain from his temples away between thumb and forefinger. *I must allow them an opportunity to vent even though I have made my decision.*

"Speak now or forever hold your peace, you lords and kings."

The Norse-Gael eorls from the many loughs and inlets of the west coast unsurprisingly screamed for blood. Some advocated contacting the lords of Dublin, Limerick and the Orkneys to forge an alliance, and march south forthwith to burn Mercia to the ground; but Mael Coluim defused that idea, pointing out that to be even seen to make alliances such as this would force Aethelstan's hand into invading at once. The Saxon king's levies were deployed and ready from his conquest of Northumbria while it would take many weeks for Scotland to ready a coherent army to face him. To antagonise him in the manner suggested by the Norse-Gael would be suicidal.

Owain of Strathclyde proposed the same plan but with different allies. He suggested that Constantine should request assistance from Hector mac Niall, the mighty King of the Northern Ui Neill in Ireland. The heroic Irishman had been winning endless battles across the Leath Cuinn of Ireland with all manner of foes and an ally such as that would make Aethelstan think twice. He had in fact considered that possibility as he saw Hector as a nephew, but the news from Ireland was dire with civil war rife in almost every major kingdom. Constantine suspected that Hector would simply have no strength to spare and needed every man to oppose the Ui Imair, the Southern Ui Neill and the many under-kingdoms in the chaotic maelstrom that was Ireland currently.

The Highlanders and Dungaill mac Giric advocated scouting the meeting place and readying an elite force to take Aethelstan captive. The men of the Highlands were savage experts at guerrilla warfare. Constantine almost laughed at that suggestion though as Aethelstan in ways was very like he himself. He was cautious, conservative, and explored every eventuality long in advance of any engagement of import. *Treachery would not suffice here as Aethelstan would see my naive Highlander friends coming miles off.* Most in the room believed in Constantine though. He had ruled them for nigh on twenty-seven years and had never failed them, and they eventually agreed with his policy of appeasement. To quell any unrest, Constantine offered to provide tribute to Aethelstan from his own stores, on behalf of all of them so that they would not be burdened by further taxes; in that respect Constantine would shield them and sue for the best deal that he could in the circumstances.

Constantine hosted the many lords there for several days, sending the uninvited under-kings and chieftains home mollified with a portion of goods and gifts, along with promises to inform them of how negotiations went as soon as possible. He insisted that they should quietly train their men in fighting in the shield wall on the possibility that the negotiations went sour. When all logistics were prepared, Constantine, Owain of Strathclyde, Dungaill of Fortriu and Indulf his son, set forth from Dunkeld with their retinues. Constantine had left Mael Coluim in command in Dunkeld on his departure, with Ceallach as his lieutenant. He left strict instructions that if negotiations failed or the Saxons proved typically treacherous, they were to bring all people and food possible behind the walls of the forts and brochs that protected Scotland and try and defeat their army through guerrilla warfare and starvation; and if a chance arrived, they were to sue for peace and submission and protect the people. It would be the only chance they had.

The journey south was uncomfortable, cold, and wet. The nights gave no reprieve as Constantine was agitated and plagued with flashbacks of darker times and visionary nightmares of potential wars yet to come. He had to rely on strong drink to put himself under but hated the hangovers such consumption left and feared the potential cognitive side effects of this abuse for when the time came to face Aethelstan.

In four days, they arrived upon the banks of the River Eamont and it was obvious that Aethelstan's small host had been encamped there for some time. There did not seem to be any Saxon camps north of the river and Constantine suspected that this was an attempt to deflate any suspicions he or his companions may have held of being taken prisoner or ambushed. Regardless, Constantine crossed the river with only a few men and the three other invitees. On reaching the far bank in the cold afternoon light, they were escorted by a formidable squad of Saxon warriors to the small village of Dacore. There was large, burned patches etched in the bare earth, evidencing great heat and fire and the many tumbledown ruins there gave Dacore an unwholesome dilapidated look. On the outskirts of the village, they were escorted to a burned-out and gutted church. Their accompanying guards were taken away from the four nobles, and they were told to walk forward into the shambolic detritus at the base of the collapsed church and there, for the first time ever, Constantine of Scotland and his under-kings encountered Aethelstan, the king of the fledgling concept of England.

He was a strong but lean and spare man of relative youth but possessed a physical fitness that shouted discipline in his day-to-day life. A jagged scar ran down his face, and he carried a small dagger at his hip. A small circlet of gold around his head was the only indication of kingly ostentatiousness about his person and Constantine could not help but feel a burgeoning respect for the young king. Ealdred son of old Eadwulf of Bernicia was there along with his son Uhtred, and the great rotund and bearded Welsh nobleman Owain ap Hywel nDa stood there, proud but somewhat unhappy-looking. There were several other ealdormen and Danish eorls from the Danelaw there too who Constantine did not recognise. The English king did not waste time and immediately got down to business.

"My kings and nobles, I have… invited… you here for a simple reason: to offer you a choice. Before I get into specifics, please take a moment to look around you."

Constantine did as he was bid and looked around him. He could see the other lords and kings doing the same. All he could see was the moss-stained ruins of the church itself.

"This used to be a major trading town on the west coast of our island. Britons, Saxons, Scots, Welsh and even the occasional Irishman used to come here and trade their wares. The great historian, the Venerable Bede, has written that where we stand here stood a magnificent monastery that served as the headquarters of the bishopric of all Cumbria. Everybody lived in peace and prosperity."

He paused for dramatic effect. Constantine risked a quick glance around to see what effect this charismatic king was having on his guests, and he could see that each were rapt to various degrees.

"But some fifty years ago, Ivar the Boneless, one of the commanders of the Great Heathen Army, led a splinter of his fleet down the River Eamont and they sacked the town, enslaved the people and tore down the monastery. What we see now are its ruins."

Constantine looked over at Owain of Strathclyde. He knew that his kinsman was partially versed in this story as this land at the time of its ruination lay under the control of Dumbarton Rock, the former capital of Strathclyde, which in turn was also sacked and devastated by Ivar the Boneless.

"I am going to rebuild this church, beginning today, and I will rebuild this settlement and here also will be erected a monument to our... unification. A Christian cross I believe would be appropriate. It is through our mutual religion in Christianity that we will build a united island and no longer will heathen barbarians be able to prey on our divisions. I propose that each of you will retain your independence and will only in name cede power to me as your overking. This will be the price of peace and prosperity and safety for our lands, our island. You will submit to me, witness my charters, and defend our island, our Britain."

Owain of Strathclyde interrupted him.

"King Aethelstan, by what right do you claim to rule over us, in name only or otherwise? Where we stand has never really been under Saxon control at all, but my Lord Constantine says that you now rule all of Northumbria, as well as the Danelaw, Essex, Sussex, Mercia, Dumnonia and some of the Welsh kingdoms. Has your ambition no limits? You have no right to claim rulership over us north of the Humber estuary as far as I am concerned. No right at all. We are a different people to your own. Sovereign and independent."

The King of Strathclyde stood belligerently with his arms folded across his chest, staring at Aethelstan.

The English king only smiled. "I have the only right. I am the strongest. I have the largest armies. I have alliances across Germania and Francia and Rome. I foster the son of the King of Norway and recently have converted him to the Christian faith. I have oaths of fealty from Owain ap Hywel here and through him the other four major kings of Wales."

The Welsh son of Hywel nDa looked angry to Constantine's eyes but nevertheless he nodded his agreement at Aethelstan's statement.

"I have driven the Ui Imair from Britain for the most part and any of the remaining warlords allied to them now pay me tribute. My lords, I hold sway over this island, and I urge you not to defy me. It is true, I demand sovereignty over all of you, but I have proved that I am the strongest and therefore it is my right. God protects only the strong and through his grace I can protect you all."

Silence reigned for a minute or two. Constantine himself was the next to speak.

"King Aethelstan, it is true that you control huge swathes of the island, but without our help you cannot hope to indefinitely subdue the people. You want our submission and to relinquish our independence, but what do you offer in return? Why should we not unite as one and throw you from Northumbria as your Wessexian and Mercian ancestors have been thrown back, for hundreds of years?"

Constantine was gladdened to hear several ayes from those assembled and even some of the Danelaw eorls looked uncertain, treacherous as they were.

"I offer you peace, King Constantine. I do not even ask for tribute. But in times of war, only then will you pay money into my coffers and raise soldiers at my command. You will protect not just your own lands, but all our mutual lands when called for. The Ui Imair will be back or some other fell power, but I will usher in such a time of prosperity that your strength will be unshakeable. For example, in Ireland right now, king fights king and eorl fights eorl, but eventually someone strong enough will emerge to threaten us once more, you can be sure of it. And when that happens, combined, we will be ready. We will begin by ushering in some new laws which each of you will witness and all your kingdoms will adhere to, and we will begin the process of forging a new army, made up of men from all our disparate lands. An army that I will lead, in our mutual defence."

Aethelstan looked around, into the faces of each of the nobles present.

"Under my rulership, what occurred here more than fifty years ago on the very ground we stand on, will never happen again. I swear it before God almighty. Are you willing to submit, you lords and kings, to a new vision of a unified Britain, or will you denounce me and become my enemy here today? Choose wisely and think on the fate of your people."

Constantine had predicted exactly what would occur to the letter. In fact the terms were not as severe as he suspected they would be, with little to no tribute required except in exceptional circumstances. Indulf, Dungaill and Owain were prepared already, and Constantine had stressed that none were to act before he did. Ealdred and Uhtred of Bernicia were the first to kneel before Aethelstan and receive his blessing. They controlled only perhaps a third of Northumbria and as such were not as significant as Constantine himself, who could call on several disparate kingdoms as his own to rule and hundreds of warlords and chieftains. Judging by the way the son of Hywel nDa stood it was apparent that he had already submitted. *Rhodri the Great must be rolling in his grave,* Constantine thought ruefully, but then he admonished himself for his arrogance as he was about to do the very same thing. Cinead mac Alpin his ancestor had forged modern-day Scotland with his bravery and force of will and to an extent here was Constantine, giving that hard-won sovereignty at least partially away. After Ealdred had sworn his oath, Constantine was about to step forward to do likewise when he was stopped in his tracks by Aethelstan.

"King Constantine, our oaths of loyalty and fealty to this idea of an alliance between the peoples of this island are conditional upon the one thing that spiritually binds us – our faith in God. To prove this, your son Indulf must forgo his newfound heathenism and once more allow himself to be baptised. He may one day be king in your stead. You and Owain ap Hywel nDa are the second and third most powerful men on this island respectively, below me. I will not accept a heathen in charge of more than one third of the island I rule as a Christian Regulus Maximus."

Aethelstan turned to his son. "Indulf, you will step forward and once more become Christian here today. I will stand as your godfather to further bind us together in the light of God. Do this and I will know Scotland as a true friend and ally."

Constantine looked over at his son. Indulf looked every bit the Viking warrior, not a Scottish nobleman. They locked eyes once, father and son, and Indulf stepped forward. He took out a small dagger, knelt before the Saxon king and cut off his long braid of hair and laid it at Aethelstan's feet, to show his submission. Constantine himself bent the knee then and spoke:

"On behalf of all of the nobles of Scotland, I accept the title of Sub-Regulus and agree to vassalage to the kingdom of Aethelstan, in exchange for prosperity, protection and military alliance." *May God forgive me…*

CHAPTER 2

THE SUPPRESSION OF THE DAL NARIDI (MID-933 AD)

The wind whistled through the cold stone slits in the wall of the church in Dunkeld, compounding King Constantine's inability to find peace. His knees were raw from kneeling and the damp leaked into his weary bones. Every day he found himself coming to this private chapel at the back of his own apartments, searching for not just solace on the death of his wife, but solitude from the weight of kingship and the demands of his lords and people. Queen Mildred had died of a flux the previous winter leaving Constantine unmarried and, due to his advanced age, he had sworn to not wed again. His eldest two daughters were already married off to two other noble Scottish lords. His youngest Aileen did her best to make his lonely life comfortable, but the sorrow that surrounded him was palpable and almost overwhelming.

It was an effort just to rouse himself from the cot and uphold a public persona of authoritative calm. It was exhausting. His heir Mael Coluim battled him every day on policy decisions, and it was a rare night in the hall of Dunkeld where their disputes did not result in a shouting match. Constantine perceived what the real problem was though; Mael Coluim was thirty-four years of age and impatiently wanted his turn upon the throne, following in his father Domnall's footsteps. Constantine was in the way, a faded and depreciated echo from an older time and a hindrance to Mael Coluim's vision of Scotland. *Maybe he is right,* mused Constantine sadly. Several times a year, Constantine had to make the humiliating trek to Winchester or Tamworth, or wherever Aethelstan the King of England deigned to hold court; all to witness charters and accept new laws that affected Constantine's people.

He was only saved from the ignominy of yet another trip south in the previous month by the untimely death of Aethelstan's half-brother Edwin, who had drowned on the dangerous crossing to West Francia. Whispers had reached Constantine that the drowning may not have been all that accidental and may have occurred upon the orders of the English king himself, due to a succession dispute. *Nothing would surprise me with the treachery of the Saxons and the House of Alfred,* he thought. His decades-long night-time suffering had persisted and at times were even compounded during the day when he found himself staring quietly into space, thinking of his dead wife and his mighty deceased cousins, Niall Glundub mac Aed Findliath and Domnall Dasachtach. The memory of his predecessor Domnall had weighed the heaviest upon his soul of late, particularly as the man who had caused his death, Harald Fairhair of Norway, had finally succumbed to old age. The great unifier of Norway had almost reached the age of ninety, but his kingdom was quickly unravelling due to the bloodthirsty ambitions of his son, the notorious Erik Bloodaxe, who was busy settling scores around Scandinavia. A civil war in Norway though was always good for Scotland, Constantine knew.

His daughter appeared in the archway of the chapel and inquired as to his wellbeing.

"You have been here for hours, Father. I did not wish to disturb you, but King Owain awaits you in your hall along with an Irish prince by the name of Domnall."

As Constantine slowly dragged himself to his feet his mind raced at his daughter's surprise announcement. He had not sent for Owain for half a year, and he knew not of a prince called Domnall, unless…

"Daughter, is the prince by any chance of the Ui Neill of Ireland?"

She nodded. "He is Domnall mac Muirchertach mac Niall, a prince of the Northern Ui Neill. That is how he was announced to Mael Coluim. And Mael Coluim has sent me to fetch you. It is news of some import, Father. Will I prepare your chambers for rest after your meeting?"

Constantine's heart leaped in his chest. His thoughts had been dark of late and to meet the grandson of his greatest friend would possibly dismiss his malaise temporarily to the background, a reprieve from his depression.

He answered Aileen, "Thank you, daughter. I will come to the hall right now. Yes, prepare my chambers with the servants and we will have supper together later and discuss setting up a decent marriage for you," he said with a wink.

She laughed at that little running joke. Being fourteen she was probably a year or two too young and if Constantine was honest, far too precious to him. He favoured a religious life for Aileen despite her beauty and she had hinted that she would be positively inclined to a life of religion rather than marriage.

He made his way by himself to the hall and entered. A fire burned in the hearth and as the dark descended outside, he was pleased to see that the servants had well-lit the hall with candles. There were several guards stationed around the room but everybody else had been cleared apart from Owain of Strathclyde, Mael Coluim to the right of the dais, and a strapping lad who looked delightfully similar to Constantine's old companion, Niall Glundub.

Without saying a word, he approached the young paragon who turned to face him upon hearing Constantine enter. He was six feet four, young, with shoulder-length brown hair and a moustache. He was dressed simply as an Irish prince should and mirrored physically the great men that he was descended from. He partially bore a resemblance to not just Niall Glundub, but Flann Sinna, Aed Findliath and even the long dead aunt of Constantine, Mael Muire the famous queen. He could not resist placing his hands on either side of the face of this apparition, to peer into his eyes, looking for some ghost of his fastest friend, the bravest man he had ever met; Niall Glundub mac Aed Findliath.

"What age are you now, lad?" Constantine rasped, barely containing the emotion in his voice, and rapidly blinking away a tear of joy.

"I am sixteen, King Constantine", the lad answered, "and I come bearing a message from my father, Muirchertach mac Niall. He asks you, lord, for the love you bore his father, to reinforce him urgently. The Kingdom of the Northern Ui Neill is on the precipice and we may fall or fracture without your help."

Constantine frowned, nodded, and walked back slowly to his throne to sit. Once there he turned and spoke.

"Speak on, Prince Domnall, and let us see what Scotland can do in your time of need."

Domnall spoke at length and the story he told was horrifying. It was quickly apparent why Owain of Strathclyde had made the journey to Dunkeld, accompanying the young prince, as his kingdom was in a perilous position should the Northern Ui Neill fall. He was clearly here to advocate for Constantine to intercede. Mael Coluim was less moved by their plight, Constantine could see, but at least he had the manners to wait until Prince Domnall's descriptive tale was done. The Dal nAridi tribe on the northwest coast of Ireland had forged an unholy alliance with several heathen Norse and Ui Imair warlords, to foment rebellion against Northern Ui Neill rule.

Two kinsmen, by the names of Matudan and Fergal of the Ui Loinsigh, another subclan of the Ulaid, had raised many of the other clans of the Ulaid, including the Dal nAridi, in revolt against Hector mac Niall, knowing that Hector's power had somewhat waned due to his endless battles with the Ui Imair, and the warlord known as Ailche's son of Limerick. Hector had slain Torulb, a Hebridean eorl, the previous year in a pitched battle around Lough Neagh, and the attacks on his kingdom had dissipated somewhat, but he had lost good men in the process. Knowing this fact, the Dal nAridi and some of the Ulaidian tribes like the Ui Loinsigh had then offered land and tribute to Godfrith of Dublin, his son Blacaire, Rorek Haraldsson of Norway and Uathmaran of Mann, in exchange for joining forces with them. The fell Northmen had agreed, ever quick to capitalise on the maelstrom of Irish politics.

At Mag Uatha a moon's turn ago, Fergal mac Domnall, Amlaib Cuaran, the young but dread spawn of Sihtric the Scourge, and a younger brother of Uathmaran of Mann by the name of Sicfrith, defeated the army of Muirchertach and his son Conaing. Two of the Dal nAridi under-kings that had stayed loyal to Muirchertach – Maelgarb of Derlas and Conmal of Tuath Achaidh – were slain in the fighting. Prince Domnall finished his tale with a harrowing statement: "If the Northern Ui Neill fall, the Ui Imair will control two thirds of the island of Ireland effectively. And make no mistake, the Vikings of Limerick, the Kings of Connaught and Brega will fall to their power eventually as well. All that will be left to oppose them will be Donnchadh Donn of Meath, standing alone against the heathen tide. Once he is defeated, Godfrith and his sons, and all the young sons of Sihtric the Scourge, will sail to Britain with a force that will dwarf the Great Heathen army of sixty years ago.

"King Constantine, my father says that if the Northern Ui Neill fall, Scotland will not long holdout. The Ui Imair will come for you too as certain as the grass is green."

A familiar shiver of fear rolled down Constantine's old spine. It was not the description of the scenario as it was laid out before him that bothered him, but the prophetic metallic taste of blood in his mouth which shouted that this outcome was certain if Scotland did not intervene. The many possible outcomes and possibilities of the coming conflict narrowed rapidly to a single likelihood. Muirchertach was his father's son and Constantine knew he would try and force a battle with the Dal nAridi, the rest of the rebellious Ulaidian tribes and their savage Viking allies, but if they lost, all what Prince Domnall described would come to pass, Constantine was sure of it. Owain of Strathclyde broke his train of thought by speaking next:

"King Constantine, cousin, we must intervene. Surely you can see that. There are only twelve miles of water at the neck of the Irish Sea between my kingdom and the northwest coast of Ireland. If the Ui Imair or the Kingdom of Mann should be simply allowed to walk in and set up shop, my people will suffer with constant raiding and probable invasion before any other kingdom of Britain. The Dal nAridi are distant kin of mine and yours, as are the remnants of the Dal Riadans to their north, but they have betrayed our joint heritage. They have invited the devil into their house, making alliance with people they don't fully understand."

Owain shockingly went to his knees, bringing his hands to plaintive prayer before Constantine.

"Please, my lord, if you will not come, at least lend me part of your strength and let me travel to Ireland. The Northern Ui Neill must hold, or we will all burn in the fires of Viking aggression and vengeance."

Constantine could feel the fear and doubt creep into Owain. He was as brave as he was loyal to Constantine and had stood beside him through thick and thin. To see him grovel in desperation grieved Constantine but a determination to stand by the Irish was tangibly growing inside him. The fear and horror of old battles he had suffered through and endured, rose like bile in his throat, but he suppressed it. Just as he was about to agree though, Mael Coluim intercepted him.

"My lord, uncle, surely you must consider Scotland first? From the forces arrayed against the Northern Ui Neill, we would have to send many of our own men to their aid, men who will fall and die in a foreign land for no good reason. You are on the cusp of agreeing to reinforce the Irish, I can see it in your bearing, but for what? If they lose, all you will have done is hasten our defeat. I cannot condone this course of action. You must not do this. Sadly, in my view, we must leave the Northern Ui Neill to their fate and look to our own defences. We are beset by enemies all around us and even our allies to the north and west are uncertain. It is madness to fight."

The outburst from Constantine's heir visibly distressed both Owain and the Irish prince. But Constantine was sick of being badgered, bullied, and argued with by his subjects, kin or no. He rose from his chair to the fullness of his height and glared down upon Mael Coluim.

"You infuriate me, Mael Coluim. You show the insane belligerence of your father but without any cunning. I have sworn that you will inherit my crown, but that time has... not... come... yet, Mael Coluim. For now, the rule of Scotland is mine and no other's. I will decide her fate rightly or wrongly. And I have decided. I will honour the memory of my greatest friend and the greatest warrior I have ever seen in the flesh, and I have seen them all, young Mael Coluim; Erik Bloodaxe, Ragnall Ui Imair, the dreaded Iron-Knee of Dublin and none of them could hold a candle to Niall Glundub. I owe him so much; Scotland owes him everything. I will lead the elite of my army to Ireland within the week and we will fight for the Northern Ui Neill and save the people there, or we will die in the attempt."

Mael Coluim had no option but to turn red-faced and, suitably chastened, retreat from the hall.

It took a frustrating eleven days for Constantine to muster a force he deemed adequate to swing the coming conflict in Hector mac Niall's favour and march them to the coast, but when he looked on the thousand Scottish warriors assembled, backboned by elite veterans, he felt nothing but pride.

They boarded the fleet of ships commandeered for the passage across on the Strathclyde coastline, but only after Constantine ordered for a gaggle of clergymen and monks to bless the fleet and warriors. There was a small auxiliary of Norse-Gael warriors from the west coast included in the force and the pagans amongst them respectfully stood aside as the prayers were spoken. They sailed west and north on the morning tide and the water was choppy but safe. The fleet kept close together, but Constantine had ordered for speed to be of paramount importance and for some risks to be taken. Apart from the Norse-Gael contingent of his force, who travelled in two sleek longboats reminiscent of the Ui Imair, the remainder of his force travelled in basic cogs, wallowing tubs, and the occasional fishing skiff. It took them the entire day to travel around the northeast coast of Ireland and to reach the estuary of Lough Foyle, where they anchored at its mouth. At break of dawn, they continued down the River Foyle, and toward one of the main settlements deep in Ui Neill territory, close to Aileach, the capital of Muirchertach mac Niall.

It was decades since Constantine had last set foot on Irish soil and despite his advancing age, he leaped from the boat that carried him and onto the dock. A contingent of Cenel nEoghain men were waiting for them and accompanied his force for two hours through the woods and fields of the land controlled by the Ui Neill. People from small villages and forts stood out to meet them on their way through which gladdened Constantine's heart; these were the people they had come to save. When he reached Aileach and entered the gate through the ditch and palisades that guarded it, his legs were aching, and he was exhausted. He ruefully regretted not requesting a horse to ride but he did not want to show his men weakness in a time like this, on the eve of battle. He ordered his men to set up camp outside the walls and share provisions to regain their strength from the crossing, while he and Owain of Strathclyde entered the main stone hall of Aileach, to take council with its king.

Muirchertach "Hector" mac Niall was a colossus, a titan amongst Irishmen. Constantine could see the deep respect for him emanating from all the chieftains and under-kings present. They each tapped their three fingers to the centre of their foreheads, the warrior's way, on receiving any command from him and always spoke deferentially to him with never a moment of doubt or dissent. Hector embraced Constantine like a long-lost brother upon seeing him and introduced him to the senior commanders of his forces. Constantine clasped hands with Fogarteach mac Donnegan the King of Argialla, Ceangalach mac Cathalainn the new King of Breffni, and several chieftains of note. He also was greeted by Conaing, another son of Hector who bore an uncanny resemblance to the old High King of Ireland, Flann Sinna. Hector divulged in depth to Constantine the composition of his forces available, and they were impressively considerable.

They could put together four thousand men within thirteen days; combined with Constantine's Scots, that would make five thousand. He explained to Constantine that if he had another three weeks, he could gather another three thousand men as well. The problem was that every day they wasted, longboats from Dublin, the Isle of Mann and the Hebrides were swelling the ranks of the Dal nAridi and Ulaidian forces that opposed them. If they waited too long, the host gathering would be too powerful to rout in open battle cleanly and the only victory would be a pyrrhic one at best, where most of the land would be devastated anyway. Even before Constantine's arrival, he had reached consensus with his commanders. They had decided that they would march within the week and break the back of the rebels. That way, the Northmen would have nobody to reinforce. Constantine's arrival had erased any doubt, any hesitation on the decision to attack, his thousand men had hardened Hector's mind. They would march east very soon.

That night King Hector held a feast for the kings and captains and Constantine was afforded the place of honour on the dais in gratitude for his reinforcement and his commitment to the cause of the Northern Ui Neill. Constantine and Owain of Strathclyde had dozens of toasts raised in their honour. Constantine was roundly drunk when he retired to his bed and for once the nightmares that usually plagued him did not make an appearance, dulled by the copious amounts of mead consumed. But his first decent bout of sleep in some time was interrupted harshly in the depths of night when he was summoned to Hector's hall. All the senior kings and chieftains had been roused and summoned too, each looking as tired and dishevelled as Constantine felt. King Hector did not waste time with any preamble.

"My lords, we must march by morning. My scouts have raced to Aileach with some dreadful news. The Dal nAridi and the Ulaid have split their forces in two and are already on the march. One force under the command of Sicfrith of Mann and Fergal mac Domnall circled north around Lough Neagh and approach from the east. The second force has moved south and around Lough Neagh under the command of Matudan mac Aed, Blacaire Godfrithsson and the young warlord known as Amlaib Cuaran, the spawn of the savage who killed my father. This force is devastating the lands of chieftains loyal to me to the southeast."

"If we do not act now, despite not being fully assembled, we will lose most of the province in a week and when that bastard Godfrith of Dublin reinforces them, we will lose most of Argialla and the land east of the Foyle forever. Summon your men. I will go south with Constantine and the Argiallans to face Matudan and the two young Ui Imair warlords. We believe that is where the main strength of their men has gone. My son Conaing will march east and then north with a smaller force and face Fergal mac Domnaill and the Vikings of Mann."

Hector mac Niall Glundub mac Aed Findliath, the mightiest Irish warrior of the age stared around at the assembled chieftains and kings.

"Tomorrow, or the day after that, we fight. We win or we die. There is no more to say, now go."

The next three hours until the dawn were frantic as men were roused, gathered, armed and fed before marching. A half hour before dawn, Prince Conaing and his two brothers marched first as their smaller force was ready first. A thousand men marched with them, leaving Constantine's forces with the Argiallans and some Cenel nEoghain and Breffni men under the control of Hector himself. Constantine had ceded control of his own men to the Irish king, settling for an advisory role in the army. He knew his limitations as a warrior and general and Hector mac Niall was born for this, a true scion of the Ui Neill. All the men he had brought with him had quickly accepted Hector mac Niall as their general with no complaint; many of the veterans remembered his legendary father and saw his resurrection in his formidable son. His aura and reputation quelled any issue of their own king and commander assuming a secondary state. An hour after the first host leaving, the second force set out on the road to Argialla.

The pathway that the rebels would presumably take was a predictable one, but Hector had sent scouts to monitor their advance anyway, and horses for them to relay messages. The enemy were ravaging the lands around Sliab Betha and were moving further west as far as the settlement at Mucnam; and it was there that Hector and Constantine's force intended to ambush them, where the topography was most suitable. Constantine was present beside Hector when the scouts had brought word mid-afternoon on the strength of the southern detachment of the rebels and their heathen allies.

They would face only nine hundred, which heartbreakingly meant that the bulk of the rebels would then face Hector's son's meagre force north of Lough Neagh at Ruba Con Chongalt. The King in his haste had guessed wrong. Constantine told his senior captains and Owain of Stratclyde the news, and they were exultant that they would have almost twice the number of their foes combined with the element of surprise, but Constantine berated them. Hector the lord of the Northern Ui Neill had sent all his own sons into the jaws of the enemy, outnumbered perhaps by as much as two to one. If the element of surprise did not give them the impetus to break the lines of the rebels, it was probable that one or all of them would not see Aileach again. Constantine had offered to take four hundred men and march north to try and reinforce Hector's sons in time, if possible, but the legendary Irish king had stubbornly shaken his head. They would proceed as planned.

It took most of the day to reach the settlement of Mucnam but their timing was perfect. All Constantine remembered of the fighting was his terror on entering the fray, even with two thousand warriors around him. Hector mac Niall though was unforgettable. He led from the front as his father had always done, the tip of the spear, the edge of the axe. At the head of the host, Hector smashed his way into the rebels. In minutes Matudan mac Aed had fled, and it was only a rearguard action from the Viking Ui Imair warriors that prevented a total rout and a massacre. The rebels suffered almost two hundred casualties to very few on Hector and Constantine's side. Instead of pursuing the foe, Hector ordered an immediate march toward his sons to the north, allowing the leaders of this southern force of rebels to escape with most of their men. Owain of Strathclyde was furious and demanded that they capture the Dal nAridi traitor Matudan and put the two Ui Imair warlords to the sword, Blacaire mac Godfrith and Amlaib Cuaran; but he wisely vented to Constantine instead of King Hector himself. With the lives of his sons on the line, Constantine had no doubt at all that Owain's life would have been forfeit on the spot, ally or not, had he complained directly to Hector.

They marched through the night. By morning, the men were exhausted. The wounded and the remains of the dead were left at the fort of an allied chieftain on the way, but the rest kept going. Constantine was ahorse but several times he nodded off in the saddle. The men were commanded to take bread and water on the march with no relenting, and Constantine briefly considered bringing it to Hector's attention that should the men arrive potentially to a battle they would not have the strength to fight. They would be lambs to the slaughter, but one look at Hector discouraged Constantine from raising his concern.

Constantine secretly felt that the battle would have already been fought and that this host would come upon the victors, one way or the other.

He began privately calculating potential strategies for the worst-case scenario, should it occur. How could he extricate as many warriors as possible from that potential catastrophe? Should he retreat to Aileach if Hector fell and rally every man under Northern Ui Neill control to crush the Ulaid, the Dal nAridi and their Viking allies? He briefly considered retreating to the River Foyle with his own men should defeat overtake them, but he discounted that option as a betrayal of his best friend Niall Glundub mac Aed Findliath, and all he had stood for. Niall Glundub would never retreat in the face of a threat like this, never surrender and would have fought to the death. Constantine had made up his mind in memory of his greatest friend that he would fight and perhaps die beside these Irishmen as Glundub had been willing to do for Scotland on many occasions.

In the afternoon of the next day, the exhausted army reached the hills around Ruba Con Chongalt. It was heavily wooded, and the light did not easily penetrate the trees. There were no sounds except for the squawking of an enormous murder of crows that lazily circled the sky. *The battle has been fought then,* Constantine sadly acknowledged. The battle that would decide the fate of Ireland and perhaps Scotland too, was fought without either of the two senior kings present. The crows were circling a specific hill to the north. King Hector commanded his host to form up in a line and wait and he began walking toward the ridge on top of the crow-crowned hill, through the trees.

Constantine dismounted and joined the mighty Irish king and they walked together to ascertain the fate of Hector's sons. Constantine could see an emotion written on the face of Hector, an emotion that was alien to his father Niall Glundub and clearly had never encroached upon his son. Constantine was familiar with that emotion; he knew it all too well. It was fear for his children. He had sent his own sons south to battle once with the Ui Imair in Corbridge many years ago; Ceallach was sixteen and Indulf just a year younger. Constantine had not slept for four days awaiting the outcome, but even on news of their defeat at the hands of Ragnall Ivarsson, he had been euphoric on hearing of the survival of his sons. And here, now, a far more tremendous king and warrior faced that same fear, the potential death of all his sons in one fell swoop.

They crested the ridge and witnessed a massacre, a field of green that had been metamorphosised into an abattoir. Hundreds of bodies littered the field, but Constantine could see the Irish banner standing in the afternoon breeze, proudly and brazenly showing the harp and the cross and the red hand, in a background of green. Constantine exhaled a breath he did not even know he was holding. *The Northern Ui Neill and the sons of Hector had been victorious then.* The rebels and their Viking allies had been scattered and driven off; their hopes of independence had been dashed and the Ui Imair had been denied a foothold in the north. Scotland also had likely been saved by the outcome of this battle. But Hector was not delirious with joy.

He purposefully walked toward the centre of the battlefield. The warriors who encountered him recognised him instantly, standing back and tapping their fingers to their foreheads in respect. Hector barely acknowledged them. Three men emerged from a circle of bloodied and battered warriors and approached the King. Constantine stood a few yards back to give them space. Conaing mac Muirchertach knelt before his father and spoke, his brothers Domnall and Flaithbertach standing on either side.

"Father, we have won. King Fergus and his forces have been scattered and the warlord Sicfrith Uathmaranson has been slain by Domnall. The rebellion is over. The Ui Neill have possession of the battlefield."

All King Hector did was reach out and place his hands on his son's head and meet the eyes of his other two sons. Constantine understood, at that moment Hector mac Niall was not a mighty Irish king victorious in battle, he was simply a father glad to see his sons alive.

CHAPTER 3

THE DISPUTE OVER BABENBURG (934 AD)

"**M**y Lord, I beg you to bring our lands under your protection," Osulf the young Eorl of Bernicia pleaded with Constantine. "If you do not, we will be swallowed whole by Aethelstan. Bernicia will be no more and become just another minor province at the mercy of his whims. We are descended from the Saxons, Angles and Jutes, but this should not mean that we must lose our autonomy to a stronger English king. I would rather lose it partially to you, than fully to him."

From his dais, Constantine considered the young nobleman before him. He was small and runtish, but surprisingly articulate, practical, and wise for his age. His more famous older brother Uhtred had died in battle in the previous summer after a skirmish with Norse raiders and Babenburg and all its surrounding lands and incomes had come under Osulf's control. *The runt of the litter,* Constantine mused, *but perhaps he is wiser than his warlike siblings, and here he is offering up Bernicia as a bastion of Scottish control within Saxon lands, all to preserve a modicum of independence.* Constantine hesitated; it was almost too good to be true, but it looked on the surface at least that the pros outweighed the cons on acquiescing to this request. Constantine cleared his throat and spoke to the young man standing on front of his court.

"Eorl Osulf, my late queen was an aunt to your most noble father and as such we are tied by blood. I understand that the people who live in your lands are hesitant to submit to a southern ruler, but why is it that you believe that they will accept me, a northern ruler, as over-king? What difference is there between Aethelstan and I, truly?"

The question clearly pleased Constantine's heir Mael Coluim who sat beside Constantine upon the dais. It was so rare that they agreed upon policy decisions that it almost shocked Constantine to see Mael Coluim agree with his sentiments and thoughts.

Young Osulf answered, "King Constantine, you are powerful in your own right and your lands are far removed from Aethelstan's effective control. He taxes all the nobles of Northumbria unmercifully, beggaring our people, ealdorman and peasant alike. My people are starving under his control, but he does not care. Earlier in the year he conscripted hundreds of my warriors to fight for his ward Haakon the Good, in Norway, against his brother, Erik Bloodaxe. None have yet returned to me, and the burden of taking care of their families has fallen upon me as a result. It is ridiculous that Northumbrian men are fighting for the ward of a Wessexian king, in Norway, and he is depopulating Bernicia all to fuel the fires of his ambition. My lord, if you make me a vassal of Scotland, I believe that he will have no option but to relent upon his exploitative policy and leave us alone. If you do not intercede, I fear Bernicia is doomed and Babenburg will fall to his greed and malice. You will have an unfriendly English king upon your border directly with no buffer zone."

Constantine considered all of what the young Saxon noble desired of him. The enormity of the choice was apparent. For the price of annexing a huge portion of Northumbria under his direct control with all its men and incomes, he would have to weather a possible political and military response from Aethelstan. It was true, the English king had slowly begun to renege on the promises he had sworn in Cumbria seven years ago and begun taxing some of the under-kings who had submitted there. Young Osulf was not the first eorl, thegn or ealdorman to come to Dunkeld with a similar complaint, searching for Constantine's support. So far, he had refused each of the petitioners on the grounds that it would antagonise Aethelstan, but Bernicia was a significant kingdom that was being offered freely to him, falling into his lap as it were.

Constantine and Owain of Strathclyde had, in fact, also been pressed to send conscripts south, to inflate Aethelstan's armed might, but they had elected to ignore the command. Two of Erik Bloodaxe's brothers, Olaf Haraldsson and Sigurd the Destroyer, had offered battle to their older brother but both had been defeated and killed on Norwegian soil. The remnants of that beaten host had requested that Haakon the Good, the youngest of Harald Fairhair's many sons, return to Norway to continue the fight against his despotic older brother. Aethelstan, greedy for influence and power, had agreed to send Haakon home, but not alone. He would sail at the head of thousands of Saxon, Dane and Welsh warriors. To spread the attritional risk to his military strength, Aethelstan had forced each kingdom under his control to send warriors to augment Haakon's army and dilute the risk to his own Mercians and Wessexians. Constantine and Owain had not publicly refused the Saxon king but had simply ignored his request and stayed silent on the matter, lest they draw Aethelstan's ire. Tenth-century communications were untrustworthy after all. At length Constantine spoke:

"Eorl Osulf, please let me retreat from the hall to confer privately with Prince Mael Coluim. We will return promptly with an answer."

Osulf bowed and Constantine and his heir retreated from the hall.

"So what do you think?" Constantine asked his heir.

They sat on either side of a wooden bench in a room adjacent to his own quarters. His daughter Aileen was flitting in and out with food and wine while they discussed the matter. Mael Coluim grimaced before answering, "I think we should accept his vassalage. The land of Bernicia is rich and fertile, and it would increase Scotland's lands by almost a fifth. If Aethelstan is angered by such a move, we can say that by right of marriage we have legitimate claim to those lands, through the blood of your late wife. If this is not enough, we will offer some token tribute to placate him and his nobles. He will have two choices: accept it, or escalate. He will lose men in Norway if he goes up against the Bloodaxe. Haakon is a pup. We have both met him, he barely has hair on his balls. How could he unite the jarls and chieftains of Norway underneath him? Nobody can defeat the Bloodaxe. Nobody. Aethelstan will lose thousands of men if he pursues this folly in Norway and will be in no position to march north to face us. To accept the fealty of Bernicia is not without risk, but it would be lucrative for Scotland."

Constantine sat back and considered Mael Coluim's words. He always listened to his council, even when it came from a place of impatience and anger. It allowed Constantine to form perspective even if they clashed often. The question was, how strong really was Erik Bloodaxe? *Can the battle with his vanquished brothers have weakened him sufficiently for another force to take advantage,* he pondered. At that moment Aileen appeared with a bowl of apples. On overhearing the two men speak, she spoke herself:

"Isn't Prince Haakon a Christian now? Does that not mean that the Norse won't fight for him?"

She took a bite of an apple and left the room, but her question left an indelible mark. Simultaneously Constantine and Mael Coluim spoke excitedly.

"Haakon is going to lose."

The meaning was clear. Aethelstan's gambit for power in Norway would most fail spectacularly and weaken him. He would be in no position to oppose Scotland. Constantine returned to his hall and addressed the young Bernicia nobleman:

"Eorl Osulf, I Constantine mac Aed mac Cinead formally accept Bernicia as a fief of Scotland. Together we will forge a new, prosperous, and independent future for your lands, under our protection."

He embraced the young eorl to a round of applause in the hall. Even Mael Coluim was pleased.

"My heir will formalise the particulars and oversee the swearing of oaths."

He retreated from the hall once more to join his daughter, leaving the young nobles to discuss and inherit the future.

*

Two months to the day an ominous guest arrived at Constantine's capital, Morgan Mwynfawr the Old, one of the Welsh kings, acting as a herald of Aethelstan.

"King Constantine, you will rescind your authority over Bernicia immediately and remove any military strength that you have deployed in Northumbria. King Aethelstan's ward has been victorious in his initial battles in Norway and thousands of those soldiers temporarily lent to him, have now returned. They have been kept in the field though and are now camped at Yorvik. King Aethelstan has not yet allowed them to disperse. The fyrd of Mercia and the Danes of the Danelaw have reinforced them. King Constantine, we have an army of six thousand men sitting on your border. If we do not come to a satisfactory agreement here today, King Aethelstan will march north and devastate your lands until you concede."

A hush fell around the court. The naked threat issued by King Morgan had shocked not just the attending audience, but Constantine and Mael Coluim also. Mael Coluim was apoplectic with rage. He stood to his full height upon the dais and glowered down upon the veteran Welsh king.

"They call you Morgan the Old, maybe Morgan the Foolish is more apt. How are you going to feed this army if you come north? All our fortresses are fully stocked with provisions and will prove adequate in repelling Aethelstan. Your entire army will starve, long before you rout us. Osulf of Babenburg has freely elected to stand with Scotland on behalf of his people, no southern king has the right to interfere."

The old Welsh king was not so easily cowed or intimidated by the firebrand Mael Coluim. Constantine was happy to allow his heir to negotiate as his sentiments matched his own on this matter. Morgan spoke:

"Mael Coluim, I remember your father, Domnall. Some called him the mad. Maybe the apple does not fall far from the tree? To not relinquish Bernicia to Aethelstan is folly and will lead to an armed response. You cannot summon an army large enough to inhibit King Aethelstan's invasion of Scotland in time. It will take you weeks to rally a significant army and our forces will have devastated Scotland by then, and he will take Babenburg by force as well."

Constantine could see the Welsh king's point but he, just like Mael Coluim, was adamant that they could hold out until the English army ran out of resources and had to retreat. The main fortresses of southern Scotland were Dunkeld and Dunnottar but there were another six or seven similar forts dotted around the land and hundreds of the ancient brochs with attached walled and ditched settlements to hide in, effectively stone towers from a prior culture long lost to antiquity. Babenburg in Bernicia was arguably the stoutest fortress in the entire island and the English, Constantine was certain, would have even less luck in besieging the ancient capital of Bernicia too. To all intents and purposes, the Welsh king's threats were idle. Mael Coluim articulated Constantine's mind perfectly.

"King Morgan, you come here to bully Scotland on behalf of Aethelstan, but we will not yield. You would do well to turn and flee back to your master before your mouth draws our ire. We have heard enough from you. Our answer is no. Leave us."

The Welsh king snorted in contempt. "You will learn that not only is Aethelstan smarter than you and militarily stronger, but he is also your master whether you like it or not. You can expect a response."

With a flourish the old Welsh king left the hall. When he had departed, Constantine turned to Mael Coluim.

"War then. Send riders out to all our chieftains and kings, even the peasants in the field, from the central highlands down. Bring in all their food to the nearest burh, rath, crannog, broch or fortress and prepare for a siege. We will outlast them and cut them to pieces as they march north, bit by bloody bit."

Mael Coluim nodded confidently. "I agree."

The weeks passed quietly with no word from the south. The longer time flowed, Constantine's concern over a retaliatory and retributive attack lessened, but he often found himself on the walls scanning the countryside for messengers or invading armies alike. His last credible information had Aethelstan's force of men leaving Yorvik two weeks prior, heading southeast. On discussing it with Mael Coluim and Ceallach his son, they had come to a consensus that Aethelstan's returned force was being sent home via the

Danelaw and that he was simply using this force to campaign in that region to demonstrate strength to the Danish eorls of East Anglia and the Danelaw. *He will remind them in case they forgot about his military power. It's what I would do,* he often thought to himself. And yet, Constantine could not help but fear the worst. Aethelstan was not someone to trifle with. He wielded soft power in the courts of Francia, Brittany, Norway and even partially held sway in Rome, especially in times of selecting the next pope. To Constantine's mind, there was no way that Aethelstan would leave this challenge to his authority unchecked.

That night he was tragically proved right. A storm had risen upon the North Sea, and it made landfall near Dunnotar, washing across the lands to his capital in a howling deluge of rain. The flashes of lightning and the bombardment of thunder that had accompanied it had kept Constantine awake and the dread of Aethelstan's actions were compounding the nightmares of battles past, in his mind. He was sitting brooding in his hall with a glass of mead and staring into the fire, when Angus the Highlander, the captain of his guard, entered and informed him of the bad news. A rider from the north had arrived and informed Angus that King Aethelstan had landed in force on the Fortriu coast and was devastating the land all around there and into Moray. He had failed to take Dungaill mac Giric's capital in Lumphanon but had begun to march north to Caithness, supported by a Danelaw fleet.

Constantine was horrified by the news. He had assumed that Aethelstan would come north by land; he had never considered that he would chance a sea passage with his army. Because of this, he had never sent word as far north as Caithness of a potential attack, thinking it too far for Aethesltan to reach. Indulf, his son, would have no time to prepare properly for a siege. All Constantine had told him was to begin preparing men in case of an attack further south. *My son will never see him coming.*

The next few days were harrowing. A trickle of refugees began to make their way from the north and away from Aethelstan's rampaging host. After five days the trickle had evolved into a torrent with word that Aethelstan's host had been momentarily halted by a Highland chieftain by the name of Timo mac Duibhne and his sons Uilliam and Cathal in the mountain passes. At the end of their resistance, even Timo's queen Sinead and his daughter Maible had taken up arms. They were all eventually taken captive but not before buying time for thousands of Scottish innocents to escape the wrath of Aethalstan. As the days passed further, desperate people were arriving with carts and mules and some livestock, others were coming with nothing, already showing the signs of deprivation after a week on the road with no food. Constantine brought in as many as he could behind his walls, but there simply was not enough room for everybody although he did distribute whatever food he could, out to the masses.

He had begun summoning warriors from Strathclyde, the Highlands, and the west coast, but they were arriving in dribs and drabs, in uncoordinated warbands and militias. Mael Coluim had sent out dozens of scouts north to track the movements of Aethelstan's army. The English king had left a token force to invest Lumphanon with a siege to keep the warriors of Fortriu penned in, and he was sacking the settlements and brochs all the way to the north coast. Two weeks into the invasion, the worst news possible arrived in Dunkeld. Latheron, Indulf's capital, had had its walls breached and Indulf had been taken prisoner with his family; Aethelstan would now come south.

It took six achingly long days for Aethelstan to arrive outside the walls of Dunkeld with his army. On the scouts' reporting Aethelstan's approach, Constantine began moving his innocent civilians away from Dunkeld to the west and into Strathclyde, under a small armed guard. If he allowed them all to stay in Dunkeld behind its walls, an unmitigated humanitarian catastrophe would most likely occur, followed by a massacre. Constantine refused to allow that to happen. Aethelstan took half a day to surround the walls of Dunkeld with his host, comprising ranks of Saxons, Danes and Welsh. There were initial flurries of arrow bombardments exchanged between the hosts, but the Scots were too well protected by their walls while the English were careful to stay out of range. Casualties were minimal and the violence dissipated.

Mael Coluim wanted to sally from the gates by moonlight and offer them battle at night but Constantine commanded patience. With the military strength of Scotland still somewhat scattered and being assembled, the only option that Constantine could see was to sue for peace. Mael Coluim raged against the humbling reality of the situation, he was his father's son after all, but eventually he saw sense; especially when he witnessed a force of allied Norse-Gaels from the west coast being driven off on the fifth night and forced to make camp ten miles away in a local hillfort. There would be no help for now and no reprieve, except what they could potentially negotiate.

On the morning of the eighth day of the siege, Aethelstan, Morgan the Old of Wales, and a menagerie of nobles approached the gate under the white banner of truce. In front of them in chains stood Indulf his son, but his family were nowhere to be seen, their fate unknown. Constantine wore his most regal robes; he strapped his sword to his hip and prepared to meet Aethelstan face to face. Before the gates opened, he turned to Mael Coluim.

"If I am slain or taken captive, I give you permission to attack. If this is to be the end of Scotland, I want you to make such a war upon the English that in a thousand years from now they will still tremble in fear."

Mael Coluim thumped his fist to his chest.

"You have my word, my King. If your life or freedom is taken, ten thousand Saxon lives will follow, one way or the other."

Aileen his daughter came rushing from the crowd and embraced Constantine. He had no words of comfort to say to her and nodded for Mael Coluim to take her away. The gates were opened and King Constantine, marched out alone, to negotiate the fate of Scotland.

Aethelstan sat across from Constantine with a satisfied smirk etched across his face.

"King Constantine, you have stolen from me lands and incomes that were not yours to seize. In response I have devastated Fortriu, Moray, Caithness and some of the Highlands. Most of your people have fled before me and escaped, but there is not a single bushel of grain to be found between here and the Orkneys, barring what you have stored in your fortresses. You have sections of your army rallying across the land, but they will not gather in enough force to drive me away for some time. By then, you and every person within those walls will have starved to death. You cannot defy me militarily or defy my siege. For a long time, I have allowed you too much independence and leeway. All I asked for was for you to witness the making of law and to send me reinforcements when I required. Both you and your under-kings refused to do that for Haakon's campaign in Norway and in the assumption that I would be weakened, you seized Bernicia, a Saxon kingdom in my domain."

He steepled his fingers. "Now tell me, Constantine, why you have betrayed me and I will consider sparing your son's life."

Constantine knew he was on thin ice here. Despite his ordinary appearance, Aethelstan was arguably the most dangerous man living between Dublin and Kiev.

"King Aethelstan, the Eorl of Bernicia approached me, I did not approach him. I did not seize Benicia through deception or violence. As to withholding reinforcements from your proxy campaign in Norway, we received no word."

Aethelstan scoffed at that. "Do not insult my intelligence, Constantine, I as you know well, have spies placed in your court. You received my instructions as did Owain of Strathclyde. You both denied me."

He leaned forward across the table.

"Now tell me this, King of Scotland, if you were in my shoes in the face of this betrayal, what would you do?"

Constantine did not even try to dispute Aethelstan on his accusation. He had long suspected that his court had been infiltrated and, in his mind, being caught in a lie was nothing compared to preserving the sovereignty of his nation.

He answered, "I would demand tribute and the relinquishing of Bernician territory. Both of which, on behalf of Scotland, I would accept without complaint. You have proved your point, King Aethelstan and it has cost many Scottish lives, and probably many more if the winter proves harsh."

Aethelstan nodded his head sagely. "You are correct, King Constantine. You will now pay a tithe to England in exchange for autonomy. You will also relinquish Bernicia to my direct rule. But my trust in you has been irrevocably eroded and I will require one more thing from Scotland. For a period of two years, you will cede your son Indulf and his family to my custody. He will inhabit my courts in Winchester and Tamworth until the two years have elapsed and you have proved yourself worthy of my trust. He is my godson after all."

Constantine's heart sank. It was not an unreasonable request from the English king and the practice was relatively common in British and Irish politics.

"And what if I refuse, King Aethelstan?" he asked. Aethelstan's face hardened, all notions of affability shrivelling away.

"Then... King... Constantine, I will gather my entire army, all thirty thousand men of the Saxon fyrds, the Danelaw and Wales, and march north and decimate Scotland. And your son Indulf will be installed as my puppet to rule the remnants in your stead or be crucified, depending on the level of your betrayal."

Constantine had no option but to stand from his seat and bend his aging knee to Aethelstan. There and then he ceded Scottish independence, agreed tribute, and paid homage to Aethelstan the King of the English. The decision to accept the fealty of Bernicia had cost Constantine and Scotland, almost everything. *For now, you evil English bastard,* Constantine thought leaving the tent, *for now...*

CHAPTER 4

THE BATTLE OF BRUNANBURH
(937 AD)

Constantine mac Aed walked alone through the halls of Dunkeld searching for solace along the cold stone corridors. His servants instinctively knew to avoid him when he was in the blackest of moods, but in truth the crippling malaise that assailed him blinded him from their presence anyway. The last fortnight had been the most difficult, the cruellest, of his long reign and the choice he had made on behalf of Scotland would inevitably result in some grave consequences. His mind wandered back to the genesis of his troubles, when Owain of Strathclyde had returned north from the witnessing of King Aethelstan's latest charter in the Saxon fort at Dorchester. His joy on seeing his son Indulf accompanying Owain, finally being released as a hostage, had quickly turned to ash in his mouth when the King of Strathclyde had divulged the message that he was bidden to carry to Dunkeld by Aethelstan King.

The tribute and taxes owed by the kingdoms of Scotland and Wales, and all lands under their control, were to be doubled. A tithe of warriors was also to be provided to Aethelstan by all loyal kingdoms throughout the island, as he intended to travel to Europe in force and assist the Kingdom of Burgundy in their ongoing battles with the Hungarian horse lords of the steppe. A powerful nomadic chieftain had risen to power some decades ago and his barbaric sons had carried the Hungarian banner deep into Europe upon his death. They were descended from the dread Huns who had brought about the destruction of the Roman Empire five centuries before, and by all accounts this latest iteration of savage steppe warriors were every bit as relentless as ancient Attila and his cohorts. They now threatened the Papal State, and the Germanic and Francian kingdoms to the west.

The King of Burgundy had died in the skirmishes and had left a widowed queen and a young child as heir, and as ever Aethesltan had looked to grow his influence and power. He intended to marry the widowed queen and foster her son, Conrad I, making Burgundy effectively another powerful, if remote, under-kingdom of England. The problem for Constantine was that the existing taxes had crippled Scotland and any further tithe on the people would result in famine and death. The last two years' harvests had been moderate at best, and a sickness had emerged from Northumbria, affecting all the neighbouring kingdoms, thus compounding the suffering of the peoples of the north of Britain. The people of Strathclyde were suffering equally and Owain had demanded that Constantine and he join forces together and march south, to devastate the lands of Northumbria as far as the Humber and Mersey rivers in response to Aethelstan's demands.

Mael Coluim had rightfully insisted that they did not have the warriors to succeed in an all-out assault upon the English, so any short-term victory would be meaningless in the greater scheme of things and would only draw the ire of the implacable Saxon king. Altogether Scotland and all its minor kingdoms and associated allies could muster a force of roughly sixteen to twenty thousand men at any given time. This was a massive force, and would no doubt ravage the lands under Aethelstan's control, but eventually he would rally a sufficient force and halt their advance. At that point they would be driven back north and as soon as he was able, Aethelstan would repay the debt tenfold. The inevitable result would be the end of Scotland.

Constantine had stated his loathing of open warfare with the English, but Owain had pleaded that unless they did, thousands would starve in Strathclyde.

He begged Constantine to send word to Ireland to rally the Northern Ui Neill to their cause along with his Orkney Islands-based Viking allies through the marriage of his son Indulf. But Constantine had sadly shook his head at this suggestion. Even with a warrior as formidable as Hector mac Niall or Thorfinn the Skull-Splitter at their side, their attack would be doomed before it begun. A relatively senior eorl of the Western Isles named Skathi Svarti, who was visiting the court at Dunkeld to complain about the very same tribute being forced upon them, had cleared his throat and put forth the ally that Constantine had at first refused, but then relented and agreed upon. The young Norse-Gael noble had mooted the following,

"King Constantine, King Owain, you should approach the warriors of Dublin. They have as much to gain as you do, if not more, from the defeat of Aethelstan. My cousin serves as a captain in the fleet of Amlaib Cuaran the son of the Scourge, and he says that the Ui Imair have regained their old strength. They have brought Limerick to heel and many of the Irish kings now bend the knee to Dublin also. He has said in his cups to me on many occasions when he docks his ship at my peer, that either this year or the next, the Ui Imair will sweep in and take Yorvik for themselves anyway. Why not attach your fate to theirs?"

Owain of Strathclyde had briefly considered shouting at the man for his ludicrous and far-fetched suggestion, but on looking at Constantine's face his words evaporated away as clearly the idea had merit. Mael Coluim had looked on thoughtfully, stroking his chin with a look of curiosity etched in his brow. Constantine had requested an hour then to debate this possibility with his sons Ceallach and Indulf and of course Mael Coluim, leaving Owain and the other nobles to await their decision. The choice was clear; acquiesce to Aethelstan's demands and achieve peace with the English, but beggar Scotland bringing its people to their knees through famine; or march south and devastate the land of England with so much force that the various ealdormen and eorls of the entirety of the island would reconsider their alliance and submission to Aethelstan. There were arguments for both decisions and even entering the small room at the back of his hall to decide the fate of his country with his kin,

Constantine knew that whatever they agreed upon, Scottish men would have to suffer and die. There was no easy answer.

The Ui Imair had been long-time foes to the nation of Scotland. The ancestors of the current generation of fiends had massacred or enslaved thousands of innocent Scottish people over the past seventy years. Many times, Constantine had dreamed of forging an alliance with perhaps his Irish Kin or the Welsh kingdoms, to sail to Dublin and burn it to the ground to rid the Irish Sea of those villains forever. The Ui Imair were the wolves of the Irish Sea and all they had brought was ruination and atrocity to the free peoples of both Ireland and Britain. But as his sons and heir heatedly argued, the expression the enemy of my enemy is my friend kept repeating in his mind, and in mid-conversation Constantine had held up his hand for silence.

"We will send young Skathi Svarti and you Indulf to Dublin and broach the idea to Olaf Godfrithsson. For the price of a military alliance against England, we will help him take Northumbria once more and there will be a peace amongst us, if we succeed. Mael Coluim, you will accompany Owain of Strathclyde to Wales and forge an alliance with as many of their kings as you can. If you can sway old Hywel nDa and his son, the rest will follow. Together we will create the greatest army the Saxons have faced since the sons of Ragnar devastated their kingdoms."

He had then walked back out to his hall where Owain ap Dyfnwal, his old ally, impatiently awaited his decision. His sons and his heir took their seats beside him. The hall went quiet; every eorl, chieftain and minor noble present, straining to hear. Owain of Strathclyde broke the hushed silence.

"King Constantine, my lord… old friend… what is it to be? War, violence and hope, or acceptance, famine, and squalor?"

Constantine looked down at his hands. They were shaking. He knew what it heralded; a dreadful night of stygian horror as he drowned in the violence of his past in fear and alcohol. Slowly he clenched his fist and recalled his Latin, taught to him as a youth at the monasteries in the north of Ireland,

"The answer is this, my old friend; Parabellum. Prepare for war."

As word was sent south to Wales and west across the Irish Sea, Constantine and Ceallach prepared their army and sent word to every chieftain and under-king under their control; seven out of every ten fighting men was to be sent to Dunkeld, including the chieftains and under-kings themselves. Only their eldest sons were permitted to remain behind to defend their lands. Depending on the quality and quantity of allies secured, Constantine and Owain had created contingencies on the scope of their assault upon the English. The key, they agreed, was Northumbria. Even if all they wished for came to pass and their invasion reached into the southern strongholds of the English, they realised that they did not have the strength to hold the entire island under their power. The optimal achievement of this assault was to install a buffer, a neutral or even friendly ruling elite in the Kingdom of Northumbria; Northman or Saxon, it did not matter. Aethelstan's reach would be much diminished, geographically, politically, and militarily if their assault went as planned; and at least one potential threat to Scotland would be neutered.

The trip south to Wales would take Owain and Mael Coluim several weeks by sea and land as they petitioned each minor Welsh king, and an answer would reach Dunkeld no less than four days after that. Constantine knew that the Welsh kingdoms were under huge economic pressure also due to the demands of the Saxons and could well entertain an alliance. Years of internal strife and civil war between the descendants of Rhodri the Great had reaped a heavy toll upon the Welsh and they were in no position to deny the Saxons anything. But even still, he was reasonably confident that they would at least tacitly support his invasion of Mercia, their minimum reaction he suspected would be to stay neutral and await the victor.

Even if Constantine was driven off, Aethelstan would inevitably be weakened, and in this period of uncertainty the Welsh would no doubt seize more autonomy from Saxon rule. The same theory applied to the Danelaw. Constantine and Mael Coluim both believed that the rulers of the Danelaw, if they did not already swell the ranks of the English, would also stand back, and await the victor if left unprovoked. The eorls of the Danelaw were notoriously fickle and mercurial in their allegiances. They only ever bent the knee to the strongest regent and if Constantine could inflict some early defeats upon the English, some or all may even switch sides.

The Norse-Gael Kingdom of Dublin was a different matter. They were the only legitimate ally that could swing the numbers and balance of power Constantine's way while simultaneously possessing a legitimate claim to the Kingdom of Northumbria. If Olaf Godfrithsson could be convinced to join forces with Scotland, Constantine would be the favourite to come out on top. The Ui Imair warlord had consolidated power since the death of his father, several years prior. He had brought many rogue and recalcitrant warlords to heel that had previously been unaligned and independent from the will of Dublin. The barbarian known as Ailche's son, the spawn of the warlord the Irish called the Ceanncaireach, and at least four sea kings in the Hebrides, now all bent the knee to Dublin. Constantine's allies in the Orkneys, the three brothers, chief of whom was Thorfinn the Skull-Splitter, were in fact coming under serious pressure from two directions.

The Ui Imair were making inroads into the islands of the southwest of the Orkney archipelago, while Erik Bloodaxe and some of his supporters had seized some of the northerly islands upon fleeing Norway after the defeat to Haakon the Good. Despite the reputation of Thorfinn the Skull-Splitter, he and his brothers and sons were wilting in the face of greater powers, ceding land and influence in the North Sea. Although Constantine had sent a request north for reinforcement from the Orkneys, he deemed it unlikely that they would be willing or capable of providing men. In fact, he felt that soon, it would be Thorfinn and his brothers looking for support from Scotland in maintaining their independence from Norway or Dublin. The Ui Imair though, if all went well, would effectively border Scotland on two sides: through Northumbria and their Kingdom of the Isles. The problem was that to make an alliance with the Ui Imair against England, Scotland would effectively be inviting the wolf through the door.

Constantine stopped to think at a doorway that looked out onto the yard in front of his main hall, all these tumultuous memories and thoughts hammering his mind. There he witnessed the hustle and bustle of his people, and their ignorance of the danger looming somehow proved cathartic for him. His daughter Aileen came out of the crowd and approached him smiling and laughing. Constantine could not help but wonder, for the idea of an alliance with Dublin, what would Olaf Godfrithsson want in return. Perhaps Yorvik would not be enough….

His answer arrived ten days later. His captain of the guard, Angus of the Highlands, announced the arrival of not one but two Ui Imair warlords to Dunkeld. Mael Coluim ordered for the hall to be emptied and the typical denizens of the court did not need to be asked twice, fleeing from the savage apparitions that appeared before Constantine's dais. Both Norse-Gael warriors had been disarmed at the door but still bore their helmets upon their heads, with long braids rolling down their backs. The more senior of the two, when he took off his helmet, looked a true scion of the Ui Imair. He was young but scars criss-crossed his face and arms, and his shoulders were broad, a fighter to the bone. He was announced as Blacaire Godfrithsson, the brother of the King of Dublin.

Constantine had heard of this brutal barbarian before. He was allegedly a veteran of a dozen battles or more with the kings of Ireland, but his battle-prowess was only as renowned as his cruelty toward Christians. When he was not waging war on the kings of the Leath Cuinn, he was sacking monasteries and churches and selling clergymen into slavery. The second warrior bore a spiked helmet akin to a lethal hedgehog and was announced as Amlaib Cuaran, a son of Sihtric the Scourge; the former King of Northumbria. When he removed his helmet Constantine's breath caught in his throat, it was if his father had risen from the dead. Just looking at these two heathen barbarians sent a tightness through Constantine's chest. All his life he had defended his people from such as these and now he was forced to pursue an alliance. He was torn. In one way it thrilled him to potentially be fighting beside these avatars of violence but in another it sickened him, making him feel like he was betraying all those who had died by their hand and those innocents who found themselves in the bowels of slave ships heading to the Aifric and the Al Andalusian caliphate. And then Blacaire Godfrithsson spoke.

"King Constantine, I come on behalf of my brother the King of Dublin. He agrees with your proposal and will meet you at the south shoreline of the River Mersey in a moon's turn at Brunanburh, on the Wirral peninsula. To keep the Saxons off guard, my brother will send my cousin here, Amlaib Cuaran, south by sea to ravage their lands, drawing Aethelstan's eye from our assembling host to the north."

The younger warlord smiled and spoke, "I swear to Odin and to you King Constantine, that I will set Britain on fire from Dumnonia to Kent."

Constantine nodded. It was prudent to keep Aethelstan occupied. Amlaib Cuaran was very young, but he was renowned as a ferocious raider already and not someone that Aethelstan could afford to ignore and allow to run roughshod over the south of his kingdom. The Saxon king would have to apportion a part of his potential defence to oppose the young warlord. *All to the good* thought Constantine. But Blacaire had not finished,

"My brother wants you, on behalf of Scotland and all your under-kings, to demonstrate the same commitment. My brother will be sailing twenty thousand men to British shores, and this could shatter his power in the Irish Sea if he is fully defeated. He risks all on this venture."

Mael Coluim's eyebrows raised at the sheer number of warriors that Olaf Godfrithsson could field. He was visibly impressed, but all Constantine felt was fear. There was every chance at some point, whatever may come, that Scotland might have to face the Ui Imair once more if they turned their gaze north.

"Olaf requires that you sign a treaty and swear before your Christ God that while you are King of Scotland, you or any host of Scotland will not set foot in Northumbria once we have control of Yorvik. Aethelstan did not tolerate your interference in Babenburg, neither will Olaf."

Constantine nodded carefully but noticed that neither warlord had moved.

"What else?", he asked tentatively. "Olaf demands that you give permission for him to take your youngest daughter to wife. She is unmarried and both of his wives are dead. This union will prove to all his captains and sea kings, under my brother's banners, that this is a viable alliance with a benevolent king."

Constantine's gorge rose on hearing this last condition, but he had no choice but to hesitantly agree. His beloved sweet and innocent daughter had been revealed as the final price he must pay to secure Scotland's future. Once the two warlords had withdrawn from the hall, Indulf turned to his father, seeing his father's dread at his daughter's fate. He leant over and placed his hand on Constantine's forearm,

"Father, let me go and talk to Aileen. She is strong, she will do her duty for Scotland. She is strong."

Constantine shook his head, "No Indulf, let me tell her. It is my duty as not just king but as her father. We have agreed terms with the Ui Imair, we cannot renege. Aileen must be ready to travel to Dublin at dawn."

Constantine almost stumbled on his way through the corridors of Dunkeld. His hands shook and his heart hammered in his old chest. The servants had informed him that his young daughter was out in the gardens outside the walls, picking flowers for the hall. At eighteen years of age, she had grown to be a beauty. She was the perfect mixture of austere Saxon nobility and vibrant Celtic fire. She had intended to make her holy vows and become a nun, in the nunnery close to the monastic centre of Saint Andrews; but she had decided to delay the move, to take care of her father. And now Constantine would repay that loyalty with betrayal. She would be sacrificed for the good of Scotland, sold to a heathen barbarian in exchange for twenty thousand warriors. Outside the walls, he stood back and simply watched his daughter glide through the flowers, basket in hand, examining each one for colour and quality. Her every movement was graceful. He could barely bring himself to draw her attention but in the end, he had no choice.

"Aileen, daughter, come here for a moment."

He tried to keep the waiver from his voice but failed. His daughter noticed the inflection immediately.

"What has happened, Father? Are the people threatened?"

Even now she thinks first of the people, Constantine thought, *what a leader she would have made had she been born a man.*

"Scotland's people are indeed suffering by the unjust taxation and tribute they have to pay to England. People are starving to death, children are dying.

We have no choice but to march south and wage war for our freedom. We are going to hit hard and fast. To bolster our military strength, we have had to make an alliance with a most dreaded entity; the Ui Imair of Dublin."

Aileen's face blanched in fear. She had grown up on stories of Ui Imair attacks and atrocities and the only emotion she associated with their name was terror.

"How has it come to this, Father? Have the days of Scotland fallen so far as to make common cause with pagan monsters and barbarous savages such as these? What of the Irish of the north, they owe you their lives do they not?"

Constantine shook his head sadly. "They do not possess the strength to shift the balance of power toward our cause. Only the Norse-Gael of Dublin and their Viking and Scandinavian allies do. They have both the military strength and the political and economic motive to join us." Aileen nodded her head.

"Well, you know best, Father. You have ruled Scotland fairly and justly for more than thirty years. I speak for all of Scotland when I say, we trust your judgement, Father."

Constantine reached out with his old, gnarled hands and slowly gripped his daughter by her slim arms.

"There was a further price to pay, daughter. Your hand in marriage."

Briefly Aileen recoiled in shock but in moments she had gathered herself. She inhaled deeply and exhaled slowly. Constantine could see that she was desperately trying to keep the tears from her eyes.

"Who am I to marry, Father?" she asked.

Constantine was astounded by her courage. Women possessed almost no power in politics, they were halfway between pawns and brood mares; but instead of defiance, Aileen displayed a stoic determination, all for the good of Scotland.

"You are to marry Olaf Godfrithsson, the great-grandson of Ivar the Boneless, and the King of Viking Dublin. You are to leave at dawn."

*

Three weeks later, Constantine mac Aed had succeeded in setting Northumbria on fire. The massive force under his command had been relatively quickly assembled and they had marched to the southeast first, into Bernicia. There were warriors from every part of the Scottish nation amidst the ranks. Grig mac Dungaill of Fortriu had come south with four thousand men, which complemented the two thousand men that Constantine's son Indulf had accompanied from Caithness. There were five hundred Norse-Gael warriors there from the Orkneys, under the command of two sons of Thorfinn the Skull-Splitter. Owain of Strathclyde had come with four thousand warriors from his lands and Skathi Svarti the Norse Gael eorl of the west coast had come with a thousand warriors too. Constantine himself had more than eight thousand warriors under his and his other son's command. He had left Mael Coluim his heir in charge of not just Dunkeld but the entirety of Scotland. On departing his capital, Constantine had embraced him and wished him well.

"Long may you defend the people of Scotland should we fall," he had told him.

Then all eighteen and a half thousand men had begun the arduous march south, followed by a baggage train trailing them, almost two miles long. The smaller forts and settlements that dared defy them in Bernicia had fallen quickly, but most had sensibly thrown open their gates at the sight of Constantine's approach. The capital Babenburg had capitulated immediately too. Eorl Osulf had not only had the small garrison that Aethelstan had left behind to keep the Bernicians in line, put to death, but also decided to augment his uncle's host with five hundred warriors of his own. It took five days to reach the walls of Yorvik from Babenburg, and word had spread like wildfire before the advance of Constantine's host. All the ealdormen, thegns and eorls unsympathetic to Constantine's cause had fled behind Yorvik's walls, but not before dispersing all their useless mouths who could not fight, into the woods and hills and away from the Scottish army. But Constantine was not interested in Yorvik and even less interested in capturing or massacring the civilian population hiding there. His army simply skirted the walls of the city and continued southwest with nary a glance at the warriors manning the walls.

The leaders of each fort, village and settlement on the way to Brunanburh, were offered a simple choice; join the host as auxiliaries or be destroyed.

Most agreed to join on the spot, but many a fort was left empty in the path of Constantine's host, their people having fled to the hills rather than face conscription. The first meaningful resistance arrived at Loidis. The walls of the second largest settlement in Northumbria were manned by the warriors belonging to a belligerent Saxon ealdorman, named Alfred. Constantine had decided that to leave such a man at his rear could potentially compromise the retreat of his forces should their invasion fail, and the remnants of his host were forced to retreat north swiftly.

All his nobles concurred with Constantine; Loidis had to be taken. They had then surrounded the walls and built shelters for their archers. Once they had the defenders ducking for cover, Constantine had sent men forward to the gates with rams while simultaneously deploying hundreds of men with ladders, to spread the town's resistance. Within the hour they had broken Loidis' wooden gates down and Constantine's elite vanguard had entered the town. In minutes, the ealdorman was captured along with his family. Constantine had ordered a halt to the rape and killing of the innocent folk, but unfortunately dozens of people had been slain during the initial breach.

The violence disgusted him, but he did not have time to punish the worst offenders. On resuming the march, Constantine had left his son Indulf there in command of the town, with a thousand men. Should the war with Aethelstan go ill, Indulf and his warriors would hold the town for as long as they could, to allow a cleaner escape for any survivors north in case of disaster. Constantine had a secret motive too; he did not want to risk both of his sons in the fighting to come and this way he had a reasonable and believable excuse to protect at least one of them. Instead of a liability, Loidis had become an asset and the men had been blooded with an easy victory. Constantine was pleased and morale was high amongst the ranks.

On the seventh day the massive host reached the banks of the River Mersey. The sight that greeted Constantine, sitting upon his horse, was astonishing. The entire estuary was packed with hundreds of longboats, as far as the eye could see. Owain spoke then with Constantine.

"This Viking fleet is vast. Are we sure we are making the right decision on our choice of allies, my Lord? This fleet carries enough pagan warriors to lay the entirety of Britain low."

Constantine could see his point, but they were committed now. From here on they could only portray surety, loyalty and strength. Despite being savages, the Ui Imair were shrewd and even now most likely harboured doubts on the loyalty of Scotland. To blink now could potentially result in a battle right here between the two factions; the peace must be maintained. Constantine, after all, had been responsible for the death of their grandfather beneath the walls of Dunkeld; it made sense that his allegiance and motives would be considered questionable by the Ui Imair.

"We are committed now, my friend. One way or the other this will all be decided in Mercia or Wessex, God willing."

The Ui Imair had created a bridge of ships at two points across the river, all lashed together with hempen rope. Bands of Viking warriors stared sullenly at the massive Scottish host as it lumbered past them. The Scottish army took the entire day to cross the river. Constantine left a significant company of archers on the north bank of the river under the command of Dyfnwal son of Owain, as a surety that the bridge of ships would remain intact should a retreat be required. If the worst-case scenario occurred, they could evacuate the warriors from the south and then cut the ropes securing the temporary bridge, hobbling any pursuers.

The Ui Imair had set out a massive area inland further east upon the banks of the river, for the Scottish army to make camp. Constantine and his commanders gave orders to do just that and then they sent parties out into the countryside to hunt game, to augment their supplies. By nightfall, the Scottish host were mostly settled but Constantine had no time to oversee the final stages; he had been summoned to the captured Saxon burh formerly overseen by Brunan, the old thegn who had managed the region. Brunanburh as the men called it had been confiscated, its owner slain in the first twenty minutes of the Ui Imair landing upon the Wirral peninsula. Now it served as the headquarters of the largest host to invade the land of the Saxons since the Great Heathen Army, almost three quarters of a century previously.

The small hall at the centre of the Brunanburh was smoky and crowded. The leadership of the two sides of the alliance kept a wary distance from each other across a large wooden table. There were jugs of water and wooden cups beside them, but nobody moved to take one. To Constantine's right, there stood Owain ap Dyfnwal his old ally and friend, the King of Strathclyde, and he was flanked by Skathi Svarti, and Lyot and Skulli Thorfinnsson, the two sons of the Skull-Splitter. To his left stood his own son Ceallach, who looked tense as a bowstring, and the young King of Fortriu, Grig mac Dungaill. On the other side of the table though, stood the most threatening menagerie of murderers and raiders that Constantine had ever encountered during his long and illustrious rule. Blacaire Godfrithsson was familiar to him, the young Ui Imair prince having visited Dunkeld in the initial stages of the alliance. The huge man in the centre was clearly his brother Olaf Godfrithsson. The King of Dublin was taller and thicker-set than his brother. He was grotesquely lacerated with scars that shouted a lifetime of warfare, and he bore the familiar white stripe of hair congenital to many who descended from the line of Ivar the Boneless. It was the King of Dublin who spoke first:

"King Constantine and esteemed nobles, I am Olaf son of Godfrith, the king of all the foreigners in Ireland and the Irish Sea. I am also the rightful King of Northumbria. You have met my brother Blacaire already, in your hall. The warriors to my left are Tomrair Ailcheson of Limerick, the Cenncaireach with his two sons, Sichtfrith and Oisle. Uathmaran of Mann stands next to them, with Geabachan of the Isles, the jarl from the isles that straddle the northwest coast of your own lands."

The latter licked his sharpened teeth menacingly, while staring at the two sons of the Skull-Splitter, like a wolf eyeing up a fresh meal. There had been running battles throughout the last year between Geabachan and the rulers of the Orkneys and there was no love lost between them. A warning look from Constantine at the brothers, nipped any reaction from the warlord's provocation in the bud. They could not afford any outbursts now on the eve of battle. The King of Dublin continued:

"On my other side stand three Irish kings who owe their allegiance to me. They are Donnchadh mac Ceallaig of Osraige, Faelen mac Muiredeag of Leinster and Beollan mac Cormaic of Brega. Each of these kings and chieftains are loyal to me and will help me command my twenty thousand warriors. I will take overall command of this host Constantine. Do you dispute this?"

All eyes went to Constantine, but he had already anticipated this problem and had advised his kings what he would do well in advance.

"I do not deny this, King Olaf. You are a warrior of renown; you have the greater host, and you have the most to gain or lose. I submit to your leadership. You have command of both me and my men and Scotland is in your debt."

Olaf Godfrithsson walked around the table and took Constantine's arm in the warrior's grip.

"No, King Constantine, father-in-law, if you can assist me in winning Northumbria and then help me to keep it, Dublin and the Ui Imair will be in your debt."

The planning dragged on well into the night. King Olaf had news from Wales. Hywel nDa and some of the less formidable kings had set aside their differences, formed up upon the banks of the Severn and would join them once the Scottish and Ui Imair host reached Tamworth, the capital of Mercia. Only then would they enter the fray and sweep southeast toward Winchester. Reports had come from the south of Britain where Amlaib Cuaran was laying waste to the countryside. His splinter fleet had already sacked both fortresses upon the Isle of White. Part of the Wessexian fyrd had allegedly been raised to oppose them, but the son of the Scourge had just sailed away from this host and attacked the next vulnerable community along the coast. Olaf decided that they would split their armies once more in two, lessening the chance of infighting and the settling of scores; Constantine had deemed that prudent.

Olaf's Viking and Irish host would hug the Severn on the way south while Constantine and the Scottish army would raze the midlands to the ground. Aethelstan would have to meet one host or the other and when he did, the unengaged army would sweep around and hit him in the rear and put his host to the sword. It was a simple plan but a devastating one. When questioned on the size of the host Aethelstan could potentially raise to face them, or when he was presented with the likelihood that the Saxon king's spy network would have informed him weeks ago of what was about to occur, Olaf seemed uninterested and unconcerned. Constantine was not taken in with the Norse-Gael king's confidence and expressed his concerns. Aethelstan should never be underestimated, he fretted, even by one as mighty as Olaf. The King of Dublin and his eorls were nonplussed with the risks involved, they simply did not care if Aethelstan knew they were coming or not. There was nothing that could be done to arouse caution in them, nothing Constantine could say to sway them to conservatism, and it filled him with foreboding. Aethelstan was arguably the greatest king the Saxons had ever produced and a foe to be reckoned with, but Olaf did not care. All that remained was to march south and destroy the Saxons and any allies they could muster, or die in the attempt. And on the next morning they would set out to do just that.

Sleep evaded Constantine. He had first attended prayers with the noblemen before retiring to his tent, but his thoughts were a whirligig of chaos. His hands shook at the thought of battle as it surely would not be long in coming and the fate of Britain would be decided. It could be tomorrow, next week or next month, but at some point, there would be a reckoning. Sleep terrified him. All the old battles were lurking beneath the surface; all the violence, fear and death waiting to overthrow his mind. An hour before the dawn, his wine cup finally slid from his grasp and the roars of ancient battles past, consumed him as he nodded off.

It seemed mere moments before the dawn light streamed through his tent cover and lit up his eyes. His mind was foggy with exhaustion and the remnants of his nightmares receded, but they did not disappear completely. It took him several seconds to realise that the horrendous sounds of battle in his dreams had somewhat merged with his current reality. There were familiar awful sounds, occurring outside his tent. He rushed outside into the daylight and saw that thousands of men were hurriedly gathering weapons and racing into position on the southward extremity of the Scottish camp. He grabbed a man-at-arms racing by to enquire what was happening, only to learn that the army of the English had crossed the River Dee overnight in colossal strength. Aethelstan had not only managed to assemble a massive army in a relatively short period of time but had successfully marched them undetected northward. *I warned them all not to underestimate Aethelstan,* Constantine fumed.

The man-at-arms knew little else and Constantine let him find his position amongst the other warriors and the bawling of the sergeants. Thankfully he had fallen asleep fully armed and armoured and did not have to waste time dressing for battle. He searched for his friend Owain of Strathclyde and found him barking orders at his own men to form up.

"Owain, are our forces being mustered quickly, how do we fare?" His old friend looked grim.

"My apologies, my lord, I was about to send men to rouse you. We are under attack. Aethelstan has mustered an enormous host. Not as many as us but he has the ground at the top ridge of the peninsula a mile south of us and has almost formed his lines. He will come upon us shortly. He obviously means to force a battle now rather than endure an invasion where our forces can splinter. We are all in one place here. Here and now, he has elected to roll the dice. It is what I would have done."

Constantine's heart immediately began hammering in his chest.

"Is Olaf aware? What are the Vikings doing? Has my son begun preparation of our deployment?"

Owain nodded. "The Vikings are already forming their shield wall over the ridge to our west a half mile away and they are quickly bringing over men from the north of the river. Not all their host has landed yet though and they are only at three-quarter strength. Olaf welcomes the battle none the less. He is a madman, Constantine, he sees Aethelstan's gambit as a good thing. The inevitable battle he wanted will happen here and now, today, and in his mind, Northumbria will be won or lost in a single morning. They are saying prayers to their savage Gods in the full belief they are watching, and his host is forming up now. We must help your son do the same, Constantine, or the Saxons will be among us before we are ready. If the Saxons break us, they will roll up the flank of the Vikings too no matter how invincible Olaf thinks he is."

Constantine had no choice to make. He accompanied Owain through the hastily erected camp and toward the front of the gigantic Scottish battle line. On the route he could see the brothers of Orkney and their men whispering prayers in their own language to their Gods, their weapons at the ready. On every side he could see Scottish warriors saying prayers, shaking in fear and pissing themselves. One man was rocking over and back crying for his mother on the ground. Constantine could relate. The same fear threatened to take the heart of him here and now, but he had no choice but to lead. As he passed the massive bulk of his army, all those ranks of men, a cheer erupted as their venerable king strode past and took his place at the front of the lines. Constantine looked to the top of the ridge and there he could see undeniably, despite the distance, the largest enemy host he had ever seen in more than fifty years of warfare; tens of thousands of Saxon and Danish warriors. *So the Danelaw have thrown their lot in with Aethelstan,* he acknowledged with a sinking heart.

All at once dozens of horns were blown simultaneously from amongst Aethelstan's host and slowly the thousands of English warriors began to march slowly forward toward the Scots and Vikings. In response dozens of Scottish and Norse-Gael horns roared and the bodhrans of the Irish thundered. Nobody on the Scottish side moved a muscle, all waiting on their ancient king to command them. The bodhran drums of his own began then and the sound permeated him, body and soul. *I wish Glundub was here beside me.* There was no more time, no more choice and no room for doubt.

Fear threatened to overwhelm him, but he swallowed it down – a familiar fear that had threatened to drown him all his life, since his first battle on the slopes of Tara in Meath; but decades of experience had given him the strength to suppress it. Slowly, he drew his sword and pointed to the skies. The English had the ground and the element of surprise, but he and Olaf had the numbers. He did not bother to shout or scream or attempt to whip his men into a frenzy as his host was too vast to hear him anyway. He prayed the defiance of his fear and his willingness, even at his advanced age, to be the first into battle would inspire them. He took one step forward toward the English out on front of his shield wall. Then another. And another. And it was enough. The warriors of Scotland joined their Viking and Irish allies, and advanced to face the English in the greatest battle of their time.

AN INTERPRETATION OF LORD TENNYSON'S TRANSLATION OF THE EPIC SAXON POEM, THE BATTLE OF BRUNANBURH

Aethlestan King, the Lord amongst eorls,

The bracelet bestower, the baron of barons,

He with his brother, Edmund Atheling,

Gained lifelong glory in battle,

Slew with the sword edge, there by Brunanburh,

They broke the shield-wall, hewed the linden wood,

Hacked the battle shield,

Sons of Edward with hammered brands.

Theirs was a greatness, received from their grandsires,

Theirs that so often in strife with their enemies,

Struck for their hoards, and their hearths and their homes,

They bowed the spoiler, bent the Scotsman,

Fell the ship crews, doomed to the death.

All the field with the blood of fighters,

Flowed from the first great sun-star of morning tide,

Lamp of the Lord God, Lord Everlasting,

Glowed over the earth, until the glorious creature,

Sank to his setting, there lay many men,

Marred by the javelin, men of the northland,

Shot over shield, there was the Scotsman,

Weary of war, we the West Saxons,

Long as the daylight lasted, in companies,

Troubled the track of the host that we hated,

Grimly with swords that were sharp from the grindstone,

Fiercely we hacked at the flyers before us.

Mighty the Mercian, hard was his hand-play,

Sparing not any of those with Olaf,

Warriors over the weltering waters,

Born in the bark's bosom, drew to this island,

Doomed to the death.

Five young kings put asleep by the sword stroke,

Seven strong eorls of the army of Olaf

Fell on the war field, numberless numbers,

Shipmen and Scotsmen.

Then the Norse leader, dire was his need of it,

Few were his following, fled to his war ship.

Fleeted his vessel to sea with the king in it,

Saving his life on the fallow flood.

Also the crafty one, Constantinus,

Crept to his north again, hoar-headed hero.

Slender warrant had he to be proud of

The welcome of war-knives, he that was reft of his

Folk and friends that had fallen in conflict,

Leaving his son Ceallach too, lost in the carnage.

Mangled to morsels, a youngster in war,

Slender reason had he to be glad of the clash of war-glaives.

Traitor and trickster, and spurner of treaties,

He nor had Olaf, with armies so broken,

A reason for bragging that they had the better of perils of battle.

On places of slaughter, the struggle of standards,

The rush of javelins, the crash of charges,

The wielding of weapons, the play that they played with,

The children of Edward.

Then with their nailed prows parted the Norsemen,
A blood reddened relic of javelins over the jarring breaker,
The deep-sea billow, shaping their way toward Dublin again.
Shamed in their souls.
Also the brethren, King and Atheling,
Each in his glory, went to his own West Saxon land,
Glad of the war. Many a carcass they left to be carrion,
Many a livid one, many a sallow skin,
Left for the white-tailed eagle to tear it,
And left for the horned raven to rend it,
And gave to the garbaging war-hawk to gorge upon it,
And that grey beast, the wolf of the weald.
Never had there been larger slaughter of heroes,
Slain by the sword edge, such as old writers
Have written in their histories, happened on this isle since.
Up from the east thither, Saxon and Angle came from
Over the broad billow, broke into Britain with
Haughty war-workers who harried the Welshmen,
When eorls that were lured by the hunger of glory
Got hold of the land.

*

.

EPILOGUE

THE GREY MORNING AT ST ANDREWS (952 AD)

The Scottish sky was pregnant with the threat of rain but had mercifully held its precipitation in its dull grey clouds. The two noblemen, Indulf mac Constantine and Domnall mac Muirchertach, eased their horses along the trail as it meandered through the trees toward St Andrews, the heart and capital of Christendom in Scotland. Domnall had travelled to Scotland with grim tidings from Ireland. His grandmother Gormlaith ingen Flann Sinna had passed away months before at a tremendous age and he had been honour-bound to personally bring the news to Constantine the Great of Scotland. The ancient Scottish king had taken the pilgrim staff some years before, stepping aside to allow Mael Coluim to rule Scotland in his stead, and had retired to a monastic life amongst the brotherhood of St Andrews.

Upon arrival on Scottish soil, Domnall and his armed contingent had travelled overland toward Dunkeld to respectfully petition for permission to visit with the old king. The new king Mael Coluim was on campaign though and it was Prince Indulf, the son of Constantine, who had greeted Domnall and consented to the trip to St Andrews; on one condition, that he would join him. The journey would take no more than seven hours, but Indulf insisted on bringing a company of his own warriors to augment Domnall's retinue. The Scottish prince had explained that the death of Blacaire Godfrithsson had plunged the Viking world into chaos and it was every warlord for himself. Raiding across Scotland had increased tenfold and Mael Coluim continually had to campaign on both coasts to shout his presence to the heathens around the Irish and North Seas. Nobody, not even a formidable warrior such as Domnall mac Muirchertach, was completely safe from rogue Viking warbands or bandit tribes.

The two princes were only distant kin but had much in common. Over the years, they had encountered each other several times, and their relationship was relatively affable. After an hour in each other's company, they fell into easy conversation on all manner of subjects. They spoke of politics to the south firstly. The murder of King Edmund a few years previously had resulted in a maelstrom of chaos in the Saxon kingdoms. The throne of Northumbria had alternated between Amlaib Cuaran of Dublin, Eadred of Wessex and even the ancient berserker Erik Bloodaxe briefly, who was quickly driven off once he tried to enforce his will upon his Saxon ealdormen. Rumours abounded that the Bloodaxe, despite being a man in his seventies, was raising another host with the intention of offering the Ui Imair battle once more for control of Yorvik. Both Indulf and Domnall agreed that the Ui Imair faction under Amlaib Cuaran looked the stronger if it descended into violence.

Talk had then turned to Ireland and Domnall had divulged all the madness and tumultuous politics occurring there to Indulf, who listened keenly. Congalach mac Mael Mithig had succeeded Donnchadh Donn upon his death, as High King of Ireland, and three years previously, it was he who had defeated and slain Blacaire Godfrithsson, the King of Dublin. Congalach and Amlaib Cuaran, the inheritor of Blacaire's title as the king of all the foreigners in Ireland, were wearily stalking each other like two fighting dogs in a pit. Domnall alluded to Indulf that he suspected war was on the horizon, but when pressed by Indulf to see if he would enter the fray beside the High King, he was noncommittal. A new power had risen in the lands of the Northern Ui Neill, a chieftain called Ruaidri ua Canannain of the Cenel Conaille and Domnall was weary of his ambition. For the time being Domnall had elected to refrain from picking any side in the multitude of civil wars raging around him, lest his strength was compromised. Ruaidri was young, powerful and brave, and his star was rising. Domnall confided to Indulf that if he was not careful the Cenel nEoghain would be dislodged as the pre-eminent power amongst the Northern Ui Neill and the Cenel Connaille would rise.

As they approached the monastery, their talk of politics and war died on the vine and the sorrowful reason for their visit came to the fore. Indulf had not seen his father in several years either, but many reports had reached Dunkeld of Constantine's failing health. He had reached an astonishing age, eighty-two years, and still held on, being looked after by the clergy of St Andrews. Gormlaith, the widow of Domnall's long-dead grandfather Niall Glundub mac Aed Findliath, had always been a close friend of Constantine and they had often exchanged letters in a decades-long correspondence. With her death approaching, she had requested the use of a literate clergyman and dictated a final letter to be sent to Scotland, and Domnall her eldest grandson had honourably agreed to deliver it in person, the last request of a dying queen.

The two princes had commanded their men to make camp several hundred yards away from the monastic compound and had made their own way, just the two of them, toward the front gates. They cantered their horses through the gates which were opened for them by a pair of guards atop the walls. When they dismounted near the stables, two young slave boys took the reins and led the animals away. Indulf and Constantine walked toward the main hall and within they found the chief abbot, a man named Fergus, scribing at a table, utilising whatever light the dim grey skies allowed through a window, to illuminate his parchment.

When the two noblemen explained the purpose of their visit, the abbot sadly looked downcast and explained to them that the legendary king they once knew was a shell of himself. He explained that in the last year particularly, he no longer could distinguish people from each other and confused visitors with other people from his distant past. He had grown frail too in his dotage and the monks had to care for his every need, a humiliating end for a historic regent. "Constantine the Great, is not long for this earth, but we shall oversee his transition to the afterlife," he had told them.

The abbot had then pointed them in the direction of a stone cloister built against the southern wall and said that within they would find Constantine. The two nobles crossed the yard and reached the small stone building. Its door was held ajar with a block of wood and they entered, and there staring out of a slit in the cloister wall sat Constantine the former King of Scotland. He was dressed in a homespun brown robe, and like the monks of Saint Andrews, he had a tonsured head. White wisps of hair hung lankly around his ears. When he turned to face them, neither noble could see any hint of recognition at first in his eyes. He was wizened, much diminished from his prime and a cataract blinded him in his left eye. Domnall was about to greet him and hand the letter over, but something stilled his hand – a spark of recognition had ignited within the old man.

Ever so slowly, Constantine rose from his seat, staring intently at Domnall. He staggered toward the young Ui Neill prince, a look of wonder and awe etched across his features. Domnall risked a glance across to Indulf who had to hold back tears at witnessing the diminished stature of his father. Domnall nodded at the letter, an unspoken query to see if it was worth handing what Gormlaith had written over to the ancient king, but a saddened shake of the head from Indulf confirmed what Domnall suspected too; that Constantine would not know or understand what it was and it would be a waste of time as the abbot had advised.

When Constantine reached Domnall of the Ui Neill, he slowly and gently reached up both of his gnarled and liver-spotted hands to the sides of the young Ui Neill king's cheeks. In a rasping voice, little more than a whisper, he spoke.

"You are here, Glundub. I can't believe it. God has returned you to me after all these years."

Tears of joy rolled down the addled king's face and it took all Domnall's will to meet his loving gaze.

"Niall Glundub, you have come back to me, just as the end is near."

*

Ten days later, on the third of September 952, Constantine, the greatest King of Scotland, son of Aed and grandson of Cinead mac Alpin, passed quietly into the night.

THE WOLVES OF
THE IRISH SEA

BOOK 1: ASCENT TO POWER

BOOK 2: WRATH OF KINGS

Available now in paperback and on Kindle® from Amazon.

NOTES

As I said in the notes for Vol 1, my intention was not to blast a history lesson at the readers, but I admit I fully intended to portray my version of a series of events from the 9th and 10th century that have been mostly ignored by fiction writers so far. *The Vikings* and *The Last Kingdom* television shows focus on the Saxon and Danish experience from the period and perhaps slightly touch on the Norwegian side of things, but the Irish and Scottish perspective has been ignored or at least mentioned minimally as a source or base for rogue Viking warbands to cause problems for their main characters. What was occurring across Ireland and Scotland geopolitically at the time has been ignored. I guess for my part, it is a good thing as it has opened the door for me to write *Wolves of the Irish Sea*.

Many people have asked me, how is it that I am so familiar with the period and the answer is simple: I studied. There are a plethora of sources out there to peruse, particularly the Annals of Ireland and the Anglo-Saxon Chronicles. I must commend the University College Cork for there extraordinary work translating the many different annals from old Latin into English for all of us idiots out there. The information in those tomes has been priceless to me. It must be noted that many of the annals clash in both their chronology and the nuances of the political situation back when they were written. There is a distinctly political tone to many of the entries as the monasteries were heavily influenced by the chieftains and kings on whose lands they resided in. Therefore, when a battle occurs in the annals, different monasteries will have different protagonists and often different victors! I did my best to transport my mind back eleven centuries and estimate what actually occurred. To summarise, the annals occasionally have to be taken with a grain of salt as they were as much propaganda pieces as they were chronicles of history.

I had an epiphany last year. I found myself pondering how it is that in Ireland particularly, a man like Brian Boru is on the tip of every tongue of children the length and breadth of the land. He was the famous Munster warlord of the Dal gCais who allegedly drove all of the Vikings out of Ireland. Completely spurious I might add, but I digress. Nobody has heard of Flann Sinna of Meath or Niall Glundub of the North, who were arguably just as powerful and successful, and existed in a period that was just as formative to modern Ireland. It occurred to me the reason is political. After Ireland achieved its independence in the early 20th century, a brutal civil war occurred between the Irish. Once it was resolved, the various factions, wary of war conflagrating once more, had to carefully form the institutions that propped up the state. One of these institutions was the Department of Education and one of the most critical subjects and curriculums to create was history. And in a climate where brother killed brother over the fate of Ireland, it would not do to focus on a time where Irish Kings were as likely to forge alliances with foreign allies and mercenaries to subdue other Irish kingdoms. The tale of Brian Boru was much more tolerable as the good guys, in their eyes, won. This is my opinion only though and it could easily change if new information presents itself. And I hope it does.

Many people have commented to me on my use of the *Dramatis Personae* at the beginning of each major chapter in book one and now on book two also. I did this as I felt it was the only way I could assist the non-Gaelic or non-Scandinavian reader in not only pronouncing names, but at times differentiating between names and places. I could have anglicised or modernised my naming of characters but I wanted to preserve the authenticity of the names at the time. I did however change some names such as the old province of Mide into the modern day spelling of Meath. This is where the words *historical fiction* become applicable. I can pick and choose my naming as I see fit without offending anyone. Anecdotally, I came across the name Olaf a ridiculous amount of times in my reading. It was the equivalent of John or Mohammad in the Scandinavian world. There are various interpretations of the name Olaf in the annals though such as Amlaib, Amliab and Anlaf. I just picked whichever version sounded coolest for whatever character I was describing.

And finally, what is my next move as an author? I have actually completed the first draft of a comedic parenting book and will be releasing that in the Autumn of 2023. Post that side project though, I will be resuming my interest in historical fiction and continuing my work on early medieval Irish Sea historical fiction. At the end of *Wolves of the Irish Sea* I intend to have three two part series completed for a total of six books. I even have the epilogue of the very last chapter mapped out in my mind. So plenty to look forward to in 2024 and beyond.

ACKNOWLEDGEMENTS

Time is a finite resource and to publish a book, no matter how well you know the material, eats a lot of it. We have finally got book two over the line. Yet again my little team of Gillian Forde, Mark Thomas and Robin Seavill have delivered in whipping me over the finish line like good jockeys on a bad racehorse. Gillian has managed the project like she would one of her hospitals or football stadiums (her day job is structural engineering). Robin Seavill has poured over my work with a fine-tooth comb catching a litany of errors before I embarrassed myself publicly. Mark Thomas is a glorious artist and an IT sorcerer, the things he is capable of doing are like incomprehensible magic to me. To these three people, merci beaucoup.

There are some other people I would like to thank profusely also, who financially backed me to become characters in book two. Martin Ramshaw, Henry the Cat (Henry Loughran's bar mascot) and the warlord from the Southland who rules the Delta. You have humbled me with your support and I hope in this little way you become immortalised. To my friends and family whom I badgered relentlessly for opinions on paragraphs, characters and even the choice of cover, I hope your patience is rewarded with this book. And finally, thank you, to you the reader. I sincerely hope that this book proves a fitting finale to the first one and nicely wraps up my tale...... until the next one.

Le meas,

CB

24 April 2023

ABOUT THE AUTHOR

Conor Brennan grew up on the slopes of Tara hill, in that landscape so heavily draped in history, but now lives in Perth in Western Australia with his partner Gillian and daughter. He has studied economics, geography and has a master's in public policy, as well as having an avid interest in sports, history and politics. He works in the financial sector. Having (possibly) reached the end of his sporting career, Conor has since been writing prolifically; already having self-published a book on gambling and two quiz books, as well as currently documenting the first six months of parenting his new daughter with a view to publishing a light-hearted reassurance to other fathers of a similarly barbarian ilk. He is now determined to pursue this endeavour; to publish books and have them read. He says he'll keep going now until the day he dies and already is cooking three more ideas (at least!) and getting ready to set them in motion next.

To discover more about Conor and *The Wolves of the Irish Sea*, please visit:

conorbrennanauthor.com

BIBLIOGRAPHY

Apart from very broad and holistic sources, the following are the primary sources I used to write this book:

Bachrach, D. (2012) *Warfare in Tenth-Century Germany.*
London: The Boydell Press.
Retrieved from https://en.wikipedia.org/wiki/Henry_the_Fowler

BBC. (2004, December 20) *Brunanburh: Birthplace of Englishness.*
https://military.wikia.org/wiki/Battle_of_Brunanburh. London.

Bill, J. (2008) *Viking Ships and the Sea.* Oxford Illustrated.

Broun, D. (2020, August 20th) *The Chronicles of the Kings of Alba.* Edinburgh, Scotland.

Byrne, F. (1973) *Irish Kings and High-Kings.* London: Batsford.

Connolly, S. (1998) *10th Century Ireland.* In S. Connolly, *The Oxford Companion to Irish History* (p. 329) London: Oxford University Press. doi:ISBN 0-19-211695-9.

Downham, C. (2004) *Erik Bloodaxe-Axed? The Mystery of the Last Viking King of York.* Mediaeval Scandinavia, 51-77.

Downham, C. (2007) *Viking Kings of Britain and Ireland: The Dynasty of Ivarr to A.D. 1014.*
Edinburgh: Dunedin Academic Press.

Duffy, S. (1998) *Irishmen and Islesmen in the Kingdoms of Dublin and Man.*

Eriu, 1052-1171. Retrieved from JSTOR 30007421.

Foot, A. (n.d.) *Aethelstan: The First King of England.*
Retrieved October 1st, 2020, from
https://en.wikipedia.org/wiki/%C3%86thelstan%27s_invasion_of_Scotland

Hader, S. (1997) *Tennyson's Translation of The Battle of Brunanburh.*
New York, United States.
Retrieved from
https://victorianweb.org/authors/tennyson/brunanburh/brun.html

Ingram, J. (n.d.) *The Anglo Saxon Chronicles.*
London. doi:https://www.gutenberg.org/ebooks/657

Killings, D. (2008) *Anglo Saxon Chronicles Translation.*
London: Project Gutenberg.
Retrieved from http://www.gutenberg.org/cache/epub/657/pg657.html

Lancaster, P. (2018, May 27) *The Unknown Region.*
Retrieved from:
https://theunknownregion.wordpress.com/2018/05/27/a-lament-for-aethelflaed

Mac Niocaill, G. (1975) *The Medieval Irish Annals.*
Irish Historical Studies, 20(77), 3-20. Retrieved August 1st, 2020

Mark, J. (2018) *Flann Sinna.* World History Encyclopedia, 1-2. Retrieved from https://www.ancient.eu/Flann_Sinna

McCarthy, D. (2002) *The Chronological Apparatus of the Annals of Ulster.* Peritia, 256-283. Retrieved August 10th, 2020

NFB. (2012, January 30) *Ireland's Wars: The Second Viking Age.* Retrieved from https://neverfeltbetter.wordpress.com/2012/01/30/irelands-wars-the-second-viking-age

O' Corrain, D. (2006) *Celtic Culture: A historical Encyclopedia.* Denver: Oxford. Retrieved August 20th, 2020

Reuter, T. (2002) *History of the Archibishops of Hamburg-Bremen.* Columbia University Press.

Smyth, A. (1987) *Scandinavian York and Dublin.* Irish Academic Press, 2-62.

UCC. (2000, June 1) *Chronicum Scotorum.* Cork, Munster, Ireland. Retrieved June 1, 2020

UCC. (2000, December 1) *The Annals of the Four Masters.* (CELT, Ed.) Cork, Munster, Ireland. Retrieved June 1, 2020

UCC. (2000, December 1) *The Annals of Ulster.* (C. -c. Texts, Ed.) Cork, Munster, Ireland. doi:https://celt.ucc.ie//published/T100001A

Ulster-Series. (1999) *Kingdom of Argialla.*
Belfast, Northern Ireland, United Kingdom.
Retrieved August 19th, 2020, from http://sites.rootsweb.com/~irlkik/ihm/
colla.htm

Wiki. (2020, September 1st) *Amlaib Cuaran.*
Retrieved from https://en.wikipedia.org/wiki/Amla%C3%ADb_
Cuar%C3%A1n

Wiki. (2020, October 5th) *Constantine mac Aed.*
Retrieved from https://en.wikipedia.org/wiki/Constantine_II_of_Scotland

Wiki. (2020, May 2nd) *Flann Sinna.*
Retrieved from https://en.wikipedia.org/wiki/Flann_Sinna

Wiki. (2020, August 2nd) *Niall Glundub.*
Retrieved from https://en.wikipedia.org/wiki/Niall_Gl%C3%BAndub

Wiki. (2020, September 1st) *Ragnall Ui Imair.*
Retrieved from https://en.wikipedia.org/wiki/Ragnall_ua_%C3%8Dmair

Wiki. (2020, October 1st) *Sihtric the Scourge.*
Retrieved from https://en.wikipedia.org/wiki/Sihtric_C%C3%A1ech

Wiki. (2020, November 1st*) The Year 918.*
Retrieved from https://en.wikipedia.org/wiki/918

Printed in Great Britain
by Amazon

24823780R00229